ALSO BY MICHAEL WEAVER

Impulse

Published by
Warner Books

DECEPTIONS

Michael Weaver

WARNER BOOKS

A Time Warner Company

WARNER BOOKS EDITION

Cover design Tony Greco

Warner Books, Inc.
1271 Avenue of the Americas
New York, NY 10020

A Time Warner Company

Printed in the United States of America

Originally published in hardcover by Warner Books.
First Printed in Paperback: May, 1996

10 9 8 7 6 5 4 3 2 1

For Rhoda—who, happily for me,
continues to share it all.

A special thanks to Maureen Egen,
not only a brilliant editor,
but a reasonable one.

More thanks to Arthur and Richard Pine.
As friends and literary agents,
they're simply the best.

DECEPTIONS

1

GIANNI GARETSKY WAS thirty-eight years old and wearing his first nonrented tuxedo on the night the Metropolitan Museum of Art honored him with a grand reception.

Distinguished, elegantly dressed men and women smiled at him and he smiled back, although he knew very few of them. Still, it was a festive occasion, and there was nothing wrong with smiling. As his mother used to say, smiling required fewer muscles than frowning.

Of course his mother had always said it in her own lyric Italian, which made it a lot more pleasing to the ear. But the meaning was the same.

Highlighting that night's tribute was a retrospective of some of Gianni's earlier work, along with the museum's first public showing of *Solitaire*, his most recent painting. A leading critic had already praised the canvas as a haunting urban landscape that embodied the kind of stark, poetic imagery for which Gianni had become so justly celebrated.

Gianni himself was unimpressed by the rave. He had too clear a memory of this same authority dismissing him ten years ago as a naive candy-box painter with no true intellectual theory behind his work and therefore no real force as an artist.

So much for the judgment of experts.

A waiter brought Gianni a fresh drink, and he continued his slow circling of the crowd. Earlier, the Metropolitan's curator had made a point of introducing him to everyone of possible importance to the museum's financial and political well-being, and the artist had shaken hands and exchanged pleasantries with them all. Now it was sufficient to simply smile in passing, sparing him the need to hear his given name mispronounced with a hard G, rather than with its proper softness of Johnny.

It was a bit past ten o'clock when he saw Don Carlo Donatti enter the rotunda.

The don carried himself with his usual great presence, an impeccably groomed man of medium height and build who, by the mere thrust of his jaw and the straightness of his back, managed to project an elemental force.

Glancing past Donatti, the artist picked out the three men who had arrived with him. They were young and sleek haired, and Gianni had never seen them before. Like the don, they were dressed in the latest in tuxedos. But instead of following him into the reception area, they positioned themselves at the entry and carefully watched their boss's casual progress across the marble floor.

Gianni hurried to welcome the don. He had, of course, sent him an invitation, but only as a mark of respect and affection. Knowing the range and pressures of Donatti's commitments, Gianni had never really expected him to attend. Seeing Donatti here now, knowing how rarely he indulged himself in this sort of lavish, ceremonial affair, the artist was touched.

"Don Donatti," he said. "You do me honor."

They embraced and Gianni felt the powerful back muscles beneath the fabric of the Don's dinner jacket. Gianni had known him since early childhood, and it was always something of a surprise to be confronted by his seemingly impervious youth and strength, the dark eyes that glittered like marbles.

Donatti kissed him on both cheeks. "It's *you* who does *me* honor, Gianni. You think I'd miss such an occasion?" He laughed. "For this, I'd have made them carry me here in my coffin."

"Not even in a joke, Godfather."

Gianni escorted Donatti to a small, corner table. How easily I slip back into it, he thought. The almost stylized rituals of old-world respect, the affectionate use of the term *godfather* that custom dictated, the sudden rush of warmth that made him feel not nearly as alone as he had felt just moments before. Although Gianni's father had raised him as a Jew, it was by his mother's Sicilian precepts that he had lived the core years of his life to date. As had his father. In the end, both his parents had died of them.

At the table, Don Donatti took out a pair of glasses, wiped them clear with his handkerchief, and surveyed the elegant setting and those in it. Then leaning forward, he gave particular attention to the collection of spotlighted paintings that made up the retrospective.

Gianni Garetsky considered the canvases along with the don.

Bits and pieces of me.

Yet, there was the wonder, too. *I did this?* That special sleight of hand. You started with a blank stretch of canvas, ran in some color, and presto! A new world. And it was all yours. Whatever you wanted to see, you saw. Whatever you wanted to happen, happened. Awesome. Sometimes his brush trembled, his eyes blurred, his stomach knotted. Whom did he think he was? God? If not God, then at least a sorcerer.

Donatti nodded, as if this slight movement of his head carried his ultimate judgment of everything he saw.

"Too bad, Gianni."

Gianni looked at him.

"Too bad they couldn't be with you tonight," Donatti said softly.

The artist was silent. The anonymous "they" were his mother, his father, and his wife. His parents had been killed a long time ago, when he was not yet seventeen. Teresa, his wife, had been taken by cancer only recently. So what he was feeling mostly tonight was cheated.

The don understands this better than most. The thing was, how much did even the best of it mean without those you loved with you to share it?

A waiter appeared with champagne and filled their glasses. They sat wordless until he had left.

Donatti gazed evenly at the artist.

"It happens, Gianni. In time, we lose our cheering sections. That's when it's good to have a friend. So I'm here."

The don reached for a glass of champagne and slowly brought it to his lips. His eyes were solemn. "And not only for tonight."

Gianni sat with it.

In time, we lose our cheering sections.

He could put it no better than that.

And for how long had Teresa been cheering for *him*? Seventeen, eighteen years? Nearly half as long as he had lived. She had lifted him when he was low, had made him feel better than he knew himself to be, had gone wild over his smallest achievement.

His one love.

Would he ever have another? Gianni doubted it. He knew that in time all things, even grief, finally passed. But he had no idea what would come to take its place. Here, now, on this special night, Gianni's mind edged closer to the image of Teresa he kept like a talisman. He saw her fair hair catching an early light on her pillow, a mouth all too vulnerable to what life had to offer, the delicate tip of her nose that had always suggested the lift of something in flight, the wide, shining eyes whose color never failed to surprise.

Then his thoughts drifted to the worst of it, the part he couldn't bear but which he still held on to like some awful relic he was afraid to cast away. Which meant he saw her, too, as she had been at the end, with her hair reduced to scrabble, her flesh wasted, the source of his love staring up from the same pillow while she struggled for the strength to smile. God help her if she failed to smile for him.

His wife had a way of saying things that he could never come close to matching, wildly extravagant things that would have sounded foolish coming from him or anyone else, yet seemed absolutely right coming from her. Like saying they'd been made for each other since the beginning of time and no exaggeration . . . or how just the way his hands touched her could leave her breathless . . . or that when he was probing deep inside her, she was sure he was reaching straight to God.

All this from a devoutly religious girl who had come to him untouched by any other man.

So naturally God had gotten jealous and taken her.

While her idiot doctors, unknowing, had called it cancer.

It was close to one o'clock when Gianni paid off the cabbie in front of the converted loft building where he lived.

There was heavy fog and the downtown Manhattan streets were deserted, left to the mist as though the night itself were a public disaster that the inhabitants of SoHo were wisely avoiding by staying inside their apartments. As the cab drove away, a dark sedan swung around the corner and stopped at the curb.

Gianni saw two men get out. They were wearing tuxedos, and he remembered seeing them earlier at the museum.

The taller of the two was carrying an attaché case. It was he who spoke as they approached. "Federal Bureau of Investigation, Mr. Garetsky. I'm Special Agent Jackson, and this is Special Agent Lindstrom."

They took out wallets and showed Gianni their identification. The artist glanced at them by the light of a street lamp.

"What did I do? Put the wrong postage on a letter?"

Their smiles were polite. But they gave Gianni the feeling they had been taught to smile exactly this way in a course at the FBI Academy.

"It's no big deal, Mr. Garetsky," said Jackson. "Could we just go upstairs and talk for a few minutes, please?"

Gianni stood there, unmoving. So if it was no big deal, why were they here at one o'clock on a Sunday morning?

Then he turned and led them through the front door of his building and into an old iron elevator.

They ascended slowly to a dull, clanging sound while Gianni felt the air being sucked out of his lungs. It was as though he had fallen asleep in a deep wood and wakened to find the trees burning. His mind searched for possible reasons and came up with none that he liked. It's nothing, he told himself. Yet he did not believe it for a second. A small hidden part of him said he had been waiting for this moment for no less than twenty years.

They stood in silence, no one quite looking at anyone else.

Then the elevator clanged to a stop at the tenth floor and they got out.

There was just the one big metal fire door facing them, and Garetsky unlocked it, preceded the two men past the threshold, and switched on the light.

The loft took up the entire top floor of the building and had once belonged to a manufacturer of men's clothing. There were three skylights and a wall of windows at the far end, facing north . . . which was the studio area. Gianni's living quarters were closer to the entrance. There were a few rooms partitioned off for privacy. The rest of the space was open.

The artist saw everything along with the government agents. They all saw the same things, but what he saw was marked inside him.

The two men stood in the center of the living area, courteously waiting to be told where to sit.

Gianni nodded toward a couch and chose a straight chair for himself. The agents sat down side by side. They were big men and their bulk made the oversize sectional couch appear small.

"We just need a few questions answered," said the one named Jackson, a balding, smooth-faced man with blank eyes. He sat with the attaché case on his lap and was evidently the senior agent of the two. "Then we'll get out of here and let you go to bed."

"Questions about what?"

"They concern an old friend of yours."

Jackson opened his case, took out some papers, and shuffled through them.

"I'm talking about Vittorio Battaglia."

Gianni sat there, his face showing nothing.

"We'd like to know when you last saw him and where he can be reached."

"Why?"

Special Agent Lindstrom broke in to speak for the first time. "I'm afraid we don't have that information, sir. Our instructions are only to locate Mr. Battaglia."

"Why come to *me*?"

Lindstrom had an acne-marked face that looked shadowed

in the overhead light. "Because since you were boys together, you've always been closer to him than anyone else."

"That was more than twenty years ago. I haven't seen or heard a word from Vittorio since we were both seventeen."

"That's hard to believe," said Jackson.

"It's the truth."

Gianni saw the two agents exchange glances, and something passed between them.

Lindstrom rose and walked to the wall of windows at the far end of the studio. Then he just stood gazing out at the row of darkened buildings across the street.

Special Agent Jackson sat in silence. He appeared to be studying the sheaf of papers in his hand. But Gianni understood that there probably was nothing in those papers that he did not already know by heart.

"A few basic facts, Mr. Garetsky," said Jackson. "The same year that you and Vittorio Battaglia were busy being seventeen, both your parents were murdered by a mob enforcer named Ralph Curcio. Who was then shot to death by you in retribution. Two days later you left the country for Italy under false papers and didn't come back for seven years. You used a thirty-eight caliber Smith and Wesson for the shooting, and we still have the gun and your prints as evidence."

Jackson paused to give the artist his most ingenuous government-issue smile.

"So you see, we have it all on file, Mr. Garetsky. And there's no statute of limitations on murder. But if you'll just cooperate on this little business of Vittorio Battaglia, I'm sure we can work something out on Curcio. Who was vermin anyway."

Somewhere inside himself, Gianni Garetsky had started to shake, as with a chill. He wondered if it showed. It seemed very important at that moment that these two men not be aware of what was happening inside him.

Lindstrom returned from the windows. "What do you say, Mr. Garetsky? Is it a deal?"

The artist held himself completely still.

"Don't be a fool," said Jackson. "You're a successful and

famous painter. You have a long, wonderful life ahead of you. Why throw it all away over a nickel-and-dime punk?"

"Even if I wanted to tell you where Battaglia is, I couldn't. I don't know."

Special Agent Jackson sighed. "I don't think Mr. Garetsky realizes just how serious we are about this. Would you say it's time to show him, Frank?"

"Yeah," said Lindstrom from behind Gianni, "I'd say it's time."

Gianni never saw the hit coming. It came over his right shoulder and caught him across the cheek with almost no force. It was no more than a light, token rap with the knuckles, yet its overall effect was greater than that of a hard punch. For it diminished him. It made him see exactly what he was worth to these two men. And that was nothing.

Seated in front of Gianni on the couch, Special Agent Jackson still considered him without particular malice, a strong professional in impeccable evening clothes whose blank eyes offered no hint of what was going on behind them.

"Let's try again," he said quietly. "When did you last see or speak to Vittorio Battaglia?"

"Twen . . ." Gianni's tongue groped slowly, almost numbly, and he had to start over. "Twenty years ago."

This time the blow came over Gianni's left shoulder. It was as light a tap as the first, but it carried the added weight of an established order. It told him that he and his flesh were not inviolate, and that this was merely the beginning. The artist felt the blood rushing to his face. His heart turned. *These are not FBI agents,* he thought. Until he remembered certain unpleasant things he had seen and heard a great many years ago, and then he was not so sure.

"Where's Vittorio Battaglia?" Special Agent Jackson spoke quietly, patiently, a controlled man with plenty of time to do whatever might be necessary.

"I don't . . ." Gianni shook his head and tried to get himself ready for the next hit from the right.

But this time nothing came. Instead, Jackson took a revolver from his shoulder holster and screwed on a four-inch silencer. He held the weapon pointing at the floor. To Gianni, the silencer was the clearest indication yet of the men's ultimate intent. Or was it only bluff, a showpiece?

"We have a job to do here, Mr. Garetsky," said Jackson. "And one way or another we're going to get it done. So why don't you make it easy on us all and answer this one question?"

"Because I don't know the answer."

Jackson lifted his revolver until it was aimed loosely at Gianni's chest. "A few hard facts," he said. "The credentials we showed you are false. Which means you can forget about any of the little niceties you might be expecting from us as federal agents. So either you start talking, or I start shooting."

Gianni sat there, dry mouthed. "You'd really kill me for this?"

"Killing you won't tell us where Battaglia is. But a few well-placed bullets might encourage you to talk."

They stared at each other.

Gianni figured it was time to give them something. He knew about interrogation under threat of physical pain. Finally, you had to talk. Even if it was only lies.

"Could I have a drink of water?" he said to stall it further. Jackson nodded to Lindstrom, who went into the kitchen and came back with a filled glass.

Gianni brought it to his lips with less-than-steady hands and they watched him drink.

"When did you last see Battaglia?" said Jackson.

Gianni gripped the water glass with both hands to keep it from shaking. "Three weeks ago."

"Where?"

The artist took another drink and coughed, still playing for time.

"Where?" repeated Jackson. Hardly seeming to move, he lifted a leg and kicked the glass out of Gianni's hand. Trailing water, it rolled along the floor without breaking.

"Chicago."

"What part?"

"Oak Park."

"Address?"

Gianni sucked air. He stared into Jackson's eyes and saw

himself dead. Whoever they were, there was no way they were going to walk out of here and leave him alive. *And I'll never know why.*

"I can't remember the exact . . ." The artist breathed deeply and seemed to grope for remembrance.

"Address," said Jackson again. He was beginning to sound bored.

Gianni slowly shook his head. Then he kept shaking it as though he were suddenly an old man from whose brain all detail had fled.

"I want his address."

Once more, Jackson lifted his leg. But this time the kick was aimed at Gianni's groin.

The artist saw it coming. Grabbing the foot in midair, he yanked and twisted until Jackson was off the couch and on the floor, with Gianni all over him and rolling them both in case Lindstrom had his own weapon out and was looking for a clear shot.

Get the gun or you're dead, Gianni told himself.

For a moment everything inside him was calm and slow. He saw Jackson's smooth face as he stared at him, saw his blue eyes, cold as glass, and felt an insane joy, as if death at this moment might not really be the worst thing that could happen to him.

Something exploded in Gianni's head and he caught a glimpse of a bright red fall that opened like a crack in the earth. Then there was a shock and things began to spin. But he did not lose consciousness or let go his grip on Jackson's gun hand.

The next blows came one after another and in such swift succession that he lost count. They caught him in the face and neck and he choked, swallowed blood, and retched all over himself and Jackson. He knew now that Lindstrom was using a leather covered lead billy and was good with it. Good enough to do the required damage without fracturing his skull or killing him. Good enough, too, for the shock and pain to start closing off the light, leaving him awash in all the shameful juices of living.

Then rage took over and Gianni had a brain full of blood that sent his teeth into Jackson's wrist with such force that they hit bone and stayed there until the fake FBI agent cried out and dropped his revolver.

In what seemed a single motion, Gianni grabbed the gun, rolled away from the steady pounding of Lindstrom's billy, and squeezed the trigger. There was just the soft whooshing sound of the silencer as the bullet sucked in Jackson's face and turned him old.

Gianni swung around.

Lindstrom had dropped the billy and was struggling to free his revolver from his shoulder holster, but it had hooked into the lining of his tuxedo. His acne-scarred face was suddenly terrified. Gianni saw it and was terrified, too. Then he swallowed, tasted his own blood, and fired twice.

Lindstrom went over backward. Two crimson buds flowered on his white dress shirt. When he hit the floor, he never moved.

Gianni Garetsky lay there.

He breathed the acrid smell of cordite and let the anger drain out of him.

The nausea, the illness, remained.

2

THE ARTIST ROSE slowly. His head, neck, and back were a single blob of pain, he saw floating spots, and he stank from an assortment of his own bodily discharges.

Why had they done this to him?

What had Vittorio Battaglia done to *them*?

Gianni expected no answers. What the questions did was make it easier for him to look at the two men.

The agents lay as they had fallen. They were on their backs, eyes staring up through a skylight as fixedly as if they were counting stars. And they were dead. There was no question about that. They were certainly dead.

Gianni fought an urge to go into his bedroom, lie down, and fall asleep in the mad hope that when he awoke the two bodies would be gone and everything in his life would be the way it had been.

Still, he was calm. It was a fragile calm, but he could feel it growing stronger. And he knew that whatever had to be done, he would finally do.

In the meantime he poured himself a generous shot of brandy, walked to the wall of windows at the north end of the studio, and stared down at the street ten stories below.

Nothing was moving. But some cars were parked at the curb, and Gianni was able to pick out the dark sedan that Jackson and Lindstrom had arrived in. The artist had lived and worked on this street for more than ten years. He knew it well. Yet he suddenly felt himself lost in an alien land.

He glanced at his watch. It was not quite two o'clock. He had arrived home less than an hour ago. The wonder was that it had all taken so little time.

Gianni carried his drink back to where it had happened. Everything was in place. No furniture, lamps, or pictures had been damaged or disturbed. Other than for the two bodies, it was a peaceful-enough scene, a quiet setting where a brief encounter had taken place.

Other than for the two bodies.

Gianni breathed deeply and felt the pain filter through him. Then he tossed off his brandy and tried to see if he could learn anything.

He went through the men's wallets and FBI identification, and everything tied together as authentic. Credit and insurance cards, driver's licenses, assorted other plastic, all confirmed their stated identities. If any glitch existed, Gianni failed to pick it out. Which suddenly added to his confusion. Were they real or not?

Jackson's attaché case held its own items of interest . . . among them, a vicious-looking electrical shock device that would have been applied to his more sensitive body parts if their other efforts failed to produce the desired answers.

In an envelope was a faded snapshot of Vittorio Battaglia

and himself as a couple of grinning teenagers at the beach, caught and held in a moment of summer sun.

Another photograph showed Vittorio standing beside a beautiful Asian girl who was staring solemnly at the camera with luminous almond eyes. A name and address on the back of the photograph identified her as Mary Yung of Soundview Drive, Greenwich, Connecticut.

Garetsky wondered if the two alleged agents had been to question the girl before they came to him. If they had, was she now lying dead or crippled somewhere? He hoped not. He very much wanted Mary Yung to be alive and communicating.

The attaché case also contained two computer printouts. One had to do with Mary Yung. The other dealt with him. He read the girl's first.

MARY CHAN YUNG (one of several names for MOPEI LINLEY FOO). Born in Hong Kong, U.K., and brought to U.S. as child by parents, now deceased. Current age, 34. Yung works on and off as a sometime actress, singer, photographer's model, fashion reporter. Apparent independent means as parents' sole heir of record. Unmarried. Yung is known to have had close and lengthy relationship with Vittorio Battaglia just prior to Battaglia's disappearance approximately ten years ago. Yung is known to have worked and traveled throughout Europe and the Far East.

The artist moved on to his own printout.

GIANNI SEBASTIANO GARETSKY. Born N.Y., N.Y. Current age, 38. Single known alias, JOHN CARPELLA. Parents, María and David Garetsky, both deceased. Murdered in internecine syndicate crime war of early eighties.

GARETSKY avenged parents' murder by killing Ralph Curcio, fleeing to Italy, and living there as John Carpella. Vittorio Battaglia's closest friend and confidant since early childhood.

FBI EVALUATION: There is no hard evidence but it

is assumed that the two men have maintained covert contact for most of the past twenty years. Although GARETSKY's father was a lifelong soldier in the Donatti crime family, there is no evidence that GIANNI GARETSKY himself, once past the age of seventeen, was ever involved in any kind of syndicate business. He is currently recognized as one of America's foremost artists.

Gianni slowly put down the two printouts. So much for any hope of this not being a genuine FBI operation. And who would believe his having had to shoot them in self-defense to save his own life?

He stood listening to himself breathe.

There really was nothing more to think about. Whatever came next, he first had to clean himself and take care of the bodies.

He stood naked in front of a bathroom mirror and looked at what they had done to him. A strange bloody creature quivered in its own violet light. Beneath the blood, his flesh was swollen, formless, purple. His eyes peered dimly through a velvet mist.

"Why?" he said aloud to the thing in the mirror.

When Gianni came out of the bathroom, he put on a fresh shirt and jeans and set about scrubbing the floor clean of blood.

With that done, he wrapped the bodies, using bedsheets as shrouds and tying them with strong nylon cord. He worked methodically and with full concentration, doing his best to keep his mind empty of all else.

But after a while a cold rage broke through that made him hate the two agents even in death. They had robbed him of his future, fouled all that might have been good in his life. Insanely, he wished he could do them additional damage.

Still, all he finally did was what needed doing. He went downstairs, drove their car several blocks away and left it parked at a curb. Then he moved his own car, a jeep wagon, to the just-vacated space in front of his building, loaded the two bodies into it in a panic of sweat and strength, and shortly after 3:00 A.M. drove out of lower Manhattan and headed west to the Hudson River, then north toward the upper reaches of Putnam County.

He drove carefully, staying well within the posted speed limits. What was his rush? Regardless of how fast he drove, two government agents alleged or otherwise would still be dead in the back of his wagon, and he would still be in the worst trouble of his life.

Vittorio Battaglia!

The name alone was impossible. Imagine a helpless little kid being launched into life as *Victory Battle*. It was a joke. Unless, like Vittorio, he started right off taking the name seriously.

Vittorio himself, apparently, was still alive. Gianni had spoken the truth when he told Jackson and Lindstrom he had not seen Vittorio in twenty years. His friend had already disappeared by the time Gianni returned from his flight to Italy. He could not even remember the last time he saw him.

What Gianni *did* remember was the first time he saw him . . . when they were both eight years old and attending Mulberry Street Art School. Vittorio had instantly determined to live up to his name by trying to beat Gianni to death with his bony little fists. Almost everyone at the school was Italian, and Gianni considered his own half-Jewish blood a near-fatal handicap. How could a measly half-Italian compete artistically with a full-blooded line that had produced the likes of Michelangelo, da Vinci, and Raphael?

Vittorio, being pure, 100 percent Italian, suffered no such problem. And it showed in his work from day one. He had a flair and brilliance that Gianni admired and felt he could never achieve.

Parts of Gianni still felt that way. And it was not just foolish modesty. He knew exactly how much he had accomplished. Yet when he envisioned the absolute best he could do, and imagined it alongside something by Vittorio, it was like seeing a good rhinestone next to a perfect diamond. The rhinestone was created out of knowledge, discipline, and hard work. The diamond was a gift of nature, a flash of the purest light that had nothing to do with anything but God.

Deep in a patch of woods off Interstate 95, Gianni buried the last mortal remains of Special Agents Jackson and Lindstrom and felt the first piercing chill of a tracked animal. He felt nothing for the men themselves, not even his earlier rage. They had, after all, just been following orders. Now there was only the chill.

3

AT THE EDGE of a forest twenty miles north of Zagreb, Yugoslavia, the gunman sat near the edge of a forest and waited for the dawn that was still an hour away.

A rifle lay across his lap, and he fingered its stock, trigger guard, and barrel in ritual order. *My rosary*, he thought. Except that he had no prayers to recite, only the vague wish that everything would go well, quickly and without surprises.

He was close to the top of a hill that rose steeply above a cluster of houses a short distance below. Closer to where he sat, another house stood apart from the rest. There were lights in several rooms, but they had been on all night and did not mean anything.

He could see clearly through the lighted windows with his field glasses, and from time to time he had watched the guards talking and moving about. There were five of them, and they tended to huddle together for company instead of patrolling their posts in and around the house. Croats. Whatever their good points, disciplined soldiering was not one of them. Had they done their work right, he could never have moved in this close. As it was, he would have a clear shot, from good cover, at an effective range.

The sky slowly lightened. He loved this time just before the rising of the sun, with shadows fading to the soft grays of Whistler. These days, all anybody seemed to remember Whistler for was that uptight portrait of his mother, but it was his misty watercolors of London that were the best. You just had to look at them to breathe the Thames. He had always envied Whistler those paintings. There was such purity of purpose there, so clear a knowledge of what was right, that it made him wonder if the artist had ever been unsure of *anything*.

Beginning to grow stiff, he shifted to a prone position, careful to keep the rifle muzzle off the ground. The few trees below were clear now. He could see a table and chairs on the second-floor veranda of the solitary house. The veranda was open to the sky, and in the distance behind it, the more modern part of Zagreb's skyline rose above medieval walls.

Farther west, the first of the early morning flights took off from the city's airport, and he watched the plane's lights until they disappeared. If all went well, he would be up there himself in a few hours, heading home. And if it didn't go well? Then he might be delayed. Like forever.

For a while he just lay there quietly as the sky lightened further and the day came, a shining spring morning without clouds, and the colors running to soft pinks and purples. To distract himself and help pass the time, he imagined how he would paint it. You had to be careful about the softness because that was the thing in this . . . not so much the color, but the mood, which was of an absolute serenity.

You paint a great picture in your mind, he told himself. *We'll see if you can paint it as great when you're home with a brush in your hand, instead of out here holding a rifle.*

The gunman wished he were home right now. This whole assignment was confusing. Until he had gotten his orders, he had thought Stefan Milokov was high on the State Department's most favored list in the Balkans: a strong Croatian leader with democratic leanings and a genuine interest in a united Yugoslavia. Evidently he had been wrong. But these days there were so many changes in political alignment, so much switching about of friends into enemies and enemies into friends, that you needed a new briefing each morning.

The sun came up and shone on the house he was watching. He glanced at his watch. Soon, Colonel Milokov, a man of unswervingly regular habits, would be out on the veranda having his usual breakfast of croissants and coffee.

It was time to get ready.

First, he moved a small rock into position for support.

Then he stretched flat-out on the ground, rested the rifle barrel on the rock, and squinted through the telescopic sights. The chair in which the colonel would soon be sitting showed sharply behind the crosshairs. The gunman inserted a clip of special explosive rounds into the magazine, worked the bolt action that sent a round into the firing chamber, released the safety, and waited.

One of the guards came out first. He stretched, scratched himself, and leaned lazily against a wall of the veranda. A heavy-set woman brought out a full tray and prepared the table with a single place setting, a pot of coffee, a basket of croissants, and a folded newspaper. Then she went back inside.

Moments later, Milokov appeared. He spoke briefly to the guard, who laughed and went into the house.

The colonel sat alone at the table with the sun shining on him, a husky, thick-chested man with dark hair. He poured himself a cup of coffee and gazed thoughtfully up at the wooded slope.

The gunman dug his elbows into the damp earth, steadying himself, feeling the rifle stock smooth against his cheek. He let the crosshairs ease down from the dark gloss of Milokov's hair until they centered between his eyes. *Sorry, Colonel,* he thought, and meant it, because this had always been the worst time for him and the years had never improved it. He was the best there was at what he did, and he still believed in its final purpose, but the act of killing gave him no joy. It never had. He thanked Christ he wasn't one of those.

Then with a touch as sweet and light as a baby's breath, he squeezed off the round and saw it explode on target.

There was no need for a second shot.

Then the sirens went off. One was near the house itself, and the others sounded as though they were howling from the direction in which the gunman had left his car.

He swore softly. He had not known about the sirens and this bothered him. It was exactly the kind of thing that should not have happened.

So he sprinted, ducking low, through the brush in this place of green presence and flickering sunlight. He ran easily and without panic, centering everything about himself as

though no other world existed. In his mind there was almost
a symmetry to where he was that made it the perfect place to
be. He swept around trees and under vines, avoiding the
whip of branches, while beneath the sound of the sirens,
birds chattered and fluttered in fright.

Then he was going generally downward as the air became
cooler and more pine laden. He breathed deeply and evenly,
feeling as though he could run like this forever, with the sun
catching him in moments of heat and moments of cool, dark
shade. He was going just like this through a patch of purple-
green darkness when he suddenly came upon the soldiers.

There must have been a full squad, patrolling no more
than fifty yards from where he had hidden his car beneath
some thickets and branches. Bunched much too close together for effective patrolling, they whirled in shock as he
came dashing down the slope.

It was too late for him to change direction or take cover,
and he was quite prepared to die for his blunder. And by any
reasonable show of logic, he should have died, because he
just kept running straight at them like a maniac, his rifle
slung over one shoulder and both hands working at the
grenades, pulling and throwing, pulling and throwing, a mad-
man at a carnival, grabbing at brass rings and tossing fire-
balls.

But whatever cosmic forces could have gone right for him
during the next few moments did so. The sun angled blind-
ingly over the hill behind him. The soldiers were startled
enough by his lunacy to throw off their fire. His grenades exploded precisely where they should have. And if the heavens
themselves had opened and rained steel, the shower could
not have been more deadly.

Then still running, he had the rifle off his shoulder and in
his hands, feeling it spit at the smoking earth that smelled of
gunpowder and seared flesh, at the faces that rose up out of it
with open mouths and blood and dirt darkening the skin.

Seconds later, he was over and past the carnage.

The sirens were still going, but he saw no other soldiers.
Sprinting to his car, he removed the camouflage branches
and drove out from behind the brush to the dirt trail just be-

yond. In fifteen minutes he was mingling with the traffic on the main highway to Zagreb.

Before he reached the city, he made a short detour and dropped his rifle and remaining ordnance into a convenient river. Then he continued on to his hotel.

There he showered and trimmed the full moustache and neat Vandyke beard that had become so accustomed a part of his carefully chosen persona that it was hard for him to remember how he had once looked without them.

Adding to the changed appearance were the contact lenses that turned his hazel eyes an electric blue, and the fair, sun-streaked hair that had replaced the almost blue-black color with which he had been born.

He dressed and checked his papers.

At home, he had stashed away passports, driver's licenses, and credit cards under half-a-dozen different names and nationalities. But on this trip he traveled as Peter Walters, an American businessman born in Miami, Florida, and living in Positano, Italy. A name he had lived under for almost ten years.

Carrying only a single carry-on bag, he left his hotel room and paid his bill in cash.

Then he drove himself to the airport and returned his rental car at the main terminal.

His 5:00 P.M. flight to Naples was airborne at exactly 5:17. *I'm going home.*

There were severe electrical storms on their flight path so they were diverted to Rome and forced to lay over for several hours. When the man known as Peter Walters finally walked off the plane in Naples, it was well into the night and he was stiff with frustration.

But he had left his car parked at the airport, and once he was behind the wheel and moving, he could feel himself ease out of it. There was a full moon, and with its light catching the calm sea, the trip along the Amalfi Drive was even more spectacular than usual.

Walters drove slowly, wanting to stretch the vista. He had been living on the Amalfian Coast for close to nine years. How familiar it had become. Yet he still remembered the sharp pain that had come with his first sight of it, with his understanding of how much he had missed in his life, and how much his parents had missed and would now never have a chance to experience.

Still, he was trying.

When he finally reached Positano, he saw the moon silver the old Arab-Saracen–style houses rising up the mountain from the sea, and felt the place enter him.

His own house was among the highest, almost halfway up the cliffs, and he left the main road and began the winding climb. Here and there small, twisted trees and bushes had broken through the rock formations . . . tired, he thought, from struggling to get out to the sun. He understood that. He would not have wanted to stay covered over, either.

He parked beside his wife's tiny red Fiat and started up the seventeen curved stone steps that led to the arched entrance to his house. As always, he silently counted each step as he took it. He had forgotten when and why he had started the small rite. But it had become a kind of talisman for his family's well-being, a crazy little offering to the gods of good fortune that he knew he would probably do until he died.

A night light was burning in the entrance hall, and he took off his shoes and left them on the tile floor with his bag.

Upstairs, his son's bedroom door was open and he quietly went in.

My son sleeps, he thought, as though he were keeping a secret as desperate as mine. And to him, it undoubtedly was. At the age of eight, Paulie was still a secret thumb-sucker. Though not so secret. Asleep, he couldn't control it, and the thumb was in his mouth now. Even awake, he had occasional lapses and the kids hammered him unmercifully.

Pound for pound my son suffers more real pain without complaint or self-pity than anyone since Jesus, and there's no way I can help him.

Walters bent and kissed his cheek, feeling the skin still smooth and baby soft against his lips.

Paul stirred, the thumb instantly out of his mouth.

"Dad?"

The whispered word was in English, although he was truly bilingual and could just as easily have awakened in Italian.

Walters stroked his hair, as silky and blond as Peggy's had been before she dyed it. Physically, Paul was mostly his mother, with the kind of fair, classic good looks that everyone said was wasted on a boy but which Walters hoped he would one day learn to use to his advantage. What came from his side was the wide mouth, the deep-set eyes, and the vague hint of melancholy that was as much a part of him as his easy smile and hard core of stubbornness.

When all else failed, it could be a saving grace.

"Shhh . . . ," he said. "Go to sleep. We'll talk in the morning."

Seconds later, Paulie's breathing was easy and regular, and his thumb was back in his mouth.

Peter Walters undressed and showered without waking Peggy. She half awakened and reached for him as he slipped into bed.

"Aah, this is better," she sighed, adjusting her body to his. "I hate sleeping alone."

He smiled, holding her. "I never knew that."

"Everything all right?" she asked.

"Everything is fine."

"Miss me?"

"Like crazy."

"Isn't that lovely," she whispered and drifted off, still holding him.

She had no idea what he had been doing, of course. Although he had once tried to tell her, feeling that much need to share.

"How much do you love me?" he had asked.

"As much as it's possible."

"No matter what?"

"You should know that by now."

"Yes, but sometimes there are things that I have to do. They don't always make me feel very lovable."

"If you do them," she had said, with the absolute certainty of the young, the foolish, or the very much in love, "then it can't be too wrong."

"Some might think it is."

"Do you?"

"Sometimes. But even then I believe it has to be done."

"Then, it's all right," she had said, granting him final absolution.

4

GIANNI SAT IN the stationwagon about fifty yards down the block from his studio. It was late afternoon and he had been watching the building since early morning. He was waiting to see whether there would be any immediate follow-up to Jackson and Lindstrom.

It was just an ordinary day on the block. People walked quickly and with purpose on the sidewalks. Cars, taxis, and trucks passed in steady streams. The spring sun reflected at Gianni off cans and pieces of glass, off the windows of stores and buildings. He breathed slowly and evenly, and the air seemed to breathe with him.

Earlier in the day, near dawn, he had caught brief snatches of sleep in the wagon, followed by breakfast at an all-night truck stop. It was characteristic of the place that no one looked twice at his battered face. And sitting there, he had suddenly envied the truckers the sweet, simple clarity of their lives, of their daily comings and goings. As never before, he understood the appeal of what they did in their big rigs. Everything was open, known, laid out for them like the rules of a supportive religion. Unlike him, they had no mortal decisions to thrash out with their eggs and fries.

The thing was, would it be better for him to go back to SoHo and watch for more visitors? Or head straight for Greenwich and find out if Mary Yung was dead or alive? Gianni settled for getting the woman's number and making a call. But all he heard was a voice on an answering machine saying she was unavailable at the moment and to please leave a name and number.

Yes, but is she dead or alive?

So now he sat behind the tinted windows of his Cherokee, on his street in SoHo, lunching on the sandwich and soda he had picked up early that morning, and popping aspirin to keep his head from going off like a bomb.

Shortly after 4:00 P.M., two men Gianni didn't recognize stopped on the sidewalk in front of his loft building. They wore business suits and dark ties and, from a distance, might have been blood brothers to Jackson and Lindstrom. After peering at the cast-iron facade of the old building for several moments and looking up and down the block, they went inside.

Gianni fixed his eyes on the entrance and kept them there for almost two hours before the men finally came out, walked down the street and disappeared. Then Gianni waited another fifteen minutes and went upstairs.

What he found was a charnel house with the gore removed.

Nothing was whole.

Floorboards were ripped up and scattered like driftwood. Upholstered pieces, chairs and couches, were disemboweled, their insides streaming. Whatever paintings he had in the studio, both completed and in work, were cut to shreds. Closets and drawers had been emptied onto the floor. Not even Teresa's things, still undisposed of after all these months, had been spared.

None of this stuff had been alive, yet things had died here, thought Gianni, and felt he had just lost his wife into another depth of separation.

Teeth clenched, he moved through the ruin.

These men in their quiet ties and neat suits. They were looking for connections to Vittorio, but this was far more. Where did such rage and savagery originate? What was its purpose? He knew. The invading Germans in World War I had called it *Schrecklichkeit* . . . frightfulness . . . and it was meant to demoralize the enemy. A calm, deliberate horror.

Searching for answers, all Gianni found was the fine residue of ruin from a trash pit.

There was nothing left for him here.

Wrong. There were still a few things.

He found a small leather bag that had escaped the general

destruction and filled it with a few toilet articles, a couple of shirts, and some slacks and underwear.

Finally, he climbed a ladder, dug behind a lighting cove under the ceiling, and pulled out a 9mm automatic wrapped in an oil-soaked cloth. He checked the ammunition clip and found it fully loaded.

Then he tucked the gun inside his belt, closed his jacket over it, and walked out of the door without glancing back.

He tried calling Mary Chan Yung once more but still reached only her answering machine.

It was a bit past 8:00 P.M. when he drove over the Williamsburg Bridge and headed for Long Island.

5

CARLO DONATTI LIVED in a house, comparatively modest for its five acres of land and Sands Point address, but it *was* built of brick and stone. For an Italian, thought Garetsky, a house always had to be built of brick and stone. Otherwise, it was considered lacking in substance and unworthy of respect.

An electronically controlled gate stood across the driveway, and Gianni Garetsky pulled up to the security phone beside it. Such precautions seemed a holdover from the old days. Things were calmer, more intelligent, and better organized now. The current trends all leaned toward legitimacy, and gratuitous violence was frowned upon by the leading *famiglia* as the worst possible public relations. These days, when a body did occasionally turn up in the trunk of a car, it was more the exception than the rule, and usually the work of some not very bright loose cannon.

Generally, wiser heads prevailed, and Don Carlo Donatti was considered high among the wisest, with a law degree from Yale and a carefully nurtured public persona that at

least made him appear to fit in anywhere. He had been his father's *consigliere* at twenty-five and had taken over entirely
at the old don's death two years later.

Gianni picked up the security phone and heard it ring at
the other end.

"Who's there?" said a man's voice.

"Gianni Garetsky."

"*Who?*"

Gianni repeated his name. Few in the new crowd knew
him, and he was just as pleased to leave it that way.

"What d'yuh want?"

All charm, thought Gianni. "To see Don Donatti."

"What about?"

"Just give him my name."

"He doesn't see anybody this late."

"Just give the don my name."

Gianni spoke softly but something in his voice must have
gotten through.

"Hang on," said the man.

Moments later the iron gate swung open, and Gianni drove
up a long driveway edged with Belgian block. He parked the
wagon in front of a porticoed entrance and got out under a
wash of floodlights.

A solidly built, big-chested man was waiting at the door.
He looked just as unfriendly in person as he had sounded on
the phone.

"You carrying?" he asked.

Gianni nodded.

The man held out a king-size hand, and Gianni took the
automatic out of his belt and gave it to him. Then he patted
Gianni down, front to back, and felt his legs for an ankle holster.

"Let's see your driver's license."

He checked the photo against Gianni's swollen, discolored
face and grinned. "You used to be prettier. What happened?
Her husband come home?"

"How'd you know?"

"Hey, I been there." The man nodded past the stairs. "First
room on the right. The door's open."

It was a big room that served as a combination sitting

room and study. The don rose from an oversize armchair beside an open fire. He wore an exquisitely tailored silk robe over his pajamas, and his hands fussed with an unlit cigarette in a holder.

Gianni Garetsky went through the formal greeting ritual, then sat down farther from the fire. The heat was inside him, a slow burning.

"I'm sorry to disturb you at this hour, Godfather."

Don Donatti sat looking at his face. He might have been weighing and measuring the damage, adding it up for a final total.

"Who did this to you?"

"Two men. They said FBI and had all the right credentials, but who knows?"

"Where are they now?"

"Buried in some woods."

The don sat in silence. He shifted in his chair, barely disturbing the robe and pajamas.

"You got a light?" he said.

Gianni took out some matches and lit the don's cigarette. The man closed his eyes and inhaled deeply.

"So what happened, Gianni?"

The artist lit a cigarette for himself and began his curious devil's tale. There was little light in the room, just that of a lamp and the glow from the fire, and the mood was that of a cave. By the time Garetsky finished, he no longer felt connected to himself.

Donatti sighed. "You have the woman's picture?"

Gianni showed it to him. "Did you ever see her with Vittorio?"

"I never saw any of Vittorio's girls," said the don flatly. "The great lover's comedies with women he played somewhere else." His voice was disapproving. "*Cinese*," he said.

"Why would the FBI want him this bad after so many years?"

"Who knows with those *zotichi*? They sniff after their own assholes. But my feeling is they were not really FBI. As for Vittorio, he just went off on a job for us one day and never come back."

"You didn't think it strange?"

Muscles worked like wires along Donatti's jaw. "Let me tell you something about your friend. He was good at what he did, and I trusted him, and he never hurt the family, but there were always spaces inside him I couldn't reach. Anyway, you live long enough, nothing is strange. It just happens."

Cigarette ash dropped on the don's robe and he brushed it off.

"But you've got the trouble now, not Vittorio," he said. "So I like it that you came to me. But I won't fool you, Gianni. You've got a bad one here. And you know where they're coming next? Right here to me."

"I'm sorry."

Donatti waved his cigarette impatiently. "Vittorio was one of mine. Where else would they go if they want him? But I can still handle those *strunzi*. What bothers me is you can't stay here. By morning they'll be buzzing around like flies on shit."

"I didn't come to stay. I just hoped you might know what this is all about."

The don shook his head. He stared dimly for a moment at a wall of pictures. The photos showed him with an assortment of the famous and powerful at every level.

"America's leaders, Gianni. And they're all happy to accept our money. But only anonymously."

Donatti rose, opened a hidden wall safe, and took out a black bag. "Do you have a good gun?" he asked the artist.

"Yes."

"Well, there's another one for you in this bag. The serial number's filed off and it's got a beautiful silencer. Also, I'm giving you a hundred thousand in cash so you don't have to worry about getting picked up in some bank."

"I don't—"

"Just listen to me. You don't know how long this *contaminazione* could drag on or where it could lead. If you need a safe passport, credit card, or driver's license, there's some of each in the bag all under clean names. All you need is your own picture taken and stuck on."

Don Carlo Donatti closed the safe, walked over to Gianni

Garetsky, and placed the black bag on his lap. When Gianni started to protest, the don held up his hand for silence.

"I want you to keep in touch, Gianni. Listen to this number . . . two four six, two four six eight. Remember it. Don't write it down. It's my safe phone. Buried in lead cable. No taps. If you hear any voice but mine, it means I'm *morto*. So hang up. I made the number easy. Even panic won't block it out. Say it for me."

Gianni said it. A schoolboy, he thought, repeating an important lesson in survival.

"I can't call you," said Donatti, "so you have to call me. Don't worry. I won't be sitting with my *coglioni* in my hand. All my old friends aren't gone. Somebody has to know something."

He moved closer to the artist and stared at his eyes. "How do you feel about having to do the job on those two men?"

"They did it to themselves. So I don't feel anything."

"Fine."

The don reached out a hand and stroked the back of Gianni's head as he would a child's. "I should know by now what you've got. At seventeen you dealt with an *assassino* as few made men could. Your head is on straight. Just don't get careless."

They looked at each other. Being with the don in this room, listening to him, Gianni could feel exactly what Donatti had become in the strict order he had imposed on himself in his chosen life. He was an educated man, the best of the family's new breed, but he still insisted on control.

"About Vittorio?" said Gianni. "That last job you sent him out on before he disappeared? What was it?"

Donatti shrugged. "I think you were in Italy at the time. We had us a crazy, a real *pazzerello*. He was screaming his head off, couldn't be reasoned with anymore. So we sent your friend to quiet him before he caused the family terrible trouble. And that was it. No one ever saw Vittorio or the *pazzerello* again."

"Who was the crazy?"

The don needed a moment. "Frank Alberto. An old Moustache Pete from downtown. I doubt that you knew him."

Gianni sat holding the black bag on his lap. He had known

the man's son from art school, a fat, curly-haired kid named Angie who was always getting beat up on. Gianni remembered protecting him once, then regretting it because the kid was so grateful he became a pest.

"One more thing," said the Don. "Don't tell me where you're going when you leave here, and don't tell me where you are when you call. That way you can be sure I won't start singing if they put a hot iron to my balls."

"I'm not worried about you, Godfather."

Donatti's eyes went dark. "You're not stupid, Gianni, so don't say stupid things. Finally, everybody talks."

6

PETER WALTERS WOKE to the sound of a bird and the old man staring at him, one-eyed, from the easel. The eye was a glittering amber that caught the rising sun and threw it back like chipped glass. The other eye, the blind one, gazed out of a milky pool. It had been blinded by the Germans when the old man was a young partisan.

Now, almost fifty years later, the result gazed out of a still-wet canvas in a corner of his bedroom. The old man had a peasant's horror of the image and had not wanted to pose. But he needed the lire so he had sat for three hours in Peter's studio, alternately dozing and mumbling into his beard.

The painting had life. The old man was there. Not just flesh, bones, rags, hair. The rest, too. It blazed out of the one good eye and hooked across the artist's chest. The old man hated him, hated anyone young, strong, whole . . . hated the little he'd had and the still less left to him. And every brush stroke screamed it.

Other than for Peggy's soft breathing at Peter's back, there was no other sound in the room. He soaked it in, lost himself in it. A wonderful sweetness gathered in his throat. This morning, he was an artist.

It was that first waking glance that told everything. Good or bad, it hit the moment you opened your eyes. The easel was always placed so that whatever canvas was in work would be seen instantly, without time to prepare defenses. And today, at least, he had won.

He stretched, lengthened his body into the cool margins of the bed, and felt Peggy come awake beside him.

"What time is it?" she whispered.

"Love time," he said and reached for her.

My reward.

Coming together now, they made love almost without preliminary. Yet even the heat was cool in mood and without the urgency to take pleasure. Peter's eyes had been closed but he opened them now and looked at Peggy in the soft dawn light. How familiar, how dear she had become.

Once years ago, before they had left America, she had come up to him in a large room full of people and said softly, "Don't go away from me. I couldn't bear it if you ever went away from me."

She had been standing close, seemingly unaware of anyone else about them, looking up at him very seriously. With some wonder, he had thought, *She means it, she actually does mean it.*

When they made love for the first time later that night, she called it her first resurrection. Wasn't she being raised from a particular kind of death? Still, when she saw all the scars on his body, some of the joy went out of her celebration.

She had cried, and held him.

He had tried to prepare her by saying he had been in Vietnam. It was a lie. He had not been near the war. Not that one, anyway.

Later, she let her anger fly. "The bastards! I hate them all."

"Who?"

"The politicians, the generals, all the damned war lovers," she said bitterly. "All those who got rich and famous and made glorious speeches while thousands of kids like you were out getting shot up for *God* and *country.* How I despise those two words."

"Why?"

"Because sooner or later people are asked to die for them."
God help me, he had thought, *if she ever finds out what I really do.*

All she knew was that his work had to do with something unofficially governmental, and no more than that. The ground rules had been set early. You loved, you trusted, and you asked no questions. It was how they had lived for more than nine years. It was how they were living still.

She was above him now, all sweet balm to his flesh. The things she aroused in him. It was a mystery. All this time and the excitement remained. How?

Finally, the original coolness was gone and the rushing had taken over, that wild blend of flesh and feeling that always made you begin. Then with a sudden urgency at his back, she had hold of him and he felt her dissolve, and himself with her.

The school year had ended so Peter took Paul out for a few hours of painting.

Art was not something he had ever pressed on his son. The feeling for it was simply there. And his Paulie was good. Not only in the technical skills, which could be learned. But he was good in the quiet, stubborn passion you either had or didn't have.

His son looked at things. He saw them. He sat for hours in his father's studio, silent, unmoving, watching him paint. He felt the emptiness of a room before he entered it. He enclosed himself in stillness until the absence of sound took a shape of its own. Sometimes the shape filled him until he was afraid there might not be room enough inside him to breathe.

He knew such things about his son because Paul told him about them. The boy had no idea how extraordinary they were.

He thought everyone experienced the same stuff, and his father was careful not to let him know they didn't. To a kid, being different meant not being as good.

Today they had set up their easels on a rocky promontory overlooking the Bay of Salerno and the houses, olive trees, and citrus groves of Positano. Edging the water were the stone towers that had defended the villagers of a thousand years ago against Saracen pirates. Perhaps a mile out to sea rose the great black rocks from which beautiful sirens had once tempted Ulysses.

They worked about ten yards apart, their canvases shaded by a pair of carob trees. They painted steadily and in silence, though one would sometimes turn to see what the other was doing. When their eyes met, they would smile. But Paul always waited for his father to smile first. He was afraid that if he smiled too much, his father might think he didn't take his painting seriously enough.

Next to painting with his father, Paul loved just being with him. Even if it was only taking a walk through the village, and maybe along the beach and finally stopping for a while where the rocks came down to the water.

They had been to the rocks just last Sunday. It was a clear morning, and his father sat smoking and looking out at the sea. There was no sound but that of the wind in a few trees, and his father had looked up into the leaves and past the leaves into the wide blue sky, not smiling, but with his face as pleased and young as Paul had ever seen it. Then Paul felt his father's hand on his head. It pushed the hair back from his forehead and smoothed it while Paul pressed his head backward against the big hand until it slipped over the side of Paul's face and drew his head down against his father's chest. Paul could feel the beating heart. He heard his father sigh once. Then the hand lifted from him and they both stood up. Walking home, Paul held his father's hand. He liked it that they could be together without anybody speaking.

This afternoon they painted until the sky clouded over and the light turned bad. Then they gathered their things and started back toward the village. It was a long climb over steep, twisting paths, and they stopped at one point to rest.

"Papa," said Paul.

He was speaking mostly in Italian today and that was how Peter answered. "Yes?"

"Can I ask you an important question?"

"Why not?"

"But will you tell me the truth?"

"Don't I always?"

"No."

"Hey! You calling your papa a liar?"

"You know what I mean," said the boy. "It's like when you don't want me to know something, so you make a kind of joke out of it."

"All right. What's the question?"

"Are you a mafioso?"

Peter Walters laughed. "That's some question."

"See? You're laughing. You're making it a joke."

Peter looked at his son. Serious. Always so serious. He wished the boy would laugh more.

"I apologize," he said. "It's just that it's a strange question for a boy to ask his father. So which of your friends said I was a mafioso?"

"Pietro Dolti. He heard his father talking."

"What did his father say?"

"That you weren't somebody to fool with. That he thought you knew a lot of bigshots in Palermo. That you always had plenty of money and nobody knew how you got it."

"And what do *you* think, Paulie? You think I'm a bigshot gangster?"

The boy looked down at his hands. He wondered if his hands would be as big and strong as his father's one day. He wondered if all the things that were kept so secret inside his father were hidden somewhere inside him, too.

"I don't know," he said, and took a few extra moments to work up his courage. "You go on these trips. I keep wondering where you go. I think about what you do."

"I work for a big American company. Sometimes I have to meet with people. They're in all different places. You know that."

"I don't care if you're a mafioso, Papa. I don't care *what* you are." Paul felt his lip tremble and covered it with the back of his hand. "I just don't want anything to happen to you."

"I'm no mafioso, Paulie. Forget about Pietro Dolti's old man. He talks with his tongue dipped in shit."

Paul gazed blindly at his father. He pictured him lying in a gutter with blood gushing from his mouth. He had seen *The Godfather*—parts I, II, and III. He knew all too well what fi-

nally happened to even the best, the toughest of gangsters.
He tried to speak, but something was stuck in his throat and
no words came.

"Listen to me, Paulie." Peter gripped his son's arms, feeling how slight they were, how delicate. "You know how I
feel about our Lord, Jesus Christ, don't you?"

The boy nodded, although he had no idea how his father
felt about Jesus Christ. In fact he could not remember his father ever saying anything at all about Him.

"Well," said his father, "I solemnly swear in the name of
our sweet Lord, Jesus Christ, that I'm no mafioso."

They stared at each other.

"Do you believe me now?" Peter asked.

Still not sure he had a voice, Paul nodded.

"Good. And what do you have to say about Pietro Dolti's
shit-eating old man?"

The boy finally found a kind of voice. "Fuck him."

It was the first time he had ever said the word in front of
his father. But it was the single word that seemed able to
come out of his throat.

"Exactly," said Peter Walters.

7

GIANNI ASSUMED THAT by now there would probably be an
all points bulletin out on his wagon, so his first move was to
leave it at JFK's long-term parking area and to pick up an in-
nocuous gray Ford Fairlane from Hertz. He used one of the
credit cards the don had given him. It was under the name of
Jayson Fox of Richmond, Virginia, and went through the
computer with no problem.

Gianni's second move was to again try to reach Mary
Chan Yung. This time a live voice answered and he felt instant relief. They had not gotten to her yet.

"Harriet?" he said.

"There's no Harriet here. What number did you want?"

Her voice was pleasant, light, and with no trace of an accent. But what had he expected? An updated dragon lady?

Gianni recited her correct number with one digit altered.

"You have the wrong number," she told him.

"I'm sorry," he said, and hung up.

It took him close to forty minutes to reach Greenwich and another fifteen to find the house, a cedar ranch overlooking Long Island Sound. There were no cars in the driveway and lights were on in several rooms.

Still, being cautious, he drove his rented Fairlane a good hundred yards past the driveway, pulled it off the road, and parked behind some brush. Then he walked back to the house, bent low behind the shrubbery, and peered through the corner of a living-room window.

Gianni had a moment then. For something in the sight of the woman he saw reading beside a lamp, some curiously tender sense that this beautiful, alien stranger was under the same threat of pain and death as he, set a small forest of nerves going inside him.

Sitting motionless, Mary Chan Yung had the stillness of a photograph. Then as if aware of Gianni's presence, she looked up toward the window where he crouched. She could not have seen him, yet her gaze gave him the feeling of being illuminated. She returned to her reading, and Gianni left to check the other lighted rooms: a kitchen, a study, and a bedroom. All were empty.

He went around to the front and rang the doorbell.

A floodlight went on and Mary Yung opened the door without first looking to see, or even asking, who was there. It seemed more a matter of style than of carelessness or bravery.

What she saw was a badly battered stranger, and no sign of a car in the driveway.

Her hand went to her mouth. "Dear God. You've been in an accident."

Gianni forced his lips into a kind of pained smile. "All this happened last night, Miss Yung. And it was no accident."

In his mind he was still smiling, but it was actually more of a grimace.

"My name is Gianni Garetsky," he said. "I'm an old friend of Vittorio Battaglia's."

Mary Yung stood looking at him.

"Of course. You're the artist. I saw your picture in this morning's *Times*. Vittorio used to talk about you a lot." She paused to let things come together. "But what . . ."

"I have to talk to you. It's important. May I come in?"

She nodded. "Please."

But once inside the brightly lighted living room, Gianni just felt exposed. Others could be arriving at any time, and he was afraid of being blindsided. Outside, everything was black.

"I know this sounds crazy," he said, "but you're in serious danger here. I was beaten half to death last night because two men with guns wanted to know where Vittorio was, and I couldn't tell them. And I'm afraid you're next on the list."

Lips parted, she stared at him. The lamplight caught her forehead and threw a shadow across most of her face. What remained visible might have belonged to some classic figurine.

"Who were the men?" she finally asked.

"They said FBI."

"The FBI goes around beating famous artists half to death these days?"

Gianni shrugged. He had no idea what she was feeling, but he was impressed by her surface calm. "I don't think they were real FBI and I'm sure they weren't about to leave me around to tell anyone."

"I haven't seen Vittorio in years. What makes you think I'm next?"

Gianni showed Mary Chan Yung the photograph of her and Vittorio, along with her biographical printout. She studied them both, a striking woman of cool lavender shadows and hidden ghosts.

"They gave these to you?" she said.

"They didn't *give* me anything, Miss Yung."

Her eyes were flat. "Vittorio always said you were a hard-head. Even as a boy."

He left that one alone.

"So what do we do, Mr. Garetsky?"

"First, we talk. But not in this room, and not with any lights on."

They ended up in the adjoining study with a bottle of Napoleon brandy and the house silent and dark around them. Other than for a patch of moon silvering the floor, everything was black.

"Do you know where Vittorio is?" said Gianni.

"No."

"When did you last see him?"

"About nine years ago."

"Is that when you broke up?"

"Pretty much."

"What happened between you?"

She lifted her snifter and breathed the brandy. "The usual. First, the excitement fades and everything becomes habit. Then one of you meets someone new."

"Which of you met someone new?"

"Vittorio."

Gianni found it hard to imagine. "Who was she?"

"I never knew."

Mary Yung rose and settled against a wall. She seemed to be leaning on a shadow.

"You're a celebrated artist," she said. "You're not just anybody. Why can't you call the police?"

"And tell them what? That a couple of supposed federal agents beat me up and were going to torture and kill me, so *I* killed *them* instead?"

His actually putting it into words appeared to affect her, and she began pacing. In the reflected moonlight, he saw her in parts . . . slender, graceful legs, a hip's curve, high perfect breasts, a China-doll face under sleek blue-black bangs. *How could Vittorio have left her?*

"Then we spend the rest of our lives hiding in dark rooms?" she said.

"Hardly." He could make out her eyes, deeply set in the oval of her face. "But we can't do much of anything until we find out why Vittorio's suddenly important enough for those two men to have come after me as they did."

"How are we supposed to manage that?"

"By taking one step at a time. By grabbing whoever walks in here looking for you and asking questions. But that's *my* job. What I'd like *you* to do right now is pack a bag, check into a local motel, and wait for me to call you."

She considered him through the dark. "And if you're dead and can't call. Where do I go then?"

"I don't expect to be dead."

"No? You mean that's not included in your one-step-at-a-time plan?"

Mary Yung came over and sat down facing him.

"Well, here's what *I* don't expect, Mr. Garetsky. I don't expect to be anyplace but right here with you when some stranger comes into my house. I'm not a delicate, eyelash-fluttering innocent. I own a licensed firearm, I know how to use it, and I've rubbed knees under the table with some very bad boys. So since Vittorio seems to have dumped my life on the line right along with yours, it looks like you're stuck with a partner."

Gianni saw no point in arguing. Besides, it would help to have her with him.

There were things to consider.

How many men would be coming?

Would they play it straight and come right up to the front door, or pick a lock and come in on their own?

If they did ring the bell, should Mary Yung open the door or let them break in and then surprise them?

They discussed everything as equals, their lives weighted the same on some invisible set of scales. Her calm, Gianni decided, was more than just surface. She was cool straight through.

She showed Gianni her revolver, a snub-nosed, nickel-plated .38 that looked, in her hand, as though it had been specially designed for her by Ralph Lauren. Gianni had never known a woman who actually owned a gun. His wife had hated and feared simply the sight of one. She despised violence. All life was sacred to her, even a fly's. He teased her about it at first but soon stopped. She took it too seriously.

"Why do you have this?" he asked.

"Because I live and travel alone and there are a lot of crazies around."

"Have you ever shot anyone?"

"So far, I haven't had to."

"But you've fired the piece on a range?"

"Yes."

"Are you any good?"

"I can hit what I aim at."

"It's different when you aim at a person."

"I'm sure it is," she said. "But whatever I have to do, I'll do."

Gianni believed her.

By 2:00 A.M. they were drinking coffee, crushing out cigarettes in ceramic ashtrays, and listening for sounds. Gianni felt tired yet strangely easy. Now there was just the waiting. But that could be minutes, hours, or even days.

They took turns dozing.

Once, asleep in her chair, she showed a soft, child's face. Until some passing dream made it change and her features became harsh, sensual, those of a woman with product to sell. Then this mask, too, cracked and a smooth-faced girl of eighteen showed herself to Gianni, skin almost luminous, a Chinese virgin with everything good still ahead.

Her eyes slowly opened.

"That's unfair," she said. "Watching a woman sleep is more intimate than seeing her naked. Now you know all my secrets."

Gianni breathed her fragrance in the air around her. It teased the edges of memories just beyond his reach.

"But I know all about you, too," Mary Yung said. "Over the years, I've looked long and hard at every painting you've ever done. You don't hold back a thing."

"What would be the point?"

"It's always safer to keep something in reserve."

"I don't paint to stay safe."

In the early dawn Mary Yung was pacing again, and Gianni watched her silhouette move back and forth across the windows.

"Maybe they're not coming," she said.

"They'll come. But it's daylight now, so they won't be breaking and entering. They'll be ringing the front doorbell. That's what we have to be ready for. Do you have it all straight in your head?"

"Yes."

She made orange juice, toast, and coffee for breakfast. Gianni ate four slices of toast. He was hungrier than he had expected.

Now, as they talked, they had become just plain Mary Yung and Gianni.

Then they began the waiting again.

8

AT 9:10 A.M. a car rolled into the driveway and parked in front of the garage.

Mary Yung and Gianni watched it from behind the living-room curtains, a blue Chevrolet sedan with a high antenna and yellow fog lights that cut through the dark-gray morning and steadily falling rain.

A couple of men got out, and Gianni recognized them as the two who had torn apart his loft. Then a third man appeared, carrying an attaché case.

Two weren't goddamn enough, thought Gianni, and a vein was suddenly pulsing in his neck.

He touched Mary Yung's shoulder and felt her warmth. Then he left the living room and took his position in the study.

The doorbell rang, and a moment later Gianni heard Mary Yung's footsteps in the entrance hall and the front door being opened.

Enclosed in his own stillness, Gianni listened to the double charade: the phony agents, playing out their polite ritual of authority . . . Mary Chan Yung, projecting surprise and concern.

Then Gianni heard them all entering the living room, where the delicate part would be to get the three men seated with their backs to the door and Mary Yung facing them.

How much suddenly depends on this woman.

Still, using her own subtle blend of charm, deference, and sexuality, Mary Yung seemed to be doing just fine.

And the men?

Without seeing them, Gianni could almost sniff their heat at the prospect of interrogating a woman like Mary Chan Yung. And that was before they were even exposing her flesh to their dirty little toys. You had to be born to stuff like this.

I'm ready for the sonsofbitches.

He waited for Mary Yung's signal. As soon as the three agents were properly settled on the couch with their backs to the door, she would ask if any of them had a cigarette, and Gianni would be off on her words. Mary's own revolver was tucked just under the edge of her chair cushion and would be in her hand the instant Gianni appeared.

Their worst-case scenario was that one of the men would suddenly decide to leave the living room and search the house. If that happened, Mary Yung would warn Gianni by going into a fit of coughing. Then she would pull her gun and cover the agents until Gianni came in and disarmed them.

It all seemed simple enough in the planning, but Gianni knew better.

With his ear to the wall, he listened to their interrogation. But he was hearing more than just words. One of the men was walking, not sitting, and Gianni followed the sound of his footsteps on the flooring. The sound hung in the air, numbing everything. It made what followed seem dreamlike and slow.

First, there were the footsteps sounding louder and coming closer.

Then Gianni had the earliest notion of leaning toward the door, his body getting ready, starting with the tiniest bones in his feet. He knew instantly what was coming next, as though the don's personal gun carried its own black powers of perception.

He and the gun knew.

It was the truth, and he was moving a good few seconds before the sound of Mary Yung's coughing came through the wall. He actually noticed a pair of watercolors as he swept past them, along with his own blurred reflection in a hall mirror.

Then he was in the living room and one of the men was coming toward him, his eyes suddenly wide as he groped for his holster. Gianni started to raise his gun, but there was an explosion before he could bring it to bear and the man went down on his knees and then on his chest.

Gianni looked at the others in the room. His ears rang from the gun blast and he saw streaks that might have been rain. Mary Yung was still sitting in the chair. The other two men were half off the couch and pulling at their guns as she fired again.

One of the men went over backward.

The other man was still tugging at his holster as Gianni caught him in the head with his gun butt. He fell and lay still.

Mary Yung sat with her revolver in both hands, continuing to aim where the man had been before Gianni hit him. Then she slowly lowered her gun.

"Have you forgotten?" said Gianni. "We need someone alive to question."

She just looked at him.

Smoke drifted in the gray light. The air smelled burned and felt humid with blood.

Gianni bent to the two men Mary Yung had shot. They were both dead.

"Will any neighbors hear the shots?" he asked.

"No. The nearest one is acres away."

Gianni lifted the unconscious man onto the couch. He found a pair of handcuffs on him and cuffed his hands behind his back.

Mary Yung sat watching him, not moving.

"You all right?" he asked.

"Why shouldn't I be all right? They came into my house

to hurt and probably kill me. I just wish I could do it all again."

Gianni didn't believe it.

"Better feed this one some brandy," he said. "We've got to get him talking."

Gianni went through the attaché case and found its contents an exact duplication of the one in his loft—same photographs, same computer printouts, same electroshock persuader. Apparently, this was standard equipment on the hunt for Vittorio Battaglia.

He heard a groan and saw Mary Yung working some brandy between the agent's lips. He was a chunky, muscular man with a jaw like an ax blade, and ochre animal eyes that seemed to live for a contest. His identification said he was Spl. Agt. Tom Bentley.

Gianni allowed him a few minutes to come out of it.

"Your buddies are dead," he told him. "So you're all we've got to answer our questions. You can do it easy or hard. It's up to you."

The agent looked at Gianni Garetsky and Mary Chan Yung. Then he looked at the electric persuader lying prominently beside the couch.

"What are your questions?"

"Why is Battaglia being hunted? Who wants him? Are you people really FBI or just playing at it?"

"That's all?"

"Yes."

Bentley lay there with it. The things he knew settled on him with a certainty that accepted no misunderstandings.

"And if I don't answer?"

Mary Yung cut in. "Then you'll end up as dead as we will. Only a lot sooner."

Bentley considered her with his pale, yellow eyes. "You're sure one beautiful woman, Miss Yung." He grinned. "And one beautiful shooter, too."

"This is no joke," she said.

"I know it's no joke. But what I don't know is what happens to me if I give you your answers."

"You won't be hurt," said Gianni. "We'll leave you in the

basement. When we're out of here, we'll let the police know where you are."

The agent was still staring at Mary Yung. When he spoke, it was directly to her. It was as though Gianni had left the room.

"Killing me won't get you your answers," he said. "Neither will hurting me. I can take as much of that as you've got. So that leaves you only one way to get what you want."

"What's that?"

"Giving me what *I* want," said Bentley. "And that's half an hour in bed with you."

Mary Yung's face showed nothing. "Are you serious?"

"I've never had a chance at a woman as beautiful as you, and probably won't again. Why wouldn't I be serious?"

"Because if I agree and you don't come through, I'll kill you."

Gianni shook his head. "I don't believe I'm hearing this."

"Why?" Mary Yung said. "Is it that offensive to you?"

The artist looked from her to Bentley, as if measuring the distance between them. The centers of his eyes had widened.

"Listen, Gianni," she said flatly. "My body's not sacred. I'm thirty-four years old and I can't even remember the names of half the men I've fucked. What can one man more or less do to me? Especially if it gets us answers that could save our lives."

"There are other ways to get answers."

"How? By torturing a man half to death? You think that's better? More moral?"

Gianni was silent. He was not even close to figuring this woman. For the moment, he had stopped trying. Somehow, he could not help comparing her to Teresa. They were that different. Or was that what fascinated him?

"All right," Mary Yung said to Bentley. "It's a deal."

She turned to the artist. "Gianni, you're going to have to give us a hand with this."

It wasn't that simple a situation. Logistics and security were involved, so it took some figuring. But the end result was at least workable, leaving Bentley on his back in Mary Yung's bed with both wrists handcuffed to the brass headboard. A man on a sexual cross.

And Mary Chan Yung?

To the artist she had a separate set of expressions for each passing scene in her act. It was little different from watching her doze last night. At moments, she seemed to draw cupidity out of the air, a whore's knowledge that wore the sour look of multiple betrayals and disappointments. Then that ridiculously tiny nose would sniff the same air and all would change, leaving her an uncertain child fearful of getting caught in some dirty act she didn't really understand.

Then Gianni's part in the arrangements was finished and he started to leave the room.

"Hey, Garetsky," said Bentley from the bed.

Gianni turned.

"Don't you want to stay and watch?"

The artist stood there. The windows were closed and the air was full of burgeonings that might have carried their own sly, bright fever. Mary Yung looked at him and her face was quite apart from her now, with that special female look that said everything in sight was hers and if you didn't like it, too bad.

He left the room and closed the door behind him.

Not wanting to go back to what was waiting in the living room, Gianni sat with a cigarette in the study. He tried to keep his head empty and simply stare out the window at the streaks of sun that had just broken through the trees and onto the grass. But he kept thinking of the two dead men lying on the living-room floor, and of what was happening on Mary Yung's bed.

Occasional sounds came from the bedroom, and Gianni made a great effort not to listen by thinking about his wife and how it had been when they made love. But he might as well have been thinking of two other people. No. Another species from another planet. Neither of them were there for him anymore. After a while, he just sat smoking.

He was on his fourth cigarette and the sun had disappeared once more when the shot exploded. A certain feeling settled and he watched himself jump out of his chair, knocking it over.

Gun in hand, he burst into the bedroom.

Mary Yung stood naked beside the bed, holding her

nickel-plated revolver. Her face was flushed, moist, and without expression.

Bentley was naked only from the waist down. His wrists were still cuffed to the bars of the brass headboard, and there was a small hole just off-center in his forehead. A fine trickle of blood ran down his face and dripped from his chin. Supported by the spread of his arms, his head drooped only slightly.

Gianni took a deep breath. "What happened?"

"It was all so stupid. I got careless and he got his legs around my neck and was choking me. I had no choice."

Gianni Garetsky just looked at her. The only thing he felt clear about was that she was lying.

Mary Yung bent to pick up her clothes. Her bottom glistened. Then moving quickly, she dressed herself where she stood.

"Let's get out of here," she said.

She went straight for the Napoleon and said nothing until she had swallowed a fair amount.

"Here's what we've got," she finally said. "The FBI part is real. Though not officially. Bentley called it a code-three operation."

"What's that?"

"Nothing in writing or on wire. And at their level they never know where the orders come from. It could be CIA, State, Justice, or even the Oval Office. But it's always from very high up, and always top priority."

"All this to pick up a small-time hood?"

"Yes."

"Did they know a reason for the hunt?"

"Not a whisper."

"What were their orders on us?"

"Do anything to get answers. But no killing."

"Terrific. That's everything he told you?"

She nodded.

"You think it was the truth?"

"Pretty much."

"Then why did you kill him?"

"I told you."

"I know what you told me," said Gianni.

Mary Yung looked at him over her brandy. "Why would I lie to you?"

"That's what I have to find out." The artist lit a cigarette. "We're way over our heads, Mary Yung. Between us, we've wasted what now seems to be five feds in three days. We were under the gun for four, so it's only this last one that bugs me. You made a deal with the guy. He was handcuffed to the bed. Why did you shoot him?"

This time Mary Yung didn't even bother explaining. Her words seemed to be stuck inside her head.

"We've got only each other in this," said Gianni. "But if I can't trust you, I'm walking out of here this minute. Is that what you want?"

"No."

"Then I want to know why you lied to me."

"Because I was afraid to tell you the truth."

"And what's the truth?"

She needed a moment to collect the words. "I didn't want him around to tell about my shooting the others. This way I can at least get rid of the bodies. Like you did with your two. Then all they can do is suspect."

"You had it planned when you went in there with him?"

"Yes."

"Why did you keep it from me?"

"Because I had the feeling you wouldn't be happy about it."

"And *you're* dancing with joy?"

"I do what I have to do, Gianni." Her voice was so low her teeth and gums seemed to be in it.

Gianni was silent. But there was something bad in his face that got through to her.

"I'm sorry if I disgust you," she said.

"I'm not that holy. I just don't understand you."

"How can you understand me? You don't even know me."

At least that much is true, he thought.

"All you know," she said, "is what you read in that dumb computer printout. And that was nothing but a pack of lies I made up for my press releases."

"Then tell me the truth."

She shook her head. "I'm afraid you'd leave me flat."

"Try me."

"I can't take that chance. Not now. Not with three dead Fibbies hanging around my house."

A look of hers went through him.

All right. So he knew she was a liar and little better than a whore in her thinking. But he also knew there was absolutely no way he was about to leave her.

9

HENRY DURNING, A tall, physically imposing man with intense eyes, was delivering a lecture before an overflow crowd at Columbia Law School in New York. It was one of many such talks he gave at regular intervals from some of the country's most prestigious platforms.

Durning used these and other forms of public address because they allowed him to be seen and heard as he wished to be seen and heard. He believed every occasion had its propaganda potential. You had an idea, a conviction, a wish, and you disseminated it. If you were good enough, if your words took, those who heard you were influenced to feel the same way.

In his own case, Durning, the United States attorney general, tried to make it known to thinking audiences everywhere that even the best of laws were all but worthless unless their true spirit was generally understood, accepted, and put into practice.

And what was Durning telling his audience today? What quick-fix solutions to the country's statutory ills was he projecting with his usual dynamic thrust?

No easy solutions. Only his core message that as long as the lawful rights of a single American—male or female; black, white, or yellow; native or foreign born—were threatened by prejudice, then the rights of every other American were equally threatened.

Durning's message.

Even-toned, clearly enunciated, it sailed across the auditorium on wings of metaphysical logic. Here on this podium he was an authority, the respected head of the United States Department of Justice and onetime war hero, to whom large audiences listened with attention bordering on reverence. Were they and he crazy? At times, Durning believed so. But more often he knew it was the strength to master your own weakness, and do what you had to do daily and without complaint, that made the only true heroes.

Still, they had hung the Medal of Honor about his neck for a different reason and made another sort of hero out of him. A war hero. Maybe they had even made him a symbol. But a symbol of what, Durning didn't know. Unless it was the image of him as a onetime intellectual, a professor of law, no less, who could be trained to kill the enemies of his country with exceptional skill.

The attorney general did not stay long after the lecture. He usually enjoyed the follow-up questioning, the student adulation, the coeds with their nubile heat, all moving flesh and shining eyes, the flattering deference of the faculty. Ego food. *Lord, my days are vanity.* But today, in his current mood, Henry Durning was not even tempted.

Instead, he had his driver take him directly to La Guardia, where a plane was waiting to fly him back to Washington.

Durning was barely aboard and seated when he was handed a two-hour accumulation of telephone messages. He chose two for immediate reply. One was from Arthur Michaels, the White House chief of staff, the other from FBI Director Brian Wayne. Durning called Michaels first.

"What's doing, Artie?"

"I don't like what's happening at that cult standoff in West Virginia. There's been more gunfire, and the head nut is talking mass suicide if the siege isn't called off by five this afternoon."

Durning glanced at his watch. It was 11:46 A.M.

Michaels said, "Have you spoken to Brian yet?"

"No. But there's a message he called. I'll get to him next."

"When you do, calm him down. A couple of his agents were hit in this latest fracas and he sounded edgy as hell. What we *don't* need is another Branch Davidian disaster."

"Don't worry," said the attorney general. "I'll handle it."

There was a short pause. "Hold on a second. The president wants a word."

Durning heard a click as the chief executive came on the line.

"Hank?"

"Yes, Mr. President."

"I know you're on top of this, but all I keep thinking about are the twenty-seven women and children in that compound."

"I'm thinking about them, too, Mr. President. And I promise you. This will not be another Waco, Texas."

"What about the five o'clock deadline?"

"I'm going to fly down there right now. I'll either have them out before five or call off the siege."

"Then we're taking the mass suicide threat seriously?"

"After the Branch Davidians, Mr. President, how could we *not*?"

When he hung up, the attorney general told the pilot they would be heading for Huntington, West Virginia. Then he called FBI Director Brian Wayne, his oldest and closest friend.

"It's me, Bri. I've just spoken to Artie and the president, so I know most of it. How bad was this morning's shooting?"

"A state trooper and two of my agents took hits. Nothing fatal. But who needed it?"

"What about the Olympians?"

"No reported casualties, but they probably took a few, too." Wayne's voice was flat, morose.

"Who fired first?"

"I'm afraid our people."

"Didn't they have orders not to?"

"Yeah. But they've been out there nine days now. Everyone's getting impatient."

"Impatient for what? To kill or to die?"

The FBI director was silent.

"I don't like the suicide threat," said Henry Durning. "It's probably just a copy-cat bluff after what happened at Waco, but we can't take that chance. So I'm going down right now."

"I'll meet you."

"There's no need for you to go, too."

"Yes, there is," said Wayne.

The attorney general's plane landed at 1:00 P.M. at Huntington Municipal Airport, where two state troopers were waiting with a car on the tarmac.

They drove through curving mountain roads at a steady fifty-five-mile-per-hour clip and arrived at the besieged religious sect's compound at about 1:40. *A sylvan feast gone bad,* thought Durning. Slowly, he got out of the car and looked around.

The Olympian site lay out of rifle range in the middle distance, a sprawl of barns and outbuildings clustered about a large central structure, where an estimated forty-three men, women, and children were barricaded against a small army of county, state, and federal officers. Standing bareheaded in the summer sun, Durning felt himself turn cold.

How do these things happen?

He knew, of course. Knowing was part of his job. Yet no two of these often deadly confrontations were ever entirely alike. In this instance, the trouble began when about fifty agents, troopers, and sheriff's deputies raided the Olympians' communal compound to serve a search warrant and arrest their leader, the Reverend Samson Koslow, on weapons charges. In the resulting shootout, two FBI agents and five of the religious cultists were killed and many more were wounded. Since then, until this morning's violence and the announced suicide deadline, the tension-filled standoff had held for almost nine days.

The scene along the dirt road where the attorney general's car had stopped might have been part of an extended country carnival. Colored lights flashed everywhere. Tents were scattered across the fields. Media vans, ambulances, and fighting vehicles stood in unmoving convoys.

Durning saw the big, converted recreational vehicle that served as the FBI command post and started toward it. He waved away a growing crowd of reporters and photographers who had recognized him, and they backed out of his path a step at a time. They shot pictures from all sides and shouted questions that were never answered.

When Durning entered the command post, Brian Wayne was already there, along with some of his top, on-site brass.

"Give us a few minutes," the FBI director told his agents, and they left him alone with the attorney general.

Durning picked up a pair of high-powered binoculars, went to a window, and surveyed the area under siege. None of the Olympians were visible in their compound, but he was able to spot the surrounding network of FBI sharpshooters lying within rifle range of the central building.

He put down the glasses. "I'm ending this botched-up mess right now. I'm not taking any chances on that crazy deadline."

Wayne just looked at him. A lean, spectacled man with a mournful, prematurely lined face, the FBI director knew his friend too well to argue. At least not until he heard more.

"How do I get this Samson Koslow on the line?" Durning asked. Wayne reached for a phone, hit two buttons, and handed him the receiver. "This is direct."

Durning heard two rings. Then a soft voice said, "Yes?"

"Is this Reverend Samson Koslow?"

"It is."

"This is Attorney General Henry Durning."

The only audible response to his name and title was a baby crying in the background.

"I'd like for us to talk, Reverend."

"We have nothing to talk about, Mr. Attorney General. Either remove your unlawful shooters by five o'clock and let us live in peace, or stay right there and watch us die for God."

Samson Koslow hung up.

Durning stood staring off through the window. Then he

tried again. This time he counted six rings before Koslow came back on.

"I'm calling in good faith, Reverend."

There was a long silence. Then, "That's easy enough for you to say. You're not risking anything."

"What do you want me to risk?"

"What all of us out here are risking. Our lives."

Durning was silent. He motioned to Brian Wayne and watched as he picked up a phone and listened in.

The cult leader said, "What's happened to your good faith, Mr. Attorney General?"

"I still have it."

"Show me."

"How?"

"By walking out here alone, sitting down, and talking to me across a small wooden table."

Durning felt something pleasantly warm enter his chest. "I'll be there in about twenty minutes," he said and put down the receiver.

The FBI director stared at his friend. "Are you mad? The sonofabitch will either take you hostage or kill you."

"No. He has himself and his disciples as hostages. He doesn't need me. And whatever else he is, he's not a murderer."

"How do you know?"

"Because I've done my homework on Koslow and his Olympians. They'll only fight when attacked. Otherwise, they're peaceful and nonaggressive. If they suffer from anything, it's an apocalyptic vision that could lead to mass suicide. Which is right where they are now."

"And if you're wrong?"

Durning didn't answer.

"For God's sake, Hank! You can't do this. You're the attorney general of the United States."

"I know who I am." Henry Durning smiled. "That's why I'm the only one here qualified to talk to Samson Koslow and God."

They stood staring at each other.

"It just occurred to me," said Durning. "That business of finding Vittorio Battaglia?"

"What about it?"

"On the outside chance I don't make it back, you can forget about him."

Wayne's eyes were blank.

"I know I never did explain any part of that," said Durning. "But if I turn out to be wrong about Koslow, nothing about Vittorio Battaglia will matter anymore."

Henry Durning walked across the open fields.

At first it almost seemed he was back in 'Nam, with the green, quiet menacing, the sun hot on his face, and a sense of hostile eyes watching him.

Then he picked up the faint whirring sounds of the Camcorders and still cameras at his back and sides, and he knew exactly how different this was.

Yet some of his fear was very much the same. Never mind what he had told Brian. He was dealing with religious cultists, zealots. Part of their theology was the theology of death. *If you want to die for God, you have to be ready to kill for God.* Also, with all their own dead and wounded, the Olympians would be seeing this by now as a holy war provoked by a repressive government.

The attorney general pushed through high grass under a cloudless sky. He walked steadily past the agents, troopers, and deputies positioned along the government perimeter. He could feel their eyes on him.

My army.

Yet at one particular point, Durning came near to feeling more like a halfback who had caught a forty-yard pass and was running another fifty yards for the longest touchdown in the history of the team.

Then he was past the last of their positions and there was only the heavy part ahead, with the steel-shuttered windows showing clear, and the gun muzzles aimed at him through their firing ports, and the solid, half-round logs of walls that could stop any rifle bullet made. But most especially there was the knowledge that at any second, depending upon the unpredictable impulses of fanatics steeped in a dogma of death and dying, he could be blown away.

Durning just stared straight ahead, kept placing one foot in front of the other, and tried to read the air. Until, at a distance of about fifty feet, a massive door swung open and he saw the Reverend Samson Koslow waiting to greet him.

A thin, middle-aged, shaggy-haired man with tired eyes, Koslow might have been the third-generation West Virginia miner he had started out as, with the coal dust freshly scrubbed from his face. Dressed in faded denim, he stood in the center of the open doorway, not moving from the spot until he had taken Durning's hand.

"Bless you for coming," he said.

Then Durning was inside, the door was closed and bolted, and he smelled his own excitement. When he turned, there was a world to see.

The compound's central building was cavernous, a great enclosed space in which the Olympian sect's forty-three surviving men, women, and children had gathered to either live or die. Riflemen were on watch at the windows and gunports. Clusters of children were gathered in a far corner, shepherded by young women. Wounded lay stretched out on bare floors and bloodstained mattresses. The bodies of a man and woman were arranged side by side on a table. Candles burned at their heads and feet, and kneeling figures circled them in silent prayer.

There was barely a sound, except for that of a baby crying. Dimly, Henry Durning wondered if it was the same child he had heard earlier on the telephone.

At last he saw the worst, and his heart pounded and his mouth turned to flannel.

He counted four of them altogether, one against each of the outside walls, where they stood like markers in a cemetery. Each made up of its own deadly conglomerate of dynamite and wires and detonators and five-gallon jerry cans of gasoline. Set off in concert, they were instant doomsday, total do-it-yourself obliteration.

Very serious stuff, thought Henry Durning. If he'd had any doubts about the declared deadline before, he had none now.

Koslow touched his arm. "Come," he said, and led Durning to a small wooden table beside a window.

A fragile, gray-haired woman brought two cups of water,

set one before each of them, and walked away. Since their water had been cut off for days, Durning knew exactly how precious each cup was.

"All right," said Samson Koslow. "You're here. You see us as we are. Nothing is hidden. So do we live or die?"

"Too many have died already. I want no more dying."

"Then you'll fold your tents and leave us in peace?"

"It's not that simple, Reverend." Durning's voice was soft, his tone and manner patient. He might have been speaking to a child. "There are still laws against shooting government agents."

"Not if the shooting was in defense of our lives, our liberty, and God. Not if the raid on our compound was unwarranted and unlawful. And certainly not if the attorney general understands justice as well as he understands the law and is willing to act accordingly."

They sat looking at each other. The religious leader's thin face was reflective, ruminating, as if the complexities of their little discussion were already dragging after them the futures of forty-three lives.

"Go ahead," said Durning. "I'm listening."

"If I were a defense lawyer," said Koslow, "I'd tell the jury my clients were victims of a wrongful attack designed as a publicity show by a desperate local FBI unit. I'd say—"

"Wait." The attorney general held up a hand. "You're losing me. Please explain that."

"You mean you don't know about these things?"

Durning slowly shook his head.

The reverend took a tiny sip of his precious water. "Well, maybe you don't. You're the attorney general and way up there next to God. The FBI is just one of your departments, and West Virginia is only a poor little state. You couldn't be expected to know about every piece of petty downstream business."

"Then tell me about it, Reverend."

"The FBI's Huntington office is facing tight budget hearings. They have to look good to keep from being closed down. So that's what their unlawful search for illegal weapons and warrant for my arrest are all about."

"Why are their search and warrant unlawful?"

"Because they had no hard evidence to back them up . . . only suspicions."

"Suspicions of what?"

"That we'd converted semiautomatic weapons into illegal automatic ones."

"And had you done that?"

"No, sir. But even if we *had*, and the illegal weapons were found, there's plenty of case law that says no search can be justified by what it turns up. Or am I wrong?"

"You're not wrong. But how do you know all this?"

"By reading about the law and believing it's not only for lawyers."

Henry Durning sat with it. There was no sound anywhere and just about everyone appeared to be watching him. Those who weren't were silently praying.

"Did you tell these things to anyone?" asked the attorney general.

"Of course."

"Whom did you tell?"

"God and an anonymous voice on the FBI line." The reverend studied the tips of his fingers. "I did much better with God. At least he sent me you."

The two men sat completely still.

"Do you trust me?" said Durning.

"I suppose as much as you trust me."

"I trusted you enough to walk in here alone. Didn't I?"

Koslow nodded. "Yes. You did."

"Then can you trust me enough to walk out of here alone with *me*?"

"Under what conditions?"

"That if everything you've just told me checks out, I'll have you back with your people within twenty-four hours."

"With no charges filed?"

"With all your reading you should know the law is more complicated than that. But I promise you this. If the original attack on your compound proves to have been unwarranted, you and your people will have nothing more to worry about."

Samson Koslow's pale eyes were wet and angry. "You mean except for burying and praying for our dead?"

Durning was silent.

"I'm sorry," said the reverend. "You didn't deserve that. Without you, we'd all soon be buried. And with no one left to pray for us. Of course I'll go with you."

The attorney general looked out the window and saw a bird rise from the tall grass. Vaguely, he was aware of the same baby starting to cry again. Or was it another?

Not that it matters, he thought.

It's a baby.

Henry Durning could imagine nothing sweeter than the way he felt at that moment.

10

FORTY-FIVE HUNDRED miles east of Huntington, West Virginia, in the Italian coastal town of Sorrento, Peggy Walters unlocked and entered the Leonardo da Vinci Gallery of Art at exactly 9:00 A.M.

The gallery didn't officially open for business until ten, when Roberta, Peggy's assistant, arrived at work. But Peggy was always there at least an hour earlier. She needed the extra time for settling in. Each day was new for her. In an odd sort of way, she still felt like a transient.

The small gallery faced the Tyrrhenian Sea. It catered mostly to tourists passing through town, staying at local hotels, or riding the ferries to and from Capri. Peggy represented and sold the work of perhaps a dozen artists, three of whom were actually Peter himself, painting under three different names and using three different techniques. Every six weeks or so, she traveled to Rome, Florence, and Palermo as Peter's agent and sold more of his paintings there.

The gallery was cool and still and carried a faint smell of the sea. Occasionally there was the mournful call of a ship's horn in the distance. In the back office, Peggy put up her usual morning espresso and tried to catch up with her paperwork. She felt the emptiness of the place settle over and about her and suddenly shivered.

For a moment she held herself still, breathing very carefully and taking as much air into her lungs as they could hold. Then the sense of chill passed and there was only the clamminess on her forehead. She patted it dry and began breathing normally.

Fear.

It could happen like that, stalling inside her, filling her with its shape until there was no air left for her to breathe. Nine years and she still never knew when or where it would hit or what might set it off. It could be no more than the sound of a man's voice in her gallery, or the way a stranger looked at her in the street or maybe just a few stray bars of a song to which she and Henry had once danced.

The persistent fear was only the residue.

Of what?

Henry's love?

The thought was coldly mocking. Even so many years after the fact, what remained with her most strongly of Henry Durning was of having passed through a carnal transaction with some sort of exotic, enormously appealing animal. The man was exciting. Everything about him was a passion. More than twice her age, and at that point perhaps the most celebrated of Wall Street's golden ring of celebrated lawyers, he had swept her straight out of law school and into his firm, his bed, and his own shining aura of the senses.

Henry Charles Durning told her once, seriously, that he could feel the soul of any living creature if he could just touch the tip of a finger to its heart. And she was so far gone by then that she was ready to believe him.

Not even with the wisdom of hindsight would she call herself a fool. What she had been mostly, she supposed, was young, awestruck, infatuated beyond measure, and gutsy, curious, and uninhibited enough to try just about anything at least once.

But where were the limits? Weren't there always supposed to be limits?

Evidently not for her. Not with the psychic bombardment of Henry Durning's love exploding in and about her. Because with all his vaunted urbanity and sophistication, he never hesitated to use the lush, old-fashioned sentiment of the *L* word to push and persuade her into joining him in whatever happened to be the latest of his more bizarre erotic entertainments.

She could almost hear his voice now. *Come on, love. Don't take it so seriously. It's only fun and games.*

Some fun and games, she thought. All those bodies twisting and rutting about like a bunch of nesting snakes, all those hot, licking tongues boiling their way up from the devil's own kitchens.

Yet why fool herself? She could hardly lay claim to being the martyred innocent. Henry may have led her to the playing field, but she did her own playing. And while it was going on, there was always that incredibly wild excitement in it, and she never backed away. The shame, the self-disgust, the final tragic horror, came only at the end.

Of course, she never told Peter about any of that. Even now . . . *especially* now, after nearly nine years as his loving wife and devoted mother to their son . . . she would sooner die than have him know the raunchy, deviant lust of which she had so enthusiastically proven herself capable. And if the worst of her recurrent fears ever materialized, dying was exactly what she might one day be called upon to do.

Mean thoughts for a bright, summer morning.

Was she getting more paranoid with time? The truth was, the only one she had to worry about there was Henry Durning. And as far as her once-revered mentor was concerned, she was lying quietly at the bottom of the Atlantic.

11

GIANNI GARETSKY LAY listening to Mary Yung's breathing from the other bed. It was soft and regular, and Mary was unmoving, but Gianni knew she was awake.

They were in a motel in Dobbs Ferry, just off the Saw Mill River Parkway, and it was their first night together away from Mary Yung's house. They had spent the day wiping her place free of blood and fingerprints and burying the FBI's latest dead. Now they were here.

There was still no way of knowing what sort of bulletin, if any, had been sent out on them, so Gianni was being cautious. Registering at the motel, he had left Mary in the car. Anyone who saw her face would remember it. They'd remember his face, too, but for different reasons.

The lights of the parkway traffic flashed through the blinds. The sound came in like that of rolling waves. When the traffic occasionally died, the sudden silence and darkness caught Gianni's chest.

He heard Mary laugh softly.

"What's so funny?" he asked.

"This is an all-time first for me."

"What is?"

"Being in a motel room with a man but not in his bed."

"How does it feel?"

"Luxurious. Also, a little lonely. Maybe even a bit insulting."

Gianni was silent.

"Thanks for taking me with you," she said.

"They can kill you with me as easily as they can kill you alone."

She thought about it. "Maybe," she finally said. "But since I've lived my entire life alone, isn't it nice not to have to die that way."

It was always easier to lose yourself in crowded areas of large cities, so in the morning they drove straight to Manhattan.

Gianni checked them into a giant Sheraton as Mr. and Mrs. Thomas Callahan, paid in advance for three nights with cash, and went up to the room alone. Mary knocked on the door and joined him ten minutes later.

"Much nicer than Dobbs Ferry," she said. "What do we do now?"

"Start trying to find Vittorio."

"I wouldn't even know where to begin."

"I don't expect you to know. That's *my* job."

"What's mine?"

"To stay inconspicuous." He looked at her. "If that's possible. Though I guess you can always put on dark glasses and make yourself up as a tourist."

"Is that what you're going to do?"

"I'll figure out something."

They stood considering each other.

"Be careful," she said.

He hadn't heard that since Teresa died.

"When do you expect to be back?" Mary Yung asked.

Nor that, he thought.

"I don't know. If I'm going to be very late, I'll try to call. You do the same. Just don't contact anyone you know. That's important. No exceptions."

She nodded.

"One last thing," he said. "We need a danger signal. If I ever call you here or anyplace else and ask how things are, give me one of two answers. If everything's fine, just say 'fine.' But if there's a gun at your head, say '*never better*,' and I'll know. If you're the one calling, the same signal holds. OK?"

"Yes."

She looked curiously abandoned as he left. Or was he imagining it?

At a theatrical costumer's on Ninth Avenue, Gianni took care of his camouflage needs with an iron-gray hairpiece, a matching moustache, and a pair of plain-lensed horn-rims that gave him the look of an aging accountant.

Trick or treat. Still, it was strangely effective . . . almost as if he were being offered a furtive glimpse of himself, a full thirty years into the future. *I should only live so long*.

Feeling much less exposed in his home city of suddenly faceless hunters, he went to work. His primary target was his onetime fat, curly-haired art school classmate, Angie Alberto, whose father, as reported by Don Carlo, had been Vittorio Battaglia's last assigned hit before Vittorio's own disappearance. He had no idea what Angie could tell him about Vittorio, or whether Angie was even still alive and in the city. But he was all he had at the moment.

Gianni found a Manhattan phone book and immediately got lucky. There was only one Angelo Alberto and he had both a home and a studio listing at the same Riverside Drive address.

Twenty-five minutes later, Gianni got out of a cab in front of a vintage Art Deco building that faced the Hudson with the faded elegance of the early thirties. A frail doorman of about the same age as the building was studying a racing form in the lobby.

"Angelo Alberto," Gianni told him.

The doorman barely glanced up. "Apartment twelve C."

In the elevator, Gianni removed his brand-new hairpiece, moustache, and glasses and put them in his pockets. No point in scaring Angie any more than he had to.

On the twelfth floor, he walked along a musty corridor, rang the bell of apartment 12C, and a moment later was staring into the round, aging face of a no-longer boyish, but even-fatter-than-before Angelo Alberto.

"Hello, Angie."

Angie's dark eyes blinked and his lips worked. Emotions passed like shadows over his face. "Gianni?"

"It's me." Gianni grinned broadly, working to show good intent. "How're you doing?"

"Hey! Not as good as da Vinci and you. I keep reading about you." Angelo gathered some composure. "Come in . . . come in. Jesus, this is some surprise. How long's it been? Twenty years?"

"Feels more like two hundred."

Gianni walked in on Angelo Alberto's life.

One careful look exposed it all . . . gloomy hall, kitchen,

combination studio–living room, single bedroom. Angie's work was freelance advertising and catalog art, specializing in men's fashions. At best, it was third rate. His family pictures showed a fat boy and girl, but no wife. Poor Angie was still getting beat up on. You smelled it the minute you walked in. The odor was sour, as if Angie himself secreted it. Being kind, Garetsky pretended to notice nothing.

In the studio–living room, Angie cleared a couple of shirts, a sweater, some socks, and old newspapers off two chairs. He fluttered nervously about. Gianni wondered when someone had visited him last.

"Sit down, Gianni. I'm honored you're here. Can I get you something? How about a cold beer?"

"I could use one. Thanks."

Gianni looked out the window at the brick wall of another building. That was the view. Faded brick.

Angie returned from the kitchen with two sweating cans. Handing one to Gianni, he noticed his bruises for the first time.

"Jesus! What's with your face?"

"A couple of Fibbies worked me over."

"You kidding, or what?"

It was a good lead-in.

"That's why I'm here, Angie. I'm in real deep shit. I was hoping you might be able to help me out."

Angelo stared dumbly. "Me?"

"These two feds who did me? They were looking for Vittorio Battaglia. Never told me why. But since we used to be close, they figured I knew where he was. Which I don't. But the bastards wouldn't believe me."

"They took you apart for *that*?"

"The going-over was just a friendly start. It looked like they were gonna waste me."

Angelo worked his beer can, squeezing, bending. "But they didn't."

"Only because I grabbed one of their pieces and used it."

The 220-pound fashion artist sat looking at Gianni. He had to work it through twice before he was ready to accept it. When he did, his plump face was flushed red and sweating.

"You blew away two feds?"

"It was that or get done myself. So now I'm on the lam and don't even know why. And I could die not knowing unless I find Vittorio."

"You think *I* know where he is?"

"I'm hoping."

An all-too-obvious attempt at innocence crossed the fat man's open face. *The guy can't even lie effectively,* thought Garetsky.

"Why me?" said Angelo. "What did I ever have to do with Vittorio after art school?"

"I spoke to Don Donatti. He told me your dad was the last contract Vittorio handled for him before Vittorio himself disappeared."

"And that's supposed to make me the murdering son-ofabitch's buddy? Because he did my old man?"

"I'm sorry about your father, Angie. It just hit me as very strange that he should happen to disappear at the exact same time as Vittorio."

"So?"

"Wouldn't you call that kind of a coincidence?"

Angelo mopped his face with a soiled handkerchief. He was sweating heavily now. "So it's a coincidence. So what?"

"So I don't really believe in coincidence. Never did. It makes me wonder how you knew it was Vittorio who did your papa."

Gianni stared long and hard at Angelo Alberto. "How *did* you know, Angie?"

"You just told me."

"You're lying, Angie."

Angelo did his best to manifest anger, but it came out more like a whimper. "You shouldn't call me a liar."

"Then you shouldn't lie. You weren't even surprised when I said Don Donatti told me your dad was the last hit Vittorio ever did for him. So you had to know it before."

About to protest, Angelo changed his mind and drank his beer instead. The can shook in his hand. Beer dripped from his chin.

"Who told you?" said Gianni.

Angelo began to smile, tried it, then let it go.

"I think it was your papa who must have told you, Angie."

"You mean from the grave?"

"What grave? Your father was never in any grave. There was no body to bury. He just disappeared. Remember? Like Vittorio."

Gianni looked evenly at Angelo's sweated face. "Your father's alive, isn't he?"

"You're crazy."

"Where is he, Angie? I won't hurt him. I swear. I've no reason to hurt him. All I want is to talk to him. Ask a few questions."

"He's dead. You wanna ask a fucking dead man questions?"

The way Angelo said it made Gianni remember how he always said things as a kid, half-whining and cringing as though he expected to get whacked and was just waiting for it to come.

"I'm giving you a choice," said Gianni. "You can tell me where your dad is, or you can tell it to Don Donatti after his soldiers chop off your thumbs. If you tell me, nobody knows or gets hurt. If you tell the don, you can kiss your papa good-bye and go looking for your thumbs."

His expression set for another denial, Angie's face suddenly seemed to melt down like butter in the sun.

"Why are you doing this to me, Gianni? You were never like the others. You always treated me decent."

"I'm still treating you decent. Just don't be stupid about this."

"My dad'll beat the crap out of me if I tell you."

"He'll be dead if you don't. And you'll wish you were."

Angelo slumped in his chair, sank back. Then he seemed to continue sinking, beyond even the chair and himself.

"Shit," he moaned. "I was always a lousy liar."

"That's not such a bad thing. Sometimes it's even good."

"Sure. It's terrific. Except maybe if you want to sometimes get through a whole stinking day without getting ripped apart."

Angelo pushed himself to his feet and wandered absently about the room. He stopped in front of a closed closet door and rocked gently back and forth like an old Jew praying at the Wailing Wall. Then without changing expression or missing a beat, he suddenly smashed his head against it.

The door splintered at the point of impact.

Angelo turned and looked at Gianni where he sat. His eyes were vacant and a trickle of blood ran down his forehead and dripped onto his shirt. For several seconds Gianni could feel himself living inside Angelo Alberto. It was not a happy place to be.

Like Gianni Garetsky, Mary Yung took care of changing her appearance as her first priority.

Being Chinese, of course, limited her options. So she settled for one of those dark, curly-haired, Kewpie Doll wigs with which more and more beautiful Asian women were trying to westernize their looks, but were really only perverting themselves into a far less attractive hybrid species.

For the rest of her new persona, she took Gianni's advice and modeled herself after the battalions of tourists currently crowding Manhattan. Which meant trendy designer jeans, T-shirt and sneakers, wraparound sunglasses, and oversize shoulder bag.

Thus disguised, Mary drifted along busy Fifth Avenue, thinking things Gianni Garetsky knew nothing about, but which she had been carrying deep inside her head for more than nine years. Although it was only for the past few days that it had started to hold any particular meaning for her.

The fact was, she had lied to Gianni about never having known the name of the woman for whom Vittorio Battaglia had allegedly broken off with her.

She knew, all right.

She definitely did.

The things we do when we're alone inside ourselves.

And why had she done it?

Part curiosity, part wounded pride, part the nature of her instincts. Men didn't usually walk out on her like that. Certainly not for another woman. So she secretly followed Vittorio one night and found out who the woman was. And followed the woman herself the next day and learned where she worked and what she did there. And followed her again at night . . . in fact for several nights . . . and each time saw her with a man. *Who was not Vittorio.* And found out too who that man was. Which, in a vindictive sort of way, amused her. The two-timing bitch.

Poor Vittorio, she had thought, and was almost able to feel sorry for him. Soon he'd be knocking at her door again.

Two weeks later she saw in the paper that the woman, Irene Hopper, had died when the plane she was flying crashed into the ocean.

But Vittorio somehow never knocked at her door, or called, or answered the phone when she called him. Eventually, his phone was disconnected. When she went to his apartment, other people were living there. All they knew about Vittorio Battaglia was that strangers were always coming around and asking for him.

Eventually, she officially buried him.

Good-bye, Vittorio.

And now? Nine years after the fact? With the FBI seemingly willing to torture and kill to find him.

Maybe not so officially buried.

Moving with the well-dressed, confident-looking Fifth Avenue throng, Mary Yung tried to make herself feel one with them. At times she could do that. At times she was able to make herself feel as much a part of America's golden dream as anyone on this beautiful golden street.

But not today. Any such dreams she had today were quickly reduced to no more than foolish flights of fancy. And she became what she knew herself to be, a scrawny little kid with matchstick arms, afraid of closets, and broken dolls, and hunger. Afraid of darkness, and open boats, and black water. Afraid of reaching, touching hands. Afraid, finally, of breathing. She might use up all the air.

I'm a banana child. I look like an unripe banana. Yellow mixed with green, and full of stomach cramps.

Mary Yung had started for the hotel, but now she changed her mind and found a pay phone in the lobby of an office building. Feeling the need for information she didn't have, she called Jimmy Lee, who either knew or could very quickly get to know just about anything.

"Your little hyacinth needs a great big favor," she told him, speaking their usual Cantonese.

"Just hearing your voice brings the sun to my day," Lee said in the same dialect. "What's your need?"

"I need to know as much as you can find out about a woman named Irene Hopper." Mary spelled the name for Jimmy Lee. "She died in a plane crash about nine years ago."

"Where was she from?"

"Right here in New York."

"Was it a major crash with a lot of fatalities?"

"I don't think so. In fact, if I remember correctly, she was flying her own plane."

"Was her death reported in any of the newspapers?"

"Yes. That's how I found out about it."

"All right, sweet thing," said Lee. "I'll take care of it."

"You never fail me. I bless you."

"I'd rather have you love me."

"Ah, Jimmy. I'm an empty husk. I'd only disappoint you."

"Please," he whispered. "Disappoint me."

"When should I call you?"

"Every hour on the hour."

They had dinner in their room that evening. Gianni had asked Mary Yung to do the ordering, and she turned the meal into an occasion, with champagne, good French wine, and a chicken *contadina* that Gianni found superb.

"You make being on the run seem like the thing to do this year," he told her.

"May as well make the best of it."

She checked the bill the waiter had left. "Expensive. How are we fixed in the money department? We certainly can't use any plastic."

"No problem there. I've plenty of cash and a couple of clean credit cards under phony names."

"Lovely." Mary sighed and poured more champagne. "Now I can truly enjoy it."

For different reasons, they were both in a better mood than they had been yesterday. Earlier, checking out each other's newly disguised appearance for the first time, they had laughed.

"I'd never recognize you," Mary had said. "Would you know *me*?"

"I'm not sure I'd want to with all that scrambled hair."

She had instantly snatched off her curly wig and disappeared into the bathroom. When she returned, her own hair was brushed out, straight and shining against her face.

"You didn't have to do that," he had said.

"That shows how much you know about women."

After dinner they found some brandy in the minibar and settled down with it.

"How did you spend your day?" Gianni asked.

"Like you told me to spend it. Taking care of my disguise, staying inconspicuous, and not contacting anyone I know." She looked at Gianni over her drink. "What about you? Were you able to do us any good?"

"I hope so," he said and told her about his meeting with Angie and finally prying loose the fact that his father was alive and living in Pittsburgh under another name.

"Which means what?"

"That I go to Pittsburgh tomorrow morning."

"Me, too?"

"There's no point. You can't really help me there."

"I just feel so darn useless."

"You'll get your turn," Gianni said. He had no way of knowing she had already started on it.

For the second night in a row they lay in their separate beds in the dark. It was late but neither of them was asleep.

"Isn't this kind of crazy?" she said.

Gianni didn't have to ask *what* was crazy. He knew.

"How long ago did your wife die?"

"About six months."

"Was she sick very long?"

"Yeah."

"When are you going to bury her?"

Gianni stayed silent on that one. Was he doing something wrong? Suddenly feeling defensive, he resented Mary Yung's intrusion.

"I'm not a dog in the street," she said through the dark.

"I never said you were."

"You don't have to say it."

He took a deep breath. "Leave it alone, Mary."

"I can't. I may have to die with you."

"So?"

"I don't want to die with someone who doesn't even know who I am."

"Then for God's sake tell me who you are," said Gianni. "Then, if we don't die, maybe we can at least go to sleep."

She allowed herself several moments to think it through. When she spoke, her voice was flat, toneless.

"I'm a liar and schemer with a soul of a drifter," she said. "I'm an exiled alien who's never had a home. My only friend is a starving, dirty-faced, three-year-old gook with shitted pants who lives inside my chest. Someday, if I'm lucky enough and find the courage, I'll cut both our throats."

The room enclosed them, silent and dark.

"Now you know me," she said.

Gianni didn't believe her for a minute.

12

PETER WALTERS TOOK a morning flight from Naples to the Spanish border city of Andorra, picked up a rental car, and drove high into the lush summer green of the Pyrenees.

He parked at the edge of a five-thousand-foot elevation where he had a clear view of the road winding up toward him and any traffic that might be approaching on it.

After about twenty minutes, a gray Mercedes rounded a curve a few hundred feet below and stopped at a turnoff. Peter sat there another few minutes and watched a few cars and trucks pass in both directions. Then he slowly circled down and eased alongside Tommy Cortlandt, his company connection.

Cortlandt slid into Peter's car, a tall, slim man with fair hair that appeared to be leaving him by the hour.

He smiled. "Good to see you, Charlie."

They met perhaps nine or ten times a year, and after eight years the brief exchange had become their standard greeting. Cortlandt always addressed Peter as Charlie because that was his signature on coded communications, and his assorted aliases meant nothing. As for Cortlandt's name, that was old Boston and very much his own. It was his alleged duties as an embassy trade attaché in Brussels that was his cover for his real work there as CIA chief of station. Cortlandt was Peter's only live contact with the Company, but even he had no idea who Peter really was, where he lived, or what he did there.

"Nice clean job you did in Zagreb," said Cortlandt, and handed Peter the plain, sealed envelope that contained his pay in deutsche marks. "Congratulations."

Peter stuffed the envelope into his pocket without opening it. "Not so clean. Sirens went off that I didn't even know about and never cut."

"It didn't hurt anything."

"No? Try telling that to the poor bastards I had to waste just getting my ass out of there."

Cortlandt was silent.

"The thing was, I should have known. It was nothing but carelessness."

"It happens."

"Not to me."

Cortlandt looked at him with his pale New England eyes. "You can't be that different from the rest of us. Even you are allowed a mistake once in a while."

"Not when nine or ten people end up dying of it."

Peter stared off at the mountains fading into the distance. They started green, went blue-purple, then ended a misty gray at the horizon.

Cortlandt touched his arm and brought him back.

"There's some news," he said. "We're doing Abu Homaidi."

Peter looked at the COS and waited. A small, cold action began somewhere inside him.

"That last horror in Amsterdam finally did it," said Cortlandt. "Our consul's whole family. His three little kids and his wife. And not enough left to mop off the sidewalk."

"That's the fourth. I told you right after the first how it would be. You should have taken the sonofabitch out then."

"It wasn't that simple, Charlie. It still isn't."

"Bullshit! In the meantime, between the TWA flight and the other bombings, you've got almost three hundred dead that could have still been walking around."

"That's unfair."

Peter had to work to put down his anger. The effort alone made him sweat. And this sort of thing was getting worse, not better.

"We don't operate in a vacuum," said Tommy Cortlandt quietly. "Remember. At first we weren't even sure it *was* Homaidi. Then the peace talks were going on and we couldn't risk fouling them up. And after that there was some hope of Syria handing him over for trial."

"Does all this mean I'm getting him?" Peter asked.

"Do you want him?"

"You kidding? Someone like that, it's why I'm in this shit to begin with."

"As I said, it's still not that simple. So before we decide, let's talk."

"What's there to talk about? He needs to be hit, so I'll hit him. The guy's a real crazy."

Cortlandt gazed at Peter Walters. He seemed to be way ahead somewhere and thinking of other things.

"That's just the point," he said. "Homaidi's far from a crazy. He's a brilliant fanatic with a cause he's willing to kill and die for. He's never alone. He has better security than most heads of state. And he's already cost us two good men who were just as gung ho as you for a go at him."

"You mean I'm the *third* choice for this?"

"You might not even be that. I haven't decided yet."

"You really know how to build up a guy's confidence."

"The first two weren't mine. They came from other stations. You were my ace in the hole. I didn't want to use you unless I had to."

"Why the devil not?"

"Pure self-interest. Homaidi's such a dangerous longshot, I didn't want to risk losing my best."

Cortlandt leaned toward the gunman, studying him, intrud-

ing into every corner with his eyes. "And also because I
know you've got a wife and little boy who need you even
more than I do."

Peter sat there with it, unmoving. A light breeze came off the
Pyrenees and he breathed it in, but its scent was that of a freshly
opened grave.

When he spoke, his voice was flat. "How long have you
known?"

"Almost as long as I've known you. Which makes it close
to eight years. I could never entirely trust a man I knew nothing about, a man who had no human ties. So I stuck a beeper
on your car when we met one day near Rome, and followed
you back to Positano."

Tommy paused. "You needn't worry. That was solely for
my own needs. No one else has ever known."

Peter just stared at him, his eyes were cold, chipped glass.

"It's been all these years," said Cortlandt. "If I meant you
harm, it would have happened a long time ago."

"What else do you know?"

"Your real name."

"Say it for me."

"Vittorio Battaglia."

Just hearing it from someone else's mouth after nine years
brought a chill.

"How did you find out?"

"I lifted a set of prints from a car door and checked them
when I was in Washington. You don't have to worry about
that, either. I hit the computer buttons myself. No one else
saw."

Peter's automatic was suddenly in his hand, its muzzle
against Cortlandt's throat.

"If no one else saw it," he said coldly, "why shouldn't I do
you right now and not have to worry at all?"

If Cortlandt showed any expression, it was one of total absorption in Peter Walters' question. "You mean you want
reasons?"

"Damn right."

"Because for one thing," said Cortlandt, "you know by
now I'm your friend, and it's not your nature to shoot
friends."

"If I feel my wife and son's lives are threatened, I can change my nature and find another friend."

"I don't believe you really think I'd betray you and your family."

"Maybe not willingly. But when our balls are in a wringer, we'd all happily sell our own mothers." Peter's gun was tight against Tommy's throat. "Go on."

"Well, you do have to be wondering why I'd suddenly be idiot enough to tell you all this after eight years of silence. You know there has to be a reason, and you're certainly not going to do me without hearing what it is."

Something stirred in the car, and Peter lowered his automatic. He had been watching Tommy's eyes all the way, and they hadn't blinked once.

"I guess I'm ready to hear."

"It happened the other day," said Cortlandt. "It was in one of those bulletins Interpol is always circulating to consulates, embassies, and police stations. It said Vittorio Battaglia was wanted by the FBI on assorted counts of murder and kidnapping."

He paused, waiting for Peter Walters to react, to say something. But Peter just sat gazing off somewhere, with the automatic in his lap.

"There was a picture, too," said the COS. "But it didn't look anything like the way you look now. No one could ever spot you from it."

Peter nodded slowly, somewhat tiredly. "Did it say why they suddenly wanted me after nine years?"

"No."

Peter was silent. He was looking off at the mountains again, as if everything would be explained for him there if he just stared long and hard enough.

"Understand," said Thomas Cortlandt III. "I'm only telling you all this so you'll know, be warned and forearmed. For me, it doesn't mean beans. There's nothing new here for me. I've known your history, your work with *la famiglia*, from the day we met. Those were your credentials, as far as I was concerned. What gave you value to the Company. And you've never failed or disappointed me."

Tommy smiled. "I even liked what you said when I asked

why you wanted to get into all this hellish stuff for us. You remember that?"

Peter silently stayed with the mountains.

"You said it was to help your poor old Guinea grandpa finally make his claw marks on Mount Rushmore. Then you grinned like it was some kind of joke. Only I knew it wasn't."

Peter turned, and he and Tommy considered each other in a curious way.

"My grandpa died about a year before I ever told you that."

"My condolences. But Mount Rushmore's still alive, and you're still making some of the best claw marks I've ever seen."

Peter felt himself off somewhere, watching them both from some distant, unfamiliar place.

"What about Abu Homaidi?" he asked.

"He's yours, of course. He always was. But, for all our sakes, including God's and grandpa's . . . please. Be careful."

Vittorio Battaglia's grandfather, having been newly resurrected, flew all the way home with him.

Vincenzo Battaglia had been a broad, low man with thick eyebrows and a dark face burned brown by the sun and bruised by hurt. Still, he'd had a softness in his eyes and an abiding love for America in his heart.

Young Vittorio saw him last in St. Vincent's Hospital. His hands and face were yellow. He had cancer of the liver. He also had a few dozen tiny American flags he had brought from home and arranged in plastic cups around his hospital room. He died on a rainy day in autumn, and Vittorio planted six of the little flags on his grave. Sometimes, in his dreams, Peter Walters was still planting them.

He touched his grandfather through the flags. They kept the old man alive for him. At times, it seemed, they kept him alive as well.

He said nothing to Peggy about the Interpol bulletin.

She was living with enough fear.

13

THE BEST, THE most erotic dreams were sometimes like that. Your hands going over soft, pliant flesh. A shadowy, sweetly scented body pressed close. The sounds of her breathing a warm, whispered promise in your ear.

As she appeared to sleep.

Then she erupted against him and Henry Durning knew it was no dream. Nor did he want it to be. What he wanted was for it to be exactly what it was, with every part of it real, with the fevers of his lust real, and the brandy in the maze of his stomach, and the pressure in his chest, and the straining of her every fiber as she fought him . . . all real.

And Lord, how she did fight.

Not that she was especially big. She was rather on the small side, actually. But young. Very young. Increasingly, youth was becoming a factor for him. Also, she was one of the new, trendy breed. Which meant she ate sensibly, worked out with weights and aerobics, and made a working religion of her body.

For all of which, considering the results, Durning was immeasurably grateful.

One of her strong rounded arms hooked around his head and caught his throat.

"Sonofabitch!" he gasped, struggled, and finally worked the arm free.

His eyes were closed, and with his body now fully against her chest, and one knee prying between her legs to work them apart, he had the mental image he was pressing against a secret barrier that would soon give way and allow him entrance to a beautiful, sunlit garden.

He ripped her gown and she cried out.

"Don't! Please . . . no!"

But her cries and pleas only excited him more, with heat packed behind heat and the pressure building in his groin.

He went at her gown again, hearing the fabric tear, feeling

himself ready to hurt, even to kill her if he had to, and loving the idea that he was capable of inflicting that much damage.

Streaks of light flew from his brain to his arm, and he had a hand on her, then part of it working its way through the damp heat, fingers taking greedy control as if all the world's knowledge of such things was centered at their tips. Oh, he knew her at that moment, knew the burgeoning warmth that was rising from her and would soon be his, knew exactly where it would be right to touch and where it would be wrong.

She was still fighting him, but Durning could feel her beginning to weaken. He could hear a murmuring in her throat that was now merely begging him not to hurt her. Holding her body in place with his full dead weight, he began stripping off his clothes.

No lights were on but there was a moon and its pale wash came in through the same open window by which he himself had entered less than ten minutes earlier. That was always one of his more pleasurable moments. The actual breaking and entering. The climbing across the darkened sill of a sleeping woman's window and getting his first glimpse of what was waiting for him. That wondrous bower of the libido. And there she was . . . unknowing, vulnerable, her body still her own secret and not yet violated. While he stood there trembling in his excitement. While he listened to her breathing and watched the gentle rise and fall of her breasts. While he saw, too, the smooth curve of her belly and the mound of Venus below.

All that waiting for me.

Sweet Jesus Christ.

I'm fifty-four fucking years old.

I'm the attorney general of the United States.

When will all this degraded clowning finally stop being the absolute core of my life?

Fervently, Henry Durning hoped never.

With his clothes off, naked now, he smothered her cries by covering her mouth with his.

She bit into his lip. Hard. It hurt.

"Do that again and I'll cut off your nose," he said.

She didn't do it again.

But she was still fighting him even as he entered her. Which he didn't do gently. He certainly didn't do it as a lover. Nor even as a friend. If anything, it was with anger, with the sense of a man driving spikes. But that was part of it, too, and not to be missed. He had never felt more greedy in his life. Nor as powerful.

I have the devil's own strength.

It was true. Nothing was beyond him at this moment. If some inner voice told him to climb to the top of the Washington Monument and fly off, he was sure he'd be able to do that, too. There were all these lovely sounds inside his head. New dreams were being born to him.

I'm my own field of force.

He roughly grabbed a fistful of her hair, rolled her over onto her stomach, and began sodomizing her from the rear.

Struggling for a poor quarter of an inch at a time, he listened to her screaming all the way.

"My God, you're killing me!"

And that was how he made his final run. Which was always something of a mystery. Maybe even a part of larger mysteries. There were times when he almost despised the entire act, when he found it a hopeless void from which nothing was ever achieved but exhaustion, a psychic and physical draining that left him hollow.

But not tonight. Tonight it was better. Tonight, somewhere near the end, he actually had a rare moment that spoke to him of the aching sweetness of love.

Even for those who had spent their lives betraying it.

She lay holding him close in the dark.

"I do love you," she said.

He kissed her. It was neither more nor less than a conditioned reflex to her words.

"I'm sorry about your lip," she told him.

"I'll live through it."

"I guess I got a little carried away."

"You were wonderful," he said.

"It's *you* who were wonderful. You make everything so incredibly exciting."

"You mean even something as incredibly boring as sex?"

She laughed. "And you're so funny besides."
"That's because I'm really a clown," he said.

I can touch and save lives. But I'm more than just a clown,
Durning thought as she slept.
I've done it.
I did it the other day in West Virginia.
And I'll do it again.

Yet, even with that, it was hours before he was able to sleep.

14

IT WAS AN area of small truck farms about fifty miles north-west of Pittsburgh, and Gianni Garetsky had driven through a long, depressing stretch of rustbelt to get there.

Following Angelo Alberto's directions, he turned east on a dirt road that ran through alternate patches of woods and open fields. When he came to a weathered gray farmhouse on his left, he turned into a dusty driveway and parked.

An R.F.D. mailbox carried the name Richard Pemberton. A big ethnic change from Frank Alberto, thought Garetsky.

He climbed a front porch, knocked on the door and waited. Then he knocked again, more heavily. When there was still no response, he walked around to the back of the house.

A pickup truck was parked in front of the barn. But other than for some goats and cows, the barn was empty. A scattering of chickens pecked at the ground.

Gianni shielded his eyes against the sun and stared off across the fields. A man was working with a hoe in the distance. Gianni started toward him, being careful to keep both hands empty and visible.

The man seemed to see him when he was about a hundred

yards away. He stopped working, dropped the hoe, and just stood watching Gianni Garetsky approach. He wore faded overalls, a peaked cap, and didn't seem to move at all. Then he slowly bent until he was squatting on his haunches between rows of what Gianni took to be some sort of beans.

When only about ten yards separated them, the man rose. He had a shotgun in his hands.

"That's far enough." He had a distinctly New York accent.

Gianni had the feeling Alberto was never without the gun. What a way to have to live. *Like me*. Except that Frank Alberto had been doing it for nine years. The same as Vittorio Battaglia, wherever he was, had probably been doing.

"Whatta yuh want?" Frank Alberto asked.

Gianni looked at him and saw nothing of his son, nothing of the lifelong victim. No excess fat here. Angie's papa was big, muscular, and clearly tough. A real *pazzerello*, Don Donatti had called him, a *crazy*. The kind that couldn't be reasoned with, so you finally had to end up killing.

"I just want to talk," Gianni said.

"What about?"

"Vittorio Battaglia. I'm his friend, Mr. Alberto. I mean you and Vittorio no harm."

Alberto's eyes darkened. "Who the hell are *you*?"

"My name's Gianni Garetsky. From the old neighborhood. I studied art with Vittorio and your Angie."

"Bullshit. I've seen pictures of Garetsky. He sure didn't look like you."

Gianni carefully peeled off his hairpiece, moustache, and glasses.

With the sun bright and strong overhead, they stood in the beanfield, facing each other.

"Then it was my Angie told you where I was."

"Don't be angry with Angie. He had no choice."

"Everybody's got a fucking choice."

"It wasn't his fault, Mr. Alberto. I said if he didn't tell me, I'd give him to Don Donatti."

Frank Alberto walked slowly, almost casually toward Garetsky. When he was no more than three feet away, he stopped and looked at him. Then seeming barely to move, he brought the butt of his gun across Garetsky's chin.

Gianni fell among the beans.

He came out of it like a scuba diver, resting a little at each level. There was pain, but that had become nothing new for him lately. Trying to figure things out, he kept his eyes closed longer than he had to. When he finally opened them, he was ready.

He was sitting in some woods, propped against the trunk of a tree. It was cool and shady, but shafts of sunlight struck down through the leaves. The bark of the tree felt rough and solid against his back. Frank Alberto sat a few feet away, his shotgun across his lap.

Alberto pointed to his right. "Look over there."

Gianni looked. He saw a large, freshly dug hole with dirt piled around it and a shovel standing in the dirt.

"That's for you."

Gianni closed his eyes and said nothing.

"What kinda shit is this?" asked Alberto. "I mean, I'm a goddamn dead man. No one in this whole fucking world . . . except my son and Vittorio Battaglia . . . even knows I'm alive. And you walk up to me in the middle of my field and say you want to talk. Just like that."

He snapped his fingers.

Alberto took out a pack of cigarettes and lit one. Gianni watched his hands. They were strong and steady.

"I'm dead nine years," said Alberto. "Vittorio's my own God. He resurrected me. He's who I pray to at night. And you wanta talk to me about him? OK. Talk to me. You've got ten minutes. Then you talk to Jesus."

His mouth dry and tasting of blood, Gianni told his tale for the fourth time. Alberto listened without interruption, smoking, looking faintly bored. He seemed to be balanced on some shrinking spot on the ground.

When the story was finished, the woods were quiet. That was the first thing Gianni noticed, the quiet.

"That's it?" said Frank Alberto.

Garetsky was silent.

"You mean now we come to the real shit? What you want from me? Like maybe where Vittorio is?"

"That's important, Mr. Alberto."

"To who? You and the *cinese* lady?"

"To Vittorio, too."

"How d'yuh figure that?"

"He doesn't even know the feds are out looking for him. If you give me some idea where he is, I can at least warn him, let him know what he might be facing."

The man Carlo Donatti had referred to as an old Moustache Pete sat quietly thinking about what Gianni had said. He tossed his cigarette into the open hole. *My grave*, thought Garetsky. Watching Alberto's face, Gianni thought he had the look of a man with so many problems, he couldn't decide which one to worry about first.

"You called Vittorio your own God," said Gianni. "You said he saved your life. Don't you think you owe him a fair shot at his own?"

"You don't have to goddamn tell me what I owe him!"

Gianni said nothing. But the anger in Frank Alberto's voice was more defensive now and actions were taking place inside him.

"Anyways," Alberto grumbled, "I ain't seen the guy in maybe nine years. So who even knows where he is?"

"What about the last time the two of you were together?"

"What about it?"

"Maybe you both talked," said Gianni. "Maybe you both said things about where you might be going and what you'd do when you got there. Maybe you could have said something about always wanting to do farming, and this was your chance. You remember anything like that?"

A black-and-yellow bird flew onto a branch and Alberto stared up at it, watching the way it ruffled its feathers. Alberto had a remote, thoughtful expression on his face. Then the bird flew away and he looked at Garetsky.

"Painting," he said. "Vittorio talked about how he wanted to do nothing but knock out all these pictures. I remember that for sure. My Angie always said he was the best painter in the school. Angie said you were good, too. But he thought Vittorio was better."

"I thought so, too," said Gianni. "But what about where he

might be doing all this painting? You remember him mentioning anything about that?"

"He wouldn't be dumb enough to tell me that. Just as I wouldn't be crazy enough to tell him where I might be going. Not that I knew. It just worked out I'm here."

Alberto studied the shotgun in his lap. He seemed vaguely surprised to find it there. "But he did say he was getting the hell out of the country fast. And he said it would be the smart thing for me to get out, too." He grunted. "But when have I ever done the smart thing?"

"If you did get out of the country, where do you think you'd have gone?"

"I don't have to think. I know where I'd have gone. *Italia.* Where else?"

They looked at each other.

Alberto nodded slowly. "If I was looking for him, that's where I'd look first. He speaks the language. He wouldn't feel strange. He wouldn't stand out like no foreigner."

"Not Sicily?"

"Hell, no. Too close to *la famiglia.* Don Donatti still owns half the goats on the island."

They considered each other again and there was something between them that went a long way back.

"Would you really have given my son to the don if he didn't tell you where I was?" asked Alberto.

"I knew Angie back when he was eight years old. I didn't expect to have to do a thing to him."

"Hey, we can't all be heroes." Alberto shrugged. "Like I ain't feeling so great myself about having to do *you.*"

It went through Garetsky like a dose of salts. Somehow, with all the talking, he'd assumed they'd left his newly dug grave behind. Evidently not.

"I thought you said everybody's got a choice."

"Yeah, but I don't like mine. Mostly, what I don't like is you walking away knowing I'm alive and here. My own son knew, and even he sent me you. Now you know and who do you end up sending me? My own fucking angel of death? Carlo Donatti?"

Alberto's words hung in the stillness, numbing the air, and Gianni knew there was nothing more to talk about. He had already accepted it as part of what had happened and what would probably happen next.

He briefly closed, then opened his eyes. "If you're in no great rush, how about a last butt?"

"Sure. I just wish my Angie had your guts."

"Why? So he could die young, too?"

Frank Alberto was reaching for his cigarettes when a handful of dirt caught him in the face and eyes.

An instant later Gianni had Alberto's shotgun by its barrel and needed to swing it just once.

The old Moustache Pete was still unconscious but breathing evenly when Gianni left him beside the open grave and headed for the Pittsburgh airport.

Gianni had done the express drop-off on his rental car and was approaching the gate 10 boarding area for his return flight to New York, when he spotted the two men.

There really was nothing unusual about them. They were dark haired, of medium build, and dressed respectably enough in sport coats and slacks. But Gianni had been born into and lived his entire life with this sort of thing, and all he had to see were those ever-so-slight bulges around the left armpits, and the restless, searching eyes. Of course they might just as easily have been local plainclothes cops, not feds. But he didn't think so.

He picked up a courtesy phone about forty feet from where the two men were standing, and he called the Passenger Service Counter in the main terminal lobby.

"Could you please help me?" he said. "I'm calling from gate twenty-five, and I've somehow missed some friends who were supposed to be meeting my flight."

"What's your name?" the attendant asked.

"Gantry . . . Kevin Gantry," said the artist, which was the name on one of the clean credit cards that Don Donatti had given him, and the card he had used early that morning to book his round-trip flight from New York to Pittsburgh.

"Please stay just where you are, Mr. Gantry."

Moments later, the announcement came over the public address system. "Attention, please. Will those meeting arriving passenger Kevin Gantry please go to gate twenty-five, where your passenger is now waiting."

Watching the two men, Garetsky saw them turn and stare at each other as the words faded. Then half jogging down the crowded corridor, they headed in the direction of gate 25.

Bingo!

Gianni swore softly to himself.

Don Donatti?

Impossible.

Until he remembered the don's own words.

You're not stupid, Gianni, so don't say stupid things. Finally, everybody talks.

But it still didn't go down easily, and he stood there, trying to work it through. You didn't give up a lifetime of that kind of feeling . . . that kind of friendship, loyalty, even love, without a fight.

Then the very intensity of his sentiment sickened him and he lost patience with it.

Think, damn it!

Flying directly back was out. They'd be monitoring every flight to New York for at least the rest of the night. Maybe longer. Although after the fake paging of Kevin Gantry they'd know he was on to them and expand their surveillance to other flights. Possibly even to rental cars and bus terminals. It depended on how many people they were using. He couldn't believe he was that high a priority. Until he remembered it wasn't him. It was Vittorio Battaglia. Yet even that explained nothing.

A sudden weakness filtered through him. The past days had taken their toll, and he was beginning to feel like an aging fighter near the end of a grueling twelve-rounder, when his legs were rubber and he could barely hold up his arms. In the distance, he could still make out the bobbing heads of the two hunters on their futile run to gate 25. He was nothing but game to them, a fox in a swamp with the hounds baying all around.

The bastards, he thought, and the anger itself brought a much-needed rush of adrenaline.

Checking the posted flight schedules, he rushed to a ticket

counter and booked himself onto a 6:15 to Boston, which would be taking off in less than ten minutes.

He paid with cash, wishing he'd done the same with his Pittsburgh tickets, instead of trying to preserve his hard currency for possible future emergencies. Although he was probably lucky to have found out where he stood with Don Donatti while he could still control the damage. At a different time and place, using another of the credit cards, licenses, or passports so graciously provided by the don, he might have been picked up cold.

Gianni Garetsky thought about Carlo Donatti all the way to Boston.

Every act of betrayal carried its own level of hurt, and this one cut deep. The don wasn't of his blood, but since the deaths of his parents, Carlo Donatti was the closest thing to blood that Gianni had left.

No more than five nights ago the don had come to the Met to honor and embrace him with flooding eyes. One night after that, he had given him a gun, a hundred thousand in cash, allegedly clean papers, his heartfelt blessing, and a warning not to trust even him.

This was the man he had known all his life.

At Boston's Logan Airport, he caught the next shuttle to New York without incident and arrived at La Guardia less than an hour later.

He called the Sheraton from the first phone he saw on leaving the arrival gate, and heard Mary Yung's voice say hello.

"How are things?" he asked, according to their agreed-upon code.

"Terrible."

Something ran cold in him. "What's wrong?"

"I've missed you like the devil."

He stood there, the receiver shaking in his hand. "For Christ's sake, Mary!"

"Oh. I'm sorry. I mean fine. Things are fine."

The wire hummed between them.

"But I still missed you like the devil," she said.

* * *

It was well past eleven, but neither of them had eaten so Mary Chan Yung had room service send up a late supper.

Gianni found something curiously domestic in it. The breed was insanely adaptable. Their fourth night together, and there was already a sense of shared histories. Another two nights, and they'd be hanging new curtains and going into family planning.

He decided to say nothing about Don Donatti and the two men at the Pittsburgh airport. But he did tell Mary Yung what happened with Frank Alberto, his shotgun, and his waiting grave.

"Your *compaesano* sounds like a real doll," she said flatly. "But after sleeping with a shotgun for nine years, who can blame him for being a little cautious?"

"Not *you*. Right?"

Mary Yung looked at him long and evenly. Then she decided to let it go.

"So what do we do now?" she said. "Take an all-inclusive Parillo Tour of Italy?"

"I'd like to pick up a bit more to go on."

"How?"

"By talking to a couple of people."

"Who?"

"You're beginning to sound like a district attorney."

"That's the nastiest thing you've said to me yet."

Gianni laughed. It felt strange, and he wondered if he'd ever be laughing again on any kind of regular basis. The warm, sweet feeling this woman was giving him felt even stranger, and he wondered about that, too.

"I want to talk to my gallery rep and my old art teacher. My teacher was also Vittorio's teacher."

"What can they tell you?"

The artist worked on his third glass of the special chardonnay that Mary had ordered to go with their dinner. She seemed to know and care a lot about such things. He didn't. But neither was he finding it especially painful.

"I don't know," he said. "Maybe nothing. But since wherever Vittorio is, he's probably painting, each one of them knew him well enough as an artist to be able to come up with something I might not think of myself."

* * *

Something awakened Gianni.

He sat up with a start and stared into the darkness.

Then he heard Mary Yung cry out and he knew this was the sound that had awakened him.

Now it just kept coming, a keening, almost childish wail, so sharp and shrill that Gianni felt it enter him like a blade.

He turned on a lamp between the two beds and the room quivered with a yellow light.

Face contorted, eyes tightly closed, Mary Yung thrashed about her bed. She might have been fighting an invisible army of wizards and fiends.

Gianni caught her wrists and held them. "Easy," he whispered. "Easy, it's OK."

She worked against him, testing his grip. She was surprisingly strong.

Then her eyes opened, went wide at their centers, and the wailing sound stopped. She lay staring at him, her face and body wet with perspiration, her gown plastered to her skin.

"It was only a dream," Gianni said. "Everything's all right."

Everything's all right.

She'd shot and buried three government agents who'd come to question, torture, and probably kill her. She was homeless and on the run. Powerful, anonymous forces were out hunting her even now. If she had any future at all, it would more than likely take place in some as yet undefined chamber of horrors.

How much worse could a mere dream have been?

She began shivering. It became very bad. It became so bad that Gianni could hear her teeth chattering. He went into the bathroom and brought back a towel and a terry robe.

"You'd better get that wet gown off," he said.

Mary struggled with it. But she was shaking so violently, he had to help her. Then he dried her with the bath towel.

Naked, she all but took his breath away.

His reaction was involuntary, pure reflex. Nevertheless, it shamed him. The human animal. It might not always prevail, but it sure as hell was going to survive.

Back under the covers, Mary Yung was still trembling.

"Hold me, . . ." she pleaded.

Gianni lay close and held her. She held him. They lay there holding each other. Finally, the trembling stopped.

But neither of them let go. They might have been imprisoned in each other, which was almost the way Gianni had begun to think about it. Still, good sounds were taking place somewhere in his head, and something bent on pleasure was loose. The fact was, he couldn't bear to move apart from her. Yet he had an intimation he mustn't think too much about it. Certainly, not now.

It was she who offered the first kiss, of course. God help him if *he* had been the one to start. Some disastrous break in the heavens might have resulted. But when he touched a hand to her breast, he was ready to commit the rest of his life to contemplating the sensation. It was as if something was demonstrating to him that until this instant he had never even come close to understanding the true miracle of a breast.

Determined to miss nothing now, he moved on to further miracles. And with what a state of grace. Even the excitement held its separate measure of calm. He looked at her eyes, at the lovely riddle of her face, and had never seen anything more open to him. It was true. Whatever he wanted was his. He had only to reach for it.

And the cost?

Who could tell with a woman like this?

Yet, somewhere near the middle of it, like a bonus he didn't deserve, something wistful and good took root in him, as if a new part of his life had begun. So that going up with it, then down, then up once more, he was able to look at her soft alien eyes, suddenly alight with pure gold, and hope for something he knew in his heart wasn't there.

It was only later, when Mary was asleep, that he thought of his wife and went cold with it.

This has nothing to do with you, he told Teresa. *Not Mary Yung, not any woman, can ever touch what we had.*

I'm making progress.

15

Gᴉᴀɴɴɪ ᴡᴀs ᴀʙᴏᴜᴛ to call Don Carlo Donatti on his private *safe* phone . . . *buried in lead cable, no taps.*

He had decided he couldn't live with it this way. The evidence was strong, but totally circumstantial. After so many years, the don deserved at least the chance to talk.

He was at a gas-station phone on Northern Boulevard, just across the Nassau County line and about a twenty-minute drive from Donatti's Sands Point home. It was a bright, sunny morning, and a cool breeze carried a whiff of the sea off the quiet waters of Little Neck Bay. It was much too nice a day for what he was doing.

Gianni dialed the special, easy-to-remember number, *even panic won't block it out* . . . and heard the don answer on the third ring.

"It's me," he said.

"Gianni! I've been worried sick. You OK?"

"I'm alive, Don Donatti. How are *you*?"

"I asked you to keep in touch. It's been four days. I didn't know what to think."

Gianni heard the reprisal of the neglected parent in his tone. "I'm sorry. That was thoughtless of me. But it's been a hard few days, with a lot of running. Still, that's no excuse and I apologize."

"*Grazie a Dio* you're all right. Something bad happened and I had no way to warn you."

Garetsky waited in silence.

"All that safe stuff I gave you?" said Donatti. "Burn it. None of it's any good."

"What do you mean?"

"This is a terrible embarrassment for me, Gianni. It's lucky you didn't use any of the credit cards. They would have had you if you did."

"But I did use a card."

The wire hummed briefly.

"Whose name?" asked Donatti.

"Kevin Gantry's. It was for airline tickets."

"And nothing happened?"

"It could have. But I spotted a couple of agents at the departure gate before they spotted me, and took a different flight."

Donatti swore softly in Italian.

"What you must have thought of me, Gianni."

Garetsky watched the flow of traffic on Northern Boulevard. He didn't think there could be any trace tie-in with the don's phone, but he still kept an eye out in both directions.

"Accidents happen," he said.

"This was no *accidente*. Someone I trusted like my right arm sold you to the FBI to get his brother out of Leavenworth. My deepest apologies, Gianni. What more can I say?"

"You don't have to say anything, Don Donatti." In the distance, Garetsky heard the faint sound of police sirens. "Have you learned anything about why they want Vittorio?" he asked.

"*Niente*. But it's the Bureau that wants him, all right."

The line hung soundless between them.

"I'm so sorry, Gianni."

Donatti didn't seem to know what else to say.

"What about your right arm?" said Gianni. "The one who sold me?"

"I cut it off. You'll call me again soon?"

"Of course. I'll try to do better with that."

"It's good just hearing your voice. Take care, Gianni."

"You, too, Godfather."

The sirens were only a few blocks away and getting closer as Gianni hung up. His car was parked just around the corner and he got in and circled the block.

Three Nassau County police cruisers were clustered around the phone booth as he drove past.

Naturally, there was no good right arm to be cut off, and no brother waiting to be released from Leavenworth. The need to deal had been strictly the don's. Who knew what the feds had on the godfather these days? The only real thing in the whole conversation was his apology. Gianni didn't doubt that part. He *was* sorry.

But Gianni Garetsky had to go back twenty years to get the true feel of what Carlo Donatti had been to him.

It was the don himself who came to tell him about his mother and father the evening it happened, just appearing unannounced at the door and letting him see his eyes.

Then he stayed all night, staring through and filling Gianni's silences with his lush tales of *la famiglia* and all it meant. In Don Carlo Donatti's world there was no evil, no calamity, that couldn't be considered as a source of good. This was what sentiment did. It cut the sharp edges off reality and taught that what you did out of necessity was far more precious than what you did from choice. Sentiment reconsidered tragedy as a test of courage. Suffering, personal loss, became purification rites on the road to manhood.

"It'll pass, Gianni. It'll make you stronger."

Strength, of course, being the ultimate good. When the only thing Gianni wanted was to get even. In his mind there was a chill, blue haze. In this light there were only his murdered parents. It drained meaning from everything else and left him dry.

"Who killed them?" he asked Don Donatti.

"A man named Vincenzo."

"Why? What did my mother and father ever do to him?"

"Nothing. It wasn't personal. It was to make a point with *la famiglia*. Don't worry, Gianni. We'll take care of him."

"With all respect, Godfather. *I'll* take care of him."

Donatti looked at him. "Do you know what you're saying?"

"Yes."

The single word hung in the air between them. Donatti spent time considering it.

"All right," he finally said. "I understand your feeling in this. But I won't have you going off like some crazy and getting yourself killed. I must prepare you."

He did.

He brought Gianni a well-oiled, 9mm automatic, explained its workings, showed him how to field-strip and put it back together blindfolded, and taught him how to shoot properly, with live ammunition, in a basement firing range. Donatti prepared him for the almost ceremonial act of killing with as much love and care as any offered novice matadors being sent out to face their first potentially lethal bulls.

When the don felt Gianni had the knowledge and physical skills to properly do the job, he tried to prepare him psychologically.

"This is no game," he said. "There are no rules. If you don't kill him, he'll kill you. Forget any ideas you might have about being fair. This is an assassination, an *assassinio* . . . not a tennis match. He wasn't fair to your mama and papa. He shot them in the back of the head. You understand what I'm telling you, Gianni?"

Gianni Garetsky understood.

When the big night came, he stood in the shadows outside the riverfront warehouse where Vincenzo worked and would soon leave to walk to his Cadillac's parking space. He had a silencer on his automatic and his mother and father heavy in his chest. He was so frightened he couldn't squeeze out enough saliva to spit. But he welcomed even the fear. He could touch his parents through it.

He saw Vincenzo come out of the warehouse and start toward his car. His plan was to wait until Vincenzo passed him, then fire into his back until he went down. Gianni had been envisioning it for almost a full week. All very clean and simple. What could go wrong?

What could go wrong was *him*.

Because when it finally came to doing it, to actually squeezing off the shots, when he had Vincenzo's broad, unmissable back squarely in his sights from a distance of no more than ten feet, he couldn't get himself to do it.

And it wasn't even a matter of being fair. There was just no meaning in it for him this way.

So he called out, "Vincenzo!"

The man turned and they stared at each other. It seemed quite natural that just the two of them should be there, that their brains and bodies should be linked at this moment.

"I'm Gianni Garetsky," he said, and saw Vincenzo's eyes as he went for his gun, saw the gun itself as the muzzle swung toward him.

Then there was some meaning in it for him, and he got off a burst of three quick shots.

The cluster was right in the killing zone.

The price was high. He had to leave the country and live a fugitive life for years.

But the prize was wholeness.

And Don Carlo Donatti was the one who helped give it to him, who offered comfort, money, protection, who did for him whatever needed to be done, who finally taught him how to make his way in the dark.

Until this.

16

THE HAND OF God, thought Peter Walters. The blood, the devastation, was stunning. All of it was right there in Peter's living room, with his wife and son sitting alongside him and watching it on the seven o'clock news. The bomb had exploded in the main concourse of Rome's Fiumicino Airport, while a dozen or more camcorders, on hand to record the arrival of some ranking American delegates to the latest Mideast peace talks, recorded this horror instead.

The explosion had taken place only minutes before the cameras began picking up the results, and the sounds and pictures carried all the bone-chilling immediacy of the best combat reporting. The dead lay about like bundles of old clothes. The wounded screamed. Those able to move ran wildly in every direction. While through and above it all, smoke and dust drifted in the misty gray layers of Dante's personal vision of hell.

And *the hand of God?*

Merely Peter's considered reaction, on watching the tragic disaster unfold, to the fact of his leaving in the morning to do Abu Homaidi.

Not that this particular bombing was necessarily Homaidi's work. So far, no one had claimed it. But its style was typically his. Which meant there was no advance warning. The bloodletting was pitiless and indiscriminate. Women and children suffered their full share of the damage. The primary targets remained American. And the bombing itself took place on European soil.

Peter Walters glanced at his son, who sat cross-legged on the floor in front of his mother. Watching the seven o'clock news together had become something of a family ritual when Peter was home. But this evening, considering the frightful nature of its content, Peter would rather not have had Paulie exposed to it.

At the moment, the boy was sitting very still, transfixed. It was as though he knew something terrible was unfolding on the screen in front of him, but he didn't understand what it meant. Until a camera closed in on a young girl's screaming, blood-streaked face, and it was terrified. Then Paul's face became terrified, too.

"Papa, . . ." he said softly, just that, not even knowing he was saying it, then slowly shaking his head back and forth, back and forth, like a suddenly bereaved old man.

Peter watched him instead of the television screen. He already knew enough, too much, about what had happened inside the Rome airport. He would never know enough about what was taking place inside his son.

But he did know what was going on inside him now. Paulie was imagining himself at the airport with the screaming girl, was seeing himself with the blood streaming down his face, was hearing his own terrified cries.

Peter also knew that Paul wanted him to touch his head. So he sat down on the floor behind him, worked his fingers through his hair, and heard him sigh.

"Papa?"

"Yes?"

"How does a terrible thing like that happen?"

"They said it was a bomb."

"I know. But why? I mean why does anyone want to kill so many people for no reason?"

Peter looked at his wife. She refused to meet his eyes. Which meant this was all his, and he shouldn't expect any help from her.

"I guess whoever did it thought they had a reason," he said.

"Like what?"

"To me there can't be any reason to hurt innocent, helpless women and children. But whoever did this was probably trying to frighten people and get attention for something they wanted."

"Why can't the police catch them?"

"I'm sure they're trying."

Paul thought about it, his eyes dark. "They'll never catch them," he decided.

"Why not?"

"Because they never do. But I bet *you* could if you tried," said Paul.

"Me?" Peter was mildly startled. "I'm no policeman. What do I know about catching crazy bombers?"

The boy turned to look at him.

"You know everything, Papa."

Peter was planning to leave very early in the morning, so Peggy was helping him pack before they went to bed.

During their early years together, she had given him a hard time before each of his mysterious little trips. Resentful of his leaving her, she had started arguments without apparent cause, had hurled recriminations, had frozen him with long, cold silences. But not anymore.

Peter thought, she accepted his need to go in much the same way a mother accepted a beloved child's permanent disabilities. She considered him rather simple in what he felt about his responsibility to America. She believed that in a way his feelings were almost juvenile, that at the age of thirty-eight he had somehow been spared the destruction of certain naive sentiments the way a pet duck was spared the ax.

But she no longer fought it. And because she didn't, he felt doubly guilty. Watching her help gather his things, seeing her neatly arrange each item, he nearly wished she would rage at him instead of trying to be so damned helpful.

"I'm so sorry Paul had to see all those awful things on the news tonight," she said. "It's going to hit him hard for the next few days. Too bad you won't be around to soothe him. He thinks you're Jesus Himself."

It was a not so subtle reminder that he was abandoning the needs of his son. Her first lapse.

"What are you telling me? That I'm *not* Jesus?"

She had stopped lining up his socks to study him, and he spoke cautiously, taking pains to give an impression of complete normalcy. Still, it must be noticeable that he wasn't in a normal state. Surely his eyes must be dilated with excitement at the prospect of what he was heading for. How could he be so eager to leave this place, this boy sleeping in the next room, this woman close beside him? Peter looked at her face, at one of the most deeply familiar and best loved of all human faces, looked at her in a way that couldn't be mistaken and thought, *Socks and underwear, look how she touches even my goddamn socks and underwear.*

Peggy smiled at his poor little joke and went back to her packing. With what control she'd learned to handle herself, he thought, and what a lot she had to hold down. The anger was still there, of course, but the explosions were all kept inside. And where fire once showed, the darkness came bit by bit. Where was it hiding, the rage of Irene Hopper, now known these many years as Peggy Walters? Under a curtain of poise and quiet humor? *Come on, Peggy. Shout! Scream! Make me explain, justify. Make me tell how I am what I am and you can't teach an old dog new tricks.*

So why fight it? Or was that just the easy way? Well, it didn't really matter, did it? One way or another, he'd still go after Abu Homaidi and she'd still be left without him. One way or another, he'd still walk out of this house in the morning and, through actual choice, not necessity, maybe never see it or her again.

He stood helplessly.

"Peter, please get some of those handkerchiefs from your drawer."

He did as she asked. Then he wandered into the bathroom, dumped his toilet articles into a leather kit, and handed it to her as his contribution.

"You'll have to shave and brush your teeth in the morning," she said.

He returned his kit to the bathroom.

Then he stretched out on the bed to watch her do the rest of his packing, finding something intensely touching in just the way she moved. What a woman. She struggled, she fought, she made do with what was finally handed her. Courage was needed to hold such control. She had a lot of it but at times it was unsteady. At times it trembled. Now, as she bent her head to look for something in a corner of his bag, Peter saw her cheek quiver.

He closed his eyes. He didn't want to watch that. It hurt too much.

"Where's your Kevlar vest?" she asked.

Peter opened his eyes. He hated wearing the body armor, and rarely did. Besides, Kevlar couldn't protect him from a head shot. But Peggy had an almost religious faith in the vest's ability to keep him alive and undamaged, so he took it along for *her* sake. Not that she ever knew where he went on his trips, or what he did when he got there. All she did know was that danger, injury, and death were always distinct possibilities.

"It's in my closet," he said.

"No, it isn't."

"Maybe it's in the hall closet."

Peggy went to look. She came back without it. "It's not there, either. Where else could you have put it?"

"Beats me."

"You're the one who unpacked it last time."

He was silent.

"This is infuriating," she said, and the quiver spread from her cheek to her lower lip like a traveling ague.

He rose from the bed. "Peggy . . ."

"It couldn't just get up and walk away. The damn thing's got to be here *someplace*."

"Did you try the refrigerator? The way my mind's working these days, I might have put it there or in the freezer."

She didn't smile. Here and there the cracks began to show. *All that poise,* he thought with regret, *all that great control.* His insides felt suspended, as before some dangerous action. She touched her cheeks in a youthful gesture, and he remembered her as she had been nine years ago. Then she let her hands hang heavy beside her hips, and she almost seemed to tumble into the beginnings of middle age. Surprise! *He* was no boy.

"You think it's funny, don't you?" she said. "You think I'm being silly and stupid about a crazy bullet-proof thing you take along just to soothe me and probably never wear anyway. Admit it."

He said nothing.

"Admit it!" she wailed.

Her brow was troubled, and she had slid into that state where the pain was coming right through her skin. Looking at her, and against all thought and wish, he said, "Do you have any idea how much I love you?"

Peggy looked as though he had clubbed her. It was unfair, he thought. You don't say things like that to a woman you've lived with for so many years. And surely not when you're about to go off and leave her.

"Yes." She sounded tired. "I know how much you love me. Only sometimes I wish you didn't love me so damned much. Sometimes I wish you'd love me less and consider me a little more."

She got back her control, and Peter found the Kevlar vest hanging under a jacket in his closet.

Then he quietly finished his packing.

But in bed later, with the dark soft all around and the moon patchy as quicksilver, they made love for what might possibly be the last time, and Peggy said, "I didn't mean that before. About wishing you didn't love me so much. I lied."

"I know."

She sighed. "The things I can get my mouth to say."

"You don't have to explain."

"Yes, I do. That's a cheap, wife's trick. Trying to load you with guilt. I'm ashamed of it." She held him. "I'm glad you love me as you do. I wouldn't have had it any different. Not for a minute."

He looked down at the drawn, wounded, beloved face, pale and a little misty in the moonlight. If I come back to her all right from this one, he swore, I'll never do anything to hurt her again. Never.

Yet, even at that moment, swearing to every word, he just wished he could believe it.

17

"THE WORST OF it is, Hank, I keep wondering where the whole mess is finally going to end."

It was near midnight and they were well into the Remy Martin in the study of the attorney general's Georgetown house. Earlier, they had enjoyed dinner and a concert at the Kennedy Center. In another room, Wayne's wife and Durning's female companion for the evening were doing their own drinking and talking.

"That is," Wayne added, "if it ever does finally end."

Durning looked at his friend's eyes, which seemed to have been without sleep for days. It gave them a roughened edge of grief. In fact, all of Wayne's features, crooked to begin with, appeared to sag in a curious mix of concern and sorrow. Not too unlike the equally sad looks of the more benighted sections of the city itself, thought Durning. Which meant that Brian and the worst of Washington's depressed areas had apparently reached the point where they both knew that many hurtful things weren't likely to get any better.

"I'm really sorry I had to pull you into this," he said.

Wayne stared broodingly at Durning and was even sorrier. They had gone all through college, law school, and the country's unholiest of wars together, and Durning had almost died saving his life. So there was no way to have turned him down on this incomprehensible manhunt for one Vittorio Battaglia. It was just that Wayne wished he knew more about what was behind it. With five of his agents already missing and presumed dead, and others still out there and in danger, he felt he had a right to know. But Hank felt differently, insisting it was enough to know that his life and future were at risk as long as Vittorio Battaglia, a known mob hitman, remained at large. The rest was simply a matter of faith and friendship. "For you to know more than that," Durning had told him, "can't do either of us any good. So please, Brian, either help me or don't help me. But leave the rest of it alone."

And that was the way it was left.

The FBI director rose to freshen their drinks.

"I guess that's how these things finally happen," he said.

Durning looked at him. "What things?"

"One's ultimate fall from grace." Brian Wayne laughed but its sound was chilling. "It creeps up on you so casually, so insidiously, you hardly notice. Like you send a couple of agents to question a man and woman as a favor to a friend, and the next thing you know you're up to your ears in shit and sinking."

"You do have a way with words, Brian."

"We've both seen enough sad examples. And in case you've forgotten, they reach as high as the Oval Office. In fact, the higher you get, the harder the disease hits."

"What disease?"

"A distorted sense of immunity. Believing you're above it all, that you can't be touched, that you're high enough up there to get away with just about any damn thing you please."

"You mean you *can't?*"

Wayne's smile was as cold as his laugh. "Next time you run into Gary Hart, Ivan Boesky, or Mike Milken, try asking one of them that question."

Durning's theory.

Like a work of art, lovemaking should never be created the same way twice. At its best it had to be a seemingly spontaneous mix of time, place, mood, and partner, blended with whatever else might happily occur along the way.

Tonight, there had been the entire evening to lead to their finally ending up in bed together. First, the gourmet dinner in perfect surroundings with the Waynes, then the always inspirational music of Mozart, then the best of brandies alone with his old friend, then working up to the penultimate pitch in the bedroom with some of the best grass available anywhere.

And the woman?

A young, recently discovered jewel of Hungarian descent named Ilona, whose family was unpronounceable, but who was an acknowledged master not only in bed but in everything leading up to it.

She believed reason could make steady progress from disorder to harmony, and the conquest of chaos didn't have to start all over again each morning. "You attack each new day, hour, minute," she had told Durning, "as though you'd never fought them before, as though you had to prove your worth all over again."

Did she mean he didn't have to?

Absolutely.

Look. He was the attorney general of the United States, a person of eminence. He should learn to relax and enjoy things more.

What things?

Her smile could be beatific. Why, her, of course.

Now, moving with her through that sweet, deep area below sex, Henry Durning felt aerated, weightless, intensely alive. All those cool, blond shadows. How sensuous, how wild she was. What joy she took in everything they did. That in itself was exciting to him. Just lying on her body was like floating on moving heat. It went out of her and took him in. When she breathed, she gave off stirrings of desire.

Then from nowhere, Brian Wayne and some of his earlier comments intruded, and Durning was put off.

Ilona felt it. "What's the matter?"

"I thought of the wrong things."

"I'll fix it."

Crouching like a golden animal drinking water, Ilona went at him. She kissed his lips, his neck, his chest, his stomach, went farther down and stayed. But Durning's thoughts, once they strayed, weren't easy to refocus, so that Ilona was working for nothing.

"I'm sorry," he said. "Maybe later."

She looked up at him, eyes stricken, looked across the flat

plain of his stomach, up between the twin slopes of his chest. "No. Wait. It'll be all right."

Then she was down and at it again.

He tried, gently, to free himself, tried to ease her away. But she held on and he finally lay back.

Strange woman. He could feel her body harden, sense hidden tensions and fears. Apart from it all now, he watched her apply what she knew, and she knew a great deal. Another expert. In bed, he seemed to have known only virtuosos. Every one a master. Where did they learn so much? And all so young. Or did it come with the genes?

And he? Eternally the god, Eros himself. Except not quite so godlike tonight. And, increasingly, other nights. *Face it, Henry. You're reaching, stretching. You're having to invent more and more.* He could still carry it off well enough in most cases, but it was starting to get humiliating.

A lamp was lit, and Durning stared at its glow on the walls and ceiling. But his thoughts were again with Wayne.

"One's ultimate fall from grace" was how his friend had described the growing threat, and it was aptly put. Except that Durning had no intention of falling. Brian was as good as they came, both professionally and as a friend, but he was a confirmed alarmist. Under enough pressure, people like that could be swayed. Which was one of the reasons Durning hadn't told him the whole miserable story. Another and more vital reason for keeping the details to himself: Brian's hardcore ethical and moral streak that might just possibly find his friend sitting in judgment on him at what could turn out to be the absolutely wrong time.

Because Durning was still not thinking of the right things, he continued to be of no help to Ilona. Then he did begin concentrating properly . . . but seeing her laboring so hard, so desperately now, struck him as terribly sad and washed out all hope. Poor girl.

He drew her up, finally, and held her.

"It doesn't have to be now."

Her face blurred, dissolved against his. Her body tensed. Her fingers clutched his chest, dug deep.

"Hey, it's no tragedy," he said.

"It is."

"You mustn't get so desperate about it."

She lay heavily, pliable flesh turned to lead. "I guess I just hate the idea of failing."

"If anyone failed, it was me. Not you."

"When a woman can't arouse a man, it's *her* failure."

"That's nothing but male chauvinist propaganda."

Ilona was silent for several moments. "It's just never happened to me before," she said.

Durning glimpsed erotic images of her successful arousals. They stretched to infinity. "I'm sorry I had to spoil your record."

But he'd had enough of this particular conversation. Too much. He knew it had gone too far when, for an instant, he stared past her head and through the window at a distant star and felt something in its mystic light, some less-than-innocent radiance out of the legions of women he had known and used through the years, leap through space and into him. So that the emptiness of his loveless couplings suddenly struck him like a blow, and a feeling passed through him that the only true path of reason was from the depth of one being to the heart of another. And that compared to this, all his usual brands of logic meant nothing.

So he was careful to avoid looking again at that pale, distant light. Although with the passage of a bit of time and a few more puffs of that magical golden weed, the star's threat did seem to lessen.

He was, after all, the one in control. He had never yet abandoned himself to any wild emotional pull. Restraint of sentiment had been his watchword, his lifelong philosophy. He was diligent in its practice. He worked at it unendingly and showed steady improvement. With luck, he expected to be in really great shape on his deathbed.

When they loved later, the last of the star's menace had faded.

18

GIANNI'S ARTISTS' REP, Marty Ellman, lived in an elegant prewar Fifth Avenue highrise that was about a fifteen-minute walk from his Madison Avenue gallery. In fact, as far as Gianni knew, walking to and from work was pretty much the only exercise his agent had done during their entire ten years together. But Marty did it unfailingly, rain or shine, six days a week.

As he was doing this morning.

With one hardly noticeable difference. This morning he was being followed.

Gianni had spotted the watcher about an hour ago, a paunchy man in a rumpled jacket and slacks, who had been leaning against the Central Park wall across from Ellman's building and reading the *Daily News*. The artist had him figured for a local, rather than a fed. But Gianni was still a bit surprised at the expenditure of any surveillance manpower at all on as remote a prospect as Marty.

Obviously not so remote.

Walking south on Fifth Avenue, Gianni kept a full-block interval between himself and the plainclothesman, who was only about seventy feet behind Ellman. Gianni wanted to be sure the cop didn't have any backup, since they often worked in pairs. But this one appeared to be alone.

Ellman turned east on Sixty-eighth Street to Madison Avenue. Then he walked downtown for two blocks and unlocked and entered the Gotham Gallery of Fine Art.

Gianni stopped walking and pretended to window shop. He saw the cop cross Madison Avenue and get into a gray sedan parked at a meter just opposite the gallery. Then the detective lit a cigarette and settled in for his day of watching.

The gallery was in a small, three-story building on the corner of Madison and Sixty-Sixth Street. Gianni walked past it and turned the corner. When he was out of the watcher's sight, he went down through a basement entrance, climbed a single flight of stairs and rang a bell beside the gallery's service door.

It was just 8:15. Marty would be alone until the place opened at 10:00 and his staff arrived.

"It's Gianni."

There was a moment's silence. Then locks and dead bolts clicked, the door swung open, and they stood looking at each other. Marty Ellman's myopic eyes went wide behind thick lenses. He stared at the gray hair, moustache, and glasses. Then he focused on Gianni's eyes, which were unchanged.

"What in God's name . . . ?"

"You alone?"

Ellman nodded dumbly, a slender man with a pink, unreasonably youthful face. "I've been calling you since the night of the reception. Where on earth have you been? And what's with the trick-or-treat hair?"

Gianni Garetsky closed and locked the metal fire door behind him. Then leading the agent into his own office, he settled tiredly into a chair. He had been on his feet for a long time.

"You'll never believe it, Marty."

"Try me."

Under the much brighter lights of the office, Ellman had his first good look at the artist's face and went pale.

"What the hell have you done? Gone back with the mob?"

"Nothing that good."

Reciting the words almost by rote at this point, Gianni gave Marty Ellman the heart of it. He told no more than was necessary for the purpose of his visit. But even this brief recital made him feel as if he were spilling his own seed, weakening some vital part of his future. Had death itself already invaded him? Unfair. Especially with Marty, who had literally changed his life, who'd had enough faith to stay with him when the art world was passing him by. His only real problem with Marty, he often thought, was trying not to kiss him too much in public.

Unable to hold himself still through it, Ellman had begun to pace. His pink face glistened with sweat by the time Gianni finished.

"I can't believe it," he said flatly. "This is the United

States of America, for God's sake! The land of apple pie and chicken soup."

"OK. So we've got a few dead cockroaches floating in the soup."

"But you're talking *FBI,* not *KGB.* Hell. Not even the Russians dare pull that kind of nonsense anymore."

Garetsky was silent. He found something oddly comforting in Marty's reaction. *Like a crazy man,* he thought, *being assured it's really the rest of the world that's crazy, not him.*

Ellman mopped his face with a handkerchief. "You took a big chance coming here. They could be watching me."

"They are watching you. I followed one of them all the way from your building. He's in a car on Madison Avenue right this minute, smoking himself to death. I'd have called, but I'm sure your phones are tapped."

Ellman left the office and walked to the front of the gallery. When he returned, his lips were tight.

"That gray Ford across the street?"

"That's the one."

"Marvelous. Absolutely superb."

Shaking his head, the art dealer took a bottle of Dewars from a liquor cabinet, filled a couple of old-fashioned glasses, and took a solid belt from one.

"It's 8:30 in the morning, Marty. Besides, you're Jewish."

"When it comes to scotch, I'm Irish."

Gianni allowed Ellman a moment to settle himself. Like Vittorio and Angie, the dealer had been part of the same boyhood group at art school. But in the end, he had found his juices flowing more toward the marketing of art than the creation of it. "I was lucky" was how he enjoyed explaining his career choice. "I discovered it early. I was simply too Jewish to ever be a major talent. Meaning, I wasn't self-absorbed enough, and I enjoyed eating too much."

"All right," he grumbled over his drink. "Now that you've got all the really good stuff out of the way, what else have you got for me? Cancer?"

"Just a few questions, Marty. When was the last time you spoke to Vittorio?"

The art dealer shrugged. "Hard to say. Had to be at least nine or ten years ago."

"How did it come about? Did you just run into him? Did he call about something? Or what?"

"He called. Said he wanted to come over and talk. Which surprised me. I hadn't spoken to him in years before that. He was strictly big-time mob by then."

Without thinking, Gianni picked up the scotch Ellman had poured for him, took a swallow, and made a face. "I was still in Italy at the time. So what did he want to talk about?"

"Nothing in particular. He came to see me here at the gallery and just sort of wandered around for a while, looking at the paintings and asking questions about them."

"What sort of questions?"

Ellman locked on Gianni's eyes. "Art questions. You know . . . style, technique, subject matter. What was most popular with the public? Which brought the highest prices and why? What percentages the gallery took? Things like that."

"You mean as if he might be thinking about going into the art business himself?"

"Exactly. In fact, I even made a joke about it. At least I hoped it was a joke. I asked him if Don Donatti was thinking of branching out into gallery protection."

Gianni leaned forward in his chair. "And then he asked you some of the same things about the European art markets?"

"How did you know?"

Gianni felt a sudden warmth. "I guess I'm just fucking psychic."

Prof. Eduardo Serini still lived in the same building in Little Italy that had once housed the Serini School of Art. It was on the Lower East Side's Mulberry Street, and Gianni Garetsky walked past the building four times, twice in each direction, and spotted nothing suspicious.

Then Gianni went up on the roof of a five-story walk-up directly across the street from Serini's house. From there he studied the action on the block for a full half-hour. Still, he saw nothing to bother him.

Even so, when he finally entered Professor Serini's tenement, it was from across several adjoining rooftops, where he had played Follow the Leader as a boy.

He slipped into the stairwell from the roof entrance and caught an instant whiff of cigarette smoke. It came floating up from below in a blue-gray spiral, and Gianni stood absolutely still, listening.

He heard a dry, hacking cough. When it stopped, Gianni eased down the stairs, his steps silent in rubber-soled running shoes. Then leaning as far as possible over the banister, he saw a man sitting and smoking on the fourth-floor landing. Professor Serini lived on the floor directly below the smoker.

The man was reading a newspaper. His jacket was off and he wore a hip holster that held a .38 caliber police special. A pair of handcuffs hung from his belt.

Gianni pulled back from the banister and thought it through. When he had it all clear in his mind, he removed his hairpiece, moustache, and glasses, and carefully stowed them in his pockets. If the cop caught a glimpse of him before he was knocked out, he didn't want him remembering his disguise when he came out of it. Then Gianni drew his automatic and started down the stairs. This time he walked normally, letting his steps be heard.

The watcher, evidently assuming he was hearing just another tenant coming downstairs behind him, leaned to one side to allow passing room. He never bothered to glance back as Gianni swung the butt of his automatic against the side of the cop's head. Making only a soft grunt, the watcher went over like a tree with rotten roots.

Gianni began moving quickly.

Kneeling, he got his shoulder under the unconscious man's middle and wrestled him up to the roof. Once there, he stuffed a handkerchief into his mouth, cuffed his hands behind his back, and tied his ankles together with some clothesline. Then he dragged him behind a ventilator and a pile of roofing equipment and went down to the third floor.

Prof. Eduardo Serini opened his door on the second ring, an old man with liver marks, a thousand wrinkles, and a full head of shining white hair. He squinted at Gianni with rheumy eyes and smiled with all his own teeth.

"*Benvenuto*, Gianni. *Avanti*. Come in, come in."

Half leaning on Gianni's arm, the old man took him into the kitchen, where he'd been reading an Italian paperback. For years, Gianni had made a point of dropping by at least once a week, so Serini showed no surprise. Gianni took his usual chair at the kitchen table, and the professor poured some espresso.

"So what did you do with the stupid *poliziotto* waiting for you upstairs?" Serini asked.

Gianni slowly shook his head. "He's sleeping up on the roof. You still know everything, eh, *Professore?*"

"Why not? What else have I got to do?"

"Then you were questioned?"

"That's their job. They don't protect people. They ask them questions."

Serini squinted at Gianni's battered face. "I see they questioned *you* pretty damn good."

"Did they hurt you?" Gianni asked.

"Nah. They wouldn't lay a finger on me. I'm too old. All I'd do for them if they touched me is die. Besides, I have *un posto nel loggione.*"

This last meant a seat among the gods, and was characteristic of the old man's speech, a patois of English and Italian that he'd developed and honed over the nearly seventy years he'd been in America. *Il professore* had arrived in New York on his honeymoon with his bride of two weeks and top honors from the Royal Academy of Art in Rome and never left. The honeymoon trip had been his graduation prize for painting, and the winning canvas itself still hung in his living room. Gianni could see it from where he sat, a huge somber oil of an actual shipwreck in which hundreds had died, including Serini's parents and sister. It gave off a bad mood.

"What did the police ask?" said Gianni.

"Where you and Vittorio were. And since I didn't know, it was a very short conversation." Serini sighed. "So what are you here to ask me?"

"The same things the police did."

"You don't know where you are, Gianni?"

"Not really, *Professore.* And it looks like I'm not going to find out unless I find Vittorio."

"What makes you think I know where that crazy *assassino* is?"

"Didn't we just agree you know everything?"

The old man nodded as if that was really an answer. Then he remained silent for several moments over his espresso.

"I'll be honest," he said. "I hear Vittorio's name and all I want to do is vomit."

"Why?"

"Because he had it all . . . everything . . . the best. And he turned himself into a first-class piece of shit. *Veramente prima classe.* I got no patience for that. I mean, I look at you. I see what he could have been. And I just get sick."

"We're two different people."

"That's garbage. You were like one. Brothers. And you both started in the same toilet. Only you got out, and he's still floating with the turds."

"That's where I'll end up, too, if I don't find him, *Professore.*"

"I don't understand."

"Just take my word for it and help me. Will you do that much?"

Eduardo Serini looked off somewhere. Finally, he nodded.

"I think Vittorio came to see you for the last time about ten years ago," said Gianni. "Is that true?"

"*Si.*"

"And what did he want?"

"To show me a painting."

"Whose?"

"His own."

"Tell me about it."

"There's not much to tell. Besides, I don't see—"

"Please, *Professore.* Just tell me what happened."

The old man allowed himself several moments to put it together.

"A surprise is what happened," he said. "Vittorio shows me this painting he says he's just done, and wants to know if I think it's any good. I tell him, yes, it's good. 'Good enough to sell?' he asks. And again I tell him, yes."

Serini looked at the artist across his kitchen table. "So, he says, it's the first painting he's done in years and am I sure

I'm not just trying to make him feel good. And I tell him I've got no reason to want to make a murdering prick feel good, that it's a stinking sin against God for a Christ-given talent like his to be wasted on shit like him, and to get the hell out of my goddamn house before I throw him out."

"And then?"

"Then the crazy *bastardo* starts laughing and kissing me on both cheeks. He says he's always loved me, too, and he's real sorry he's been such a murdering prick all these years, but maybe there's still a little time left so he can change."

"That was it?"

The professor nodded.

"And you never saw him again?"

"No."

They sat there over their black coffee.

The professor stirred himself.

"Vittorio did call me once," he said.

"When?"

"I'm not sure. But I don't think it could have been more than maybe two, three years ago."

"What did he call for?"

"Just to say a long-delayed *grazie*. Also, to tell me he had a son who was gifted with a true *talento* for *la bella arte* and wouldn't waste one fly speck of it like his murdering prick of a *padre.*"

"Where was he calling from?"

"He never said. But it must have been a long way off."

"How do you know?"

"Because it was a pay phone and he dumped in a pile of money."

"You heard the coins clanging in?"

"Yeah."

"Then you must have heard an operator tell him how much to dump in."

"*Probabilmente.*"

"OK," said Gianni. "So what language was the operator speaking?"

Serini stared blankly.

"Come on, *Professore*. Think. Did you understand what she was saying?"

"Yeah."

"Then it was English?"

The old man tiredly shook his head. *"Non.* That much, I know."

"So what other languages do you understand?"

"Solamente italiano."

They looked at each other.

Reaching an outside phone later, Gianni Garetsky called 911 to report someone lying tied-up on the roof of 45 Mulberry Street.

19

IN NEW YORK for the day on official Justice Department business, Henry Durning broke away from his staff at about 5:00 P.M. and had his driver take him to the huge Mariott Marquis Hotel in midtown.

He took one of the back elevators to the thirty-third floor, walked along the carpeted corridor to suite 3307 without passing anyone, and let himself in with the key that had been delivered that morning to his own suite at the Waldorf.

Deliberately early for his meeting, he removed his jacket and poured himself a tall Perrier from the minibar instead of his usual Jack Daniel's. Then, carrying his drink, he walked to a big picture window facing west and stood in the wash of the late-afternoon sun. On the river, a distant, incoming freighter moved slowly with the tide.

What he felt most at that moment was a peculiar apathy.

Yet much of his initial shock remained and kept breathing through. The thing was, it had all happened so quickly, so unexpectedly.

Thinking of it now, he found it hard to focus. His mind seemed to slip in and out of gear like a faulty machine. But he stayed with it. How could he not? It was suddenly the central issue of his life. His survival hung on its outcome.

It was exactly a week ago that it had all gone off inside him like a personal earthquake, and the aftershocks were still spreading.

The note had come to his Georgetown house exactly ten days ago in a plain white envelope marked *Personal*. It was delivered with the regular mail and there was no return address. But the postmark was stamped Freeport, New York, a town on the south shore of Long Island.

The enclosed, poorly typewritten message said:

Dear Mr. Durning,

Irene Hopper didn't go down in the ocean with your plane nine years ago like you and everybody thought she did.

She didn't die. I'm enclosing her old driver's license so you don't get the idea I'm just some crackpot.

If you want to see proof of this and hear the whole story of what really happened to her, call me at (516) 828-6796 and I'll tell you how to get where I live.

I'm very sick and can't leave my bed or I'd be happy to come to you in Washington.

Please don't wait too long to call me. My doctor doesn't expect me to be around all that much longer.

Mike

Henry Durning had read the note five times. Each time he felt primitive stirrings of dread in his brain. Yet, less than twenty minutes after his first reading of the brief message, he found himself dialing the man's number.

"Is this Mike?"

"Yeah."

"This is Henry Durning. I read your letter a little while ago and I have some questions."

"Not on the phone, please Mr. Durning. If you want to talk, you'll have to come to my house."

"When?"

"The sooner the better. Tonight OK? About eight?"

"Sure."

The man called Mike gave him directions.

"Just two things, Mr. Durning. Don't tell anybody about this, and nobody comes with you. No chauffeur, no security, nobody. It's nothing personal. Something like this, a man can't be too careful. Understand?"

Durning understood.

He understood enough to slip an automatic inside his belt. Then he flew his own Lear to La Guardia, picked up a rental car at the terminal, and fifty minutes later parked a few blocks away from the modest, shingled Cape Cod in which Mike lived. If there was some sort of mystic dislocation in the heavens that night, Durning was sure it had stayed very close to him all the way.

A middle-aged woman with thick, graying hair opened the door.

"I'm Henry Durning."

"I know. I've seen you on TV." She flushed self-consciously. "My husband's waiting for you."

He followed her upstairs to a small bedroom smelling of body things, sickness, drugs.

Mike sat propped up in bed. He had not been lying about his condition. His hollowed-out eye sockets, his gaunt face, the yellow-gray color of his skin, all projected death.

"Hi, Mr. Durning." His voice was hoarse, rasping. "You met my wife, Emma. You'll excuse me, but she'll have to pat you down. I can't take a chance you're wired."

"I'm not wired, but I am carrying."

"I don't mind a gun. But Emma's still gotta check you for a wire."

Durning stood while the woman searched him. She found the automatic in his belt but left it where it was. When she was through, she nodded to her husband and slid a chair close to his bed for their visitor.

"Would you like some nice red wine, Mr. Durning? Or maybe a little Irish whiskey?"

He looked at the woman, smelled the organic soup in the air, and smelled the entire rest of her life. "Thank you," he told her. "The red sounds fine."

When his wife was out of the room, Mike said, "I'm doing this whole bit for her, Mr. Durning. Between the doctors and drugs and not working and all, I'm leaving her with shit. So, if you want what I'm selling, it'll have to cost a few bucks."

Durning just sat there.

"To be honest," said Mike, "I hate like hell doing this. In my whole life I never sold out a friend. But Emma's given me thirty-eight years and I owe her."

He coughed and passed blood and mucus into a tissue.

His wife returned with a bottle and two glasses on a silver tray, and Mike watched her serve Durning and herself. Then she settled on the edge of the bed.

"OK, here's how it was," said Mike. "About nine years ago this friend of mine came to me for a favor. Because I could fly, he asked me to help him work something out. What he needed was to make it look like this woman, flying alone, got killed when her plane took a dive over the Atlantic."

Durning moistened his lips with the wine. "This woman was Irene Hopper?"

"Yeah."

"And who was your friend?"

"That comes later. That's the part you're going to have to pay for."

"Why would Irene Hopper want me to think she was dead?"

"My friend never said it was you she wanted to think she was dead. He never said anything about reasons, and I never asked. We both figured the less I knew, the better."

"Then what did you know that made you write to *me* about her being alive?"

"I saw the plane's papers. They were registered in your name. So, I just figured you might have some interest. Right?"

Durning nodded slowly. "How did you do it?"

"It wasn't all that hard. Irene just took off from Teterboro,

New Jersey, with a flight plan filed for Palm Beach. You remember that?"

"Yes."

"You also remember how she made an emergency landing in Florence, South Carolina, 'cause she didn't like how her engine was sounding?"

"Yes."

"Well, when her plane took off from Florence an hour later, I was flying it, not her."

"Where was *she?*"

"Driving off in a rented car I left in a parking lot."

"And then?"

"I just followed her flight plan off the coast of Georgia. When I was about thirty miles out over the ocean from Brunswick, with no ships or planes in sight, I got into a life vest and parachute, emptied both gas tanks, and bailed out as the plane was about to go into a stall."

Mike sucked air and began coughing again until his wife had him sip some water through a straw.

"I was in the ocean maybe five minutes," he said, "when my friend got me into his boat. We had it figured that close. Then we dumped enough flotation stuff for the Coast Guard to identify over the next few days. And that's how it was, Mr. Durning."

The room was still.

"How do I know you didn't just make all this up?"

The sick man nodded. "Emma, please get that envelope in the next room for Mr. Durning."

The woman brought it, and Durning glanced through a sheaf of creased and faded FAA forms, licenses, and flight plans. They all bore the signature of Irene Hopper, as well as the ID number of the plane she was flying on the day they both vanished off the Georgia coast.

Also in the envelope was her pilot's license. Durning held it awkwardly in his hand and felt himself disappear into emotions that didn't seem to belong to him. He looked at the attached photograph of a beautiful, fair-haired young woman whom he had been very close to for a long time but evidently had never even come close to knowing. When he felt his fingers starting to lose control, Durning put everything back into the envelope and closed the flap.

"When did you last see her?" he asked Mike.

"Nine years ago. When she got out of your plane in South Carolina and I got in."

"Did you know where she was going from there?"

"No."

"And your friend?"

"Same thing. Haven't heard a word from him since the day he fished me out of the ocean. We agreed it would be best that way. So the only thing I can tell you is his name."

Mike took in more water through his straw. "That's if you want it."

Henry Durning looked at the man propped on his pillows, and his wife sitting on the edge of his bed. He saw the fragile looks exchanged between them and understood that in these exchanges there were elements of panic.

"I want it," he said.

"Like I told you, that's the part that has to cost."

"How much?"

Mike took the long, deep breath of a man about to go over a fall. "A hundred grand. And it has to be all cash."

"Who knows about all this?"

"Just Emma and you." Mike's shame wouldn't let him leave it alone. "And even you wouldn't know if I wasn't this sick and broke."

"Did you tell anyone I was coming here tonight?"

"Hell, no. You think I'm nuts?"

Durning's eyes were off somewhere. He felt lost in the surprise of who he was.

"If it's all right with you," he said, "I can pick up the cash and be back at eight tomorrow night."

The sick man's lips worked dryly. He tried to smile, but the required muscles seemed to have forgotten what to do.

When Emma opened the door for Durning the next night, she gazed at him as though he were an exciting new suitor. She had brushed her hair until it shone, and her eyes had new lights. She half glanced at the briefcase in Durning's hand, then avoided looking at it again.

Upstairs, Mike, too, seemed to have reconstituted himself. His breathing had deepened, and new blood, ordered like reinforcements, had added color to the pale translucence of his skin. This time, his muscles remembered how to smile. A pine spray had improved even the air.

Durning opened his briefcase and placed it on the bed.

"The bills are all hundreds," he said. "They're in fifty packs of twenty apiece. You can count them."

Mike lay there, looking at the open briefcase. Then he briefly closed his eyes, and a tiny moment seemed to stall inside him.

"I don't have to count anything. My friend's name is Battaglia . . . Vittorio Battaglia."

Mike said it again, more slowly. Finally, he spelled it. Durning took out a pen and small notebook and wrote the name. Staring at the two words, he felt himself looking someplace he couldn't see.

"Where is he from?"

"New York."

"What kind of work did he do?"

"He never really talked about it, but I'm sure it was mob connected."

Durning nodded his head, looking slow and tired.

Mike started to cough again and Emma brought him some tissues and water. Then she sat on the edge of the bed, holding the glass for him while he sipped through a straw.

Durning sat watching them. He saw Emma's full, curving back as she leaned toward her husband, and the way the overhead light caught the gray streaks in her hair. He saw that Mike's eyes were closed as he lay there, as if he might be drinking the water in his sleep.

This was how Durning would remember them.

Exactly twenty-nine hours later, an explosion and fire eliminated Mike, his wife, his house, and everything in it. Evidence of a propane tank was found in the basement. Little remained above it except clouds, scarred scraps, and ashes.

Reading about it in the news, the attorney general had felt the fact of it enter him. You never appreciate the true urgency of life if you haven't seen how easily it can be taken away.

In his mind, there was nothing else he could have done, of course. Considering what they knew, there was no way he could have just left them there.

Still, it brought him no joy.

Ten days, thought Durning, and stared off at the river thirty-three stories down and half a mile west.

It had been a bad period of time for him and things showed every promise of getting worse. There was even a way in which his sudden personal trials seemed to proclaim the entire country. Like something dying in a brightly colored candy box, he thought. Terrible to watch, yet darkly fascinating. But then the dead had always fascinated him. They looked so indifferent to what had happened that dying almost didn't seem so bad.

He was well into his third Perrier when there was a soft knock and he opened the door for Don Carlo Donatti.

They embraced and the attorney general breathed the don's once familiar designer cologne. Some things did stay the same.

Donatti held him with some deep authority of feeling. But whether it was for Donatti's own need or Durning's was impossible to tell. They had not, after all, met face to face for years. But inasmuch as it was Durning who had requested the meeting, and Donatti still had no idea of its purpose, the edge remained in the attorney general's favor.

"You look well, Don Carlo. You haven't aged five minutes in five years. What's your secret?"

"Pure thoughts in a healthy body."

"Both way out of my reach."

"And mine, since your honesty shames me."

The two men smiled and something passed between.

Durning poured Donatti some scotch and handed it to him. Then he switched on the radio, tuned in a Philharmonic recording, and pushed up the volume. He had already checked the suite for possible bugs and found it clean. But these days, with the latest electronic advances, it was impossible to be sure. The music also eliminated the inelegant, always embarrassing need to pat each other down. This was all understood and Donatti said nothing. It was for their mutual security.

They sat facing each other beneath a soaring rendition of Beethoven's Fifth.

"A question," said Durning. "Regarding that little favor you did me nine years ago. Was the man who handled it named Vittorio Battaglia?"

Donatti's face was blank. Then he nodded, "Something's wrong?"

"I'm afraid a lot's wrong," said Durning, and he told Donatti about Mike's letter and everything that followed.

Don Donatti listened in silence. Then he slowly rose, walked to the big window, and stood looking out over the city. Finally, he turned.

"When did all this happen?"

"Ten days ago."

"What have you been doing for ten days?"

"Watching people disappear."

The attorney general's next witch's tale was the one about Gianni Garetsky, Mary Chan Yung, and the apparent melting away of the five men sent to question them.

Donatti shook his head. "Why didn't you come to me right away?"

Durning sipped his Perrier and said nothing.

His silence made the don smile. "You still don't trust me?"

"Nine years ago you assured me the woman had been taken care of. Now I find she's alive. Is that a basis for trust?"

"What can I say, Henry? It's an embarrassment. But Vittorio was the best I had and he told me it was done. News of the accident was in the papers. I'm as shocked as you."

"Where's Battaglia now?"

"Christ only knows. He vanished a few weeks after the crash and I haven't heard a word about him since."

"And that didn't seem strange to you?"

Carlo Donatti shrugged. "Nothing's strange in Vittorio's line of work. There are always enemies. People disappear. Even the best. So I just lit a candle and kissed Vittorio good-bye."

"What about his friend, the artist? You think *he* knows where Battaglia is?"

"I doubt it."

"When did you last see Garetsky?"

Donatti considered his scotch through hooded lids. "A few nights ago. There was a reception in his honor at the Met. I went to pay my respects."

"He didn't call or come to you for help after that?"

"No."

"Let's put the pistols on the table, Carlo. We've always been comfortably *quid pro quo*, we two. Something for something. Right?"

Donatti sat completely still.

"Many years ago," said the attorney general quietly, "as a prosecutor, I quashed a serious murder indictment against you. Some time later, in return, you were supposed to take care of Irene Hopper for *me*. Now it turns out you never did."

"I'm sorry. Until five minutes ago I thought I had."

"Maybe and maybe not. In either case, it's irrelevant. All that matters now is that I suddenly find there are two people out there who can effectively ruin me anytime they choose."

Donatti stared down into his drink. He might have been considering the entrails of a blood sacrifice. "If they haven't done it in nine years, why would they do it now?"

"You're missing the point. I can't live with this hanging over me. I *won't* live with it. For God's sake, Carlo! I'm not what I was nine years ago. I'm now attorney general of the United States. And I could be more. Who can tell the workings of people's minds? Who knows what can suddenly push them to do what they haven't done before?"

Donatti was silent.

"I'm dead serious," said Durning.

"You think you have to tell me that?"

"What I think is that you've seen this Gianni Garetsky since the night at the museum. Which means you've already lied to me."

Donatti's eyes were cold, but he said nothing.

"I'm holding you responsible for this disaster, Carlo. So when Garetsky next contacts you, as I'm sure he will, I expect to hear about it."

Don Donatti sat letting the words settle. "You're looking in the wrong place. My feeling is that Gianni Garetsky doesn't know anything."

"You let *me* judge that."

Henry Durning studied the way the late sun came through the window and painted the walls. He smiled, but there was no humor in it.

"And just in case you get any foolish notions, Carlo, please . . . just remember three things. There's no statute of limitations on murder, the evidence against you is still locked in a bank vault, and every bit of it will go straight to the DA if I should accidentally die."

Majestically, Beethoven filled the following silence.

20

MARY YUNG SAT at a table in the great reading room of the main branch of the New York Public Library. Feeling her excitement building, she was utterly unaware of those about her. For the past hour she had been studying the contents of the manila folder delivered to her there by one of Jimmy Lee's messengers.

The enclosed microfiche printouts included every detail . . . as reported by *The New York Times, Newsweek,* and *Time* . . . surrounding the crash in which Irene Hopper had died more than nine years ago. And what struck her most strongly were the many recurrent roles played by Henry Durning.

It was Durning's plane that Hopper was flying when she crashed.

It was Durning who was described as having originally hired Irene Hopper for his law firm, become her mentor and benefactor professionally, and formed a seemingly close relationship with her outside the office as well.

It was Durning who delivered an emotional eulogy for her in a moving memorial ceremony conducted a week after the crash.

It was Durning who apparently established a generous scholarship in Irene Hopper's name for the benefit of needy and deserving law students at her alma mater, the University of Pennsylvania.

But for Mary Yung, what were undoubtedly the two most meaningful bits of information she knew about Henry Durning had nothing to do with what she was seeing on the microfiche. The first was that Durning was the man with whom Irene Hopper had been two-timing Vittorio nine years ago. While the second had to do with Durning's appointment several years ago as attorney general of the United States. Which not only established him as titular head of the Department of Justice, but actually placed the FBI itself under his jurisdictional control.

Meaning what?

Perhaps everything.

Or, just possibly, nothing.

But a forest of nerves had started making sparks inside her, and she knew better than to negate it.

She had it all.

Henry Durning was behind the whole thing. He had too many connections to too many key elements not to be involved. She had no idea what his reasons were, but reasons hardly mattered. At this point, all she saw was an unbelievable opportunity. Which, if handled right, might just possibly help lift her out of the nest of snakes she'd been calling home for as long as she could remember.

Mary Yung floated on excitement as she left the library. Her new Nikes barely touched the wide, stone steps to Fifth Avenue. She sensed her own pulse in the air.

Still, she felt one of her sudden needs for reassurance, a compulsion to be sure, to remove even the smallest remaining doubt.

So fired, she again found a public phone and called Jimmy Lee.

"Aah," he said, hearing her voice. "Filled with undying gratitude, you've called to thank me for my graciousness."

"Yes. You're indeed supreme. And I've called also to put myself even further in your debt, if I may."

"You may, you may. What is it, little flower?"

"I have to call the attorney general in Washington. But I want to reach him without going through half a dozen switchboards, secretaries, and assistants."

"You're shooting high these days. What are you trying to steal from this poor shyster?"

"My life," she said. "And if I'm lucky, maybe a little something extra."

"Call me back in five minutes."

Mary Yung stood waiting. Someday she would like to spend six or seven hours just sitting and talking to Jimmy Lee. It would be like talking to the devil's private gatekeeper. When she was through, she was sure she'd know enough to have the devil himself working for her. The only trouble was, she would have to shoot Jimmy first.

She had her pencil and notebook ready when she called him back.

"Take this number down," he said, and read it to her. "It's as close to the man as the president himself can get. It's his private secretary's number and she can put you right through."

"Honest to Confucius, you're too much."

"I know. Except with you. With you I always feel I'm too little."

She prepared a fistful of quarters, dialed the number Jimmy had given her, and deposited the amount requested.

"Attorney General Durning's office," said a woman's voice. "Miss Berkely speaking."

"The attorney general, please."

"I'm sorry, but he's in a meeting. Who's calling, please?"

"Just tell him it's someone with information about Vittorio. Do you have that? *Vittorio*. And tell him if he's not on the line in sixty seconds or less, I'm hanging up."

Mary watched the second hand of her watch. Seventy seconds was generally the mean trace time on a call from an automatic switching station, and she was using that factor to add pressure. She wasn't really worried about being picked up. They'd have to be prepared in advance for something like that and they weren't.

At forty-five seconds, a man's voice said, "Durning."

"This is Mary Chan Yung," she told him. "I expect to know where Vittorio is in a few weeks or less. You interested in dealing? No questions, please. Just yes or no."

She watched seven seconds ticking off. It seemed longer.

"Yes," he said.

"I'll be in touch again," she said and hung up.

Exactly seventy-four seconds.

Now she really did know.

21

GIANNI HAD STARTED to think of the evening as kind of a celebration. On a small scale, of course, with their hotel room as its entire site, and the two of them as its only celebrants.

Still, what more was needed?

A thunderstorm was raging outside, but he and Mary Yung were dry, untouched. They had the best of food and drink delivered to them with no more than just a quick telephone call. For the moment, at least, no unseen, threatening forces were breathing down their necks. And perhaps best of all, neither of them had to be alone.

Madre Garetsky's legacy.

Whatever you do, Gianni, don't do it alone. We're born alone and we die alone. In between, it's nice to have somebody to do things with.

Even if it's a crazy Chinese who fucks like a whore, kills like a pistolero, *and probably can't be trusted for a second?*

Even so. And since when do you use the F-word with your madre?

Scusi, madre. *But she can sure do it.*

Moments later, she was doing it again.

And although it was no longer the first time for them, Gianni still had the feeling it was totally new, a sensation of something astral, a communion with cells he'd never even suspected he owned. Although the truth was he felt you didn't really have sex with Mary Chan Yung. What you had was more of a species of psychic interplay. Dispatches went back and forth, bits of information, real and imagined, over which the brain had little control. Never had he met anyone so telepathic. After less than a week with her, he'd begun to feel he was in touch with a chorus of the devil's own handmaidens, some of whom he'd just as soon have left alone.

But, oh, Lordy, Lordy . . . what she did have it within her to do to him sexually. *Don't worry,* he told Teresa. *It's only lust, not love.* I think.

Yet it lingered even later, as they lay together.

She sighed into his ear, then offered a kiss that was full of the smell of honeysuckle and very like a first kiss. Except that it was a gift, not a vow. No promises had been made between them. Even now, the act of love was very far from the reason they were in this hotel room together. It was only an exceptional fringe benefit.

She smiled at him in the lamplight. "How lovely," she whispered.

"What?"

"To be going to Italy on our honeymoon."

"Some honeymoon."

"It won't be all bad, Gianni."

"Unless they find us before we find Vittorio."

"You've got to look more on the bright side of things."

"I'm trying," he said, and looked at that perfectly lovely face on the pillow beside him, a face no longer spectacularly young. Yet there was something even more special about this face, a silver cunning in the way it was woven together, a quiet air of hidden secrets, as if once there had been a deep sadness, and now a delicate humor had formed to cover the hurt.

"But among other things," Gianni told her, "we've still got the matter of clean passports, credit cards, and drivers' licenses to take care of. Those I have are now worthless, and you have none at all that you can safely use."

"I'll handle that."

"You?"

She laughed. "Don't be so superior. How do you think I've gotten along all these years without you?"

He had started to learn how.

"Fooling with stuff like this could be dangerous," he said.

"I know, Gianni, I know."

"You really have people you can trust?"

"If I didn't, I'd have been dead or in jail twenty years ago."

He stroked her hair where it caught the light on the pillow. She smiled at him with that look of nakedness that comes after great joy, or grief, or terrific sex.

"I have a good feeling about this, Gianni. You'll see. It'll be fine. Italy'll be fine. I love that country. It's so unbelievably beautiful. I'm so glad Vittorio chose to go there. Even if we never find him, it'll be a lovely trip."

"You should tell Mr. Parillo. He'll be happy to run your testimonial in his tour ads."

The room was high in the hotel, and outside, the wind was up, whipping the rain. Lying there with Mary Yung, Gianni Garetsky could hear it too well, and it had the sound of an angry gale at sea.

God, he wanted to ask, *why can't I just lie in a room and make love to a woman with no thought reaching past her and the four sides of a bed?*

In the morning, Mary Yung called Jimmy Lee's private number from an outside phone.

"Your eminence," she said.

"My day has already reached its zenith," he told her in the same gently mocking Cantonese. "I've heard your voice. What's left for me to look forward to?"

"Seeing me for a few moments in person. If I dare presume on your time with so bold a suggestion."

"I can't believe my good fortune," said Jimmy Lee. "At this moment I'm literally trembling with it."

Mary Yung laughed. "Don't get carried away, Jimmy. If it's all right, I'll be there in about half an hour."

"I doubt if I'll be able to wait that long."

"Please try," she told him.

Mary hung up and stared out at the rain, still falling heavily after almost ten hours. It was one of those New York downpours that seem created to either wash the city clean of its sins or sweep it into its surrounding rivers. When she saw a cab heading for the curb to discharge a passenger, she dashed for it in time to beat out several slower-moving, less-determined men. She could feel her nerves wriggling at the prospect of what lay ahead for her. A web was being spun and she was at its center. It was her own web, of course, and she was doing the spinning. But she was hung there just the same, and the threads could get dangerously sticky.

Jimmy Lee lived and worked high in a soaring tower on the tip of lower Manhattan, where even the summer breezes sounded carnivorous and the views of the Lady in the Harbor could tear your heart.

Each time Mary was there, she responded with the same curious mixture of wonder, reverence, and fear.

She sensed it again this morning as she stepped out of Lee's private tower elevator and was greeted by a polite, impeccably dark-suited young Asian who could have been interchangeable with any one of a dozen others who had greeted her there before. And the feeling grew as she followed him along a wide, gently curving corridor, past large quiet rooms filled with desks and glowing computer screens at which other, equally anonymous Asians were at work.

A long way from the rice paddies, thought Mary Yung.

Then her escort showed her into Lee's private quarters, bowed formally, and closed the door behind him as he left.

Suddenly she was alone and there was a change of mood as exact as the moment of entering a place of the distant past, some ancient Confucian temple with Oriental screens, antique wall hangings, and the aroma of burning incense.

There was very little light in the room. It made Mary Yung feel vaguely disconnected from herself and everything around her. Until she sensed a presence like the ghost of a dead emperor, and saw Jimmy Lee sitting on a kind of carved teak throne in the shadows, watching her.

"Master," she said, and stood waiting with bowed head until he rose, came forward, and gently raised her chin.

They stood looking at each other.

Tall for an Asian, Lee appeared even taller in an ankle-length Mandarin robe.

"You keep growing," Mary told him.

"Only in your mind. In truth, I'm afraid I've entered my shrinking season. I must remember my posture." He smiled with perfectly capped teeth, a slender, smooth-faced man of indeterminate age who could have been anything from thirty to fifty. "But you do keep growing more beautiful."

He bent and kissed her lips . . . lightly, barely touching her. Then he slowly pulled away.

"Still soft as a bird's feather," she said. "I won't break, you know."

"So you keep telling me."

"Then why won't you take more?"

"I'm still waiting for our wedding night."

"And what if I'm dead before that ever arrives?"

Gravely, Jimmy Lee considered both her and her question.

"Then I'll mourn you until I die, and take you as I do now. In my nightly fantasies."

"While you do yourself?"

"What better way?" Jimmy laughed. "You do go right for the heart of things, don't you?"

"One of us has to."

Abruptly taking Lee's hand, Mary Yung led him back to his private throne and sat him down. Then she went back to the door through which she had entered the room, and turned the key in the lock.

"Don't do it, Mary." His voice was soft, but there was a sudden edge to it.

"How do you know what I'm going to do?"

"Because I know *you.*"

"If that's true, then you also know how I feel about people giving me orders."

"This is about more than just *your* feelings."

Mary Yung stood in silence for a moment, wanting something that didn't have a name. She went to where Lee was sitting, pressed her lips against his ear, and kissed him.

"Be nice, Jimmy."

Then she moved a few steps back and began taking off her clothes.

She did it slowly, deliberately, a single piece at a time, letting each one drop at her feet.

A few strands of hair fell across her eyes, and she stared at Lee through them. She felt his eyes on her and heard the sound of his breathing. It was the only sound in the room. The walls and ceiling might have been breathing with Jimmy Lee.

Finally, Mary Yung stood naked before him.

The air, cool against her skin, raised her nipples, and Jimmy's eyes went to them as though drawn there.

She stood absolutely still, hands hanging loosely at her sides. She, Jimmy Lee, everything around them felt delicately balanced. It seemed dangerous to move.

Until her hands moved.

Jimmy's eyes widened.

He watched her hands as she licked her fingers and touched herself.

He groaned softly. The sound was that of a man in the farthest reaches of pain.

Mary Yung watched and listened, knowing she had him now, very nearly able to feel him in her.

Better yet, she knew what *he* was feeling.

Her body stirred, flowed with sensation, and she carried him up with her. Slowly. Letting it all drift along the edge. Not wanting him to go off quite yet.

Then their eyes met, so that even apart she had him held fast, circling him. While his eyes went blank with an old darkness.

"Mary!"

Her name was the only word he spoke.

They lay close to one another, but not touching, on Jimmy Lee's near priceless Oriental rug.

He said softly, "You must want something very badly from me this morning."

"Why? Because I dared presume to bring you a few moments of joy?"

Lee stared at the ceiling. "Just tell me what you want."

"When you want to, you can be really hateful, can't you?"

"I'm sorry. It's just that I've never taken well to being manipulated."

"The key was always in the door. All you had to do was walk over, turn it, and leave."

"That's what makes it even worse." He turned his head to look at her. "But that's my problem, not yours. So please tell me what I can do for you."

She needed a moment as a buffer.

"I must have two clean passports, two drivers' licenses, and a couple of major credit cards."

"For whom?"

"Myself and someone you don't know."

"A man?"

"Yes."

Lee raised himself to a sitting position. "You're going to leave the country with him?"

"It's not what you think. We're under the gun."

"How seriously?"

"Very."

"Do you want to tell me about it?"

"It's better that I don't," she said, and could almost see his mind sniffing and picking at it.

Jimmy Lee nodded. "Of course. I remember now. You wanted the attorney general's private number."

Mary Yung was silent. Suddenly chilled, she rose from the rug and began putting on her clothes. Lee studied her, his eyes flat. Something seemed to circle inside him. Then it surfaced.

"You don't have to run," he said. "I can protect you."

"Not from this. There's too much breakage."

"I'll fix whatever's broken."

She sighed. "God, I love your confidence."

"I'd rather you loved *me.*"

"I do." She worked into her blouse. "In my own way."

"Then stop all this craziness and marry me."

Mary laughed. *"Marry?* I can't believe some of your compulsions. Your heart's in a time warp. It's a hundred years behind your brain."

He just looked at her.

"Ah, Jimmy. If I did marry you, I'd only end up hating you. And you, me."

"I'm willing to risk it."

"Well, I'm not. You'd smother me blue in a month. Then we'd lose even the little we have."

Buttoning her blouse, she considered him where he sat on the floor.

"Talk about craziness," she said. "You can have me any-time you want and won't so much as touch me. Yet you walk around with this marriage bug up your ass like some tight-lipped virgin in need of sanctity."

Jimmy Lee sat there, insulated in silence.

"Explain *that* one, Buster."

"I can't," he said. "I only know I want more from you than just another perfectly put together piece of flesh. I can pick those up by the thousand. They grow wild in the streets. It's the rest of you I want and can't get and can't find anywhere else."

"What's so special about the rest of me?"

They stared at each other as though stuck in space.

"You really don't know, do you?" he said.

Mary shook her head.

"A terminal soreness of the heart," Jimmy Lee told her. "The only kind that really disdains the pleasures of the flesh but tries to heal itself by touching others."

Mary Yung's eyes were mocking. "Does that mean I use sex for something more than just getting what I want?"

"Loosely, yes."

"And that appeals to you?"

"I cannot begin to tell you how much."

"Good. I'm in favor of whatever works."

Mary put on her skirt and picked her purse off a chair. "So what about the stuff I need? You going to help me with it, or what?"

"When have I ever refused you?"

"I appreciate it."

She took an envelope from her purse and gave it to Lee. In it were photographs taken earlier that morning of her and Gi-anni Garetsky in full disguise.

"You'll need these," she said.

Jimmy Lee looked at Garetsky, complete with gray hair-piece, moustache, and horn-rimmed glasses.

"This is the man you're running away from me with?"

"I wouldn't put it quite that way."

"What does he really look like?"

"Clean shaven, no glasses or gray hair, and about twenty years younger."

"Who is he?"

Mary shook her head.

"What did you two do?"

She hesitated, then shrugged. "Between the two of us, we seem to have caused five FBI agents to disappear."

Jimmy stared at her. "Only five?"

"Please. No more questions."

He was now studying Mary's picture. It showed her with the curly Kewpie Doll wig, which she had quickly taken off and stuffed in her purse the moment she entered his elevator.

"It doesn't improve you."

"That wasn't its purpose."

Lee got up from the floor, stood tall beside Mary Chan Yung, and straightened his long silk robe.

"I don't understand this entire thing," he said.

"You aren't supposed to."

"I've been running what amounts to about a billion-dollar operation for more than ten years," Lee said. "Most of it violates federal laws of one sort or another. Yet not a single government agent has ever ended up any the worse for it."

"What would you like? A good conduct medal?"

"I'd just like to know why you and your friend should have had to get rid of five feds." Jimmy Lee snapped his fingers. "Just like that."

Mary took a deep breath. "It was simple. To keep *them* from getting rid of *us*. That was the choice we had. And that's the last I'm going to say about it."

She picked up the completed paper and plastic from Jimmy Lee early the next afternoon.

Every piece was letter perfect.

His last kiss remained, as always, light as a feather.

"You take care now," he said in what was very near to a whisper. "You're the only truly irreplaceable piece of work I've ever known."

On her way back to the hotel, Mary Yung stopped at a public phone and made her second call to the Washington, D.C., number of Henry Durning's private secretary.

"Attorney General Durning's office," said the secretary's voice. "Miss Berkely speaking."

"Hello, Miss Berkely. We've spoken before. Would you please tell the attorney general it's Vittorio's friend, and he has to get on the line in under thirty seconds or I'm out of here."

This time Henry Durning took the call in exactly seventeen seconds.

"Miss Yung?"

"A brief update, Mr. Durning. We're getting closer, so I just want to lay out the deal. It's an even million and it has to be deposited in a numbered Swiss account when I have the information. Are you still interested? Just yes or no, please."

"Yes."

The answer was instant, without hesitation.

"You'll hear from me soon," Mary said, and hung up.

Exactly fifty-six seconds, she thought. Better than the first.

She was sure she could hear her blood. It was near to a fluttering of wings.

At home in his study late that night, Henry Durning felt Mary Chan Yung's two phone calls gnawing at him like a pair of angry ulcers that needed soothing.

How had she known of his involvement? And if *she* knew, who else knew?

It made him wonder if he'd made a mistake in telling her that he was interested in a deal. It was the same as an admission of interest in the hunt for Vittorio Battaglia and all its potentially lethal undercurrents.

It made him wonder, too, about Mary Yung herself. Exactly who and what was she?

In reviewing her FBI short-form file printout, the whole thing had suddenly struck him as curiously superficial, even false. A call to Brian Wayne for more of an in-depth probe produced a wholly different image of the woman.

For one thing, she was no jet-set glamour girl out of Hong Kong money.

Quite the opposite. Everything about her, even the air she breathed, entered Durning's brain with a history of pollution and the compromised souls of numberless dead.

Born to Chinese parents in Saigon, Mary Yung, at the age of three, sailed out of Vietnam's mortal bloodfest during the open season on boat people and ended up an instant orphan when her leaking, overloaded rust bucket foundered with almost all on board. She was later passed from one foster home to another, until finally disappearing into the rat- and roach-infested alleys of a street-gang social order so bizarre and ruthless that its very existence seemed to have broken some unwritten law of survival. Unmarried, but never at a loss for men. No criminal record, although not infrequently picked up for questioning and released. Occasional talk of her being a possible police informant, but Durning's in-depth researcher didn't believe it for a minute. Had there been the slightest truth to the rumor, said his report, she'd have turned up dead years ago.

Durning's FBI source also had described Mary Yung as an exceptionally beautiful, shrewd, and potentially dangerous woman. Since Durning had already seen her picture and heard the way she pitched him on the phone, none of these things were hard to believe.

All of which added up to what?

Easy.

A woman off the mean streets, on the make, looking for a big score.

Good, someone like that . . . she might just end up with velvet to sell.

In the nighttime quiet of his study, Durning sat staring at empty space. He stared until he filled the darkness with Mary Yung's presence. But she remained amorphous in his sight, shadowy and remote, an image suspended in dust.

Still, she was aware of him. She had risked something in just calling.

There was a measure of promise in simply that.

22

Peter Walters' reaction to his first live sighting of the infamous, even legendary Abu Homaidi was a surprised *How ordinary he is*. It often happened that way with a long-anticipated target. Emotion created its own advance images.

In reality, Homaidi was a thin, almost concave-chested young man with a scraggly beard who limped slightly as he came out of his house onto the busy Barcelona street. Two men and a girl had preceded him onto the sidewalk, a second girl was close beside him, and two more men followed as backup. When they strolled in the direction of The Ramblas, they kept this same formation. Moments later, another young man left the house and trailed the others.

Nine in all, including Homaidi. A lot of firepower.

Parked a short distance down the block, Peter got out of his car and followed the last one at an interval of about fifty yards.

It was a Saturday night and the sidewalks, cafés, and restaurants along The Ramblas were more crowded than usual after a day and a half of rain. In Barcelona, as in most Spanish cities, people rarely went out to dinner before eleven, and Vittorio assumed that was where Homaidi and his people were headed now.

So far, no surprises.

He had flown into Barcelona less than twenty-four hours ago and found a car left for him as expected, in section 34, row 5, of the airport parking lot.

In its trunk was a large suitcase packed with all the weapons that airport security made it impossible for him to fly in with himself. Included were a disassembled sharp-shooter's rifle with scope sights, two automatic pistols with holsters and silencers, and an ankle holster with a snub-nosed police special. Additionally, there were a few boxes of ammunition, a hunting knife in a belt sheath, and a wire garrote. Some of the ammunition had explosive tips.

Half-a-dozen grenades were in form-fitting holders. Three

were fragmentation and three were tear gas. There also was a gas mask.

The tools of his trade.

Yesterday afternoon and evening had been spent settling in and familiarizing himself with the area and pertinent locations. He had one of the Company's more comfortable *safe* apartments just off Catalonia Square. It was the nerve center from which Barcelona's largest streets branched out, and the dividing line between the old city and the new.

Abu Homaidi and his people occupied a collection of rooms on the two top floors of a narrow, five-story building less than half a mile away. A detailed scale layout of the place had been left for Vittorio in his weapons suitcase, with Homaidi's own room outlined in red. There too was an outline of some of the group's living habits: the approximate times of their comings and goings, the cafés and restaurants they favored, the places where they did their marketing.

The rest would be up to him.

As Cortlandt had indicated, Homaidi was never alone. Not even in bed, where the woman he slept with doubled as a security guard. As did the other women in the group. They were all Palestinians, born into exile and the *intifada*. Wanton terror, the deaths of others, was their reason for living. They had made a significant discovery. What the world respected most was killing. Violent death got people's and nations' attention faster, and held on to it longer, than anything else known to man. All the words, reason, logic on earth were nowhere near as persuasive as a single bloody corpse.

But this was something Vittorio Battaglia, now Peter Walters, had discovered for himself a long time ago. He, too, considered himself a soldier in an unending, undeclared war. Except that he recognized certain necessary restrictions. Certainly those applying to unarmed noncombatants. Abu Homaidi and his people recognized nothing but their own purpose.

It was a cool night, but Peter was wearing the Kevlar vest under his jacket in deference to Peggy, and he was uncomfortably aware of his own body heat. *I'm wearing it for her,* he thought, and this amused him. Was the chance that the armor might save his life really more important to Peggy than it was to him? Or did he just consider himself invulnerable?

Neither, he decided, and settled for the kind of long-term fatalism taken on by most of those in the dangerous professions as their personal security blankets. *It'll happen when it'll happen.*

Talk about dumb.

Peter trailed the extended group along The Ramblas in the direction of Barcelona's port, barely keeping Homaidi in view through the teeming sidewalks.

Near the harbor itself, he saw them stop at an outdoor café, put together a few tables, and draw some chairs around them. A moment later he passed them by and kept walking for about another hundred yards.

Then he turned around, came back, and took a small table at an adjoining outdoor café where he could sit and watch them with little likelihood of being noticed.

He ordered a carafe of the local wine and paella and studied Abu Homaidi and those with him.

The bitter truth was, they might have been just another one of any number of similar groups of young people out for a Saturday night of fun. Talking and laughing, it was hard to imagine them with anything more threatening on their minds than the latest soccer scores and who would be in bed with whom later that night.

From where Peter sat, Homaidi himself seemed to appear a lot more attractive then he had earlier, with an easy laugh and manner that made him the focus of the group's attention. The girl seated at his side couldn't seem to keep her eyes and hands off him. Grudgingly, somewhat sadly, Vittorio thought she was lovely, a delicately put together blonde whose every move and gesture was touched with grace.

Sorry, girl. You just happened to pick the wrong guy this time.

Then he caught the flash of a plain gold band on her finger and blocked out whatever else he might have been thinking.

Peter Walters looked dimly off toward the water.

In the near distance, he could see the dramatically flood-lighted masts and bows of Christopher Columbus' *Santa*

María, where the great man's faithfully reproduced flagship was tied up as a kind of floating museum.

More than five hundred years. Imagine. That little wooden cockle shell and a crazy Italian.

Some men live and leave such marks.

And me?

I live and leave dead bodies.

Peter slowly shook his head, the motion that of an old man no longer able to comprehend the behavior of himself and the world about him.

Then two things happened at once.

Something hard was pressed against the back of his neck, and a woman's voice whispered into his ear from over his right shoulder.

"What you feel is the muzzle of a gun," the voice said in good but foreign-accented English. "It's hidden in my purse and has a silencer attached. If you don't do as I say, I'll shoot you here and now and be gone before anyone notices you're dead. If you want to live, you'll put some money on the table for your bill, stand up, and walk slowly toward the harbor. I'll be close behind you."

She paused. "Which will it be?"

"I'll live."

"Then do it."

Peter carefully put money on the table, rose, and began walking toward the harbor as instructed.

Passing Abu Homaidi's group, he saw that no one there as much as glanced in his direction. If that meant they weren't connected with this, there might yet be some hope. But not really expecting that, his brain sought other solutions.

"Turn into the alley on your left," the woman's voice said.

Peter did it and found himself in a dark, damp, cobble-stoned walk between rows of shuttered old buildings. The air stank of sewage.

"Stop here and put your hands on your head."

He silently obeyed and felt cold metal against the back of his neck. The gun apparently was out of her purse.

Then she patted him down and felt his body armor and his hip- and shoulder-holstered handguns. She left the guns where they were.

"Who are you?" she asked and the metal was withdrawn from his neck as she took several steps backward.

"I'm a private investigator."

"Why are you following and watching those people?"

"What people?"

"I'll give you five seconds to answer. Otherwise, I shoot."

He knew she meant it, and wondered how well the Kevlar would hold up at point-blank range. But of course she'd be putting it into his neck or head, not his body.

"I was hired to do a surveillance on them," he said.

"On the whole group?"

He nodded stiffly.

"Who hired you?"

"I'm not sure. I think it's an American company operating in Saudi Arabia. I was contacted and paid in cash by an agent. He said it was confidential and I was to make my reports only to him."

"Name those you were hired to watch."

Walters slowly recited six of the current aliases he had been given for Homaidi and five of his people. He was surprised he remembered them.

Then still stalling for time, he said, "I thought I was doing OK. How did you make me?"

"I was covering their backs and saw you get out of your car. You made your move a little too fast."

"And how did you know to speak English to me back there?"

"Because that's how you spoke to the waiter when you ordered. Though your clothes are Italian."

"You're good," Peter said flatly.

"In this, if you're not good, you're dead."

"You mean like me?"

She was silent and he could almost feel her beginning to work up to it now.

"I guess you didn't believe a word I said, did you?" he asked.

"No."

"Then maybe I can do a little better for us both with the truth. If you'll give me a few minutes."

Again she was silent and Peter braced himself for the impact of the bullet. He knew she was that close to it.

"All right," she finally said.

He felt his legs go weak. "Can I turn around?"

"Why?"

"It's different when you're looking at someone."

"Go ahead. But slowly."

Hands still on his head, he turned.

She looked no more than nineteen. But he guessed that was how they all looked when they were young and you were near forty. This one had dark hair and the kind of steady, deep-set eyes that seemed to live for a contest. She wore jeans and a sweater and carried an oversize shoulder bag that left both hands free for the automatic and its silencer that she kept aimed, stiff-armed straight between his eyes.

And the only thing on her mind is killing me.

"Are you Palestinian?" he asked.

She nodded.

"You speak English very well."

"It's important to know the language of your enemy."

"America isn't your enemy."

She tossed her head impatiently. "I'm waiting for your truth. Not more lies and propaganda."

"Sure," he said, and saw little hope for him in her eyes, which had already bought, sold, and closed him out. "The truth is, I'm here to kill Abu Homaidi."

In the dark translucence of the alley, her face almost gave off a light.

"For the CIA, I suppose?"

"Yeah."

"Of course. You're the third they've sent to try."

"And I won't be the last. They won't stop until Homaidi's the one who's finally dead. And we both know that's got to be sooner rather than later, don't we?"

She just stared at him through the dark.

"Unless I stop it," Vittorio said. "And right now I'm the only one alive who can do that."

She still stared at him, eyes almost lost in their own shadows. "You?"

Translated, it meant, *A dead man?*

"Yes. Me."

"How?"

"By sending a coded message saying Homaidi's dead in the sea with two bullets in his eyes."

She stood unmoving and silent.

"Once he's officially dead," said Peter, "who's going to be trying to kill him?"

"You'd really do that?"

Vittorio flexed his arms against the top of his head to keep them from going numb. "If it'll keep me alive."

"Yes, but—"

She cut herself off. The faint sound of voices and laughter drifted into the alley from The Ramblas.

"But what do I think happens to me," he finished for her, "after I do my little act and Homaidi doesn't need me anymore?"

She nodded.

"I'll take my chances," he said. "They're a lot better than having you finish me right now. Besides, I couldn't just tell my people Homaidi's dead, then disappear. They'd get suspicious. So I'd have to be kept around for a while to contact them."

"It's too crazy."

But she said it without conviction.

"At least take me to Homaidi and let him decide. There's always time for the other if he doesn't like it."

The automatic was still steady in her hands and aimed between his eyes. Looking at the gun was like looking over the edge of a high building and feeling the fall suck at his stomach. Still, for one instant, he could sense something in her eyes waver.

That was when he went for it, hands reaching, feet leaving the ground in a flat-out dive.

He heard the soft sounds of two silenced shots and felt something burn across the top of his head.

Then he had his hands on the gun barrel as his body took her down. It was her back that hit the cobblestones. Peter was on top. He felt only the yielding of her flesh beneath him.

He had the gun.

He also seemed to have gone blind.

Trying to understand what had happened, he found blood leaking into his mouth and licked it. It poured from his scalp. It ran into the wells of his eyes, down his face, and dropped from his chin. He felt her tugging at the automatic as she tried to yank it away. Swinging blindly with an open hand, he hit only air.

He swung again, this time with his fist, and caught her.

She went loose from him and he heard her cry out. It was in Arabic, a loud, keening wail of pain.

Then everything suddenly stopped between them and he felt her break away, and he heard her feet on the cobblestone.

If she reaches Homaidi and the others, I'm dead.

He brushed an arm across his eyes and blinked through a fall of red rain. He did it once more and glimpsed her in silhouette . . . a poor stick figure, all moving disjointed parts, stumbling toward escape. Hers, not his.

Lying stretched out, prone position, elbows braced on the wet stones, he again blinked his eyes clear and got her lined up with the automatic. His finger tightened on the trigger.

Until he faltered and hung there, all grace deserting him.

He had never done a woman.

Good for you, asshole. Then widow your wife, orphan your son, and let Homaidi murder another three hundred.

He squeezed off a cluster of three quick shots, heard their deceptively innocent sounds, and saw the stick figure break apart and fall.

The girl was dead when he got to her.

Not looking at her face, he picked her up and carried her deeper into the alley. She weighed nothing. She was already air.

Peter Walters sat beside her. He kept his mind empty. He just watched himself sit there with the girl.

He felt his head. It burned like hell, but it was just a scalp wound and the bleeding had stopped. He was a good clotter. A doctor, patching him up for perhaps the fifth or sixth time, had once called him the best damn clotter he'd ever seen.

Battaglia the Clotter.

So you took your talent and celebrity where you found it.

He spit into a handkerchief and wiped the blood from his

face as well as he could. He finger-combed his hair and cleaned off his hands. There was a bad taste in his mouth and he brought it out with some phlegm. The rest he had to take with him as it was.

Then he looked at the girl.

Her eyes were still open. They stared past him, looking all the way to Palestine, where she had never really lived because it had been Israel since long before she was born.

Peter closed her eyes.

One more for Abu Homaidi.

He pushed himself up and started back to his car.

23

IT WAS EARLY morning and three boys and two dogs were playing Indians in a patch of woods near Greenwich, Connecticut.

The boys moved stealthily through the brush, shot arrows into the air, and sent the dogs to retrieve them.

Until at one point, sniffing, scratching and digging, the dogs came upon a lot more than just arrows.

Because such things always took time to filter through properly authorized channels, it wasn't until much later in the day that FBI Director Brian Wayne strode briskly into the attorney general's office and made sure he closed the door behind him.

"Some kids just dug up three of my missing agents," he told Henry Durning.

Working in rumpled shirtsleeves, the attorney general looked across his desk at Wayne's face and didn't especially care for what he saw there.

"Where?"

"In some woods near Greenwich, Connecticut."

"Which agents?"

"The ones sent to question Mary Chan Yung."

Durning put down his pen and sat there. Simply hearing her name seemed to react on him. "How were they killed?"

"Shot. All three." Wayne shook his head. "Sonofabitch," he said softly. "Once they're missing, you know they have to have bought it. But it always hits harder when the damn bodies actually turn up. Then it's for real. Now we fucking wait for the other two."

Anger changed the director's voice, made it shrill. His color had been near crimson since entering the office. Durning waited for him to gain control. *I'm the one he's really furious with.*

"But even worse," said Wayne, "it's finally out. The thing's gotten away from us. It'll be the lead item on tonight's news. 'Three FBI agents dug out of unmarked graves.' And you can be sure they'll give us the whole bit. Cameras at the open holes. Interviews with the kids who found them. Probably even close-ups of the fucking dogs who goddamn sniffed them out."

Durning fought down an urge to smile. That would really push his friend too far. Old weights shifted inside him. They turned him properly solemn. He even managed a sigh.

"I'm sorry, Brian."

The apology did its usual good work. It almost seemed what the FBI director had been waiting for, what he had come into the office to receive. Christ, the stroking people needed. But it did take the edge off Wayne's anger and allow him to sit down.

"The damn locals just handled it so badly," Wayne said. "The bodies had been stripped so they had to ID them through prints. Then the assholes turned it into a media feeding frenzy instead of letting us stonewall it."

"The press have already been at you?"

"Like sharks. When was the last time they had three naked Fibbies with bullets in them to dance around? You can imagine the questions. 'What kind of case were they on?' 'Any others on it with them?' 'Any threats to the national security?' 'Any racist overtones?' 'Why has the Bureau been targeted?' 'How much further is it expected to go?' And ad infinitum."

"How did you deal with them?"

"By the book. By saying it's under investigation and classified."

Wayne had calmed himself enough to actually produce a wry smile.

"Too bad the Soviets had to collapse," he said. "Good old Commie conspiracies were such handy scapegoats for just about anything."

Durning nodded, wondering how Brian would react to knowing about Mary Yung's two brief calls and her offer to deal. *Probably with mild hysteria,* he thought.

But about to leave the office moments later, and almost as if following some delicately balanced form of psychic interplay, the FBI director took a sealed manila folder out of his attaché case and dropped it on the attorney general's desk.

"This just came in from Background Checks and Research."

Durning picked up the folder. It was classified "Top Secret" and was otherwise unmarked.

"What is it?"

"I don't know," said Wayne. "I haven't opened it. But since you called and insisted on seeing as much as possible on the woman, I had a few people out digging for whatever they could find."

It took some effort, but Henry Durning had to restrain himself for almost seven hours before opening the folder.

First there were the last two appointments of the day in his office, both landmark civil rights cases, to keep him from it. Then there was his address to the American Bar Association and the formal dinner that followed. And finally, he had to deal with the need to briefly show his face at the secretary of state's reception for the Israeli prime minister.

Still, there was almost an exquisite pleasure just knowing it would be there, waiting for him, at the end of the evening. At moments he felt like an impatient child, forcing himself through a dull, seemingly endless meal, by concentrating on the unbelievably delicious dessert that lay ahead.

At just past midnight, freshly showered and in his study with a bottle of his favorite brandy, he ended his waiting and unsealed the folder.

A covering letter from the researcher was taped to a second sealed manila envelope inside the first. It described the primary source of much of the enclosed material as the subject's onetime manager and agent during her early years as a model and performer.

The later material apparently came from a variety of sources and was, in most cases, self-explanatory. Wherever further clarification was needed, it was generally supplied by the researcher himself or one of his assistants.

Durning opened the second envelope and took out a clutch of what appeared to be a haphazard mix of photographs and text, of pages torn from magazines, of home camera prints and glossy studio shots, some in color and some in black-and-white.

A note from the researcher indicated that everything was arranged chronologically, with the earliest material representing the subject at the age of six, and the last when she was twenty-seven.

Unaccountably, Durning felt his palms start to sweat and something in his chest catch fire.

She's coming to me now.

And she did, arriving in a mystic bombardment of childish innocence and nubile perversion so subtle and delicate that at first it was hard to tell where one ended and the other began.

Christ, they had started her early. With those two lovely eyes, black and shining as pitch, gazing so proudly into the camera while all sorts of unmentionable erotic things were being done to that perfect little six-year-old body below.

Yet her eyes stayed the same as her body grew.

Somehow, the pride was still there, and it wouldn't have been for many. Not with what they had her doing in those gaming houses of lust, with all kinds of players swarming over her open heat like teams of hungry maggots.

It was as though they had never even touched her.

So that up through the years, she was the one who remained the true handmaiden of love. The others about her, whatever else they may have thought, were never really anything more than pretenders.

Insanely, Henry Durning gazed at the filthiest of the nubile Mary Yung's dirty pictures, and felt himself all but cleansed.

As she grew older, he started seeing the hunger in her eyes and, later, the greed. Breathing deeply, he could almost smell it.

And he was sure it had nothing to do with the million she was trying to squeeze from him. It was simply her nature. Which, in anyone else, might have taken the edge off his desire.

With her, it just made him want her more.

24

GIANNI GARETSKY AND Mary Yung, about to leave New York for Rome, were careful to maintain their usual security.

They had booked and picked up their Alitalia tickets separately and paid for them in cash. They took two cabs to JFK Airport. And at the airport itself they made sure they never came within fifty feet of one another.

Gianni was working on the assumption that whatever watchers might be around would be concentrating their attention on couples made up of an Asian woman and a Caucasian man. Which didn't mean they were anywhere near being out of danger as separate individuals. It just helped edge the odds a bit in their favor.

Racial origin was the single ingredient their disguises couldn't do a thing about.

They were booked for one of the busiest and most popular departure times in Europe, and JFK's International Terminal was swarming with passengers and those seeing them off.

Which was why Gianni had chosen this flight time to begin with. The more crowd confusion, the better.

Right now he was on a long check-in line, with Mary Yung about twenty passengers ahead of him. Thinking every second, she had attached herself to a small group of Taiwanese tourists, and the camouflage was perfect. Talking and laughing with them, she was all but invisible as just another member of the tour.

Still, there was tension. The nature of what they were doing made it inescapable. From being hidden in a citywide base of nearly 8 million people, they were about to be funneled through a limited number of ticket agents . . . with one of whom, for a brief moment, they would have to abandon all anonymity, present their phony passports, and be subject to scrutiny and questioning.

If anything could go wrong, this was the most likely place for it to happen. And after what they had seen on last night's network news, and read in today's papers, the pressure was that much greater.

The worst of it was in finally knowing, with all remaining doubt removed, that the five men he and Mary Yung had shot and buried were really bona fide government agents. Until now he had known, yet he hadn't known. There had still been that tiny stubborn voice somewhere inside him that refused to be quieted, that kept insisting that such things couldn't happen to people here.

Now the voice was quieted.

Curious as to what sort of story would be offered to explain the deaths of the three agents, Gianni had read, watched, and listened to every related piece of news he could find. So far, from the local police who had uncovered and green-bagged the bodies, all the way up to the FBI director himself, there had been nothing but lies and hedging.

The director, a tall, physically imposing man with steely eyes and a square jaw straight out of a Hollywood casting office, had mourned his bureau's dead with quiet dignity and promised their killers would be brought to justice.

Up yours, Gianni had thought.

But then he had to wonder how much of the truth even this man knew.

The line of passengers slowly moved forward.

Bag in hand, Gianni edged along with it.

He watched Mary Yung . . . watched the row of Alitalia clerks checking passports, tickets, and baggage . . . watched everyone in sight who might be a possible threat.

Gianni particularly watched for blank-faced solitary men in business suits who looked as though they themselves might be watchers. There happened to be a fair number of such types about. In fact, two of them were stationed directly behind the long ticket counter.

And what if I see one coming for us?

Unfortunately, the possible responses were limited. Because of airport security, Gianni and Mary were unarmed. Earlier, they had dropped their guns into a convenient sewer. So all they could do, at best, was to duck away, run, and try to lose themselves among the crowds. If only one of them was spotted, the other had to forget any thought of foolish heroics and just quietly leave the terminal.

If they were separated and both of them somehow got away, they would try to meet at noon the following day in front of the Fifth Avenue entrance to the Forty-second Street public library. If that failed to work out, they would try again for the next three days. After that, they would cut loose and be on their own.

But of course these were their worst-case scenarios.

They were simple, of last resort, and neither Mary nor Gianni ever really expected them to be activated.

It was Mary Yung's turn.

Garetsky saw her carry her bag to the check-in counter and hand her ticket and brand-new counterfeit passport to the Alitalia agent.

She was out of there and on her way to the boarding gate in just under five minutes.

Eighteen minutes later, so was Gianni Garetsky.

About half an hour after that, the big 747 was airborne and on the way to Rome.

Parts of him took his wife along for the ride. Leaving America, he felt himself abandoning Teresa as well. He had talked for years of their taking a trip to Italy, to the "old country," but something always seemed to come up with his work. Then she was gone and it was too late.

I waited too long. I should have taken her sooner.

Stop whining, he told himself. *You did what you did, what you didn't do, you didn't do, and beating your breast changes nothing. Besides, did she ever complain?*

No.

And wasn't it always you who talked about Italy, not Teresa?

Yes.

And what did she always say?

That if Italy was so wonderful, how come so many Italians were always leaving it for America.

And what else did she say?

That she didn't really care where we were, as long as we were there together.

And did you believe her?

Yes.

All right. Then for God's sake, leave it alone and go to sleep.

25

PETER WALTERS TOOK a swallow of water from the bottle beside him and felt it cool and pleasant going down. It was just past noon, with the sun directly overhead and the Barcelona street out front barren of shade.

He sat behind the curtained window of a room he had rented almost directly opposite Abu Homaidi's house. His rifle with the high-powered scope lay across the sill, and he touched it from time to time for reassurance.

Come on, Abu. Enough's enough.

By now he felt less anger than impatience. His anger had

simply run out of adrenaline. It had just left him tired and de-pressed.

More than two-and-a-half days had passed since he'd had to shoot the Palestinian girl, and her death had affected everything. Homaidi's people rarely left the house anymore, and as far as Peter could tell, Homaidi himself hadn't ap-peared at all.

You made your move a little too fast, the girl had told him.

Now she was needlessly dead, Homaidi was warned and trying to wait him out, and he himself had lost the advantage of surprise.

So when had he started screwing up?

Certainly in his last hit, when he'd forgotten to check for sirens. And what others before?

Or was he just psyching himself out? It could happen that way. You start questioning and second-guessing yourself. You worry enough about something, build doubts, and be-fore you know it, you're making sure the very worst hap-pens.

Psycho-bullshit.

Yet it wasn't anywhere near that easy to dismiss. He was having lapses he hadn't had before. So far, he'd been lucky, but how long could he go on depending on luck? He was close to forty. Maybe too old, when lives depended on re-flexes and concentration.

At best, he was in a lonely landscape. And there was no one who could make it less lonely for him.

There had once been Gianni, of course. They'd run as close, as much in the same blood, as brothers. But that was more than twenty years ago. Now they weren't even in the same world.

Just thinking of Gianni Garetsky brought him joy. The guy had really made it. Nice that one of them had. And on his own terms. No sucking up or selling out. *Bravo, Gianni.*

The thought made Peter grin through the curtain at the street below.

An instant later, he stopped grinning.

He reached for his rifle and got down on his knees, in fir-ing position. Carefully, he kept the muzzle back out of sight on the windowsill.

Two of Homaidi's men had come out of the door. They stood there for a moment, casually looking around. One of them lit a cigarette and tossed the match into the gutter. Then they separated and walked in opposite directions. They checked people, parked cars, the houses on both sides of the street until Peter lost sight of them.

But they soon returned to the door.

A moment later, two more men came out.

They were immediately followed by Abu Homaidi and another three men.

Peter sighted through the scope, enlarging and drawing the group closer. But Homaidi was blocked from view by the bigger men circling him. Then they began walking up the street to Peter's left, mingling with other pedestrians, making it impossible to draw a clear bead on the terrorist.

They stopped at a gray sedan parked on the curb, and Homaidi and three of the group got in. The others stood talking to them through the car's windows.

Peter Walters swore softly. Damned if they weren't trying to sucker him, bait him out of hiding. He could read the whole thing as easily as that.

He spent a total of five seconds thinking about it, estimating the odds.

Then he flicked the rifle on safety, wrapped it in a light raincoat and went for broke.

He dashed down two flights of stairs, out the back door, and into the narrow serviceway that ran behind the house. He wasn't afraid of getting there too late and losing the car. They'd make sure he had enough time to catch sight of them before they drove off.

Peter moved quickly but calmly. He felt no panic. It was almost as though he had already died and accepted it.

By the time he circled around to the street, got into his car, and drove to where he had last seen Homaidi, the gray sedan was gone. But he just continued in that direction and saw it moments later about two hundred yards ahead. There were four cars between them.

Peter settled into his slot and kept it that way.

The traffic was heavy in this part of the city, so it took a while for him to pick out Homaidi's backup squad in a dun-colored Jeep with six cars in between. The Jeep held four men, and probably enough weaponry to mangle a full platoon.

You can still break out of this, Peter told himself. But it was only a token thought. This contract remained his. He could feel Abu Homaidi reaching in to a forest of nerves in his gut. It carried an old excitement.

By the time they reached the coast road, only three cars separated Walters from the gray sedan up front, and two cars, a pickup and a stationwagon separated him from the Jeep in back. Having a good idea now of how it was going to be, he settled in for a long stretch.

The final bit of game playing ended about half an hour later as they hit the start of the Costa Brava, Spain's fabled Wild Coast, where the road twisted as it climbed, the sea and mountains locking it in, one on each side. The last of the intervening vehicles had turned off and disappeared. Peter saw no more than the gray sedan in front and the Jeep at his back.

Did he have Homaidi, or did the sonofabitch have him?

Two cars and eight of them. All men, thank God.

One car and one of him.

Even money.

Peter Walters smiled at the road ahead.

He waited for Homaidi to make the first move. Behind him, the Jeep was still holding at two hundred yards. There was no other traffic moving in their direction. An occasional car passed going the opposite way.

What were they waiting for?

Peter was sure Homaidi was in touch with the Jeep by radiophone. It was the only reasonable way to keep control of an operation like this.

If I were doing it, I'd be getting off the main coast road very soon now.

I'd be sure to have a good spot picked out in advance. The important thing is isolation. No interruptions.

Moments later the gray car turned off on a road rising to the left. When Walters reached the place, he turned also.

It was a two-lane, rutted blacktop with weeds growing out of endless cracks and potholes. If three cars a day used it, that would be a lot.

Perfect.

Peter felt energy pumping through him like a crowd in riot.

Clouds had suddenly come in off the sea, and it had started to rain . . . no more than a heavy drizzle, really, but enough to cut visibility and get the wipers going. The road twisted and climbed through the beginnings of a pine forest, and Peter heard its whisperings.

Now, it told him.

He began slowing with the thought, not hitting the brakes and setting off their warning lights, but just easing up on the gas and letting the steepness of the grade do the rest.

He watched the rearview mirror.

The driver of the Jeep, maintaining his climbing speed and unprepared for the abrupt slowing, was quickly narrowing the gap between the two cars.

When the Jeep was no more than about a hundred feet back and still closing, Walters took his foot off the gas pedal entirely, pulled the pin on one of the fragmentation grenades beside him, and counted to five. Then he leaned from his window, lobbed the grenade in a high arc back toward the oncoming vehicle, and slammed down hard on the gas pedal.

The car leaped forward and quickly out of range. With frags, you don't hang around waiting.

Watching the road ahead, Peter never did see exactly where the grenade landed. But when the explosion came, he saw the fireball in the rearview mirror, saw it rise as the gas tank went, and felt the rush of superheated air catch up with him at a good hundred yards.

Whatever had to be done now was all in front of him.

The road was narrow and sharply winding here, with the undergrowth and trees pressing close from both sides. Speeding around a bend, Peter suddenly had to jam on the brakes to keep from crashing into the gray sedan, where it had been left parked across the road.

Then he was down under the dashboard as they opened up with everything they had, and they had a lot. By sound and impact alone, Peter was able to pick out two submachine guns, a high-powered rifle, and an automatic pistol. They were in the brush at the left side of the road. All four of them. He thanked Jesus, Cortlandt, and the Company for the car's heavy steel plating, standard equipment lately on his assignments. Without it, he'd now be Swiss cheese. He might yet be. But he still had a few things to do.

That's some fucking Homaidi.

Who'd have expected this?

No wonder he'd lasted so long.

There was a break in the firing as they stopped to reload, and Peter went to work.

Staying down, he groped for the gas mask above him on the seat, found it, and put it on.

Then he picked up and tossed his two remaining fragmentation grenades, carefully counting to twelve this time because his targets were no more than twenty feet away, and he didn't want the damn things getting thrown back at him.

He tossed blindly through the driver's window, head down behind the armor plating. He heard the crackling roar of the two blasts going off, then the metallic rattle of shrapnel against the car and the whine of steel flying over his head. He thought he heard a cry, but he couldn't be sure. Homaidi and his people were flat out among brush and trees, so there had to be a measure of protection in simply that.

Peter let go with his tear gas.

He lobbed all three, everything he had, and he still didn't raise his head above window level to see where they landed.

Scrunched together in the well of the car, covered with a thousand bits of glass, he waited and listened. He heard only silence. Not a bird. Not a whisper of leaves. Dead air.

The tear gas drifted into the car. It settled on the eyepieces of his mask. Staring through it, everything was gray.

Peter breathed heavily through his mask. All he wanted to do was huddle there and not move. Mostly, he didn't want to get out and deal with what was waiting for him.

Finally, he did.

Automatic in hand, he slid out of the passenger's door and crawled around to the other side of the car. Layers of gas hung like fog. The air was cool but he was sweating under the mask. Through the gray, he saw torn brush and scorched and shredded pieces of bark.

Not straight in. You don't know what's waiting. Circle around and come at them from the rear.

Peter Walters crawled all the way. He did it slowly, tortuously, pausing every few moments to listen. There was still no sound. Not a bird, not an insect.

I've killed everything.

And with that thought, dread entered him and the image of his own death passed by like a breeze. Or was it some other hired gun being blown away somewhere else at this instant, in some other wood, or back alley, or city street? The images in his mind were blurred.

Then the images passed and he wanted nothing more than to escape from that voodoo that let him know of unseen killings in one direction and his own death in another. He wanted to be free of wizardry, free of the gas mask on his face and the automatic in his hand, free of any further violence. He wanted to turn away from whatever was waiting for him a few yards ahead in the brush, and just keep going without looking back and turning to a pillar of salt.

But of course he didn't.

And moments later, he was among them.

The grenades had done well. The carnage was complete. Pockets of gas still hung in the low places, partially obscuring the bodies, but he saw enough.

The force of the explosions had torn them apart. In spots, the greenery was pulverized. The grass seemed to ooze out of the soil.

Over it all, the drizzle made the air coolly humid, blurred the eyepieces of Peter's mask. He groped for a handkerchief and wiped them clear.

More broken stick figures.

A quick glance gave him all four.

Then he took them one at a time.

In something like this, you had to be absolutely sure.

He came to Abu Homaidi first. He was still able to recognize the slight, almost concave body. The staring eyes carried a glint of ice . . . the open mouth, a silent scream. The overall mood was nothing but fear and funk and stink of the grave.

The next two were as anonymous to Walters in death as

they had been in life. One of them seemed to grin with a clown's deep gloom. The other had too little face left to show any expression at all.

Then he saw the pale blond hair spread beneath the fourth one's head. It was long, shoulder length, and evidently had come tumbling out from under the baseball cap that had concealed it.

He saw, too, the plain gold band on her finger.

Peter rocked gently on his knees on the wet ground.

Was he going crazy?

There was getting to be plenty of evidence.

But if he was, he wasn't going alone.

This is my last.

26

THE FBI DIRECTOR had originally described the press reaction as a media feeding frenzy, and it was beginning to look pretty much the same way to Henry Durning.

My God, look what I've caused.

The attorney general's thought held a curious mixture of wonder, excitement, and wry amusement, all heightened by a fine edging of fear. Or was the fear merely part of the excitement?

Either way, people certainly were frightened in the area where the three FBI agents' bodies had been dug up.

They also were wealthy, politically influential, and totally unaccustomed to having a bunch of murdered feds turning up in their midst. That sort of thing was strictly inner-city garbage. What was the point of living in Greenwich, Connecticut, if the same things were beginning to happen there?

So they wanted reasons. And at this point they hadn't heard any that satisfied them. Nor had any of their local political representatives, many of whom were coming up for reelection and saw the unexplained murders as a possible attention-getting issue.

From his office late that evening, the attorney general watched a news conference, televised live. The FBI director was a fox at bay, surrounded by yapping hounds in the guise of reporters. Wayne was generally good at this sort of thing, and he appeared no different today as he fielded the steady barrage of questions, calmly explaining that the Bureau's investigation into the three agents' deaths had top priority, and the media would be kept informed of developments.

But Durning knew Brian Wayne well, and he didn't like the way he looked and sounded in front of the cameras. There was too much sweat on his forehead and upper lip. He was blinking and shifting his eyes too often. His voice was husky and he kept clearing his throat. He was responding to questions too slowly, and several times he had to grope for a word.

Brian was definitely shaken. Worse than that, he was frightened.

Durning had lunched with Wayne less than five hours ago and he had seemed fine. He wasn't fine now. What had happened in between?

The attorney general picked up the phone and dialed the FBI director's office.

"When the news conference is over," he told the assistant who answered, "please ask the director to call me."

Wayne called Durning fifteen minutes later. They spoke briefly and Wayne walked into the attorney general's Justice Department office exactly twenty minutes after that.

Durning's immediate staff was gone for the night and the two men were alone.

"What's wrong?" said Wayne.

Durning gave him a chance to sit down. Then he poured him some bourbon to match his own. "That's what I wanted to ask *you.*"

They sat staring at each other.

"I guess you saw the news conference," said the FBI chief. Durning nodded.

"And it was that obvious?"

"Only to me."

Durning looked at the drink in his friend's hand. It was shaking enough to make the ice clink against the glass.

"I had a couple of visitors," said Wayne. "They came just before I was due at the conference, or I'd have called you." He paused for some bourbon. "Ever hear of a Washington lawyer named Hinkey? John Hinkey?"

"Sounds familiar but I don't know from where."

"Real hotshot type. Always pushing for cameras and sound bites. Started off as an agent for the Bureau, then he went private and cashed us in for a lot of big, high-profile cases and big bucks."

Durning nodded. "I remember now. The shyster almost knocked me over once getting to a camcorder."

"He came to see me with a new client. A woman. Her husband's Jim Beekman."

"Who's Jim Beekman?"

"He's one of our two still-missing agents. The ones no kids or dogs have come up with yet."

The attorney general looked at the FBI director, not moving.

"It seems Mrs. Beekman's very worried. She wants to know why her husband hasn't been home all this time and not called her. She's a little hysterical over the three bodies. She's been asking questions and getting only one answer: 'He's off on a case.' "

"Who's she been asking?"

"His section chief. Agents he's worked with. Anyone who'll talk to her. Finally she went to Hinkey because he'd been in the Bureau himself and she and her husband knew him from way back."

"What's Hinkey's attitude?"

"Tough. No nonsense. Believes in going straight to the top. Refuses to take any more of what he calls that classified top-secret shit." Brian Wayne sighed. "Then the sonofabitch actually gave me an ultimatum."

Durning sat listening to his friend's ice rattle.

"He said he'll give me just three days to either tell Mrs. Beekman where her husband is, or let her speak to him on the phone."

"And if you don't?"

"He'll do his own asking and looking around. He'll find out if any other agents have disappeared and not been heard from for more than a week. Then he'll go to the Justice Department's Office of Professional Responsibility and see if they can find out what the fuck is going on. And if they try to cover up, too, he'll call his own goddamn news conference and bust the whole thing wide open."

Durning sat four feet away from the FBI Director, studying his face. Watching what was happening there. He saw there was nothing for Brian anywhere in the world but this moment, this thing. It was consuming him.

"I've never asked you," said Durning. "These five agents you used to help me with this. How was it arranged inside the Bureau?"

"They were given special duty assignments to the Office of the Director. I thought I was being careful. I took them from five different cities."

"What were their immediate superiors told?"

"Nothing. The assignments were classified. But that won't hold up forever once Hinkey starts digging."

"But you're still the only one who knows of any connection to me?"

"Of course."

"And the term *cover-up,*" said Durning. "Those were John Hinkey's exact words?"

Wayne nodded glumly. He suddenly seemed to have lost interest in the whole discussion. He sank within himself and a deep shadow crossed his face, as if something had passed between him and the light.

Except that this shadow didn't pass. All it did was hold on and deepen further.

Henry Durning awoke in the night and remembered the carriers of Brian Wayne's syndrome, or fear, or whatever, in Vietnam.

These things were always different, of course, but small parts remained the same. Finally Durning had gotten to know the darkly fear-haunted ones, the real suicides, pretty well. They usually stared off with their hundred-mile stares and carried their pain like a skin disease on the surface, sensitive to the slightest touch, and scratched and tore at it until at last there was nothing left. Only the final, self-inflicted bullet in the brain was left.

Brian Wayne had been one of them.

But he had lacked enough of that final touch of lunacy to blow his brains out himself and had walked straight at a bunch of waiting VC to see if they could do it for him. *And they'd have done it if I hadn't been there to stop them.*

It was strange how these things worked. If you thought about them enough you could end up screaming in a rubber room. So most of the time you tried not to think about them. But every once in a while, if you woke up in the middle of the night and weren't smart enough to goddamn get out of bed and start doing something, they could still grab you.

As they were doing now. While making him a hero all over again.

Although he had his own theories about heroes. It was all circumstances, reflex, and luck. No one ever knew in advance how they'd react. But in his particular case, it also was desperation.

The thing was, as his squad's brand-new, first-time-out patrol leader, he'd gotten them caught right smack in the middle of a goddamn clearing, with grenades floating out of the surrounding jungle like black baseballs, and very little of anything left by the time the earth stopped exploding.

He himself was lifted, breathed cordite, and came down with a crash. Somehow, he was still gripping his submachine gun. He lay flat in the tall grass, oozing blood from seventeen separate shrapnel wounds. Brian lay somewhere off to his right. The remains of his patrol littered the clearing.

Everything was still.

Then he saw them coming out of the jungle. There were only seven of them, all dressed in their baggy black pajamas. They held burp guns and pistols and carried satchels of grenades. They came slowly, carefully, ready to finish off any survivors. They had smooth, egg-shaped faces, one third of which was forehead. Guns ready, moving in a loose line, they watched the high grass.

Just in case any life remained, they fired into everybody they came upon.

Durning sighted along the blued steel of his gun, feeling the barrel slippery with blood. He had to get all seven with a single burst, or he and any other survivors were dead. They'd probably be dead soon anyway, but why make it easier.

It was then that he caught sight of Brian Wayne rising up out of the grass and starting to walk toward the VC. He had dropped his gun, and blood was running from his face and head. A walking herald of death, making his own mad statement: *Here I am guys. Finish me off clean 'cause I can't do it for myself.*

It took the boys in the black pajamas several beats to react. By that time, Durning had his front sight squarely on the chest of the first VC on the left and was squeezing the trigger. He felt the quick, spastic lurching of the gun against his cheek and saw the young soldier's body pop like a large black balloon. Still squeezing the trigger, he eased his sight to the right across the six others. They seemed to go up, then down, in puffs of brown smoke.

Then he passed out.

He lay in the grass with the sun on his back, slipping in and out of consciousness. How easy it was to kill. You just had to point a gun and squeeze the trigger. Anyone could be taught to do it. But they should have taught him sooner. At the age of six he should have been put in the army instead of school. By now he might have learned enough about killing to have been able to keep his men alive.

Another patrol from his company found them less than an hour later. Durning, Brian Wayne, and a headquarters captain who'd been along as an observer were the only ones alive.

Durning was out of his head for a week. But Wayne and the captain were able to give lucid detailed accounts of what had happened. On the basis of these, Durning was hailed as a hero and received the Congressional Medal of Honor.

Thinking of it now, almost twenty years later, he still felt he should have been court-martialed instead.

So, Brian.
Under that surface crust dwelt pure mush. How long could

he hold together once Hinkey's sharp jackal's teeth began ripping at him?

Something would have to be done about the lawyer. *And* his client.

Such were the nocturnal considerations of Attorney General Henry Durning.

None of which calmed him enough to let him go back to sleep. For that, he tried drifting into an appealing erotic fantasy of the beautiful Mary Chan Yung.

It began with her body pictured in the position of ascendancy, with her face and breasts close above him. He placed his hands on the dip of her waist and studied the result for a moment. Then changing his mind, he slipped his hands beneath her breasts, cupping them lightly, his palms barely making contact, and all of it shining out of a velvet midnight dark.

There were soft purple shadows about her eyes and under her cheeks and chin.

He saw the play of light across her forehead and smooth, shining hair.

Her lower lip, he decided, was extraordinary, with the kind of sensuous fullness that could probably break some unsuspecting man's heart.

He pictured her breasts as surprisingly full for so slender a woman, with brownish-pink nipples and flesh that gave off a pale, porcelain glow.

She bent to him and they kissed and held one another.

Then he was in her.

He closed his eyes.

In his little mental charade he envisioned it being several weeks since they were last together, and they both responded to it. Separation. Still the most powerful aphrodisiac available. It made the upstairs bedroom seem much too far away. In the less than five minutes since she had entered his house, they were naked on the living room rug.

It had been a long, tiring, tension-filled day, but he could feel her pumping new life into him. For these few moments, in this warm dark, he had no brain, no plan, no wit, no care, no desire, other than the sexual. It was as if everything that had happened until now was just so much dead skin, waiting to be peeled away.

For now, they belonged solely to each other. He had some distinct notion that there might well be a world beyond the immediate reach of his body, but it held no interest for him.

Then, inevitably, at the very moment his desire seemed most insatiable, it was sated.

He kept her there beside him. Finally she brought him sleep as a special gift.

27

ROME OFFERED GIANNI Garetsky well over a hundred art galleries to comb through for something he might recognize as having been painted by Vittorio Battaglia. And along with Mary Yung, he was covering about twenty of them a day.

But Rome was, after all, one of the most romantic cities in the world, it was summertime, and the more immediate threats to their lives seemed to have eased.

So it really wasn't all that difficult to take a little time off here and there to pleasure themselves. And if it wasn't quite the sublime honeymoon idyll that Mary Yung had teased Gianni about, it did come startlingly close.

They stayed at a charming *pensione* within walking distance of the Trinità dei Monti.

They ate at delightful, out-of-the-way restaurants, where everyone seemed warm and friendly, where it was impossible to get a bad meal, and where the mandolins came close to making you weep for the years spent anywhere else.

They strolled by moonlight on the slopes of the Palatine Hill on which the emperors of Rome's golden age erected their palaces opposite the Colosseum and the Arch of Constantine.

They stood mute before some of the greatest art ever produced by the civilized world, and held hands to better share each moment.

"I can't imagine anything sadder," said Mary Yung, "than to have to look at things like this alone."

How did she know to say that? Gianni wondered.

Once, sitting on a bench opposite the Spanish Steps, he watched her walk over to a stand to buy some flowers for their room. She had on a pale yellow blouse dotted with leaves. A breeze brushed the blouse softly against her breasts as she stood in front of the clustered blossoms. Because of the sun, Gianni couldn't tell what her face was like. But he had a curious need to wave to her, so he did.

She kissed him when she came back.

"Thank you," she said.

"For what?"

"For waving to me."

He looked at her, this beautiful, solemn-faced woman who said such strange things.

"No one's ever waved to me like that before," she said. "I mean just for no reason."

Gianni had to turn away. She was reaching that far into him. He could no longer pretend the feeling wasn't there or that it was only lust.

The flowers looked bright and hopeful in their room. When the sun or the light from a lamp caught them, they seemed to dance. Mary called them her bridal bouquet and laughed when she said it. But only her mouth was laughing. Her eyes were doing something else. It was her eyes that Gianni cared about most.

In bed, they couldn't seem to leave each other alone.

Mornings and late afternoons were Mary's favorite love times. She said night was mostly for peasants, who were too bashful or ashamed to look at each other.

Gianni was like an adolescent, newly arrived at the feast. The pleasure she gave was exquisite at any time, but in his thoughts the moment he kept reliving was that of climbing the stairs to their room behind her, watching her hips move and anticipating what was ahead.

God, he would think, *this woman has got to be too much.*

On their fifth morning, they lay side by side in the after-glow.

The blinds were drawn but the early sun broke through in splinters of brightness. Gianni's body seemed weightless to him, anointed. He knew he should be getting up to start the day's search, but he felt only a vague inertia.

It was warm in the room and they lay naked on the sheets. Mary's flesh gleamed in the morning light.

Another ten minutes, Gianni promised himself.

"How many more galleries do we have left in Rome?" Mary Yung asked.

"About fifty or so."

"And if we don't find anything in those?"

"We go on to Florence."

"And then?"

"Venice, Naples, Palermo. You know the list."

She stirred beside him. "I have a terrible confession to make."

Gianni waited.

"I sometimes wish we never find anything."

He stared at the ceiling.

"That's really crazy, isn't it?" she said.

"It sure is."

"I know. It's just that these past days have been so lovely."

Gianni was silent.

"At least for me," she said.

"For me, too."

She rolled over and kissed him. "You didn't have to say that."

"Yes, I did."

"Only because you're such a nice man."

"No. Only because it's true."

Mary lay still, holding him. Golden flecks came and went in her eyes as the curtains stirred in a breeze and shifted the sun's rays.

"What if we never do find Vittorio," she said. "Would it really be that awful?"

Gianni let the possibility enter him, felt it start moving

around inside. It was no worse than swallowing ice water too quickly.

"With care," he told her, "and a bit of luck, I suppose we might survive it."

"That's not the answer you're supposed to give."

"I'm sorry. I guess I'm just not very good at these games."

"It might not be a game. There's always the chance it could happen. Haven't you ever thought of that?"

"How could I not?"

"And?" she said.

"Most of the time I just brush it aside."

"And when you don't brush it aside?"

Gianni lay with it for a long moment. "It can run pretty deep and dirty. We'd need plastic work on our faces. We'd have to live looking back over our shoulders and never stop. We'd be reinventing ourselves a day at a time and knowing it's not going to change."

"You mean like Vittorio's probably been doing for the past nine years?"

Gianni nodded, although he hadn't really thought of it in that light.

Mary sat up in bed to look at him. "You kept saying *we*. Does that mean you'd want us to be together?"

Gianni was silent and sat very still on the bed, allowing the beautiful naked body and the exquisite face to make all the more obvious arguments in her favor.

"We could end up hating each other," he finally said.

"There's always that danger."

"We'd have to be very strong and very good to make it last."

"Yes."

Then they just looked at each other until he finally pulled her to him.

"This is just bullshit," he whispered.

"I know."

He kissed her and felt drunk on her taste.

When he could speak, he said, "At worst, I'd rather hate you than be without you."

Sadly, she didn't believe it for a minute.

* * *

Having just crossed off their first two unsuccessful galleries of the morning, they walked in the sun along the Via Veneto and stopped at some sidewalk tables for an espresso and *briasche*.

The Via Veneto, thought Gianni dimly . . . where the women are young and beautiful, the men rich and distinguished, and where never is heard a discouraging word.

At least, as long as you picked up the check.

Their next scheduled stop was the Galleria Raphael on a nearby side street. Before going in, they stood studying several paintings in the windows.

"I'd buy this one in a minute," said Mary Yung.

Gianni looked at the canvas. It was a freely brushed portrait of a solemn, dark-eyed boy with the sun lighting his hair and an azure sea behind him.

Gianni stood silently staring. And he knew he had a moment then. For the boy in the painting spoke to him. Something in the deep of the boy's eyes, some familiar radiance, traveled out of a far-off past and into his brain.

"We've hit it," he said softly. "This is Vittorio's."

Mary Yung looked at him. "You're sure?"

Gianni nodded, feeling himself nothing but open, raw depths.

"How do you know?" she said.

"Because I first met Vittorio when he was eight years old, and he had the same face. If this kid isn't his son, I swear I'll eat the canvas."

He felt Mary's fingers dig into his arm.

"Also, that's his brushwork. It's the way he always handled flesh color in direct sunlight. See? Two cadmiums, yellow and red—broken, unblended, and both on the brush at the same time." Gianni was excited now. "Can't you just feel the vibration, the damn sun itself on the kid's cheeks?"

Mary bent to squint at the name in the lower left-hand corner of the painting. "Guido Cosenza," she said.

Gianni took a deep breath, let it out with a sigh, and led her inside the Galleria Raphael.

The proprietor was involved with another customer at the rear of the shop, and Mary and Gianni browsed on their own. Gianni saw two more paintings signed, "Guido Cosenza," and recognized Vittorio's hand and talent in both. A vein in his temple throbbed as though about to go into riot.

The other customer left and the proprietor came over.

"Is there something I can help you with?"

He spoke to them in fluent but slightly accented English. Like almost everyone else they'd had anything to do with in Rome, he had them instantly stamped as American. Which Gianni preferred. It allowed him the advantage of keeping his Italian to himself.

Gianni smiled. "My wife and I have fallen in love with Guido Cosenza's handling of that young boy in the window. So few artists ever know what to do with children. They always seem to turn them into undersize adults."

"That's true," said the art dealer. "But not many people are perceptive enough to see that. Are you interested in the painting?"

"It's very appealing," said Gianni. "But what we're really interested in is having Mr. Cosenza do a portrait of our son in that same style."

The man stood looking at them, and Gianni could almost feel him estimating price as measured by their ability and willingness to pay.

"I hope Mr. Cosenza accepts portrait commissions," said Mary Yung. "We'd be so disappointed if he didn't."

"To be honest, *signora,* I couldn't answer that. I'd have to speak with his representative. Is your son with you here in Rome?"

"Yes. And he's about the same age as the boy in the painting. That's what got us so excited about the whole idea. We'd certainly appreciate it if you could make a call and let us know where we stand. Is that possible?"

The dealer was busy staring at Mary Yung's eyes, a meticulously tailored connoisseur of beauty in any form who, Gianni saw, had just been inducted into his alleged wife's fan club.

He smiled with less-than-perfect Italian teeth. "Everything is possible, *signora.*"

"We'd be so grateful."

The proprietor offered a small bow with his head, went to

the phone on his desk at the rear of the gallery, and checked a number in his Rolodex.

A moment later he was talking to someone in rapid-fire Italian.

Pretending to study some of the paintings, Gianni worked his way close enough to the dealer to hear just about everything he was saying. The artist's rep was obviously giving him a hard time, and his voice kept growing louder and more emotional. When he finally hung up, he was furious.

"*Signora . . . signor . . .* I am decimated. I am so sorry . . . so sorry."

Arms waving in frustration, the art dealer was abject in his apologies.

It appeared that Guido Cosenza not only didn't accept portrait commissions, but detested them. In fact, he didn't even like children. Evidently not even his own, since the boy in the painting did indeed turn out to be his son. What normal father would put a price on his own child's head. It was like selling the child's soul on a piece of canvas. God was too careless in handing out talent. Guido Cosenza was unworthy of his gifts.

By the time they left, Mary Yung was consoling the dealer. Gianni Garetsky just wanted to fly out of there as quickly as possible. He was that excited.

"Well?" said Mary when they were outside and walking. "Talk for God's sake! I'm busting!"

Gianni was so busy thinking, it required special effort to put the necessary words together. "We're going to Positano."

"That's where Vittorio is?"

"I think so."

"What do you mean, *think*? Is he or isn't he?"

"It's not that simple. Let me tell you what I've got. Then decide for yourself."

They were back on the Via Veneto, with the traffic crawling and honking and swarms of tourists everywhere. Garetsky walked for a moment in silence, his mind still trying to catch up with what he'd overheard.

"Understand," he said. "Everything I have came from the dealer's end of the conversation. So I had to do some filling in. The artist's rep is a woman. Her name's Peggy Walters.

She's American, she's married to another American named Peter Walters, and they have a nine-year-old son called Paulie."

"Lovely. Peter, Paul, and Peggy."

"More than just that."

It took her a moment. "You mean the boy's about the same age as Guido Cosenza's son in the painting?"

"Exactly. So you can see where that points. They all live in Positano, on the Amalfian Coast. Which I know well. In fact, well enough to recognize the three tiny islands of the Sirens that Vittorio painted in the water behind where he posed his boy."

Gianni walked looking at the bumper-to-bumper traffic without seeing it. All he saw was a young kid he felt had to be Vittorio Battaglia's son, standing there with the sea and Ulysses' three rocks behind him.

"This Peggy Walters reps other artists besides Vittorio," said Gianni. "So she's got his work nicely camouflaged among the rest. The thing is, who could Vittorio trust more than his wife to sell him as Guido Cosenza and keep his true identity secret?"

The question was purely rhetorical but Mary Yung answered it. "Nobody."

"Then you agree? You think Vittorio's living in Positano as Peter Walters?"

Mary shook her head. "I don't just think. I *know* he is."

They said good-bye to their room.

Then as Gianni waited impatiently for their bill to be put together, Mary Yung went into the powder room to make her call.

She had the attorney general on the line in under two minutes.

"We've located him," she told Henry Durning. "Are you ready to carry out your end?"

"Yes." It was said without hesitation.

"Then wire the money immediately to the Banque Suisse in Berne, credited to personal account number 4873180. Do you have that?"

"Yes. But it's after four here and the banks close at three."

"Don't fool with me, Mr. Durning. We both know there's no clock running on electronic international money transfer anymore. I'm calling my bank in exactly one hour. If my account's been credited, you'll hear from me with the information. If not, forget the whole thing."

"How do I know you won't just take the money and run?"

"You don't. But I suggest you try a little old-fashioned trust, Mr. Durning. You might find it rewarding. Besides, you're not someone I'd want chasing me for the rest of my life. Nice speaking with you."

Mary Yung hung up.

Her palms were sweaty and bad things were happening in her stomach. They held the promise of extinction. She had opened a big, black hole and placed herself at its center. Still, she felt she had carried it off well. For which she thanked Jimmy Lee, who had once taught her about numbered offshore accounts and their many uses. He had even helped her open her present modest account with the promise she'd be grateful to have it one day.

She was grateful now.

In a few hours I will be rich.

28

THE FLIGHT FROM Rome took less than an hour, and Gianni Garetsky and Mary Yung were at the Naples airport by early afternoon.

They had spoken little during the trip. Their brief Roman idyll suddenly seemed distant and dreamlike, and the initial excitement of locating Vittorio had passed. In its place was the more sobering thought of what might now result from their having found him.

For Mary Yung, with her own two-faced involvement, there obviously was a double concern.

While Gianni was impatiently arguing and filling out forms at the Hertz rental counter, Mary drifted out of sight and found the public phones.

First, there was the Banque Suisse in Berne.

Put through to an English-speaking account executive, Mary identified herself with her secret code letters and account number. Then with her throat dry and scratchy, she asked the big question.

"Could you please tell me whether there were any deposits made to my account during the past few hours?"

"One moment please," said the Swiss banker in perfect Oxonion English.

There was silence, and Mary Yung had a vision of swift, practiced fingers flying over computer keys.

"Madame?"

"Yes?"

"There was a single deposit. It was received by wire at exactly 1437 hours, standard time."

Mary's mouth was a desert. She tried to suck some moisture into it, but there was only sand.

"What was the amount, please?"

"Exactly one million dollars, American."

"Thank you so much."

"A pleasure to be able to serve you, Madame."

Slowly, almost trancelike, she hung up the receiver.

Then she felt it building down below. And rising. And building and rising again.

Until she had to stuff her fist into her mouth to keep it inside. Thirty years tore through her brain like a videotape gone wild, she saw a thousand ugly things she'd done just to keep herself breathing and that she'd never have to do again.

Then she came down with a bump.

Payment time.

It was late, but she knew the attorney general would be waiting for her call. He answered the phone himself.

"Durning."

"You see?" Mary said. "I don't just take the money and run."

Henry Durning laughed and she found the sound surprisingly warm and easy.

"I appreciate it," he told her.

"You should learn to trust people more."

"I'm afraid I'm in the wrong profession for trust. I'm a lawyer. But I'm trying, Mary."

How lovely. I'm Mary now.

"OK, here it is," she said. "Vittorio's in Positano, Italy. He has a wife and son, and he's calling himself Peter Walters."

There was a long silence.

When Durning spoke, his voice was charged with feeling. "Thank you. This is very important to me."

"I know. You've already shown me its importance."

"The money's the least of it."

"Not to me, Mr. Durning."

The line hummed between them.

"Tell me, Mary. Have you and Gianni actually seen Vittorio yet?"

"No."

"When do you expect to see him?"

A warning light went on behind her eyes. "I don't know. That's up to Gianni."

"Well, do yourselves a big favor. Don't go anyplace near Battaglia for at least twenty-four hours. I can't tell you more than that. But you have my word it'll be best for you both."

Durning again gave her his best laugh. "You see? Now it's your turn to do the trusting. Thanks again, Mary," he said, and hung up.

With no more than that to go on, Mary somehow found herself believing him.

Anyway, what did she have to lose?

Picking up some tourist brochures of Capri . . . a short ferry ride from nearby Sorrento . . . Mary Yung had an overnight honeymoon extension all planned by the time she rejoined Gianni at the Hertz counter.

Gianni had no problem with the idea. He was learning about pleasure. You didn't put it off.

Whatever it was that Vittorio had to tell them would keep for one more day.

29

HENRY DURNING CALLED Carlo Donatti's private number moments after he hung up on Mary. If he hoped to keep her alive, which he did, he had little time to waste.

His conversation with Donatti was cryptic and brief. But when it was over, the two men had arranged to meet at an airport motel near La Guardia in exactly two hours.

The attorney general reached the designated meeting room fifteen minutes early. But Don Carlo Donatti was already there, waiting for him, the radio blaring at its usual high volume to cover possible bugs and wire packs.

They went through their ritual embrace and greeting with apparently undiminished zeal, but their eyes were cold.

"It's good of you to come on such short notice, Don Carlo. I appreciate it."

"It sounded important."

"It is. I've located Vittorio Battaglia."

The don slowly sat down. "Where?"

"Italy. More exactly, Positano. I believe he's living with the woman he was supposed to have done for me nine years ago. And they have a child. A boy."

"Under what name?"

"Walters. Peter and Peggy Walters."

"Who found them?"

Durning hesitated. "I suppose you have to know that."

Donatti extended both hands, palms up.

"Garetsky and Mary Yung," said the attorney general.

The don's brows lifted ever so slightly.

"So Gianni did find him." The idea seemed to surprise and amuse Donatti. "Which means you paid off the *cinese?*"

Durning ignored the question. "Time is important, Carlo. If it can be handled fast . . . say no more than eighteen hours . . . it'll be best for all concerned. Can that be arranged?"

"Anything can be arranged. But why the rush? What happens if it takes a few hours longer?"

"Then your boy Gianni and the Chinese woman might have to be done, too."

"I don't understand."

"They're just on their way to Positano now. They don't know yet what Battaglia and his wife can tell them."

"And you don't want them to know?"

"Not them and not anyone else." The attorney general looked at Donatti. "That's what this whole thing is about, Carlo."

"Of course." The don spoke softly, as if anything voiced less gently might cause him pain.

They sat considering each other. To Durning, the feel was of new mysteries being exchanged for old, and of secrets yet to be discovered.

"It'll be done," said Donatti. "This has been a deep embarrassment for me. Vittorio Battaglia has made me feel like a fool. I'll be as relieved as you to finally put an end to it."

"I'm grateful." Durning's face was grave. "Now there's just one last favor I have to ask." The attorney general paused. "With your permission, Don Carlo?"

"Ask . . . ask." Donatti smiled, his good humor suddenly restored along with his sense of honor and dignity. "You observe our little ceremonies as if you were one of us."

"I *am* one of you."

Donatti nodded. "Now what's the favor? I like it that I'll be one up on you again."

"There's this bigmouthed Washington lawyer and his client," said Durning. "They're about to cause a lot bigger trouble than they know."

"Who are they?"

"The lawyer is John Hinkey. His client's name is Beekman, Mrs. James Beekman."

"She's in Washington, too?"

Durning nodded.

"Her husband's not part of this big trouble you mentioned?"

"No."

"Then what *is* he part of?"

"The FBI."

Donatti stared at the attorney general.

"No problem," said Durning. "He's one of those your friend Garetsky buried somewhere. If he ever does turn up, he won't be saying much."

Don Carlo laughed and he didn't laugh often. "I'm beginning to understand a little about his wife and the lawyer."

"Then you'll help me out?"

Donatti was still chuckling. "Why not? There are too many wives and lawyers causing trouble as it is."

Durning sat in the helicopter taking him back to Washington and thought, *Is this really the measure of me?*

He'd had a shot of brandy at the start of the flight, and it had lit small fires in the caves of his belly. But just before that, he had calmly arranged for the deaths of four people and felt only deep relief at having acted to preserve himself.

Meaning what? That he was missing an essential human ingredient? Pity?

Nonsense.

In his current situation, pity would have been the ultimate indulgence, a futile emotional gesture that would have put an immediate end to all the good he was doing, and offered nothing in its place.

In all modesty, he was probably the best single thing to have hit the Justice Department in almost fifty years. He had taken an inert, morally crumbling agency, so desperately in need of renewal that its best and brightest people were fleeing in droves, and had restored the heart of its legal and ethical foundations.

He had pumped up the department's moribund long view of the law and forced it not just to win cases, but to live up to its tarnished precept that the United States prevailed only when true justice was being done.

And finally, he had himself inspired great numbers of lawyers with their present vision of the law as a magic wand for creating desperately needed social and political change.

It's all true. I've actually done these things. And more.

Still, if he could be so heroic, how could he also have become so villainous?

Not that he really felt like a villain. He had simply learned that when survival was at stake, you did what you had to and put the rest aside until Judgment Day.

30

GIANNI GARETSKY AND Mary Yung drove toward Positano in separate cars. Gianni Garetsky led the way. Capri had been magnificent but wasted on them. They couldn't escape what lay ahead.

Earlier, Gianni had picked up two 9mm automatics, a 12-gauge pump-action shotgun, a .30 caliber rifle with scope sights, and enough ammunition to fight a small war. Everything but the two automatics was locked in the trunk of his car. He carried one of the handguns. Mary Yung had the other.

Gianni had no special reason to expect trouble in Positano. The weapons, like their second car, were, as he had explained to Mary, just in case of the unexpected. In situations like this, he'd always found it a lot safer to have too much of everything rather than not enough.

Gianni drove at a steady fifty kilometers per hour, not rushing, swinging easily into the seemingly endless turns. The Amalfi Drive was cut out of solid rock, with a sheer drop to the sea on one side, and the mountains shooting straight up on the other. In places, the curves were so sharply angled that mirrors had been hung to help drivers see if any traffic was coming around the bend. Gianni watched the road, the sea, and in the rearview mirror, Mary Yung's car.

The road split into a one-way descent as they approached the cutoff into town.

Gianni thought about Vittorio . . . what he'd look like, what he'd say, how he'd react to suddenly seeing him like this. *Twenty years.* It was hard to believe any part of it.

Then the traffic began tying up as they circled down into the old cliffhugging town's center. Tourists were everywhere, crowding the streets and shops.

Gianni checked the mirror and saw that a car had squeezed between them. Most of the side streets were narrow, steep, broken by stone steps, and closed to all vehicular traffic. Moving bumper to bumper, he finally pulled into the town parking area and found a place. He saw Mary park a short distance away.

First, he needed a telephone directory. There was one in a tobacco shop, and he looked up Walters. There they were . . . Peter and Peggy. The address was listed as 14 Via Contessa.

Garetsky bought a street map of Positano and got back into his car. He glanced only once at Mary where she sat parked and waiting. There was no need to talk at this stage. They had made most of their plans last night. They both knew exactly what to do.

He located the Via Contessa on his map and drove in that direction. Mary Yung followed him, staying about fifty feet back.

The street circled and climbed up the mountain. Slowing down, Gianni edged around a curve and saw the house . . . white, flat-roofed, and graced by the region's typical Moorish arches. Stone steps climbed from the road up through a garden to the entrance. Below the garden, just off the road, two cars were parked in the cleared and leveled-out space.

The two cars probably meant they were both home.

Gianni kept going. The road ended farther up the mountain in a cul-de-sac and he stopped there. A moment later, Mary Yung parked beside him. There were no houses in sight, just rocks, cliffs, brush, and scrub trees. In the distance the sea.

They left their cars and stood together.

"You saw the house?" Gianni said.

Mary nodded. "Very sweet."

Her voice held more than a hint of irony. But her eyes, as sensitive to mood as the antennae of a cat, carried dark, hidden secrets. More than that, they seemed worried.

"Easy," he told her. "It'll be fine."

She was silent.

"You OK?" he said.

"Sure. Why wouldn't I be OK?"

He stepped close and held her, feeling the tension, the surprisingly frail bones so close beneath her skin.

"Come on," he said. "We're almost home free. This is the easy part."

"I know. This is so stupid. Just kiss me once for luck."

They kissed and she pressed him hard.

"You sure you don't want me to go with you?" she asked.

"I'm sure. I don't want to hit Vittorio with both of us at once. I'll be enough of a shock for him alone. And it'll be easier for us to talk this way."

"All right."

"Have some lunch at Sta Via. It's that place with the green awning where we were parked before. Give me about two hours, then come. If there's any change, I'll know where to reach you."

She stared at him.

"What is it?" he said.

"I think I could get to love you."

He laughed. "Is that why you're looking so miserable?"

"Probably."

"Stop worrying. It'll pass."

"I don't think so."

Gianni Garetsky watched her walk to her car and drive off.

Moments later he followed and parked alongside the two cars already in front of the Walters house.

Then he climbed the seventeen curving stone steps to the entrance, and lifted the brass knocker.

He felt a plunge of lead weights at the bottom of his stomach.

The man who opened the door stood looking at him.

"What can I do for you?" he asked in Italian.

Gianni would hardly have known him to be Vittorio Battaglia. Apart from what the years had added, he had a full moustache and beard, his eyes were an almost startling blue rather than hazel, and he definitely seemed taller, bigger, huskier than the Vittorio he remembered, with a fighter's chest and shoulders and heavily muscled arms. Only the paint-stained jeans and T-shirt held a touch of familiarity.

And what about how I must look to him?

Then suddenly flooded with remembered warmth, Gianni grinned and peeled off his fake gray hair, his moustache, and his horn-rims. He stood there, stripped to the truth.

"Does that help any? Or is it always trick-or-treat around here?"

Even then, it still took Peter Walters a long moment.

"I'll be a sonofabitch," he whispered in English.

"That's nothing new. You always were, buddy."

Abruptly narrowing, Peter's eyes swept past the artist and took in his car, the road, the steps, the garden, the whole immediate landscape.

Then while Gianni was still standing there grinning, he suddenly found himself grabbed and yanked into the house, his face slammed against a wall, and his automatic snatched from his belt and pressed to the back of his neck.

"Hey!" Nose mashed and bleeding against the plaster, Gianni could manage little more than a muffled grunt.

Walters shut the door and threw the bolt. The muzzle of the automatic stayed hard against the back of Gianni's neck.

"Who's out there with you?"

Gianni mumbled something that sounded vaguely like "Nobody."

"Lie to me, Gianni, and I swear I'll blow your head off." His voice was quiet, calm, but he was breathing heavily.

"I'm . . . not . . . lying."

Walters increased the gun's pressure.

"Did Don Donatti send you?"

Garetsky tried to shake his head.

"Who then?"

"Nobody . . . sent me."

Gianni Garetsky swore silently. He cursed his own stupidity for not anticipating exactly this reaction. What had he expected after so many years and God only knew what else. A fucking kiss on the lips?

A woman's voice called from upstairs. "I heard a knock before, Peter. Is someone there?"

Walters sighed. "Better come down. And don't be frightened. It's probably not as bad as it looks."

Peggy came down the stairs, saw what was there, and covered her mouth with both hands.

"Oh—" She cut it off. She'd been waiting for something like this for nine years. *Handle it,* she told herself.

"Where's Paulie?" her husband asked.

"Off painting somewhere."

"Fine. Now listen to me. This *goombah* here is my old buddy, Gianni. I don't know how he's found us, or who's with him or sent him. He says nobody and maybe that's the truth and he's just gotten stupid. But I haven't seen him in twenty years and I'm not taking any chances. So lock all the doors, close the blinds, and activate the alarm system. Then get me that gray suitcase in my closet. You know the one?"

Peggy nodded.

He smiled, trying to ease it for her. "It's OK. It'll be a good dry run for us."

She left, and Walters shoved Garetsky into the kitchen, dumped him into a chair, and gave him a towel and bowl of ice for his nose.

"Now talk," he said. "And it better be good or you're dead as Kelsey's nuts."

31

A LITTLE BEFORE 2:00 P.M., just as Gianni Garetsky was once more beginning the witch's tale that seemed to have become his most popular solo recitation, a pair of gray Mercedes sedans left the Amalfi Drive and circled down toward Positano.

There were two men in each car, and they had flown into Naples that morning from Palermo. They were attractive and solidly built, with the kind of smooth-faced, well-barbered good looks in which a particular breed of Italian men tends to take pride. Dressed as well-to-do tourists, in obviously expensive designer sport clothes, they carried several equally costly cameras to push their desired image one step further.

Yet someone who knew about such things had only to look at their eyes, which were flat and curiously without expression, to know they were anything but tourists. What they actually happened to be were four of Don Pietro Ravenelli's best soldiers, made men every one, on a very delicate mission for someone who was reputed to be the *capo di tutti capi,* the boss of all bosses, of an important American *famiglia.*

As such things went, the mission was considered a plum, a great honor. If well performed, it could bring far-reaching respect and advancement for those involved. If botched, it could just as easily destroy careers, reputations, lives.

The four men in the two Mercedes had been briefed personally by Palermo's illustrious Don Ravenelli. Great care had to be taken, he told them. There must be nothing crude or heavy-handed. He wanted no big, noisy shootouts with a lot of police, press, and international notoriety.

Moving smoothly and silently, the twin Mercedes followed the local traffic into Positano, circled the general area twice for the required familiarization, and finally parked side by side in the open space at the center of town.

Nervously waiting and eating an ice cream cone in her own car, Mary Chan Yung watched the two identical gray German cars parked no more than forty feet from where she was sitting.

She saw the four almost identical men in their expensive clothes get out, stretch their cramped muscles, and stand looking about them with their flat, expressionless eyes that somehow reminded her of Jimmy Lee.

And she noted too the slight yet all too significant bulges in their chest and hip areas that were the unmistakable marks of their trade.

Mary Yung had never seen these four men before, yet she

knew them as well as she knew the inside of her own skin. She wasn't fooled by the designer sport clothes or the cameras. Today was just another of their normal workdays, and this was where they had come to work. And she knew as surely as she had ever known anything that it was her phone call that had summoned them.

Mary suddenly felt sick.

When the four tourists left the parking area to stroll along the nearby streets, she began following at a safe distance.

She saw them separate into two pairs and go into about half-a-dozen shops, where they seemed to be asking a lot of questions. They also made several small purchases that included a map, a couple of rolled up posters, and some picture postcards.

At one point they opened the map and gathered about it for a few minutes, pointing and talking.

Then they returned to the two Mercedes and drove out of the parking area. This time three of the men were in one car, leaving the fourth man alone in the other.

Mary got into her rental and followed. Thinking no further than that, she had no idea what she was going to do about anything. It just seemed right to stay with them.

Reaching a fork in the road, the man alone bore left and headed out of town and toward the road edging the water. The car with the three men stayed to the right and drove in the direction of the Walters house, with Mary tailing them from far back.

As they approached 14 Via Contessa, Mary picked up a bit of speed and drew just close enough to catch a glimpse of the Mercedes as it came to an almost complete stop in front of the house, hung there for a few moments, then continued on up the winding road and out of sight.

Toward the cul-de-sac, Mary thought.

If she'd had any small lingering doubts before, she didn't now.

Reaching number 14, she pulled into some space beside Gianni's car, dashed up the house's entrance steps as fast as she could, and banged on the door.

It opened almost immediately.

Mary Yung looked at the fair-haired, blue-eyed, bearded

man facing her and didn't recognize him as anyone she knew.

Then she saw the automatic pointing loosely at her chest.

"Come on in, Mary," Vittorio Battaglia said. "Join the party."

The man traveling alone, a dark-haired young Sicilian named Domenico, drove only a few hundred yards out of town and parked at a scenic turnoff overlooking the water.

A short distance below, he saw the ruins of an old Saracen tower that one of the local shopkeepers had described, and started down toward it. The path was rough, with much of it carved out of rock, and Domenico picked his way cautiously, with particular concern for his brand-new Gucci loafers.

Nearing the tower, he heard the water lapping at the rocks and the cry of a gull, but he still saw nothing. That asshole bean-counter didn't know what the hell he was talking about. *Amalfians.* They were all shit-eaters. He'd never met one that wasn't.

Then he scrambled around the edge of a sharply angled carob tree and saw the boy.

He was kind of a small kid, with these skinny arms and legs that instantly reminded Domenico of his brother before he'd been mashed flat as a pizza by an oil truck. The boy's back was toward him, and the kid was standing at an easel, painting. The canvas was only about half-done, but it looked beautiful to Domenico, very real and lifelike, with the water all shiny, and the sun on the rocks bright enough to make you squint your eyes. The thing was, it didn't look like anything you'd expect a kid to be able to paint.

"Hey."

The boy turned.

"You Paulie?" Domenico said in Italian.

Paul nodded.

Domenico grinned. "That's a great picture. I couldn't do anything like that if my life hung on it."

Paulie looked at him with his serious eyes. "How did you know my name?"

"Your mom and dad asked me to pick you up. They were in a kind of rush on account of the party. My name's Dom."

"What party?"

"The one at my uncle's house that they forgot all about until a little while ago."

Paulie frowned. "They want me to come to a party?"

"They thought it would be a big treat for you on account of all these great paintings that'll be there. Not to mention some pretty important artists."

Paulie stood there staring. He was holding his palette and brushes, and his fingers kept opening and closing on them. His lips felt very dry, and he licked them.

"What's the matter, Paulie?"

"I think you're full of shit."

"Hey, that's no way to talk to a guy. It's not even respectful."

"I don't know you, mister. And my mom and dad wouldn't send anybody I don't know after me. What are you? One of those creeps that like to fool around with little boys?"

Domenico laughed. "You're some kid. Real tough. I once had a little brother was tough like you. Till a truck rolled over him. Then he wasn't so tough no more."

Paulie was suddenly terrified. Was this a real mafioso? He'd only seen the fake ones in the movies and TV, so he didn't know whether this Domenico was the real thing. He didn't look much like a gangster. He looked kind of nice. Even the way he spoke and laughed. Like he was just having a good time. But maybe there were all different kinds of gangsters, too.

"So what do you say, Paulie? You coming to the party, or what?"

Afraid his voice might turn out to be gone, Paul just shook his head.

"Stubborn, too, huh?" Domenico shrugged. "OK. Then stay and finish your painting. It's coming great. If you don't mind, I'll just watch a minute."

Feeling his knees getting wobbly, Paul turned and stabbed a brushload of cerulean blue and purple at a patch of sky.

Then a streak of really bright light suddenly popped on and off somewhere behind his eyes, and the painting and everything else in front of him quietly disappeared.

Domenico made sure he caught him as he started going

down, so Paul never hit the ground. There were a lot of sharp rocks around that could have hurt him. Domenico wanted no unnecessary damage being done to this particular kid.

The three men in the other Mercedes were parked on the cul-de-sac at the far end of the Via Contessa. Having passed and taken stock of Peter Walters' home at number 14, they had things to consider and decisions to make.

The house itself presented no problems. It was a reasonable distance from its closest neighbors, and the surrounding brush and trees, along with the twisting road it was on, made it all but invisible from other houses. So there was little chance of anyone seeing them entering or leaving. The possible complication came from the third car parked in front of the house. It meant one or more visitors. Not great for carrying out a low-profile operation.

But that would have to be dealt with. Time also was important. At least they'd learned the boy was out of the house, and Domenico would be handling that. You couldn't have it all ways. If something got fucked up, the kid would be good insurance.

It took no more than fifteen minutes of discussion. They'd go with what they had.

Leaving the cul-de-sac, they drove back down the Via Contessa, charged with the dark excitement that such things brought. They were in good spirits. Maybe the third car had even left by now.

The Mercedes slowed as it approached number 14.

The third car was still there.

So was a fourth car.

Swearing softly, they passed the house and continued on toward town.

32

Number 14 Via Contessa had already taken on the closed-in air of a position under siege.

The security system was turned on, the doors and windows were locked, the blinds were drawn, and those inside were armed.

Waiting, peering anxiously out at the road for nearly fifteen minutes, Peter Walters finally saw the gray Mercedes coming back down the mountain. He watched it approach, slow almost to a halt as it neared his house, then pick up speed and disappear around a curve.

Still, he kept everyone on alert for a full twenty minutes more. When it seemed clear that the men in the car weren't immediately coming back, he told the others to have some coffee and try to relax for a while. He himself remained on watch at a window.

Peter was almost sorry the Mercedes had passed him by. It had been simpler, somehow, when the immediate threat was there. Regardless of the danger, he could always deal with straightforward action. It was what he did best. Now there was nothing to do but think and wonder. And it had been a confusing, stress-filled time for him from the moment Gianni had knocked on his door and instantly turned his and his family's world upside down.

Was it really just an hour ago?

And for nearly half that time, he and Peggy had sat listening to Gianni's own collection of horror stories while a leaden anxiety settled on his chest, and an oppression close to strangling rose to his throat.

Yet in the end, all Gianni had been able to do was create more mysteries than he was able to solve, and pose more questions than his old friend Vittorio could even come close to answering.

What could the FBI want from him so badly?

After more than nine years of peaceful obscurity, what could he have done to suddenly turn himself into such a threat to the national security? Of course Cortlandt had already warned him he was the object of an FBI hunt. But Gianni's tales of terror pushed it much further than that.

And what about the four men in their two Mercedes that Mary had come screaming her new alarms about? Who were *they?* More FBI agents? Or Interpol police? Or maybe just some independent syndicate people joining the hunt for fun and profit?

But even more puzzling and dangerous, how had these four beauties known he was living as Peter Walters in Positano and been able to drive straight to his door? And could it really be pure coincidence that they had somehow managed to find him no more than an hour after Gianni and Mary had arrived in town?

If anything had helped keep him alive for twenty years in a very dangerous line of work, it was his never believing in coincidences. When these odds-on, seemingly inexplicable things happened, there was almost always a connection somewhere. Which meant that Mary and Gianni had either been under surveillance from the beginning and followed here, or one of them had turned informer.

Another puzzle for his growing collection.

Then he thought, *Idiot! Go back to the beginning.*

"Gianni, watch the window for me," he said, and went into his studio to make a call he'd thought about making from time to time for almost ten years.

Somehow, he still remembered Mike's number, and he decided a special kind of hocus-pocus had to be running riot in just that. But after two rings, a telephone company recording clicked in to tell him the number he had called was no longer in service.

Peter sat staring bleakly at the phone. Until it hit him that his pilot friend had a brother named Artie living in the same area of Long Island, and he had an operator look up the number and put through the call.

A man answered.

"Is this Artie Keagan?" said Peter.

"Yeah. Who's this?"

"My name's Thompson, Mr. Keagan. Your brother, Mike, used to do some flying for me."

"Yeah?"

"I just tried to reach Mike's old number, but it's been disconnected. I was wondering if maybe you had a new number where I could reach him."

Keagan made a soft, grunting sound. "Wish I did. But Mike's gone."

"Gone?"

"My brother's dead, Mr. Thompson."

Peter Walters sat listening to a dull humming. He wasn't sure if it was coming from his head or from the phone.

"I'm sorry. I didn't know. When?"

" 'Bout two weeks ago. Damnedest thing. I'd just seen him earlier that night. Then *bang!* He was gone a few hours later. His wife, too. And the house and everything in it. All gone. Like they was never there."

"Jesus. What happened?"

"Firemen said a propane tank went. Should never have been stored in the cellar. I don't understand it. Mike never had no propane in the cellar. He wasn't that dumb."

Walters offered some sympathy and hung up.

Two weeks ago. Just about the time the Fibbies started coming after Gianni and Mary to find out where I was.

Another coincidence he didn't believe for a second.

But where was the connection?

Of course. Other than for Peggy and himself, Mike Keagan was the only living soul who knew that Irene Hopper had never really gone down with that plane.

Was that why Mike and his wife were blown up?

Maybe. But why by the FBI, of all people?

Who else?

How about whoever it was that got Don Donatti to send me to waste Peggy when she was Irene Hopper?

Great. But who would that be?

His imaginary trail ended right there, and Vittorio went back to the others.

Gianni and Mary Yung were still at the living-room blinds, peering out at the road.

Peggy sat alone in the kitchen, watching out the back. The automatic Peter had given her earlier looked like a new kind of toy in her hands. He sat down beside her. As always, a few strands of hair had fallen across her eyes, and he brushed them back.

"I just tried calling Mike on Long Island." Vittorio spoke quietly, so only she could hear. "When I couldn't get him, I called his brother. It seems Mike and his wife got blown up two weeks ago. The way I figure it, whoever did them has to be the same one that was originally looking to do *you.* And the only one I can think of who'd know who that was is my old *capo,* who was given the contract and sent me to carry it out."

And I, thought Peggy. *So that makes two of us who know.*

*S*he thought it calmly, coldly, although it was her first conscious admission of the fact. Even to herself. Yet there was a distinct sense of relief in just knowing she was able to deal with it. After so many years of sublimated fear, of wondering how she'd behave if this moment ever arrived, she no longer had to wonder. She knew.

It really was quite simple. There was absolutely nothing that could make her strip herself naked, that could make her smear herself that ugly, dirty, and deviant in front of her husband.

Yes, but was it really worth dying for?

It hadn't come to that yet. It might never come to it.

And if it did?

She'd deal with it *then.*

When Paulie hadn't come home by four-thirty, Peter went to get him. It wasn't that he was especially concerned. When the light was good and holding, and the painting was going well, his son rarely quit before five. But with all that was going on, the father thought it best to keep his family together.

He walked.

The farthest of Paulie's usual painting sites was no more than a short hike away, and Vittorio Battaglia, as he now began to again think of himself, wanted to leave his car in front of the house with the others. He'd decided that the four cars parked there were probably what had kept the men in the Mercedes from stopping during their last pass. As he figured it now, they'd most likely do another drive-by just before or after-dark. Then depending on what they found, they'd take it from there.

Ten minutes later, Vittorio Battaglia saw his son's easel, canvas, and paint box close beside the Saracen tower. What he failed to see was his son.

The first place he looked was the nearby water. Paulie had strict orders never to go swimming off the rocks alone, but Vittorio had the feeling he often did.

Vittorio stood on a rock and stared at the empty patch of sea. The tide was coming in, and he heard its soft lapping against the rocks and felt the cool spray on his face.

He closed his eyes.

He stood very still for half a minute. His only movement was the rise and fall of his breathing.

Slowly, he began to feel the tightening. It squeezed something deep inside his chest. Then it let go. Then it squeezed again. Milking.

Then he carefully packed up Paulie's things and walked back to his house.

33

"DEAR GOD," SAID Peggy Walters.

She had been alone at the front window, but Gianni and Mary Yung came and stood beside her when she spoke. What they saw was Vittorio Battaglia coming up the garden steps carrying his son's things.

Peggy went out to meet him, saw his face up close, and felt everything turn cold. She tried to speak, but there was no sound. She reached for Paulie's folded aluminum easel, took it from her husband's hand, and stared at it. Her silence hung in the air, numbing those watching.

Vittorio flushed with a sudden awareness of his mistake. He never should have brought the stuff back. He should have dumped it somewhere and made up a story about Paulie going over to a friend's for dinner. But he'd had his own demons to deal with, and how long could he play that kind of game, anyway? At best, he could only have delayed the truth.

"He just wasn't around," Vittorio said. "He might have walked into town for something. Or maybe gone off with a friend. It could be nothing, Peg."

She nodded and he studied her face, an etched image that quietly turned to grief.

Vittorio took her inside and carefully laid down his son's things. He put a cigarette in his mouth and lit it. His hands were slow, graceful, and steady. Gianni and Mary Yung watched him. But he might have been in another place, lost in this moment that brought together and formed the pieces of his life.

He looked at Garetsky.

"Help me get a couple of the cars out of sight," he told him.

They went outside and walked down the steps together.

"They're going to be coming very soon now," Vittorio said.

"How do you know?"

"Because they'll want to be here before I discover they've got my son."

"You really think they've got him?"

"Don't you?"

"This is your kind of shit, not mine."

"Maybe it should be yours," said Vittorio flatly. "You sure found *me* pretty damn good."

They reached the four cars and Battaglia got into one.

"Jesus, I'm sorry about this mess," Gianni said.

Vittorio was silent.

"I swear I don't know how anyone could have spotted us and got on our tails. I was careful as hell every second. So was Mary." Gianni looked helplessly at his friend. "I just wasn't as smart as I thought. They gave me enough rope and I hung us all."

Battaglia turned the key and started the engine. "That's history now. Forget it. Let's just hide these two cars. The fat lady hasn't even started singing."

They were back in the house in five minutes, getting ready.

Less than half a mile away, in a small patch of woods, the men in the two Mercedes were making their own final preparations.

Moments earlier, a check with high-powered field glasses had shown only two cars parked in front of 14 Via Contessa. The guests apparently were gone. That had been their only real stumbling block. The rest was expected to be pretty much standard procedure.

Still, because they were all experienced professionals of the top rank, nothing was being taken for granted.

Another potential loose end, the boy, Paulie, was peacefully asleep on a backseat under a shot of sodium pentothal. He would remain that way for several hours. This was important. Had he returned home at a delicate operational moment, everything might have been thrown off.

With Sal running things, they'd be two and two in the cars. Sal and Frankie would pull right up to the house, knock on the door as a couple of lost tourists asking directions. There'd be no reason for the Walterses to be suspicious, and guns would be flashed only if needed to gain entrance or keep control. There'd be no shooting, no bullets to be found in any walls or bodies. The Walterses would just be knocked unconscious and carried to one of their own cars.

The timetable on the whole job, in and out, should be no more than six or seven minutes.

Meanwhile, in the second Mercedes, Domenico and Tony would be waiting a few hundred yards down the road with the kid. If all went as planned at the house, they'd just follow Sal, driving the first Mercedes, and Frankie, who'd be at the wheel of the Walters car, to the chosen setup point near the Ravello cliffs. If something went wrong at the house, if Domenico and Tony spotted any kind of mess-up, they'd get out of there fast with the kid and contact Don Ravenelli for further instructions.

By 6:00 P.M., with every anticipated move checked over twice, they were ready to go.

34

I⊤ WAS SIX hours earlier in Washington, exactly noon, and the man responsible for all this activity in Positano, Henry Durning, had stayed home to await the results.

By the purest of accidents, a man and woman had been given control of what remained of his life and would have to die because of it. As those others already had done, and still others might yet have to do. In human terms alone, preserving him was becoming very expensive.

Was it worth it?

The attorney general was able to smile. *Not to those doing the dying,* he thought.

Yet he wasn't really amused, and he tried to get something for them. But all he could manage to come up with was a poor, sick joke. Here he was, head of the entire U.S. Department of Justice, and he couldn't even get justice for his own poor victims.

The best he could do was sigh.

And what of his lovely phantom lover, Mary Yung? Had she been able to act on his warning not to reach Positano for at least another twenty-four hours? Or would she and Garetsky arrive just in time to die with Irene Hopper and Vittorio Battaglia?

It was Durning's deepest hope that she didn't. What a pathetic waste if she did.

Just thinking of her reached into him. Without ever having met her, without having once seen, touched or known the sweetness of her flesh, he felt her effect growing on him by the day.

To this end, he had requested and received another package concerning her from Brian Wayne, marked as follow-up material from the FBI Background Checks and Research Department. The Bureau's covering letter described its contents as early videotapes of the subject at the age of eighteen.

Durning had not yet looked at any of them, but he was

about to. Waiting to hear from Donatti was starting to get to him. He could use the distraction. For as long as he could remember, certainly since puberty, sex had been his favorite and most easily accessible opiate of choice. In this, at least, he hadn't changed. Why should he? It certainly was less damaging, long-term, than drugs or alcohol.

Unless, he thought wryly, it got out of hand and ended up dumping him into something resembling his present less-than-exalted state.

But even that, he hoped, was finally being handled.

"Come on, Mary Yung ... *distract* me."

Murmured aloud, the few words were enough to set the spark to him.

Durning drew the blinds and darkened his study. He poured himself some vodka, chose a cassette from the FBI's latest Mary Chan Yung festival pack, and clicked it into the VCR. Then he leaned back on a soft leather couch and was off into that instant bower of the libido where he could usually count on being king.

The video begin rolling.

Trying to achieve some slight social redemption for its hard-core porn base, the movie affected a rudimentary story line in which Mary Yung played the part of a heartbroken Asian high-school girl, whose first romance has just been destroyed by her young white lover's racially bigoted parents.

Crying herself to sleep that night, Mary dreams of a kinder, more tolerant world in which the color of one's skin makes no difference, and all that really matters is love.

"Holy Christ," whispered Henry Durning.

For at that point he had begun watching a girlishly slender, eighteen-year-old Mary launching her own sexual paean to the brotherhood of man with the glistening naked bodies of a black, a white, and an Asian.

In consort.

For there was this lovely flower child ... she really was wearing a garland of white in her hair ... taking on all three men at once in the lewdest of triple plays, and doing it with only the purest, most generous, and guileless of motives.

The girl had a gift, if not a true calling.

This Mary Chan Yung.

She literally romped. She was musical, her lips playing the sweetest of woodwinds. Her tongue whispered undreamed of secrets. She had choices to make and she made them, every one.

Rampant on a king-size bed, she was a living metaphor for universal love.

She was new born each moment.

She was a gold medal athlete, a sensual gymnast taking pride in her turns. Her variously skin-colored lovers were becoming hers as they'd never been, nor were ever likely to be, anyone else's.

Bending forward on his couch, watching, Durning ached to join in and make a quartet of the lucky trio. He longed to become part of her will, to share in her. This one delicate, dark-haired girl who was fighting bigotry in the most eloquent of all possible ways. See how even the men were becoming one, these three living stalks growing out of this single, smooth-skinned, amply orificed mother earth.

A hired performer in a cheap porn flick, she transformed the coldest of cash bargains into a salient act of love.

She's mine. She's custom made for me. She matches me point for point and leaves me crawling in her dust.

Never mind her intentions regarding him, or how many others she'd lain with in between. Just watching her, his chest was an empty cage from which all his dark birds had flown. He felt free of his anxieties, lighter than air. She stared straight at him through the camera's lens and perhaps fifteen years, while her black eyes rose from the surface of her cheeks in the same way her breasts rose from the surface of her body.

And all with the same miraculously unsoiled air of innocence.

There has to be a distant garden somewhere, he thought, a place where mysterious exotic objects grow . . . and there, in a lovely pink haze, the heart of Mary Chan Yung hangs like a soft, sweet peach.

"Please," he said quietly, on the off-chance that someone with influence that reached far beyond even his own, might just be listening. "Whatever else happens there, it would be the worst sort of foolishness to have her die today in Positano."

35

THEY CAME JUST about as Vittorio Battaglia had expected them to come . . . out of the early evening glow and in a single car.

The second Mercedes would have to be off somewhere with his son. The only things Vittorio hadn't been sure about was how many they'd be leaving with Paulie. As the car swung off the road and parked beside Peggy's red Fiat, he saw that there were only two men in it. So they'd left the other two to handle his dangerous son.

Three dull thumps sounded on the ceiling directly overhead. Which was Peggy, letting them know they'd seen the car arrive. Vittorio had wanted to send her and Mary Yung to a friend's house in the mountains above Atrani, but they'd refused to go. The best he could get from them was the promise to stay upstairs in the bedroom until whatever was going to happen had happened. In the event of an emergency, they both had guns and knew how to use them.

Vittorio and Gianni knelt together on the floor, peering between the blinds. The house was still. Occasionally a gull cried out as it flew up from the water, then glided back down.

The two men got out of the Mercedes. They stood staring up at the house for a moment. Then they started climbing the garden steps. One of them, Sal, still had his camera around his neck as he went on playing tourist. The other, the one called Frankie, kept laughing and talking, playing his part in their little two-character charade.

"You know them?" Gianni asked.

Vittorio shook his head. "Whoever sent them wouldn't be dumb enough to send anyone I might have seen before."

He looked at Gianni. "You OK?"

"Better than OK. I goddamn can't wait."

"Don't be too eager. They're no good to us dead."

"I know."

They stood up and moved into position on either side of the front door. They both carried automatics with attached silencers.

Gianni released his safety. He felt the sweat forming in his armpits and tried to keep his mind empty of everything but the action immediately ahead. The wall blocked his view, but in his mind he still saw the two men climbing the stone steps toward the house.

They've come to wipe out this whole family like a medieval plague, and I'm the one who brought them here.

Thinking that, he fed his rage to keep it up to full strength. Let Vittorio stay cool. He himself was at his best with anger. *Good God, they had his boy.* How could he stand there, waiting with such icy control? Simple. The guy was a pro.

The knocker banged three times and Vittorio's color-coded blue eyes met Gianni's and held them.

My once and closest friend, thought Garetsky, and knew that the human soul had more sides and corners than he would ever know or touch.

With seeming casualness, Vittorio opened the door and pointed his automatic at the head of the lead man, Sal, who was the one who had knocked. Frankie was in the middle of one of his better, more authentic-sounding laughs, and stood several feet behind Sal. Gianni showed himself and brought his own gun to Vittorio's side, and the four men stood in a silent tableau, staring at one another.

Vittorio took a few steps back to clear the doorway, forcing Gianni to move with him.

Speaking Italian, Vittorio said, "Come in. And do it slowly and carefully. Just one stupid move and you're both dead."

Neither man budged an inch. They seemed frozen in place. All they appeared able to do was look at the two long, silenced automatics and wonder why and how they had come to be aimed at them.

"What the hell's this?" said Sal. "We just got lost and wanted to ask directions to Amalfi. Are all you natives this jumpy?"

"I said come inside," Vittorio quietly told them again.

They still stood there, staring.

Without moving or taking any apparent aim, Vittorio squeezed the trigger. There was a soft, whooshing sound and Sal cried out and spun to his left. A crimson edged hole showed in the upper part of his left sleeve.

White-faced, he stood clutching his arm. He looked at it. Then he looked at Vittorio Battaglia.

"You're fucking crazy!"

"Here's how it is," said Battaglia. "The next one'll be a gut shot. And if you need any more after that, I'm going to shoot out both your eyes. So why don't you just get your ass in here and save us both trouble."

Without another word, and still holding his arm, Sal half stumbled into the house.

Gianni felt as though he had been watching the entire scene performed from a long way off and underwater. Then he saw a sudden blur of movement as the other man, Frankie, panicked and took off down the steps.

"Get the bastard," said Battaglia, now in back of Gianni Garetsky.

Gianni aimed low, for the legs. He squeezed off a single round and watched the laughing man go down, roll, and come up on his knees with a gun in his hand.

The man wasn't laughing now. He was staring at Gianni with a jester's deep gloom. Then he fired at Gianni and missed, and fired again and missed once more.

He was about to let go with his third try, when Gianni reluctantly put a bullet in his chest and saw him go over on his back. He heard Vittorio's voice behind him, but not what he said.

Gianni ran down the steps and bent over the man. Frankie's eyes were glazing over, but he was still breathing.

"Where's the boy?" asked Gianni, speaking Italian.

Frankie coughed blood and just stared at him.

"The boy . . . " pleaded Gianni. "Is he alive? Come *on,* for Jesus' sake! He's just a baby. Help him!"

Frankie moved his lips. "How . . . " Red bubbles formed, broke, dribbled down his chin. "How . . . did you know . . . we . . . was . . . "

The light starting to go out in his eyes, Frankie coughed a small gusher of crimson. Then he gave a slow look of surprise and died.

Gianni rocked gently on his knees in a patch of grass. Glancing back at the house, he saw the two women watching from an upstairs window. Vittorio and the wounded *pistolero* stood in the entrance foyer staring out at the same action.

Garetsky put his automatic in his belt and carried the dead man up to the house. He was heavy. It took hard, concentrated effort. Battaglia closed and locked the door behind them. Sal stood squeezing his blood-soaked arm, his face showing nothing. He looked at Frankie's body, accepting it as part of everything that had happened, and what was probably going to happen next.

Peggy called down from the second floor, her voice low and anxious. "Vittorio?"

"We're OK," Battaglia answered. "Just stay up there a while longer. I'll yell when we have something."

Vittorio got them all into his studio, a huge, picture-windowed room with a spectacular view of the mountains and the rocky terrain below.

Gianni placed the dead man on the bare wood flooring. One of Frankie's legs was crooked and he straightened it.

Battaglia put Sal in a chair. Then, moving slowly, thoughtfully, he sat down facing the man, his automatic pointing at his chest. Sal was still holding his wounded arm, but the bleeding seemed to have stopped. Gianni remained standing to one side. He took his gun out of his belt and flicked off the safety. Beyond the window the sun was low, slanting in over the mountains and bathing everything in a soft orange light.

Sal and Vittorio stared at each other in an odd sort of way. Each of them seemed to know what was going to happen as exactly as if they'd already been through it during an earlier incarnation.

But it was to Gianni that Vittorio spoke first. "Did you get anything out of that clown down there?"

"No. Sorry about having to waste him."

Vittorio shrugged. "What else could you do? You gave him two freebies, which was dumb in itself. If he wasn't such a lousy shot, you'd be the wasted one, not him."

He considered Sal for a long moment. "So who *are* you guys?"

"Undercover *carabinieri.*"

"Gianni, get his wallet. Read me what kind of fake paper he's carrying. The same with the guy on the floor."

Garetsky did it, and the room was silent.

"They've both got *carabiniere* IDs."

"Where does it say they're from?"

"Palermo."

"Names?"

"This one's Sal Ferrisi. The other guy was Frank Bonotara."

"Anything else?"

"No."

Several moments were chewed up as Vittorio Battaglia sat looking at Sal Ferrisi.

"You got any kids, Sal?" Vittorio's voice was so low his lungs and heart might have been in it.

Ferrisi shook his head.

"I didn't hear you."

"No."

"Too bad. Maybe if you'd had a kid of your own, you'd never have taken on this dirty a job. Then you wouldn't be where you are now."

Gripping his bloody arm, Ferrisi sat very still, afraid to move, afraid to abandon this instant. As if by staying where he was, he could somehow hold back everything he knew was coming.

"Where's my boy, Sal?"

"I don't know."

Vittorio sighed. "Take off your clothes."

Ferrisi sat there, white faced. Then using his own good

arm, he began struggling out of his clothes. Finally, he was sitting naked in his chair, a sun-bronzed, muscular young man with a 9mm puncture wound through the fleshy part of his upper arm, and a less-than-bright future.

Vittorio went to one of several painting cabinets and came back with a razor-edged utility knife.

"I really hate this stuff, Sal. Lots of guys love it, but I'm not one of them. What I love is my son. So just tell me where he is, and you can put your clothes back on and stay in one piece. Otherwise, I'm afraid your friend, Frankie, is going to end up the lucky one."

"I swear I don't—"

He was cut off by a quick flash of Battaglia's knife across his chest. The blade barely broke skin. But it did leave a faint, almost invisible line that slowly widened and deepened until a single crimson drop formed, rolled down Sal Ferrisi's lower chest and stomach, and vanished into the darkness below.

"No more lies," said Battaglia. "My wife's upstairs this minute with a great big hole in her heart, and all I've got to patch her up with is you. So give us an answer we can live with, or I swear to Christ I'll peel you like a fucking apple."

Ferrisi wasn't really listening. He was too busy staring at the tiny drops of blood that kept forming, rolling and disappearing on his body. There had been no pain in the touch of the blade. But the act itself had been so swift and indifferent that he suddenly felt like a side of beef in a butcher shop. And he knew his nakedness was all part of the softening-up process. He'd used it himself. It was the first thing you did. You took away clothes, along with an essential human dignity.

"I mean it, Sal," said Vittorio. "I'm going to tie you to this chair, do you piece by piece, and finally feed you your own balls for dessert. And I'm not just talking. Believe me."

Sal Ferrisi believed him. His problem wasn't belief. His problem was that he was dead either way. Even if he talked, they could never safely turn him loose. They'd have to bury him with Frankie. And if by some miracle they didn't, by the time Don Ravenelli got through with him, he'd be wishing they had. Ferrisi thought it through coldly, without particular malice. It was just the way these things worked. If he had any slight chance at all, it was to go for broke before they tied him to the chair. Once they did that, he was gone.

He sat gazing through the big window at the sunset, wondering why he'd never paid any attention to stuff like that before. He heard Walters asking him the same questions about his boy twice more, and heard himself giving back the same answer.

Then Walters was suddenly looking tired, like someone had cut all his strings. Even his voice sounded worn out when he told the other guy, Gianni, to go into the kitchen and get some rope he had there.

Sal saw Gianni walk slowly out of the room, not happy about the whole thing. So who was happy about it?

He and Walters were alone, staring at each other. The gun was in Walters' hand, cocked, and with the safety off. But Walters seemed to have forgotten about it. At that moment there was an emptiness in his eyes that Sal Ferrisi felt gave him an advantage, and he entered it, driving his legs like two great pistons, and for a moment everything in the room was calm and slow.

Ferrisi saw Walters' eyes widen as he came up out of the chair, not going for him and his gun, but driving past him with all his force to the high window. He took the impact on his head, shoulder, and good arm, feeling the shock for only an instant before the glass shattered and he sailed on through.

The empty stillness of falling filled his chest. The length and speed of the fall surprised him. It seemed to go on and on, making him breathless, confused.

He hit the ground before he ever understood.

Then there was no more time.

Vittorio reached him several moments before Gianni.

Sal Ferrisi lay among the rocks and shattered glass with the special awkwardness of the suddenly dead. His eyes were open, looking a thousand miles beyond Vittorio. His head and neck were twisted into the impossible angles of a broken doll.

Vittorio Battaglia looked up at the remains of his studio

window more than fifty feet above. He guessed Ferrisi hadn't seen the depth of the gully until it was too late.

A breeze came in off the sea and he turned his face toward it. The smell was as old as the world.

Now I've got nothing, he thought.

36

"THERE'S A LOT to do," said Vittorio Battaglia, "so we'd better get started."

The four of them were gathered in his studio. It was less than ten minutes since Sal Ferrisi had flown through the window. A gust of air blew past the broken glass and ruffled Frankie's hair where he still lay on the floor. No one looked at him. Nor did they look at each other. They had their own things to think about. But they were listening to Vittorio because it gave them something to do.

"I don't know who sent these guys or why," he said. "But I know there's going to be more of them coming. So we're getting out of here."

Vittorio looked at Mary Yung and Gianni. "Peg and I have this old ruin of a safe house we keep. It's way up in the Ravello mountains, and no one knows about it. I'm taking Peggy there."

No one said anything. Peggy's face was set. She was looking at the blood Frankie had leaked onto the wood flooring. Mary and Gianni weren't looking anyplace.

"Unless you two have other plans," Vittorio added.

"What other plans?" said Gianni. "We came looking for *you.* That's why we're here."

Mary Yung just stared off somewhere. She didn't seem to be listening anymore.

Peggy began to weep. She wept silently, not wiping the tears but just letting them run down her cheeks and onto her blouse. Vittorio watched her. He saw there was nothing that meant anything to her now but her son.

Working quickly, carefully, they cleaned up all traces of blood and broken glass—inside the house and out—and loaded the two bodies into the Mercedes.

Peggy and Vittorio packed a couple of suitcases and put them into their own cars. One of the bags held a full range of weapons and ammunition, including grenades, gas, and explosives. Vittorio made a final check of the house. He walked past Paulie's room without glancing in. He didn't have the courage.

Other than for the broken window in the studio, everything seemed in order. None of this was for the benefit of the police, who would probably know nothing about anything. Actually, Vittorio wasn't sure who it was for. The only ones likely to enter the house would be those sent to follow up on Sal and Frankie, and they weren't about to be fooled by anything they did or didn't find. He guessed it was mostly for himself, for his own sense of order. He didn't change old habits easily. For this, he wasn't even trying.

Peggy called Roberta at the gallery to say she was going on an unexpected trip with her son and husband and wouldn't be in for about a week. She told her assistant to bring in whatever extra help she needed, and not to worry if she didn't hear from her.

Vittorio had to walk out of the room while she was talking. It wasn't Peggy's fault. She was handling it very well. It was just that all at once, *he* wasn't doing so well.

It was shortly after dark when they pulled away from the house in a four-car convoy.

Battaglia drove the lead car, the Mercedes, with Sal and Frankie in back, neatly folded under a blanket. He headed southeast at a steady sixty kilometers, feeling like the hearse driver in a funeral cortege. And in an all too real sense, he was.

Peggy came next in her red Fiat. Temporarily shielded from her husband's eyes, she wept without control. It began blinding her to the point that she knew she had to either stop crying or stop driving. She stopped crying.

Directly behind her in Vittorio's Toyota, Mary Yung drove under the unforgiving weight of conscience and dread. For her big million dollars, she'd as good as murdered a child, and she might yet end up doing the same for his parents, Gianni, and quite possibly herself if she didn't get out of here fast. Unless, of course, she told them about the attorney general. And that would be the same as putting a gun to her head and squeezing the trigger.

Another fifty feet back in his rented Ford, Gianni Garetsky brought up the rear with his own sharply nagging brand of penance for something he hadn't even done. But thinking he had, it remained an extinction. In his mind, it no longer seemed to matter where he went or what he did. He had already done his damage.

Vittorio stopped the convoy on a winding mountain road about ten miles out of Positano.

With the three last cars parked out of sight in a pine grove, Vittorio and Gianni maneuvered the Mercedes to the edge of an almost vertical three-hundred-foot drop. What remained of a rotted wooden guardrail was broken apart with rocks. They put Sal in the driver's seat and Frankie beside him. They fastened the seatbelts around the bodies, kept the engine running in neutral, and locked the doors. Vittorio dipped a length of rope into the gas tank, reversed it, and left a saturated six-inch piece hanging out as a fuse.

Then he and Gianni leaned into the rear bumper of the car.

When it started to roll, Vittorio put a match to the end of the rope and saw it flare. They gave the car a final shove and watched it pick up speed and go over the edge.

The tank blew when it was about halfway down the cliff. The car hit bottom and a giant fireball erupted in a second explosion. It turned everything a flaming orange.

Then Vittorio got behind the wheel of his wife's Fiat, and led the remainder of the suddenly bodiless cortege farther up into the mountains.

37

Attorney General Henry Durning's anxiously awaited call from Carlo Donatti finally reached him at home at 3:16 P.M., Washington time. Which made it 9:16 P.M. in Positano.

There were no preliminaries.

"I've just heard from my connection," said Donatti.

Durning didn't like the way his heart was drumming against his chest. *Imagine. At this stage of my life.*

"And?"

"The news isn't good."

Durning sat there. He stayed exactly where he was, staring across the big walnut desk in his study. He felt a pulse going in his temple. His hand pressed the receiver against his ear as if trying to shove it clear through his brain.

"What happened?"

"We'd better meet."

"When?"

"Can you make it at six tonight?" asked Donatti.

"Same place as last time?"

"If that's all right."

"I'll be there," said Durning, and hung up.

He still sat there. Insanely, with all that could be blowing up in his face, he found himself wondering whether Mary Yung had been among those killed. There was no doubt in his mind that people had died. It was just a matter of his learning which ones they were.

Their control and timing were such that they arrived at the airport motel room within minutes of each other.

Durning started the radio going. Then he searched for a classical station and finally found some Brahms.

They embraced and Carlo Donatti poured them each some scotch from the minibar. The small act alone added weight to the attorney general's depression. To Donatti, scotch was a very serious drink.

"So?" said Durning.

"The way it sounded," said Donatti quietly, "nobody's exactly sure what happened. Four good soldiers went into Positano, and only two came out. The other two haven't been heard from. And they probably won't be."

Durning ignored his serious drink and remained silent. It was Donatti's story.

"Battaglia had to be waiting for them," said the don. "So my feeling is Gianni and his *cinese* got there first and blew the whistle."

"Where are they now?"

The don shrugged. "They were all gone when someone checked the house later. The only sign of anything was a smashed window."

"And this is what you've brought me?"

"Not quite. We've also got Battaglia's kid. So it's not all bad."

The attorney general started at Donatti. "What does that mean?"

"We've at least got a string on Battaglia. He and his wife won't just disappear on us while we've got the boy. They're going to have to deal."

"I don't want them dealing, Carlo. There's nothing to deal. I want them dead. Haven't I made myself clear on that?"

"Very clear. But first they'll deal. *Then* they'll be dead." Something in that made the don smile. "You're head of the whole damn Justice Department, Henry. You should learn more about how justice works these days at the basic levels."

Durning breathed a joyless odor in the air that had nothing to do with Donatti's expensive designer cologne.

"How old is the boy?" he asked.

"About nine or ten."

"Who's keeping him?"

"The two men who picked him up in Positano."

Durning's face was blank. "He'll be able to identify them. He's old enough."

"That won't be a problem."

Durning felt a new mix of disgust and damage take root inside him. Now he was accepting the murder of children?

"How do we find the parents?" he asked.

"We don't. They'll find us."

Durning's eyes were hard, yet curiously uncertain. He was a knowing, complex man accustomed to intricate situations. Yet he suddenly felt himself in uncharted territory.

"Tell me about it," he said.

"By now, Battaglia and Garetsky have to know I'm involved," said Donatti. "And the women certainly have told them of *your* interest. So either one of us can expect a call." He paused. "Or maybe a bullet."

Durning considered him. "You trying to scare me, Carlo?"

"Damn right. Why should I be the only one scared? And you're the guy hooked me into this in the first place." Donatti grinned without looking happy. "We've got us a couple of tough, angry boys out there. I've known them both since they were kids. When you try to waste their kind, it's best to get it right the first time. Because mostly you don't get any second chances."

"You're really making my day."

The don laughed, and this time he seemed to be enjoying himself. "Nothing like a little dose of fear to get the adrenaline going. But it's nice we've got the kid. Without him, there'd be good reason to sweat. This way, Vittorio's not going to do a thing. Except maybe call up one of us and beg."

Durning felt a faint hint of nausea drift through his lungs. "Anything doing yet with that other little favor I asked?"

"You mean John Hinkey and the Beekman woman?"

"Yes."

"It's all set for tonight."

"Both of them?"

Donatti nodded. "That's the best way to do these things. No piecework. Then you don't have one of them going around asking questions about the other."

"I appreciate it, Carlo."

"Hey!" said the don. "A couple of sweethearts like us . . . we've got to look out for each other, right?"

It was a little past ten that night when John Hinkey left his Washington law office and started the drive home. He was dog tired but exhilarated. He'd been working tough, sixteen-hour stretches, but he finally had things adding up on the Beekman case and he was almost ready to run with it.

This was going to be his big one. He may have had some of the same feeling before on other cases, and he'd done pretty damn well with most of them. But there'd never been any quite like this. Not with this kind of stature. This one was putting him on another level entirely. This fucker was taking him right over the top.

Hinkey hummed tunelessly as he drove, while his fingers tapped along on the wheel to some beat of his own.

And who'd have expected it that first day, with Bonnie running to him half-hysterical because Jim was off on a case and hadn't called her in a couple of days? No use kidding himself. If they hadn't been old friends, he'd have had her out of his office in five minutes flat. Then the Bureau had started the stonewalling and the top secret bullshit and the whole thing just took on a bad smell. So when the three bodies finally turned up, he wasn't all that surprised and he really started digging. Which led him to the wife of another seemingly missing agent, this one out of the Philadelphia office.

But the real clincher had come today, when he'd called in every favor owed him at the Bureau over the past ten years and learned that all five agents . . . the three dug up dead in Greenwich, and the two allegedly on top secret cases and out of touch with their wives . . . were all listed as being on special-duty assignments to the head man himself, FBI Director Brian Wayne.

So what's it all about, Alfie?

He had given the director three days to either tell Bonnie where Jim was, or let her speak to him on the phone. Brian Wayne had done neither, and his time was up. So tomorrow would be Hinkey's personal D day. He had decided to bypass the Justice Department's Office of Personal Responsibility, call his own news conference, and go public with what he had.

There was little doubt in his mind that Jim Beekman and the missing agent out of Philadelphia were as dead at this moment as the three agents dug out of the Greenwich woods. Which was the saddest part of all. Not that these tragic overtones were going to hold him back in any way. Just the opposite. He absolutely couldn't wait to get at it in the morning.

At about eleven o'clock, Hinkey pulled into the high-rise apartment complex where he lived, and parked in his assigned space in the underground garage. He had brought home a briefcase full of papers, and he was fumbling with an open clasp when a lead billy caught him just behind his right ear.

He neither saw nor knew what hit him. Nor was he aware of the two solidly built men in stocking masks who stretched him out in the back of a dark, compact van, bound, gagged, and blindfolded him, and drove quietly out of the garage.

Bonnie Beekman rolled over in her sleep, reached for her husband and touched his empty pillow. It was enough to wake her with an oppression close to strangling in her throat.

Oh, God, she thought, and wept.

He was gone.

Never mind what they told her at the Bureau. She knew better. He'd have to be dead not to have somehow gotten word to her. In twenty years, nothing like this had ever happened. Even stuck up there in the wilds of Maine that time, he'd arranged for someone to call and say he was OK. He was like that . . . always thinking about her, not wanting her to worry for no reason.

But no more.

And who was there to think about her now?

Maybe if they'd had children, it would be better for her. But she didn't think so. Not with what they'd had together. Kids had their own lives. They couldn't take the place of your man. And her Jimbo was some man. Jesus, they didn't come any better.

Maybe he's not really gone, she suddenly thought.

Well, no one had showed her a body.

So maybe the call would come in the morning.

She could imagine herself hearing the ring, picking up the phone, and listening to him say, as always, "Hi, hon. Miss me?"

And she could hear herself answering, as always, "You'd better believe it, love."

It was all so real and reassuring that she needed only two more pills to put her back to sleep.

Bonnie slept a dreamless sleep under a single bedsheet. A breeze ruffled the curtains at an open window, and a three-quarter moon patterned the floor.

Two shadows briefly blocked the window, then silently approached the bed.

This time they used a shot of sodium pentothal instead of the leather-covered billy.

Bonnie struggled for a few seconds, but it seemed part of a dream, and she wasn't consciously aware of it as real before the shot cut off all awareness and put her out.

38

THEIR SO-CALLED safe house was an old, half-crumbling ruin set high in the mountains above Ravello. Trees, shrubs, and cliffs made it all but invisible until you came upon it. And to come upon it, you had to know exactly where to look.

Inside the house no one said much of anything.

Gianni saw the fragile looks between Vittorio and his wife and understood that in these exchanges there were touches of panic. He sensed, too, that much of the same condition existed among all four of them. It was as if the boy, Paulie, whom Mary Yung and he had never even met, was a common anchor, draped around their necks and dragging them all down. And they couldn't as much as talk to each other.

That was what Gianni wanted. To talk. He wanted to tell the boy's parents again and again what he'd already told them . . . that he was sorry, that he'd done everything possible to keep from being followed, that it was eating his gut to have been the one to have done this to them. But he knew there was nothing he could say that they would hear.

The silence went on so long that it became unnatural. It made the old house and those in it seem unnatural, too. It made Peggy begin crying again. Then it made her go into the next room and close the door.

The rest of them sat looking at the door.

Vittorio pushed himself up and followed his wife.

Peggy sat in a straight-backed wooden chair facing the door. A small bedside kerosene lamp was on, and it threw a flickering yellow light that left deep shadows on her face and body. Her hands were folded in her lap and she was staring down at them. She had stopped crying, but she didn't look up as Vittorio came in.

"Please close the door," she said softly. "I have something to tell you."

Vittorio did it and sat down on the bed. Peggy was still staring down at her hands. She hadn't looked up to follow her husband's movements.

"I think I know who's behind all this." Her voice, besides being barely audible, was toneless. "It's Henry Durning."

Vittorio felt something flop over in his chest.

"I lied when we first met and I told you I didn't know who wanted me dead. I knew. I just didn't want *you* to know."

"Why?"

"Because there was too much I'd have to explain. And I was too ashamed."

"Ashamed?" Vittorio stared at her. "Of what?"

"Of what I was. Of some of the things I've done."

Some part of it caught in her throat then and she had to stop. A single tear appeared in a corner of her eye and slid down her face. Numbly, Vittorio watched it.

"I was afraid I'd lose you if you knew. It was all so stupid. But now they've got Paulie and I just want to die. So there's nothing else I can do but tell you."

Finally, she thought, and felt it come out in what might have been a clot of tears and blood.

39

My devil's tale.

Yet even now, in the telling, Irene Hopper knew she was giving Vittorio no more than the bare bones. To be explicit, to flesh the story out, would be too much for either of them. The bones would be damaging enough. The rest of it, the ugliest of the details, let them bury with her.

Her worst time had always been late at night, when Vittorio was away on one of what he chose to call his "business trips." It was then that her private bête noire would be let out of its cage to move in with her.

In time it became almost ritualistic.

As though seeking confirmation of her blackest thoughts, she would begin by staring into the big, baroque dressing-table mirror in her bedroom.

More lies.

Even prepared for it, gazing at herself remained a shock. Her once long blond hair was now short and dark. Her nose was lifted, turned up at the tip, instead of running straight. And with the additional magic of contact lenses, she and Vittorio had literally switched the colors of their eyes. Suddenly he had become the one with the cornflower blues, while she gazed less than serenely from her own bogus golden browns.

But her biggest lie to Vittorio was the one she invented to explain why there could have been any number of people . . . yet none she could specifically accuse . . . who might have had reason to want her terminated.

She originally told Vittorio that she had stumbled across hard evidence of insider trading in the common stock of a company her law firm was representing in a billion-dollar takeover deal. It was a serious criminal offense, and there was no way for her to conceal the fact that she had seen the evidence. Although she claimed she wasn't about to blow any whistles, there obviously had to have been at least one among the guilty parties who wasn't about to take any chances.

So said she to the man she had met, fallen in love with, and married only because he had been sent to carry out a contract on her life.

End of lie.

And the truth?

Irene Hopper would sit staring at the semistranger in the mirror, a new woman named Peggy Walters. She would picture herself as she had once been, yet feel no closer to that person than to the one before her. Maybe neither woman had anything to do with her anymore. Then feeling as though she had caught herself at something, she would abandon both images for the truth as she knew it actually to be.

It all started simply enough, driving back from the Cape one Saturday evening. She and Henry turned off the Connecticut Pike for a late supper at a country inn near Stratford. Seated alongside an attractive young couple, they were soon talking, laughing, buying each other drinks, and exchanging life stories.

The couple's names were Lucy and Hal Chanin, and they were vacationing at a cottage they had rented at a nearby lake. Near midnight, they were all carrying enough of a glow for the Chanins to invite their new friends back to their place for some brandy and whatever, and Irene and Henry accepted.

The *whatever* turned out to be several better-than-fair lines of coke. It was no surprise. None of these things were ever really a surprise to those who knew about them, and she and Henry knew about them. There were always subtle code words, glances, faint half-smiles to make sure everything was understood and agreed upon in advance.

By two in the morning there was enough heat in the air for Henry to make the first move. Peggy knew he would be the one to set it off. He always was. When he came to her on one of the room's two couches, she could feel his pulse as if it were her own, hear his heart like the electronic beat in a microphone. He was pure spark. And she was waiting. Yes, she was. So were the Chanins.

Henry took off her clothes and started on her.

Sensations passed through her body like the friendliest of

ghosts. Which wasn't to say she was free of doubt. She never was. She knew she'd despise and repel herself on certain far-off nights. But now was now, and adding to her excitement were the flushed faces, hungry eyes, and suddenly stripped down flesh of Lucy and Hal as they began their own run. Until all that damp anxiety that reaches for the brain and deadens joy was brushed aside and she was a burning, two-backed beast.

She was never really aware of the exact moment when it became Hal's face she was seeing . . . first, above, and then beneath her. Not that it mattered. By then she was well into her own magnetic field, where forces beyond reason were pulling her to do things whose only purpose was to satisfy an itch that was on the verge of driving her mad if she couldn't reach it.

There were wild sounds in her head and the sense that the best parts of two men . . . good, lovely men . . . were entering her at once. Which, God help her, they were surely doing. And she itched for more of that, too, maybe even another, but was just as pleased, finally, to settle for Lucy herself . . . pretty, full-lipped Lucy, who offered the sweetest, most knowing of smiles before joining with the men.

Breathing the freshest, most delicate of bouquets, she remember drifting off to whispers that told her she was queen.

She was.

She certainly was queen.

Whatever came later, she was ready to swear to at least that much with her last breath.

But what did come later would make her less certain about ever swearing to anything again, she thought.

They sprawled about the room, half in stupor, sipping what remained of the brandy. Clothes were scattered everywhere. They lay naked . . . exposed, uncovered, uncaring. Peggy was alone on one couch. Hal and Lucy lay together on the other, her tongue licking idly at his ear. Henry was stretched out on a rug in front of the fireplace, his head on a cushion, his eyes closed.

It was a cool country night and Hal had lit a fire earlier to take the chill from the air. With only embers left burning, he rose now to stir them alive with a poker and toss on another few logs. Then he freshened his drink and settled down on the rug beside Henry.

The new logs crackled. It was the only sound in the room. The odor of heated sex mixed with the aroma of the fire. Lucy was dozing on the couch and Peggy felt herself starting to drift off as well. On the floor, the two men talked softly and drank the brandy in front of the fire.

Peggy slept.

When she opened her eyes it was with a start.

Something had wakened her.

The two men, still naked, seemed to be struggling on the floor. She heard Henry cry out and it was the same sound that had broken through her sleep.

She froze, staring.

Hal appeared to be all over Henry. A big, powerful, heavily muscled man, his knees and body pinned Henry to the floor. His hands stabbed brutally between Henry's legs, as if seeking to grab and mangle his genitals. Then Hal did have hold of him and Henry screamed and kept screaming until the two women, both fully awake now, began screaming with him.

The room filled with their combined sound, and it was of something so far out of control and human intent, that it might have come from a rent in the earth.

Peggy never saw Henry reach for the fire iron. Maybe he never really did reach for it, but just groped wildly for something, anything, until his fingers happened to make contact with the poker. Then he lifted and swung the full, solid weight of it and kept swinging blindly, fiercely, until the indescribable pain between his legs started to ease and Hal Chanin was lying very still with his eyes open and staring and his head pumping blood.

From that point, Peggy would never be completely sure of the details or sequence of things as they happened next.

What definitely did come out of it was that Hal was dead, and Lucy was still screaming, and suddenly coming at Henry with this small-bore rifle she'd grabbed hold of somewhere in the room. She fired from the hip without aiming and missed, and was working the bolt for a second shot when Henry caught her with the fire iron and knocked her down.

Then there was Henry picking up the rifle and staring at Lucy where she lay, stunned, but not badly hurt. He looked at her for a long moment. Then he slowly raised the rifle, aimed, and shot her through the forehead. Dead center.

Peggy remembers screaming.

She also remembered Henry, gentle and loving as a mother, feeding her brandy and pointing out that there was no other way, that once the police and media were involved, both their lives would have been ruined by the drug and sexual aspects of the scandal. Not to mention the small matter of manslaughter. Christ! Just try to explain the coked-up queer suddenly going wild to sodomize him, and tearing his balls when he tried to fight him off. With his wife as an obviously less-than-friendly witness, Henry said he'd be lucky to get off with ten to twenty years. Remember, too, it was Lucy's gun, and she who started the shooting. They just got a break when her first shot missed. Her second shot wouldn't have. Wasn't it better that she, not he, was the one lying dead?

Dimly, Peggy had to agree it was better. But what a choice.

As a former district attorney, Henry knew enough about such things to do whatever needed doing. He wiped away all fingerprints. He dressed the two bodies and smeared their clothes with their own blood. He packed a bag with whatever cash and jewelry he could find, and smashed a window to make it look like a break-in burglary. The police would assume the Chanins came home unexpectedly, caught the thieves in the act, and were murdered for their trouble.

To lend detail and credence to the staged break-in, Henry Durning added the illusion of rape by stripping Lucy below the waist, ripping her bra and underpants, and bruising her thighs. The required semen, other than her husband's, had already been deposited during their earlier round-robin.

With the rest of his life on the line, Henry made sure he missed nothing. When they finally drove off, he stopped the car a few miles from the house and buried the rifle and jewelry in a patch of woods. Ever practical, he saw no point in burying unmarked cash.

* * *

It had all worked out pretty much as Henry planned. Since the Chanins were on vacation, their bodies weren't discovered for more than a week. The break-in theory was picked up by the police, and the evidence of rape was exploited by the media. As for the country inn where they met the Chanins, they were all strangers to the place and not even their waiter ever remembered the two murder victims having dined there.

The only thing that didn't work out as Henry planned was me, Peggy thought.

Because it stayed with her. She couldn't forget any part of that night. But most of all, she couldn't forget Henry picking up the rifle and looking at Lucy for that long, calm, contemplative moment before he coldly dead-centered her.

Yet she functioned normally enough day to day. She went to her office in New York every morning. She did her work in the practice of law. She saw Henry Durning whenever he asked to see her, and behaved without visible panic or hysterics in his presence. But she also kept seeing Lucy Chanin's eyes just before their light went out. They told her she was living in a sick void where things far worse than death were waiting.

She guessed it was just about then that she began seeing Vittorio Battaglia.

It was almost like a new strain of peripheral vision, she thought, in which you were only vaguely aware of these brief images. At first he was no more than a nebulous face on a Manhattan street or in an office building or theater lobby. Then it began happening in restaurants and she was able to get a better look at him, liking what she saw but thinking no more of it than that. She was usually with friends or people from her office, but he was always alone and quite unaware of her.

Until one night, leaving an old Fellini movie at an art theater on Second Avenue, she almost walked straight into him. For once, she was by herself and he was smiling at her.

"Don't you think it's about time we spoke?" he said.

What she remembered thinking was that up close he

looked like some Renaissance prince, by way of Titian. "I never thought you were even aware of me."

He looked at her, holding on to the moment. "How could anyone not be aware of you?"

They went to a nearby lounge and sat talking and gazing at each other until two in the morning.

They did the same thing for the next four nights. It was no problem for her. Henry happened to be out of town on a case and would be gone for another two weeks.

On the fifth night she invited him to dinner. To this point, they had not so much as kissed or even held hands. Which was fine with her. Still haunted by the horrors of Stratford, she was content just to be with him. But it did make her wonder a little about Vittorio. What was *his* problem?

She was about to find out.

He waited until they finished eating and were sipping what remained of the wine. Later, he told her he hadn't wanted to spoil her beautiful dinner.

What he did first was to put down his wine, take her hand in both of his, and just sit holding it for a moment.

Then he said, "I have to ask you a few questions."

"Why not?"

"They may sound strange to you, but just give me a chance. Do you have any enemies that you know of? I mean serious enemies, those who might do you harm?"

She thought he was joking, until she saw his eyes. "What kind of harm are we talking about?"

"The worst kind. Like maybe dead?"

She just stared at him.

"I'm not kidding, Irene."

Suddenly, she was frightened. Those early sightings of him, the strangeness of their meeting, all began falling into place. "My God, what are you? A cop?"

"No." A cold blankness settled over his face. "I'm the one who was sent to get rid of you."

Her heart banged against her chest. It might have been trying to escape.

"Please," he said. "Don't be afraid. I'm not going to hurt you."

She had a moment then when the prospect of dying didn't seem all that bad. This alone softened and cut into her fear.

"This is what you do? You get rid of people?"

Vittorio was silent. Her hand was still in his and he slowly raised it to his lips, then to his cheek and kept it there. The gentleness of the gesture reached her.

"Who sent you to do this?" she asked.

"A man I do work for. But he's not the one behind it. He doesn't even know you. He's just taking care of it for someone."

"And you have no idea who that is?"

He shook his head. "I was hoping *you* might know."

Of course she knew. But that in itself sent a new kind of chill coursing through her. *Henry,* she thought, and gazed deep into the madness of Hal and Lucy's all too recent deaths, and the prospect of her own somewhere just ahead. *How could he?* Stupid question. The same way he could have calmly blown away Lucy. To protect himself. Except that in her own case, he had made the mistake of contracting it out.

But all that was academic. The only thing that really mattered at the moment was this gentle, curiously appealing, if somewhat crazy killer sitting beside her.

"I'm an attorney," she said evenly. "I spend my days working with other attorneys. We deal with contracts and points of law. When we have differences, we negotiate or go to court. We don't hire hit men to blow each other away."

"Then I guess somebody just got tired of negotiating and going to court."

She considered him. "So if you were sent to kill me, why are you sitting here holding my hand?"

"Because I don't kill women."

"How gallant. How about children?"

Vittorio was silent.

"You mean it's just a matter of principle that I'm not dead?"

"No. It's gotten to be a lot more than that with you. That's why I've got this little problem."

"What problem?"

"How I'm going to keep us both alive." He grinned and

kissed her hand. "But of course you don't even know what I'm talking about, do you?"

She shook her head, wondering at this strange and beautiful young man who could speak so easily and lightly of death.

"Here's how it works," he told her. "The minute it's known I haven't done my job, someone else gets assigned to kill us both. So we've got to figure something out."

Eyes wide, she was beginning to see a totally alien world opening around her. "You're doing all this just like that?"

"No. Not just like that. I've been thinking about it a long time. I can do more and better than what I've been doing. Then they gave me you, and you were all the reason I needed."

"You don't even know me, Vittorio."

"I know you've got a lower lip that absolutely busts my heart. That's enough to start with."

It was then that he kissed her for the first time.

All very lovely, very romantic, she thought in retrospect. But there was too much fear in her during the days that followed, and too many life-sustaining plans to be worked out, for either of them to concentrate all that much on the yearnings and trappings of new love.

Because Vittorio kept pressing her for a suitable enemy, she finally had to create her big lie about the insider trading group she claimed to have discovered.

What she knew she couldn't hand Vittorio was the truth about Henry Durning. Which had nothing to do with any lingering feeling she might have had left for Henry. That had died with the bitter knowledge that he had coldly written her off. Keeping silent about Henry was strictly for her own survival needs.

With a lawyer's knowledge of such things, she wasn't about to identify herself as a material witness to a brutal double murder she not only never reported to the police, but actually helped cover up in a clear criminal act of obstructing justice.

Quite apart from that, she had no intention of offering Vittorio any hint of her true relationship with Henry Durning.

Too much shame and ugliness lay buried there. In fact, the only reason she ever brought Henry to Vittorio's attention at all was that he inadvertently became part of their plan for her phony death.

Struggling to work out a disappearing act that would hold up under investigation, Vittorio was ecstatic when she happened to mention knowing how to fly and having a pilot's license.

"Jesus, that's it!" he said. "You don't happen to have a plane too, do you?"

"No. But one of the firm's partners does, and he sometimes lets me use it."

"Great. What's his name?"

Even then, she literally had to force herself to say the two words aloud, "Henry Durning."

Vittorio hugged her with excitement. "The guy's our solution. I love him."

Irene didn't.

Nine years later, the sheer irony of it had begun to take on a circular feel. Things did have a way of coming around.

Like fear.

Yet why shouldn't she have been able to feel safe after all these years and a distance of forty-five hundred miles?

Another foolish question.

Because Henry Durning was still alive. Additionally, he was now the United States attorney general, with all the visible and invisible power and limitless reach that came with the territory.

But she, Irene Hopper, was officially dead.

Yes. Yet with a separate sadness and sense of extinction even in that. She had no siblings and both her parents were gone, so who had ever cared enough to mourn her passing? And how much of what she shared with Vittorio was built on, and could survive, the less than happy lies of her past?

As for Vittorio, he'd had to live with his own lie to the anonymous mob *capo* who still believed his loyal soldier had carried out his sworn contract as assigned. Which meant there was danger from there as well.

40

VITTORIO LISTENED IN silence to the weeping woman he loved as Peggy Walters. He had once experimented with LSD, and it had made everything quiver with a lavender light. He experienced much the same sensation now. Like ghosts, emotions passed invisibly through his body, along with the parade of cold facts leading to his son's kidnapping. They left him wet and limp.

Her tale finished, Peggy started to cry again.

"Dear God, look what I've done to us," she wept. "How you must hate me."

She squeezed her eyes shut to hold back the tears, and Vittorio stared dumbly at her. "How could I hate you? Without you, there's nothing. Don't you know that yet?"

"No, I'm disgusting. I've got layers of dirt I can't peel off. I never wanted you to know about Henry and all that filth. But now you know."

Now I know.

Vittorio felt something bleeding inside him. He lifted his wife from the chair, held her, and tried to keep his hands from shaking.

"It's my penance," she whispered. "Maybe if I'd told you sooner, you could have—"

"Stop that. There's no way I could have done anything in advance." He stroked her hair, still soft and silky even with all the years of bleaching. "But I sure as hell can do something now."

Mary Yung lay awake in the same bed where Gianni Garetsky lay sleeping. The bed smelled of dampness, and was too soft, and creaked when she stirred. It felt as old as the house, and the house felt older than the mountains around it.

Yet there was a deep, almost compulsive quiet to the place that she liked. As if that in itself could help still the disquiet inside her.

Enough, she thought.

She had to get out of here as fast as possible. What would be the point of her hanging around at this stage? So she could beat her breast and pour ashes over her head about the boy? She'd already done her bit. She'd already saved their lives and endangered her own by warning Vittorio and his wife about the four torpedoes in the Mercedes. Too bad she couldn't do anything about their son, but you can't have it all ways.

She had her million waiting. The only sensible thing to do now was to pick it up and run while the running was good.

Good-bye, Gianni.

She looked at him as he slept and was curiously moved.

It had been lovely, hadn't it?

Yes.

But hang around one minute too long, she told herself, and you'll end up as full of bullet holes as he, Vittorio, and Peggy. When the United States attorney general and his assorted allies wanted you dead, you were dead. It was just a question of details.

There was nothing more she could do to help them anyway. And if they somehow found out about her and Durning, they'd kill her themselves. And who could blame them?

I'll leave tomorrow.

Yet, something said, *nothing good comes that easy.*

41

VITTORIO WAITED UNTIL their morning coffee was poured and on the table.

"Last night," he said, "I was told who's behind this whole *aborto.*"

With his wife sitting beside him, he spoke directly to Mary Yung and Gianni Garetsky.

Gianni just looked at him.

Mary's face hardened and turned cold.

Peggy sat staring into her coffee.

Outside the kitchen windows, daylight and a misty sun showed off the wild beauty of the mountain landscape. It was wasted. None of them saw it.

"It's the head of our Justice Department," said Vittorio. "Henry Durning. The United States attorney general."

The room was so still it seemed airless.

Gianni was the first to speak.

"Is this some kind of joke?"

"I wish it were."

"I don't understand," said Mary Yung. "There's no phone and you were here all night. Who could have told you?"

"My wife."

Mary and Gianni stared across the table at Peggy. She gave them back nothing.

"I'm afraid it's personal," said Battaglia. "But I wanted the two of you to know while you can still get out of here."

The words hung in the air. It was cool in the old, thick-walled stone house, and the moisture condensed on the windows and dripped onto the floor. A splinter of sun came in and was caught in a spiderweb.

"This changes everything," said Battaglia. "Now it gets to be a lot more than just a crazy mob hit. Now it can be anything from armies of cops, to federal agents, to Interpol, to mafiosi, to Christ only knows what else."

Battaglia slowly lifted and drank his coffee. Then he looked at his wife, and Gianni was offered a glimpse of precisely how bad this was for them. Whatever Peggy had told Vittorio, it obviously had been forced from her by the taking of their son.

"What are you going to do?" Gianni asked Vittorio.

"Get back my boy."

"Do you know who's got him?"

"No. But I'll find out."

"You're that sure?"

Vittorio nodded.

Gianni stuck a cigarette between his lips and lit it. His hands were steady and deliberate. "And you expect me to just walk out of here and leave you with this?"

"Damn right. Unless you've gotten stupid with age."

They stared at each other.

"Listen," said Vittorio. "If those *strunzi* didn't have our boy, Peg and I would be out of here ourselves this minute. Like I said . . . this is personal. It's got nothing to do with you and Mary anymore."

He managed a faint smile. "So just go home and paint. Which is what you do best anyway. I may be jealous as hell, but I'm still proud of all you've done. Fact is, buddy, we need good, live painters a lot more than bad, dead shooters.

"End of discussion."

Mary Yung and Gianni Garetsky arrived at the Naples airport in plenty of time to return the rental car and book space on the noon flight to Rome, and then to New York.

They were having a final drink in the lounge when their flight was called for boarding.

Gianni looked at Mary across the tiny table. "I'm not going," he said.

The lounge was quiet, cool, and dim in the pause between arrivals and departures. Mary Yung glanced slowly around, as though Gianni hadn't spoken.

"Did you hear me?" he said.

"Yes."

"And?"

"And what?" she said. "You didn't ask me a question. You made a statement. Or is there something you're waiting for me to say, other than good-bye?"

Gianni considered her face and wondered whether this would really be his last glimpse of it.

"You sonofabitch," she said flatly. "You never had any intention of going, did you? You just played me all the way, right down to boarding time. What were you so afraid of? That I might not go without you? That I might make a big scene and throw myself around your neck so we could all die here together?"

Mary Yung offered what she thought was her best smile, but it came out a grimace. "Well, you don't have to worry. I don't share your death wish. Or your guilt. Or your need to do penance. I'd much rather get on that plane and live, than stay here and die."

"I don't want to die, Mary. But neither can I just fly off and leave these people with what I've dumped on them."

Mary seemed to be watching herself from an unfamiliar place.

"You've got it all wrong," she said quietly. "You never dumped a thing on them. I was the one who did the dumping."

"What's that supposed to mean?"

"No one followed us here, Gianni. You don't have to spend the rest of your life blaming yourself for that. It was all me. Before we even got to Positano, I called Durning from right here at the airport and told him Vittorio's new name and where he was living."

Gianni didn't believe her at first. Then he saw her eyes and knew better. Besides, who would make up something like that? Who would *want* to? He felt himself struck, then struck again.

"What did they ever do to you?" he said.

"Nothing."

"Then for God's sake! *Why?*"

"An even million in cash."

"Money?"

The disgust in his voice rendered her silent.

"You used me for *that?*" he said.

It took her a long moment. "It wasn't that way. It never had anything to do with you . . . with us."

"Jesus, how could it not?"

"I don't know. It just didn't." Her voice had dropped off to a bare whisper. "It all turned out so much worse than I expected. I mean with their little boy and all."

"What the hell did you think the bastard was paying you a million bucks for?"

"I never thought that far ahead. I obviously didn't want to. Until I saw those four pistols drive into town." She shrugged. "Then it hit me. Then I did what I could."

"It was too late to help the boy."

"I know."

Gianni sat there, gripping his drink with both hands, staring at her. How frightened she looked.

"I was the perfect patsy," he said dully. "I never suspected a thing. You didn't have to tell me now. Why did you?"

"Because I didn't want you staying here to die, thinking it was your fault."

"It's still my fault. I'm the one who got you here. Give me a better reason."

"Because I love you."

"Terrific," he said, and groaned softly. "I'd like to see what you do with those you don't love. No. I take that back. I don't think I could stomach it."

Gianni put down his drink before he shattered the glass. He felt himself that close to it.

"All right," she said, and the words were so soft as to be barely audible. "If you're staying, I'll stay with you."

"Like hell you will."

"I want to, Gianni."

"Why? You think there's a chance for another million in selling out Peg and Vittorio's safe house?"

That one reached her, twisted all the way in, and stayed.

Gianni dropped her plane ticket on the table and rose. "The only place I want you is on this flight."

He left her sitting there and went to get his bag off-loaded.

Then he watched her walk across the tarmac and board the plane. She was the last one on.

He was still watching as the big Boeing roared down the runway, lifted off, and disappeared into the haze.

The thought occurred only then. How had she known it was Durning?

He rented another car and drove past Positano and up into the mountains above Ravello. He found the overgrown trail leading to the safe house and was back there by midafternoon.

No one was in sight and the place was still.

Then Vittorio Battaglia came out from behind some brush and trees and walked slowly toward him. He had a necklace of grenades around his neck and was carrying a submachine gun.

"I didn't recognize the car," he said. "What did you do? Steal it?"

"I haven't hot-wired a car since the last time with you. And that was twenty-one years ago."

"Hey, it's like swimming and fucking. You don't forget."

"How did you know a car was coming? You got something rigged?"

"About a quarter mile down the trail. Photoelectric. Battery powered."

They stood looking at each other.

"Where's Mary?" asked Vittorio.

"Probably just leaving Rome for New York."

"And you?"

"Looks like you're stuck with me."

"Still have to be a fucking hero, don't you?"

Gently, Gianni Garetsky gave him the finger.

They walked up to the house together.

42

PAULIE FIGURED HE'D been there with the two men now for part of yesterday, all of last night, and most of today.

He remembered it being sometime late in the afternoon when the one called Dom came around with that bullshit story about a party, then whacked him out good. Now it was late afternoon again.

In between, he'd slept and had all those crazy dreams. Then he woke up with that bad smell inside him every time he breathed or swallowed, until it finally made him sick and he vomited. He still felt kind of sick, but Tony said that was just from the chloroform they'd given him so he'd stay quiet, and promised he'd feel better soon. Tony wasn't as full of bullshit as Dom, so Paulie believed him. But he still liked

Dom better. Even though it was Dom who whacked him in the head when his back was turned.

Paulie still didn't know what was going on. They kept saying he had nothing to be scared about, that he'd be let go as soon as his father made a business deal with some big shots. But he wasn't sure how much of that to believe. He figured Dom and Tony were a couple of Sicilian mobsters, holding him to make his father do something he didn't want to do. He knew all about that from the movies and TV. He guessed he was what they called a hostage. Either his father did what they wanted, *or else.*

Paulie didn't know where he was. All he saw through the windows were mountains and trees. There was no sea, no road, no other houses, and not a sign of anything he could recognize.

To keep him from trying to run away, they had him on a long chain. One end of the chain was attached to a pair of handcuffs on his ankle. The other end was locked into place around a water pipe. Otherwise, they didn't bother much about him.

There were things that came to him without his knowing how. He saw the way Dom and Tony looked at him and at each other, and understood they didn't like being stuck up here with him any more than he liked being stuck with them.

Time passed. The minutes leaked into hours and hours ran into each other. There were no beginnings or endings. Early in the day, the sun shone into the house and made the walls a pale yellow. Later on, everything got to be duller, cooler, less bright. The boy thought about how he'd paint the light on different walls at different times of day. He wished Dom had brought his paints and brushes along after he'd knocked him out and put him in the car. They'd be nice to have now.

Then, thinking of his paints, he thought about his mother and father, how they'd be worrying about what might have happened to him. When he didn't come home in time for dinner, his father would probably go out looking for him and find all his stuff down there by the water.

What would his father think then? That he'd gone swimming off the rocks like he wasn't supposed to, and drowned? He pictured his father looking for him, calling his name, not finding him, and finally going home with his painting things. He saw his mother and father crying together, and for the first time since all this happened, the boy himself cried.

Worried that one of the men might see him, he quickly dried his eyes. He didn't want them thinking he was a cry-baby. Which made him doubly careful about making sure they didn't see him sucking his thumb.

Sometimes he wandered around as far as his long chain would let him. It made him feel like a dog on a leash. He didn't think he'd like it very much, being a dog.

Other times, he thought about escaping. He decided the first thing was to somehow get hold of one of the keys. There were two of them. One for the handcuffs on his ankle. The other for the lock holding the chain to the water pipe. Tony kept both keys in his pants pocket. The boy wished Dom had the keys instead. Or at least kept one of them. Dom was always drinking wine or beer and taking naps on the couch. So there might be a chance of a key falling out of his pocket, or something.

Once, he tried sitting down next to Dom on the couch to see how it would be. His skin gave off a lot of heat and it felt warm being so close. He could tell Dom liked him. He guessed it was because he reminded him of his little brother before the truck rolled over him. Dom liked to muss his hair, and give him these little shoves, and put up his fists like he wanted to fight him. "This is some tough kid," he'd say to Tony. "He don't take no shit from nobody. Took some real hard whacks with a billy to put him out. That's the kind of tough head he's got. Watch him, Tony. Come on, kid. Hit me. Hard as you like. Give me a good one right here on the jaw."

The boy would swing at him then. With all his might. But somehow no jaw was there when his fist got to it, and Dom would laugh. Tony never laughed. He just shook his head and rolled his eyes like Dom was crazy.

Both men had guns.

They wore them in belt holsters and never took them off. When Paulie thought about escaping, his best plan was to grab Dom's gun while he was dozing on the couch. Then he'd aim it at Tony and ask for the keys. If Tony didn't hand them over, he'd shoot him and take them. He'd never shot anybody in his life, but he didn't think he'd mind too much having to shoot Tony. The boy didn't know about Dom. He didn't think he'd like having to shoot Domenico. But if he had to, he guessed he could do it.

Didn't Dom himself say he was some tough kid?

Lots of kids got killed. He kept seeing it on the TV news and in the papers. And it wasn't just a lot of make-believe stuff like in the movies. The news didn't fool around. They showed it like it was, with all these little kids getting blown up by terrorist bombs, and crashing in cars and airplanes, and getting shot, stabbed, and beaten to death by all kinds of creeps.

Paulie hoped Dom and Tony weren't going to have to kill him. But if they did, he wondered which of them would do it and if it would hurt. He'd once seen a dead little boy lying by the side of a road after an accident. The kid lay there all bloody, and Paulie had never forgotten it.

He imagined himself lying on the floor the same way, and the thought of it made him wish things.

It made him wish he'd painted more pictures.

And given his mother and father more hugs.

And looked at more of those big, white, puffy summer clouds.

And eaten more ice cream.

And been more able to stop sucking his thumb.

43

To be able to appreciate and be amused by the mixed blessings of irony had to rank high among life's more underrated gifts.

So thought Henry Durning as he sat listening to himself being eulogized as that year's recipient of the Washington Press Corps Honor in Government Award, a distinct and almost instant outgrowth of his peaceful solution to the Olympian standoff.

The citation itself, being read now to a large and distinguished black-tie audience, was intended to embody and convey the full spirit of the award.

"Attorney General Henry Durning reminds us all," said the speaker, "by his personal example both in and out of office, of our moral obligation to confront those tragedies of the human condition that continue to haunt the world in good times as well as bad.

"All who have enjoyed even the briefest association with this man feel as if they have had a glimpse of greatness in the guise of justice and compassion."

A standing ovation followed the reading. The ovation went on and on and on, while Henry Durning sat there on the dais, eyes suddenly brimming and no longer amused, and felt himself losing what remained of what he had always been pleased to consider his mind.

It was close to midnight and he was riding home in the back of his official limousine.

The sound, the sight, the full heart-stopping emotion of the ovation rode with him. It was impossible to lose. The fact was, Durning didn't want to lose it. He felt it as a core moment in the days and years of his life ... beyond irony, beyond not caring, beyond even the easy, knee-jerk cynicism of his usual defenses.

It was prima facie evidence of his contribution, of the always reassuring fact that he was something more than the poor, less-than-admirable creature he was increasingly discovering himself to be. And it couldn't have come at a better time. Other than for this, it had not been his greatest day.

None of the news from Italy was good. Another brief meeting with Don Donatti had established the fact that Irene and Vittorio—and the two men who had been sent to take care of them—were still among the missing and had contacted no one about their son.

The single positive piece of information from Donatti was that John Hinkey and the Beekman woman had been taken care of. That problem was over.

But even this had its negative side when Brian Wayne reacted to the news with more than his usual panic.

"You had them *killed?*"

Durning had looked into the FBI director's eyes, heard the shrill pitch of his voice, and poured him a generous shot of bourbon.

"What did you expect?"

"I don't know. But Christ! Not this!"

"They were about to blow everything wide open, Brian. How would you have handled it?"

"I'm no murderer."

"And I *am?*" Durning had asked.

"I don't know how much more of this I can take," said the FBI director.

Durning had looked hard at his friend's eyes. Clearly, not too much more.

That had been this morning, and the attorney general had neither seen nor spoken to him since. Wayne and his wife were supposed to have been at tonight's award dinner. But Marcy had called to say that her husband had come down with a touch of something and wouldn't be able to make it.

Durning had a fair idea what the "touch of something" was. He even knew its name. It was called fear.

Not good.

Poor Brian. He's definitely not made for this. But then, who is?

I am.

He must have dozed off.

When he glanced out the car window, they were almost in the area of Georgetown where he lived. The streets glistened and he opened a window and felt a mist of rain on his face. He breathed deeply and the air smelled sour going into his lungs. Was it an omen? Was there suddenly something out of place in the heavens that was following him?

He sometimes had such presentiments. Not that he really believed in this kind of voodoo. If he had a problem in this realm, it was in not believing in anything outside of his own sight, sound, touch, and mortal limitations. Which automatically cut him off from both God and the devil, and this in itself left him pretty lonely. Where did that leave him to go for comfort?

They pulled up in front of his house, and the chauffeur opened the door for him.

"What time in the morning, Mr. Durning?"

"The usual."

Tommy saw the award plaque in the attorney general's hand.

"Congratulations, Sir. I heard the presentation. I've listened to a lot of them over the years and they're mostly bullshit. But not yours. Every word they said was true. I feel honored to be working for you."

"Thank you, Tommy. I appreciate that."

Durning stood in the drizzle as the limousine drove off.

He didn't see the other car until he turned and started up the brick walk to his house. The car was parked about fifty yards down the block, and he probably wouldn't have noticed it at all if the door hadn't opened at that moment, putting on the interior lights.

A woman got out and started toward him through the mist. She was slender, almost wraithlike, and she moved with a certain grace. Watching her approach, Durning had the sense he had seen her before.

Then she passed beneath a streetlight, and for a brief moment he was almost sure he had seen Mary Yung's face.

I'm twice mad, he thought, and everything he had felt and fantasized about her all these past days was suddenly packed so solidly inside his chest that it was hard to breathe.

She stopped three feet away and they stood staring at each other.

"It *is* you," he said.

Mary Yung nodded, not quite ready to trust her voice. She had an automatic aimed at him through her jacket pocket, because you never knew about these things and she had tried to come prepared. What she wasn't prepared for was his sheer physical presence. He was imposing. Yet it was more than just that. She could feel him prowling around inside her.

"What I was most afraid of," he said, "was that you'd be dead before I ever got to see you."

Then he took her into his house before she could disappear as suddenly as she had arrived.

He wore the comfortable elegance of his house like a second dinner suit, she thought. It fit him in a way that no house she had ever been in could fit her. Unless it was a grass hut.

The study was Durning's favorite room, so this was where he sat her. Even so, he felt himself moving trancelike through an alien landscape.

"Would you like to take off your jacket?" he asked.

She shook her head. "I'm all right."

"I just want you to be comfortable. You can hold your gun in your lap, if you like. Or put it in your purse."

Mary Yung was able to smile. "Have you ever in your life been caught off balance?"

"It's happened to me twice tonight."

"I can't imagine it."

He handed her his plaque, which he had not yet put down. "The first time was when I was given a standing ovation."

She read the inscription. "Very impressive. But why should that fluster you?"

"Because we both know I'm a lot less than those words make me out to be."

"And when was the second time?"

"When I saw your face under that streetlight, and was affected as I've rarely been in my life."

"But you don't even *know* me."

"I know you, Mary."

With that, Durning opened a closet, took out a carton, and placed it on the coffee table in front of her.

"What's this?" she asked.

"You. Your file."

She sat staring at a bunch of folders, photographs, magazine tear sheets, and videocassettes.

"Just look through them," he told her. "Please."

"Why?"

"So you'll understand certain things. So that we can go on from there."

Mary Yung gazed into Durning's eyes and saw herself reflected there. What a curious man.

Then choosing a photograph at random, she saw herself again. Except that this time she was naked, and in the company of two equally naked men.

She looked to be no more than seventeen, although the men were older. They were no one she recognized or remembered. All things considered, how could she? Caught by the camera at a moment of less-than-classic drama, she was frozen forever in an act of fellatio with one man while being sodomized by the other. It was all very concentrated, very joyless, an act of intimacy in which no one was intimate. Each was alone. If she were to choose a title for the picture, Mary Yung would have called it *Solitude*.

She felt some mild, initial surprise, then nothing. If the distinguished attorney general was watching her face, hoping for fireworks, he would be disappointed.

Mary never glanced up to find out. Instead, she quickly and quietly went through the entire carton: she was vaguely amused by the diligence of the FBI Background Checks and Research Department, and the official comments that were sprinkled in along the way. As though from the age of six on, she and her pathetic little sexual fumblings had constituted a continuing, insidious threat to the internal security of the country.

When she was finished, Durning poured some brandy into two large snifters and handed her one.

"Why did you go to all this trouble?" she asked.

"So I'd know you."

"And do you?"

"As I know myself."

"Meaning what?" she said.

"That there's probably nothing either one of us wouldn't do to survive."

"Is that a compliment or an indictment?"

"A compliment for you. An indictment for me."

"Why the difference?"

"Because you started naked, abused, and alone. I started with everything."

They sipped brandy and considered each other. There were no sounds. The night and the drizzle closed them in.

"As I mentioned before," he said, "I was just afraid you'd die in Positano and never come to me. Then I'd have been truly bereft."

Mary Yung shook her head. "You sound absolutely crazy, Mr. Durning. Women must go wild about you."

"Women, per se, no longer interest me."

"What does interest you?"

A distinctive fragrance was in the air around her. It teased the edges of his thoughts, just beyond his reach.

"*You* interest me," he said. "Or haven't I made that clear enough?"

They sat silent and unmoving for half a minute.

"From your pictures alone," Durning said quietly, "I've been fantasizing about you like a tumescent schoolboy. I want you more at this moment than I've ever wanted any woman. And you obviously want something equally strongly from me, or you wouldn't have come rushing here straight from Positano."

Elbows on knees, he leaned toward her over his brandy. "Tell me, Mary Yung. Exactly what is it you want from me?"

"The boy."

It came out as quickly and easily as that.

"Are you so great a lover of children?"

"No."

"Then why is this child so important to you?"

"Because I was the one who did this to him."

"You mean you still have it in you to suffer remorse?"

"Yes," she said. "Don't you?"

Durning slowly nodded. "If I believed in God, I'd say, thank God!" He smiled. "As it is, I have only myself to thank."

"Why is remorse so important to you?"

"It's the one thing that separates us from the apes."

He got the brandy and added to their drinks.

"Please understand," he said, "I had nothing to do with the taking of the boy. I didn't even know about it until it was done."

"Fine. You're a great human being. Now set him free before your Italians bury him."

"It's out of my hands."

"Nothing is out of your hands."

"I've overly impressed you. I do have my limitations."

The air in the room suddenly seemed to be getting tired, used up. Mary Yung sat staring at the walls of books, at the signed photos of the attorney general with the great and near-great. The man had reach. She wanted so badly to get this whole thing right.

"Would you at least be willing to try?" she asked.

Durning was silent. He felt as though he wanted something that didn't have a name. He seemed to see her in separate sections . . . hair, eyes, nose, lips, the curve of a cheek. And they were real, three-dimensional, not parts of a paper photograph.

"I've never asked for a handout in my life," Mary Yung said. "And I'm not asking for one now. I'll pay my way."

"I don't care about the boy," said Durning. "It's his parents I need. Can you give them to me? You never fully came through as promised, you know. In fact it was you who warned them about the Sicilians, wasn't it?"

"I don't know where they are."

He didn't believe her.

"You said before that you wanted me," she told him. "Or was that just talk?"

He stared at her eyes, two black marbles in the pale oval of her face. When she lit a cigarette, they glowed with exhaustion in the flare of the match. When had she last slept?

"It wasn't just talk," he said.

"All right."

His mouth was suddenly dry. The brandy didn't help.

"I can't promise you anything," he said. "You know that, don't you?"

"I know."

"Will you stay here with me?"

"Is that what you want?"

"Yes."

"For how long?"

"I have no idea."

She shrugged. "Why not?"

He knew her thinking, of course. All she felt she needed

was enough time with him. Her confidence alone was exquisite. In its particular way, inspiring. For his own needs, whatever they were or turned out to be, it couldn't have been better. Durning assumed she felt the same way.

As long as they understood each other.

Their deal, like the surrogate marriage contract it resembled, was consummated in bed an hour later. And like the best of such arrangements, both parties believed they had gained the advantage.

Maybe they both had, thought the attorney general.

To him, it was an emotional rite of passage, a knowing, burning, drowning experience . . . a trip to a sensual Holy Land, with him as the barefoot pilgrim, and Mary Yung as his priest and guide.

And this time it was no fantasy. Yet even alive, even right there with him, her face and body had about them something shadowy and elusive, something prematurely aged or still so young they were not yet fully formed. This smoky creature. She made him weightless. He floated free, knees and body vibrating. Touching her, his hands felt so magical they threatened to fly off at the wrists.

She had brought her life with her. On the open grounds of his king-size bed, in the half-darkness of his room, they had company. She was breathing an endless parade of her erotic pictures into his brain, all those full color glossies of multiple couplings, all that rosy flesh and those romping bodies.

Mary Yung's army.

I have them all, he thought.

Mary Yung was thinking something else.

She had made her plan, put it into action, and was carrying it out as simply a job that had to be done.

It was no more to her than that.

Something she had always been able to do. Most women couldn't. But she wasn't most women. She had her own secret place, and once in it, she couldn't be touched. It was never that hard for her. The flesh, the body cover, didn't matter all that much. It was just a protective shell for the important stuff beneath. Nothing sacred lived on top.

People were only locked rooms to each other, anyway. Even if you heard someone crying in one of them, you couldn't get in to help. That was the saddest thing of all. The body was just a toy, a plaything. Except that she'd never really had that much chance to enjoy it. It had to be her work tool too early. A very serious thing, very serious flesh. Whatever she'd wanted or needed, her very serious flesh had helped her get. It didn't matter what men did to it, or it did to men. It was all mechanics. Maybe it was getting to be something more with Gianni, but she'd sure messed that one up good. Now he wouldn't even spit on the best part of her, and so much for that.

What the hell. At this point she just wanted to get the boy out of there in one piece, and Durning was the guy who could do it. The *sonofabitch*. Imagine him so hooked on her and her shit life. As if she'd done something wonderful and holy.

Fucking and sucking.

Jesus, look at the sonofabitch go. The attorney general of the whole United States and she was playing him like a hooked fish.

She could feel him starting his final run, sense it coming from the farthest parts of him.

Then he broke the surface and she heard him scream, heard him cry out as though he were dying. And she screamed and cried out with him because that was what they always loved and wanted, along with all the lies that came after.

Enjoy it, she told him deep inside her. *Enjoy it while you can. Because if you don't get me that boy and something happens to him, I swear on the holiness of this less-than-sacred act that I'm going to blow your fucking head off.*

44

THE WORST OF it for Vittorio was having to leave Peggy behind and alone. He had stalled the going, but he had finally run out of reasons and Gianni was waiting in the car.

For the past half hour of preparations Peg had been on the edge of something, the wide eyes growing wider and darker, the small mouth stretching flat. A confused hurt had slipped over the smoothness of face like a net. Through it, Vittorio felt her anguish.

"It'll be all right," he assured her for the third time. Or was it the fourth?

Peggy nodded mechanically, not believing a word.

"They won't hurt him. He's their only hope of reaching us. *We're* what Durning wants, not Paulie."

"No," she said. "*I'm* what he wants. *I'm* the only material witness against him. You're just another innocent bystander. Like my poor baby."

Tears welled, clung to her lids, and Vittorio pressed her to him. How thin she felt, how frail. When had she gotten so breakable?

"Listen to me," he said. "We've lived together ten years. Right?"

She nodded.

"Have I ever lied to you?"

"No."

"And I'm not lying now. I swear it, Peg. I'll bring Paulie home to you."

She drew back and nailed him with her eyes. "When?"

It was a child's question. *When, daddy?*

"I don't know. Just finding out where they've got him could take days. So don't sit watching the clock and worrying."

She shook herself out of it. "I'm sorry. I know I've only been making this harder for you."

Peggy kissed him and forced a smile.

"I'll be fine," she said.

Sadly, Vittorio didn't think so.

Vittorio and Gianni left the safe house at about 6:00 P.M. They went in Gianni's rental car because it was unidentifiable. But it was Vittorio who drove.

They rode in two separate silences for almost half an hour before Gianni finally spoke.

"How are we figuring this?"

"There's not all that much to figure," said Battaglia. "We start with the names of the two pistols we sent over the cliff, find out who sent them, then keep a gun up his ass until he tells us where Paulie is."

"Just like that?"

Vittorio watched the road as a big tourist bus crowded them uncomfortably close to a wall of solid rock.

He shrugged. "That's the core stuff. The rest is detail."

"I like detail."

"You've got a right. It's the detail that can end up killing you. Or did you think this was going to be a piece of cake?"

"I've learned something in the twenty years since you saw me. Nothing's a piece of cake."

Vittorio groped out a cigarette and lit it with the dashboard lighter. The orange glow reflected on his face.

"There's this old man in Naples who owes me a few big ones," he said. "He knows every *famiglia* in the area, and what he doesn't know he'll find out. So we go there first."

"You mean the United States attorney general has Neapolitan mafiosi in his back pocket?"

The car was quiet.

"A little background," said Battaglia. "I first met Peggy almost ten years ago when Don Donatti sent me to kill her. It seems clear now that it was Durning who took out the contract for the hit. But I'm sure it's the don who's got the long reach."

Battaglia glanced at Gianni and saw his confusion. *What the hell,* he thought. The guy'd been dragged into this only because they'd been friends. Didn't he at least deserve to know what he might be dying for?

"You'd better hear the rest," he said, and went into it as he drove.

Vittorio told the full story, and just the fact of putting it into words and sharing it with someone brought a measure of comfort. Then carried away by the further euphoria of the confessional, he threw in his covert government work as well. Something that not even Peg knew for certain.

"Now you have it all," he said. "Or have I just confused you more?"

Gianni felt the full weight of the tale pressing him. *While I've been painting my pictures.*

"You haven't confused me," he said. "You've just made me see the kind of self-absorbed, make-believe life I've been living all these years."

Vittorio came up on a slow-moving truck, hit the horn, swung out of lane, and passed it.

"You're not complaining, are you?"

Gianni was silent.

"For Christ's sake!" said Battaglia. "You've done it all. Everything we ever used to dream about and more. While I've been swimming in blood and crawling through shit."

"I'd change with you in a minute."

"You're out of your skull. Where the hell do you think I'm goddamn sitting?"

"I know the kind of trouble your family's in. And it's awful. But at least you've got a family."

Vittorio looked at Gianni's face. He glimpsed what crossed it and disappeared.

"I read about your wife," he said. "I'm sorry."

Gianni nodded. At that moment Teresa and all his years with her suddenly seemed very far away. It almost panicked him. Then he put things in place.

The car stayed quiet for a while. It was nearly dark, with the last of the light turning the distant sea red.

"Listen," said Vittorio Battaglia. "I talk big about getting my boy back, but it's just talk. I'm so scared I could puke. They're going to keep him just so long. Then that's it. Past a certain point, he's too dangerous to hold."

Gianni remembered enough from the old days to know it was true. No matter what anyone wanted, sometimes you got into things and there was no way to get out.

Battaglia sighed. "You know how I keep my lid on? I'll tell you my secret. I just think about what I'll do if the sonsofbitches kill my Paulie. In my mind I do them one at a time, and nice and slow. First I do Henry Durning, then Carlo Donatti, then everybody over here who had anything at all to do with it. And that's how I keep from screaming and beating my fucking head against the wall."

For a long time they rode in silence.

"I'm glad you're with me," said Vittorio. "I can still talk to you like to nobody else. Peg is my life, but some things I could never say to her. Stuff she couldn't take, or understand, or might sit in judgment on. Know what I mean?"

They were in the center of Naples by 8:30 P.M.

Vittorio stopped at a gas station, left the car, and made a phone call. He was back in five minutes.

"Our man is home," he said. "He'll have the apartment clear and be alone by the time we get there."

They headed north on the Via Santa Rosa.

"Who does he think you are?" asked Gianni.

"An Italian-American businessman with good connections."

"And I?"

"A close friend. Anonymous. It's all right. He knows better than to ask questions."

"You said he owed you. What did you do for him?"

"Save his life. Also, his wife's."

"What do I call him?"

"Nothing. You won't be introduced."

Vittorio parked on a poorly lighted street three blocks west of the Via Santa Rosa. They crossed a cobbled courtyard, entered a building lobby, and rode up three flights in a highly polished brass elevator. Vittorio knocked three times on the door of apartment 4B, and they stood waiting.

Gianni heard slow, halting steps and the tap of a cane. Then the door was opened by an elderly, gray-haired man with the bearing of an Italian general out of central casting.

"Come in, come in. I'm honored."

He had a husky smoker's voice and a cigarette between his teeth. He embraced Vittorio, shook Gianni's hand, and led them into a large, high-ceilinged room crammed with heavy furniture and dark oil paintings. As Vittorio had promised, no introductions were made and no names were mentioned.

The old man seated them around an elaborately carved coffee table and filled three glasses with red wine. He made a small ceremony of it. The aromas of that night's dinner still hung in the air.

They all sipped the wine and put down their glasses. It was only then that Vittorio Battaglia spoke.

"I need your help, my friend," he said. "I have one child. A young boy. I'm sorry to say that yesterday he was taken from me."

The old man had a high forehead that was knotted by veins. Gianni saw one of them begin to pulse.

"He was *taken?*" said the man.

"Abducted. Kidnapped."

"Ah. By whom?"

"I don't know." Battaglia paused to light a cigarette. "Four men, strangers, were seen coming into Positano in separate cars. One behind the other. Two of the men took my boy, who was alone by the water, and disappeared. The others came to my house to do away with my wife and me. But with the help of my friend here, they were killed instead."

The old man slowly nodded. "And ended up at the bottom of a cliff not far from Ravello?"

"Then they've found them?"

"It was on tonight's news. There was no identification yet. The explosion and fire didn't leave much to identify."

"I took their wallets," said Vittorio. "Their names were Sal Ferrisi and Frank Bonotara."

The old man was silent.

"Do you know them?" asked Vittorio.

The old man looked at the two men facing him, suddenly dreading having them in his home. Gianni Garetsky understood his fear, along with the reasoning behind it. Just their presence here could kill him.

"I've never met them," he said.

"But you've heard of them? You know who they are?"

The old man nodded and cigarette ash dropped on the front of his shirt. He didn't seem to notice.

"They're local mafiosi?"

"Not so local."

"How far away?"

The old man drank some wine. His eyes were off somewhere and he appeared not to have heard the questions.

"How far away?" Vittorio asked again.

"Sicily."

"Where in Sicily?"

The old man's face went slack. He sat diminished in his chair, no longer looking quite so militarylike. He stared appealingly at Battaglia, but Vittorio's face was cut stone. Watching the man's silent struggle, Gianni found himself almost feeling sorry for him.

"Palermo." The answer was little more than a hoarse whisper.

"Who did they work for?" asked Vittorio. "Who would have sent them on a hit like this?"

"You know what you're asking me?"

Vittorio didn't answer.

A fly buzzed around the room and the old man's eyes followed it hopelessly. He seemed to be growing more inert by the second. Then something took hold in him, and Gianni saw it as an image of a man reconstituting himself out of sheer will.

"I'm in your debt," he said. "But what you're doing is pointing a loaded gun at my head and asking me to squeeze the trigger."

"No one saw us come in here. No one will see us leave. And no one will ever know who told us."

"Unless they got one of you alive. Then they'll know soon enough."

"That's not part of our plan."

"Men plan and God laughs," said the old man.

Vittorio stared long and hard at him. It seemed to Gianni that for a full minute there was no sound anywhere in the room, in the building, or in the city of Naples.

"You're embarrassing me," Vittorio finally said.

The old man reached for his wine. But when he picked up the glass, his hand was shaking so badly that he had to put it down without drinking.

"But even worse," said Vittorio quietly, "you're shaming yourself. Which you're too good a man to be doing."

The old man tried to swallow but couldn't scrape together enough saliva.

"How old are you?" Vittorio asked.

The man looked startled. "I'm seventy-nine."

"My son isn't even *nine.*"

The old man stared out of his age and frailty. "And that makes his life more valuable than mine? You think being old makes me ready to be thrown out with the garbage?"

Everyone understood that Battaglia had said the absolute wrong thing. It lay in the room like a long dead rat, numbing the air and the three men breathing it.

"I'm sorry," said Battaglia. "I apologize." He gestured tiredly. "I'm getting desperate. It's making me cruel and stupid. I didn't mean that."

"Yes, you did," said the man. "You were just being honest. And who can blame you? You love your son and you'd happily sell ten old farts like me to save him." He sighed. "One of the things about getting old. Instead of making you smarter, it makes you more afraid. It's crazy. The less you've got left to lose, the more worried you get about losing it. And you were right about my shaming myself. A few years ago I'd never have behaved in such a disgusting way."

He made a small bow with his head. "It's I who apologize to you."

This time he was able to drink his wine. Gianni looked at his hand. It was an old hand with sunken, spotted skin, and every bone was visible. But it suddenly seemed strong.

"So much for that poor misery," said the old man. "The boss you're looking for, the one who sent those men, is Don Pietro Ravenelli. He lives in a big house about ten kilometers west of Palermo, off the coast road to Punta Raisi. I wish you and your boy luck. I'm glad I'm seventy-nine and not nine. Who wants to go through it all again?"

They were back in the car and driving out of Naples.

"I'm not what I used to be," said Battaglia flatly. "And I just hope we don't end up paying for it."

Gianni looked at him. "What are you talking about?"

"If I was smart, I'd have pumped one into his head before we left."

"Why? He gave you what you wanted."

"Yeah. But there's still a better-then-even chance he'll call Ravenelli just to cover his ass."

45

HENRY DURNING WOKE in the soft dawn light, looked at the sleeping face of Mary Yung on the pillow beside him, and smiled. Then it hadn't been just another improbable, wildly erotic dream.

She sleeps, he thought, *with the total innocence of the young, the pure, and the dead.*

Here in my bed.

The telephone rang on the table beside him. It set off a forest of jangled nerves. No one ever called with anything good at 6:10 A.M. Then he remembered it was six hours later in Italy and picked up the receiver.

"Hank!" said Brian Wayne's voice.

"What's wrong?"

"Tune in. Fast. Neal Hinkey is coming on in a minute."

Durning felt Mary Yung stirring awake beside him. "Who the hell is Neal Hinkey?" he said.

"John Hinkey's son. He evidently works for his father. I don't like the whole smell of this, Hank. I'll call you when it's over."

The FBI director hung up.

Durning hit the remote for his bedroom television. Then he kissed Mary's cheek.

"Good morning," he said. "You even sleep beautiful. And that's something hardly anyone ever does."

The screen came alive in a wall unit, and Durning saw a thin, nervous-looking young man sitting with the CNN commentator.

"Do you always start your day with the box?" Mary Yung asked.

"No. I hate the thing. But there's something coming on I have to see."

Then the attorney general turned up the volume as the interview began. Although it quickly became apparent that this was not going to be the standard question-and-answer interview format, but something more like a breaking news item in the form of a prepared statement.

What the commentator did was introduce his guest as Neal Hinkey, a son and law associate of John Hinkey, the nationally known Washington attorney. He had an announcement to make that could have grave implications.

Hearing no more than that, Durning knew instantly just how bad it was going to be. And knowing it, he accepted it. For now, at least, what else could he do?

Hinkey spoke in a young voice stretched thin with emotion. He was here this morning, he told a network audience of millions, because his father and a woman who was a client as well as a close friend had been missing for close to three days and had to be presumed dead.

The young man's voice broke on the word *dead,* and he took a moment to compose himself.

When he continued, he explained that his father had left instructions as to what he should do if anything happened to him, and that he was simply following those instructions now. He said that by appearing on national television this morning, he was hoping to make the facts in the case known before they were buried by the same tainted power structure that had buried his father and his female client.

Then Hinkey went into the specifics.

The mysterious disappearance of five FBI agents, the discovery of the three bodies, the futile efforts of Mrs. Beekman to learn what had happened to her husband, the stonewalling by the Bureau were all laid down block by block until they formed their own wall of indictment. And when each of the missing agents was discovered to have been on special-duty assignment to the FBI director himself, there was no denying the smell of something rotten.

Durning glanced at Mary Yung and found her watching

his face. Their eyes met and held, and there suddenly seemed little that each didn't know about the other.

Hinkey was still going on with his injustice recital, but they were no longer paying attention.

"I guess it's going to get a little sticky for you now, isn't it?" she said.

Durning took her hand and could almost feel some of her serenity flow through to him. Yet how many of those three dead agents sent to question her had she killed herself? No matter. They would have buried her if she hadn't. But what he liked most was that she showed no visible pleasure in the turn of events against him. If anything, she seemed warmer, more gentle. Lord, this one did carry grace. Even with her loaded gun.

"Very sticky," he told her.

"Will you be able to handle it?"

"I'll certainly try."

"You have a lot to lose."

"No more than anyone else." He shrugged. "We all leave the same way. Naked and alone."

Durning put on a robe and excused himself. He wanted to call Brian Wayne from the safe phone in his downstairs study before his friend got back to him up here.

Marcy answered on the third ring. She obviously was crying.

"I don't understand," she wept. "He's your oldest and dearest friend. How could you have done this to him?"

Her apparent knowledge of it was his second shock of the morning. But he still needed to be sure.

"How could I have done *what* to him?" he asked.

"Whatever he did, he did for you. Now you've ruined him with your selfishness. Ruined him." She dissolved in sobs.

"No one is ruined. There are ways to contain this. Just get hold of yourself, Marcy. Brian needs support, not hysterics. Now let me speak to him, please."

It was several moments before the FBI director came on. "Sorry about Marcy," he said. "She—"

Durning cut him off. "When did you tell her about my part in all this?"

"I don't know," Wayne said dully. "But she'll quiet down. You don't have to worry."

"I'm not worried. We're stamping out this fire before it starts. I know exactly how to handle this." Durning paused. "How do you feel?"

"I had a couple of bad minutes, but I'm OK."

"Good. Now listen carefully. We're going down to your place on the shore. Marcy, too. I want us all incommunicado until we've talked and gotten everything straight. Just make one call to your secretary. Tell her you'll be at Cove Point for the day and to cancel all appointments. And make sure she tells no one else. The last thing we need is the whole Washington press corps streaming down there after us. And for God's sake, muzzle Marcy and keep her away from the phone! You with me?"

"Yeah."

"Then I'll see you down at the point in about two hours. Everything's going to be fine, Brian. Drive carefully."

The attorney general hung up and made two brief calls. One, to his secretary to cancel the day's appointments. The other, to Tommy, to say he wouldn't be using the limousine.

Upstairs, Mary Yung was in the stall shower. Durning took off his robe, quietly opened the door, and joined her.

Had flesh ever promised so much?

Yet it wasn't only that. He was aroused before he entered the shower and touched. The tension, the fear, the excitement of the past half-hour had all added to it in advance.

Still a crisis junkie.

The things it took to get him started. And now here she was to finish it, with the warmth of the misty spray, and the soft, slipping, sliding of her lips and hands, and his own hands on the two perfect spheres of her bottom to lift and enter her right there, seeing her eyes with their yellow rims where he could see himself reflected.

Then he held and moved with her across spaces crowded by the bodies of five dead agents, and the murdered widow of one of the agents, and the equally wasted lawyer of the widow, and the sudden living presence of the lawyer's son, who was even now blowing everything to hell.

Durning felt sensations pulsing through her. He felt her moved by things far beyond him, of which he was less than a vagrant thought, just someone to be used by her. As he was using her. As they were using each other.

Wide-eyed, clearly startled, she touched his cheeks. "Why are you crying?"

"Why are you?"

"Because people are horrible. And we're two of the worst."

"Maybe we can get better," he said.

"Wouldn't that be lovely." She stared at him. "Why don't we start by saving that little boy?"

Henry Durning took every shortcut he knew. Also, he drove fast, but not so fast as to risk being stopped for speeding. He didn't want any involvement with the police on this trip.

And much of the way, when his thoughts should have been focused on what lay immediately ahead, he was thinking of Mary Yung.

He had given her a house key before he left.

"This is yours," he told her. "And so is the house and everything in it."

"For how long?"

"For as long as you want it."

"You're a very generous man."

"No. I'm a very selfish man. All I can think of around you are my own needs, everything I want most."

"Just like the rest of us."

Durning made it to the Waynes' shore house overlooking Chesapeake Bay in exactly an hour and seventeen minutes. He had been coming here for so many years that the place felt like his own.

Marcy and Brian were not there yet, and he hadn't expected them to be. At best, Marcy was notoriously late, and today she had good reason to be even later.

Durning parked in the gravel driveway and glanced around. The house itself was modest, but it had been in Brian's family for four generations, and the hundred acres it stood on were now worth millions. So it had the kind of privacy that was impossible to find these days at the shore, with no other houses anywhere in sight, and a view of the bay for which developers would happily sell their souls.

The attorney general found the key in its usual place under a rock beside the front lamppost. Then he opened the door and went inside.

The gun cabinet was in the den. Its key hung from a nail in the wall behind it. Durning took out a 12-gauge, double-barreled shotgun. It was well oiled and cleaned. Brian had always taken meticulous care of his guns. In the army, he used to call his carbine his best friend. Durning broke the shotgun open, closed it, then broke it open again.

The ammunition was kept in a drawer next to the broom closet, and Durning found a box of 12-gauge shells. He slid two of the shells into the shotgun's chambers and closed the breech. Then he put back the box, brought the gun into a downstairs bedroom off the kitchen, and put it behind some clothes in one of the closets.

He stood there for a while listening to the hum of the refrigerator, and the engines of a plane passing overhead, and the sound of crows in some nearby trees.

Well, he thought, and wondered how it had ever come down to this. Not that he really had to wonder. He knew. It was just one thing leading to another, getting you in deeper and deeper until it seemed the more you struggled, the further you sank.

But that was some John Hinkey. Who would have expected that whole piece of business with his son? Who even knew he *had* a son?

But that was enough to do it, all right. And it was easy enough to see the whole progression from there ... with the appointment of a special prosecutor, and the media sideshow that would follow, and Brian inevitably splitting apart at the seams, making a full confession, and throwing him to the wolves as he turned state's evidence.

So what options do I have other than this?

Blow my own brains out? Quietly waste away in prison?

Which in a practical sense meant no options at all. Maybe for others but not for him. Never for him. He had firmly established that part of his nature ten years ago, when he had chosen to cover an accidental killing with his first deliberate one. That was the *biggie* right there. That was the one that programmed him for everything that followed. After that, it was just a matter of hitting the right buttons.

As the bodies kept piling up.

And with this thought, the sickness hit him. Sudden and unexpected. One moment he was standing in quiet contemplation. The next, he was puking his guts into the kitchen sink. He had never known such a sickening. It was as if whatever good had been left in him after all these years was leaving. It was a dissolution, a final revolt of the cells. Only instinct was left to hold him together.

Then the moment passed and he put his face under the faucet and washed himself clean.

Durning was sipping scotch and listening to a Chopin étude in the living room when he saw the Buick enter the driveway and pull up in front of the house.

He watched through the window as they got out of the car. Marcy was talking nonstop while dabbing at her eyes with a handkerchief. Brian just stared off somewhere.

Durning rose to greet them as they came in. He kissed Marcy on the cheek, embraced his friend, and handed them each a perfectly chilled martini.

It was their house but he had taken over as host. Then wasting no more time on amenities, he moved right into it.

"The worst of it was the initial shock," Durning said, "and that's over."

He spoke to Wayne. "Did you know Hinkey had a son working for him?"

The FBI director shook his head. "I met him only that one time in my office, and he never mentioned it."

Marcy was crying again. "What would you have done if Brian had known?" she asked Durning. "Had the man's son murdered, too? And what about other possible law associates and partners? Or would you have just planned on putting a bomb in their offices and getting them all at once?"

Durning looked at Brian Wayne. "What else did you tell her?"

Wayne sipped his martini and didn't answer.

"I only wish to God he'd told me more," said his wife. "I'd have screamed so loud none of these disasters would have happened." She bit her lip to stop its trembling. "Friendship! The next time I hear that word I swear I'll spit."

For the first time Wayne met Durning's eyes and something passed between them, something they both understood and Wayne's wife never would.

"Marcy, please," said the FBI director. "What's done is done. We're not here for recriminations."

"Like hell we're not," said Marcy. "That's exactly what I want. Recriminations!"

She took down half her martini in a single gulp. Then she breathed deeply and stared at her husband.

"I'm going to tell you something," she said, suddenly calm and very cold. "I hate your friend Henry Durning. And I despise what he's done to you all these years. He's cold and he's self-serving and he doesn't care if you or I or anybody else lives or dies as long as he gets what he wants. You amuse him because he once saved your life, and you've been paying him homage and kissing his ass ever since. You're basically the most ethical man I know. Yet when he asked you to betray yourself and your office for a reason he wouldn't even tell you, you sacrificed the lives of five of your agents without batting an eye."

The FBI director closed his eyes as though in pain. "For God's sake, Marcy—"

"Don't you 'for God's sake' me!" she rushed on. "Then when he has two more people killed to cover up the first five, and the whole rotten mess explodes in *your* face, not *his*, he has the nerve to talk to *me* about my hysterics."

She turned to face Henry Durning. "Well, Mr. United States Attorney General," she said softly, her eyes dry and hard now, her voice and face like glacial ice, "you haven't even begun to see my hysterics. Because if you've got the idea I'm just going to sit quietly by while my husband is crucified and you're left untouched, you're not as smart as I think."

The room was silent.

Durning and Wayne stared at each other in a strange, almost embarrassed way. Marcy didn't look at either of them. She just stood there finishing her martini. Then moving very deliberately, she walked to the far end of the room and began mixing herself another drink.

Gently, Durning took his friend's arm. "Forget all that," he said. "It's a bad time for everyone. But it might be easier if we talked alone for a few minutes and got a couple of things settled."

His hand still on Wayne's arm, Durning guided him to the bedroom as if he were a blind man, and followed him in.

Wayne never had a chance to turn around.

Durning swung the pistol butt only once, a flat solid shot to the back of the head that caught Wayne exactly right and dropped him without a sound. He didn't seem to fall as much as crumple.

The attorney general stood looking down at his friend. The calm Durning contained seemed delicate and he didn't press it. It was enough to just stand there for a moment, letting things settle. Then he returned to the living room.

Marcy had finished mixing her second martini and was standing at a window, gazing out and drinking as he quietly approached.

She must have heard him, yet she didn't turn until he was almost on her. When she did see him, it was the moment he was taking that final step, arm raised, and he faltered before her stare, all stomach for it leaving him. Until the sound of her glass smashing on the wood floor shook him free of her eyes and he put her out.

I never knew she hated me so much, he thought, and carried her in to join her husband.

Moving more quickly now, he laid them side by side on the bed.

Worlds circled as in a dream.

Both their faces seemed flat and they stared at him out of their own darkness.

Durning put on a pair of rubber cleaning gloves from the kitchen, took the 12-gauge out of the closet, and wiped it and the shells free of all prints.

The rest would be all iron discipline.

Apart from everything else, there were certain details to be considered in a purported murder-suicide. Sometimes the murdered party would be a willing victim . . . other times, not. In this instance, either way would be feasible. Shotgun shells made a much bigger mess than rifle bullets but also carried a couple of advantages. At close range, the result would never be in doubt. And any possibly embarrassing evidence of earlier blows to the head would be eliminated.

He had, after all, been a prosecuting attorney.

All right.

He did Marcy first, of course, feeling his arm jump with the recoil, and going briefly deaf and numb from the explosion in so small an area.

Jesus!

Cotton-mouthed, fighting nausea again, Durning carefully laid the shotgun on Brian's chest. He placed the muzzle under Brian's chin, Brian's left hand around the double barrel, and his right hand on the trigger.

Then kneeling beside the bed, Durning kept his head down and away as he squeezed Brian's thumb against the trigger until the second shell exploded.

He knelt there, neither moving nor looking at the result, but just breathing the smell of cordite as though it were a new antidote for death.

He felt a scaling wash of sorrow for which he was unprepared.

We were friends once, and young.

Still, it was said the best way to die was with someone you loved. And how many were able to arrange that?

Holding to his discipline, Durning spent fifteen minutes wiping prints from everything he had touched.

He swept up the bits of broken cocktail glass from the living room floor and threw them in a pile of trash out back.

He washed his own glass and put it back into the liquor cabinet.

About to leave, he closed his eyes and felt cold, quiet waters flow over him.

Then he started home.

46

DON CARLO DONATTI was engaged in a long-term love affair with his life. He adored it. Each day he saw it with new and freshly appreciative eyes. It was the thing about him that made him appear and feel younger than his years.

This morning he was having breakfast on the terrace of his Sands Point home. The house overlooked Long Island Sound, and the don saw the acres of evenly trimmed lawn sweeping down to the water, the specimen trees catching the early sun, the sky as pure a cerulean blue as any he had ever seen over the Mediterranean. And he consciously savored everything he saw.

The fact was, Donatti took nothing he had, nothing around him for granted. He knew it did not have to be this way. Not his imposing home, not the respect and power he enjoyed, not the soaring midtown Manhattan headquarters of the Galatea Corporation, where he spent the better part of his days and years. In a way, the office tower itself had become the prime symbol of his good life, of his long-hoped-for and ever-growing legitimacy. On clear days, when the light was right, he could sometimes see the tallest of its spires. They gleamed even from here. And suddenly, it was threatened.

Just the thought of it ruined Carlo Donatti's mood, brought beads of sweat to his forehead and upper lip. And it took only one man with a safety-deposit box to be able to do this to him. But it was a box that could be more dangerous than a gun. Henry Durning could be dead and the box could still ruin Donatti, send him to prison, take away everything that mattered, force him to march through his remaining years in lockstep.

Who would have expected anything like this? And all because of something that had happened nearly ten years ago. Or, rather, something that had *not* happened. Durning had wanted a woman dead. Donatti had thought he had taken care of it for Durning. And now, a decade later, she'd suddenly turned up alive—while all these others kept dying for no better reason than that this woman is still breathing out there someplace.

Some woman, thought Carlo Donatti.

He looked off at a scattering of birds working some of the feeders he kept around the grounds. He sipped his second cup of espresso. He thought about the woman whom Vittorio Battaglia, one of the best made men ever, had decided to disappear with almost ten years ago.

Considering Vittorio's reputation with women, she had to be something very special. And considering Durning's need to have her dead, she also had to be very dangerous.

At least to Henry Durning, Donatti thought.

Then having thought this, Don Carlo Donatti wondered at his never having thought it before. But he did think about it now, letting the concept drift through his mind while he nibbled at the sudden sweetness of its possibilities.

Donatti continued to think about Peggy Walters as he finished his espresso and was driven into midtown Manhattan in one of the three identical Lincoln towncars he used to confuse his enemies. And he was still thinking about her as he settled behind his oversize desk high in the Galatea Building like a man who has finally arrived at either the beginning or the end of something.

Peggy Walters had been alone in their so-called safe house now for more than a day. She had heard nothing from Vittorio. And she was becoming more certain by the minute that no news had to be bad news. If her Paulie was going to end up dying sometime during the next few days, she knew better than anyone that the ultimate blame had to lie with her.

Yet she did have her moments of hope.

It was, after all, Vittorio himself who was looking for their son. If anyone could find him, he could. Vittorio knew about such things.

In her mind, she took to playing out the small progression of hope . . . the searching, the finding, the coming home . . . all so real that she was able to weep genuine tears of joy. It was one of the things that helped keep her sane.

Another thing that helped was staying busy.

She prepared meals that were not eaten. She scrubbed walls and floors that were already clean. She gathered wildflowers into endless bouquets until the small stone house resembled an indoor garden.

Finally, although Peggy Walters had rarely if ever prayed, she prayed now.

It was nighttime and she stood barefoot in the damp grass, feeling the earth under her feet, her face raised in the darkness like some supplicant to the stars. Although she supposed it was probably less a matter of praying than of trying to work out some sort of deal.

Take me for my Paulie, Lord, and You'll never get Yourself a better bargain because nobody will ever work harder for You than I'll work.

Or was deal making with God just another form of blasphemy?

If it was, no offense intended.

Anyway, she was doing her bargaining with the wrong party. Because if she was at all serious about this, the one she really had to deal with was the devil, Henry Durning.

Which was precisely how the idea was born.

Still, it did take one of her worst waves of fear to convince her of what she must do. It hit her when she realized the odds against Vittorio and Gianni getting themselves anything but dead in what they were attempting to do, and that this was finally going to have to be all hers.

Paulie was *her* baby.

It was decided as simply as that.

She sat with it for a long time in the grass in the night, loving the new calm that came with it.

She breathed the cool night air and studied the way the dark rim of the mountains stood out against the lesser dark of the sky. All her reverence for life, all the love she felt for her son and husband sang softly inside her. For a while it kept her from feeling quite so alone.

It was quiet in the small house high among the Sicilian hills. Paulie was doing a pencil sketch of Domenico as he sat posing. Tony was sprawled on the couch, glancing through a picture magazine and sipping beer.

At the moment, Paulie was having a problem with Dom's mouth. It was closed and didn't seem to look natural that way. But that was how Dom kept it, so that was how Paulie was sketching it. Mouths and eyes were always the hardest for him. They kept changing. They looked different every minute.

"What are you working on now?" Dom asked, intrigued by the whole process of reproducing his face on paper.

"Your mouth," said Paulie.

"Women tell me that's my best feature. They say it drives them crazy. Be very careful how you handle that mouth. It's my whole future."

The boy sketched the same way he did everything. With quiet solemnity. He wished he had his paints and a canvas so he could do a proper, full-color portrait. But a pencil was still better than nothing, and drawing did make the time go faster. And he liked Dom's face, liked the rough, crooked features. They looked as if they had once been broken apart in the middle, and never been put back together exactly right.

Although working on Dom's face, Paulie was watching Tony as well. He felt it important for him not to miss anything about either of the two men. He saw how Tony kept glancing around even as he flipped through his magazine. It seemed to him that Tony was always looking around and waiting for something to happen. Even when he was very still, his eyes were moving. The boy guessed they were gunfighters' eyes. In Westerns he had seen about gunfighters, they always watched a man's eyes to know when he was going to draw.

"Why is it taking so long?" Dom said.

"This isn't long. Leonardo da Vinci took seven years to do the Mona Lisa."

"Hey. I'll be dead in seven years."

When the sketch was finished, Paulie gave it to the mobster to see. Dom laughed and shook his head in wonder.

"That's me, all right. You're a genius, kid. You even got my beautiful mouth." He showed the portrait to Tony. "Great, huh?"

"Just what the world needs. Another face like yours to look at."

"You want me to do one of you?" the boy asked. He was trying to be nice to them both. It had come to him that it would be better if they got to like him and believe he liked them, too. Then they might get a little careless and give him a chance at something.

Tony shook his head. "The *carabinieri* got too many pictures of me as it is."

Later, Paulie sat at the end of his long dog chain watching Domenico clean and oil his gun. The boy appreciated the way he did it, touching and holding the separate parts as though each was something special. Paulie guessed that in a gangster's business, everything had to be special. If just one tiny part wasn't right and got messed up, you could be dead.

Dom glanced up at him. "You like guns?"

"I don't know. I never had one. I don't know anything about them." Then by way of explanation. "I'm only eight."

Dom laughed. "When I was eight, I'd already shot four guys."

Paulie stared gravely at him.

"Hey, I was only joking."

The boy was silent for a few moments. "If you teach me about guns, I'll teach you how to draw."

"It's a deal, kid. Then maybe you can grow up to be a rich made man, and I can retire and be a famous artist."

The pistol was a 9mm automatic, and Domenico explained the parts and the way they worked, with the weapon's mechanism automatically throwing out the empty shell after each shot, putting a new one into the chamber, and preparing the pistol to be fired again.

When Paulie understood all this, Dom taught him about shooting.

Tony sat shaking his head. "I don't believe I'm seeing this shit."

The boy noticed the change that came over Domenico, how serious he became as he talked and described how things should be done. There was none of his fooling around now, no teasing him as a child. Paulie understood that Dom wanted him to know that guns were a man's business, not a kid's, and that people got killed by them. You didn't play games with guns. You didn't point one at somebody unless you were ready to shoot that person. And if you ever did have to shoot, there was a right and a wrong way of doing that, too.

The right way was to first make sure that if the gun had a safety switch, you turned it off. Then you aimed the pistol with both hands, extended your arms, held your breath, and gently squeezed, not jerked, the trigger.

With the ammunition clip removed, Dom demonstrated how all this was done. Then he handed the empty automatic to Paulie and told him to try it himself.

The boy felt the weight of the gun along with a sudden trembling in his knees. He released the safety. He gripped the butt with both hands, extended his arms, and aimed the front sight at a crack in the wall. He held his breath and gently squeezed the trigger.

"Bang," he said.

The big surprise was that it was all so easy.

47

THE HOUSE OF Don Pietro Ravenelli was just about where the old man in Naples had told Vittorio and Gianni it would be. It stood in the foothills of northeastern Sicily, about ten kilometers west of Palermo, and not very far off the coast road to Punta Raisi.

It was a big, white, Mediterranean-style villa, with an orange tile roof, a high wall surrounding its several acres of manicured grounds, and four heavily armed security guards patrolling the areas between the wall and the house itself. Additionally, there were strategically placed floodlights and closed-circuit television cameras to cover whatever the guards might miss.

It was getting close to early evening, and Gianni and Vittorio had been reconnoitering the house and grounds for the past four hours, locating whatever they had to, noting everyone who entered and left the compound, and of course making absolutely sure that Ravenelli himself never drove out of the place.

In position near the crest of a wooded hill, at a distance of about three hundred yards, they spelled each other behind a pair of high-powered field glasses. Their car was out of sight in back of some brush, and far off to the right they could faintly make out the traffic to and from Palermo along the coast road.

It had been a long, sleepless night and day of travel, planning, and surveillance, and now they took turns stretching out in the high grass and dozing. They would not be making their move until close to midnight, and it was important for them to be as rested and sharply tuned as possible when they finally went in. It would have been much easier to have just flown over and rented a car at the Palermo airport, but there had been their trunkful of weapons to consider. And because they had missed the last ferry of the night from Naples, they had been forced to drive over four hundred kilometers on the Italian mainland, take the ferry to Messina, and drive another three hundred kilometers west along the Sicilian coast road to Palermo.

They watched the sprawling white villa, and waited, and dozed, and felt the growing tension of what lay ahead.

At about six o'clock, two men who had been working on the shrubs and flower beds got into an old pickup and drove off.

The housekeeper, a heavy-set woman in a black dress, left an hour later.

A car arrived and picked up another woman, probably the cook, at shortly after eight.

By then it was growing dark and the stillness of evening drifted in and muted all sound. They saw the warm yellow glow of the houselights come on, and the cool white of the outside floods. The guards threw long shadows as they walked.

"Just so you understand," Vittorio Battaglia's voice came

softly through the dark. "One sound from a guard, and we're as good as gone. And so is my boy. That means we do them all with silencers. Four outside, patrolling, and one inside, at the closed-circuit monitors."

Gianni said nothing.

"You OK with that? " asked Vittorio.

Gianni Garetsky nodded.

Vittorio took a long, deep breath and slowly let it out.

They began blackening their faces and hands. They already were wearing the necessary dark shirts and trousers.

The second-floor bedroom light went off just before eleven.

At midnight, they silently went over the wall and dropped into the shadows of some bushes. Earlier, Vittorio had checked and determined that neither the wall nor the house was wired.

Two guards with submachine guns stood together about fifty meters to the right. They were smoking and talking. They should have been apart and patrolling. Gianni and Vittorio crouched in the shadows and waited.

One of the moving floodlights passed over their heads, and Gianni saw the television camera timed to go with it. He felt himself sweating and was disgusted by his fear. *It's allowed,* he told himself.

The two guards strolled their way, still together and still talking. As they were going they would pass within five feet of the bushes where Garetsky and Battaglia were waiting.

"Let them pass," whispered Vittorio. "Then you take the nearest one and I'll take the other. Make it a head shot. We can't have them crying out. So for Christ's sake, don't miss."

Gianni wiped the sweat from his eyes.

The guards came by and Gianni and Vittorio aimed and fired. Their silenced shots made only a single, soft whooshing sound. The two men made no sound at all. They fell forward on their faces and didn't move. Gianni and Vittorio dragged them behind the bushes before the traveling floodlight and camera swung back.

Keeping to the shadows, they moved cautiously around to the rear of the house.

The next security man was dozing, sitting up, his back to a tree. Vittorio shot him once through the forehead without waking or stirring him.

They crept forward, looking for the fourth and last of the exterior guards.

At the back of the house, they heard rather than saw him. He was softly humming what Gianni recognized as the most lyric segment of the love duet from *La Bohème. Italians,* he thought sadly.

Vittorio pressed Gianni's arm. He motioned for him to stay where he was, and disappeared in the direction of the man's voice. Moments later the humming suddenly stopped, and Vittorio seemed to float back out of the dark.

They approached a lighted ground-floor window on the far side of the house. It was the only interior light on and they had not been able to see it from their position on the hill. A single, uncurtained window was open to the cool night air.

His back to the window, a man sat reading a newspaper in front of a bank of television monitors. He never so much as glanced at the screens.

Vittorio stepped close to the window. He drew a careful bead on the back of the guard's head and fired once. It was done.

My God, thought Gianni Garetsky. *Five.*

He looked at Vittorio in the reflected light. His face showed nothing, and Gianni wondered what he had expected to find there. Then they were climbing through the open window and he had stopped wondering about anything at all.

Vittorio led the way through the room, along a short corridor and into the front entrance hall. They had bought rubber-soled running shoes on the drive down and they moved without sound on the tiled floors.

An orange night-light burned on the second-floor landing, and they climbed the stairs in its glow. Gianni felt himself moving as though in a fever, his face hot, the sweat running like tears.

There were five doors facing the second-floor corridor, but only one was closed. Vittorio eased that door open. Then Gianni quietly followed him into the darkened room, breathed air redolent with sex, and hit the light switch.

A naked couple lay sleeping on a king-size bed. The man was big, middle aged, dark skinned, and going to fat. The woman was young, beautiful, and wore a look of sweet, almost holy innocence.

Their silencer-lengthened pistols leveled, Gianni and Vittorio stood at the foot of the bed waiting for the light to waken the sleeping lovers.

It was Ravenelli who stirred and blinked open his eyes first. He looked at the two men with their blacked-out faces and hands and their guns pointing loosely at his head. He half turned to see them better. Gianni admired his control. He did not make a sound and his face revealed nothing.

The young woman came awake a few seconds later. She cried out just once. Then she carefully held herself silent and unmoving. It seemed so deliberate a performance that it might have been mistaken for an act of faith. Gianni made no such mistake. He knew exactly how frightened she was.

The silence stretched until it ran out of air.

Then Vittorio broke it. "You know who I am?"

The don slowly nodded. "What I don't know is how you got in here to point a gun at my head."

"Yes, you do."

Gianni saw the dark face become a lesson in controlled pain. "They were five good men."

"I'll cry later," said Vittorio. "Right now I just want to know where you've got my boy."

"What boy?"

Vittorio fired without warning or movement and a small hole appeared in the girl's pillow. It was only inches from her head. Her eyes widened, but that was all.

"The next one does her," he said. "Now let's try it again. Where's my boy?"

"About a half-hour drive from here."

It came without hesitation this time.

"Your boy is all right," said Ravenelli. "You don't have to worry. We're not animals here. We don't make war on children. There was never any intention to do your son harm."

Vittorio Battaglia just looked at him.

"On my honor," said the don.

Vittorio's silence told him what he thought of his honor.

Ravenelli turned to Gianni for the first time. "You must be Gianni Garetsky. I have great respect for your work. I've felt that way for years. Long before the critics. I myself own two of your paintings. They're hanging downstairs in my living room. Maybe you saw them coming in."

Gianni stood there. The only pictures he had seen and still saw were the framed photographs across the bedroom walls . . . ancient family pictures of children and old people posing stiffly and unsmiling in their Sunday best. He wondered which of the little boys pictured was Don Pietro Ravenelli.

The don turned to Vittorio. "You want to listen to me talk to your son on the telephone? Would that make you feel better about how he's being treated?"

"What I want is to talk to him myself."

"That wouldn't be a good idea. Not for any of us."

"Why?"

"Because there are two men with him who would know I'm under the gun the second they heard your voice. Then they'd just move the boy someplace else before we got there. We'd all be unhappy."

Gianni watched as his friend considered it. He saw Vittorio study first the telephone on the bedside table, then the don and his wide-eyed, virginal-looking young woman lying so unself-consciously naked together in bed, then the telephone once more.

"What's your name?" Vittorio asked the girl.

"Lucia." It was the first word she had spoken and it half stuck, hoarsely, in her throat.

"I'm sorry you had to be caught in this, Lucia. But you won't be hurt unless your man is lying to me. If he *is* lying, and you don't tell me about it now, I'm going to shoot you before I shoot him. Do you understand what I'm saying?"

The girl nodded.

"Do you believe I'll do it?"

"Yes."

"All right. Has Don Ravenelli been telling me the truth so far?"

Lucia took a moment. "As far as I know. But there may be

things Pietro hasn't told me. It's unfair to blame me for those."

"What's happening to my son is even more unfair."

Vittorio looked at Ravenelli. "Where's an extension I can listen on?"

"In the next room. On your right."

"Watch them carefully," Vittorio told Gianni, and went to hear his son's voice.

He stood listening to five rings on the other end before a man's voice finally answered.

"Who's this?" said the don. "Tony or Dom?"

"It's Tony, Don Ravenelli."

"Everything all right?"

"Sure. Everything's fine."

"No problems with the boy?"

"Not one, Don Ravenelli. Right now he's sleeping like a little angel."

"Good. Wake him up and put him on the phone. I want to talk to him."

"You mean now?"

"No. Next week. Just put the boy on."

"Sorry, Don Ravenelli. I'll get him."

Waiting, Vittorio gripped the receiver so hard his fingers began to cramp. Then he heard the small, sleep-clogged voice say hello, and felt something go soft inside him.

"Sorry to wake you, Paul," said Ravenelli, "but I just wanted to make sure Dom and Tony are treating you OK."

"Are you the big boss?"

Ravenelli laughed. "I don't know how big, but I'm the boss."

"Dom and Tony are treating me good, but I want to go home. When can I go home?"

"Pretty soon now."

"What does that mean?"

"Maybe a couple of days. Maybe sooner."

"Will you tell that to my mom and dad so they won't worry?"

"Sure."

"Are they OK, too?"

"They're great."

"All right," said the boy.

A moment later Vittorio heard the connection broken. *My son,* he thought, and for the first time in days he was able to consciously allow himself the luxury of hope. Still, even this was a fine, delicately balanced thing, and he walked cautiously going back to the next room for fear of disturbing some part of it.

The three-figure tableau appeared unchanged as he reentered Don Pietro Ravenelli's bedroom.

"Let me explain something," the don said. "This whole thing isn't my operation. It's just a courtesy I've been pressured into doing to accommodate Don Carlo Donatti. And that courtesy has so far cost me seven good men and a lot of dignity. So you don't have to worry about me. I'm just as happy to end the whole misery right here."

Vittorio Battaglia nodded. "Good. Now you and Lucia can put on your clothes and I'll make you even happier."

48

PAULIE WAS BACK in bed. But he was very far from falling asleep. His mind was too busy trying to make sense of the phone call, trying to figure out what it meant. Because the only thing he was sure of at that moment was that it had to mean *something.*

The thing was why would the big boss call up in the middle of the night and get him brought to the phone just to ask if Dom and Tony were treating him OK? As if the boss cared how he was being treated.

Even that business about his going home in maybe a day or two had to be nothing but a lie. If it wasn't a lie, Dom would have said something about it after the call. Not Tony. But Dom would have. Yet Dom hadn't known a thing about it when Paulie asked him later.

Then there was all that excitement after Tony hung up, with he and Dom arguing, and Tony making his own phone call and yelling at whoever was at the other end of the phone. The trouble was, they had their bedroom door closed through it all, and Paulie couldn't make out what they were saying. They were still going at it, and the boy saw the crack of light under the door that meant they weren't even thinking about going back to sleep.

When the whole thing got to be too much, he slid out of bed and trailed his long chain into the living room. He wanted to get closer to Dom and Tony's bedroom door. If he got near enough, he might be able to hear something.

The boy never reached the door. He went only as far as the big, overstuffed armchair that Dom had been dozing in earlier. It was here that he saw the mobster's holstered automatic, complete with belt, pressed half under the back of the seat cushion.

For an instant, it froze him in place, and something cold ran through his stomach. Then barely breathing, he snatched up the holstered pistol and attached belt, carried it back to his bed, and slid it under the sheet with him.

Paulie was no longer cold. Suddenly, he was sweating. From barely breathing, he was sucking in great gulps of air. The air made him dizzy and things started to spin. He closed his eyes and lay without moving until his head settled. Finally, he was able to think.

He needed just one thing . . . the key to the handcuffs that connected the long chain to his ankle. But Tony always carried that in his pants, and the pants were with him in his bedroom. Paulie had once seen some guy in a movie shoot off a pair of handcuffs with a gun, but that wouldn't work here with him. Dom and Tony would just come flying out after him with the first shot. So the only way was to go in after the key.

It took him five minutes to prepare his head.

The first thing was to release the safety, which he did now because he was afraid he would forget later in all the excitement. Then he went over the rest that Dom had taught him about using a two-handed grip, and extending his arms, and holding his breath at the right moment, and squeezing and not jerking the trigger.

All that, he thought, and wondered how he was ever going to remember everything at the moment of shooting. But he did not really expect it to come to that. They would see the gun, Tony would give him the key, he would be gone from here, and that would be the end of it. In his mind, there was no way he could imagine himself actually shooting either one of these two men.

Then moving with care, Paulie approached the bedroom door, quietly turned the knob, and entered the room. He walked in like an undersize sleepwalker, gun and extended arms leading the way, and every visible part of him aquiver.

Domenico was the first to see the boy. "Oh, Jesus," he whispered.

He and Tony lay in their underwear on twin beds, and the boy swung his arms and gun back and forth from one to the other. His dark eyes were wide, his mouth tightly set. The men stared at the shaking muzzle of the automatic. Neither of them moved.

"Easy, kid," said Dom. "That fucker's got a hair trigger. Just stay nice and easy and talk to us. Just tell us what you want."

"The key. I want the key to these handcuffs."

"Sure," said Tony quietly. "No problem. Things can be worked out. We're all friends here."

The boy swung the automatic toward Tony and held it there. "I don't want to be friends. I want the key."

"Hey, it's yours, Paulie. It's right over there in my pants. Draped over that chair. If you'll let me, I'll get it for you."

Paulie licked his lips and tried to swallow. He couldn't. And the trembling inside him was getting worse, not better. In a crazy way he found himself glancing at Dom, as if for advice. Would it be safer to go for the key himself, or let Tony get it and give it to him? Dom's blue eyes shone in the overhead light. They told him nothing.

"I feel bad about this," said Tony, and smiled, which he never did. "I thought you were having kind of a good time here with us. I never thought it was that terrible for you."

"It was great for me. I love being chained up like a dog. Try it sometime. Maybe you'll love it as much as I did."

Domenico laughed. "I told you he's a tough kid, Tony. He takes no shit. Give him the damn key and let him go."

"I'm waiting for permission to move. You think I want to get shot by *your* gun? Talk about bright moves. Imagine going to sleep and leaving a loaded piece lying loose out there."

Dom was silent. His eyes had stopped shining.

The boy spoke to Tony. "OK. Give me the key. But do it real slow. Because I'm very nervous right now."

Tony nodded and took the two steps needed to reach the chair.

"Tony." Dom's voice stopped him before he could pick up his pants, and he turned.

"Yeah?"

"Give Paulie the key."

"Sure. That's just what I'm going to do."

"I'm serious, Tony."

"Good. 'Cause I'm serious, too. And I know the kid here has got to be serious as all hell. So I guess that means all three of us are serious, right?"

With all his shaking, the boy stood as still as he was able. He understood that something was going on between the two men, but he had no idea what. Not that it mattered. Because what he was concentrating on mostly was Tony and Tony's pants and the all-important key to freedom that lay somewhere inside them. He saw Tony's face as he bent over the chair and picked up his pants. He saw the muscles in his jaw and the way his eyes narrowed as he dug a hand deep into one of the pockets.

Then the hand came out of the pocket, and Paulie saw not a key or a bunch of keys, but the dull, blued steel of a gun barrel. And it was pointed at him. *Him.*

He froze. Everything he had learned was forgotten.

His trigger finger might have been a piece of wood. It would not move. He heard an explosion off to his right, where Dom was, and Tony cried out and was slammed against a wall.

There was another explosion as Tony pointed his gun barrel at Dom. Then there were more shots, with the explosions coming one after the other from both sides of the room until they all seemed to roll together like thunder.

Through it all, the boy stood paralyzed, the gun forgotten in his hand, and smoke and sound settling around him.

Finally, it was quiet.

Paulie breathed the bitterness of the gunpowder, which seemed to have a yellow smell, and saw Tony lying on the floor. The gangster's legs were bent crookedly under him, he had a small hole in his forehead, and his eyes were staring at nothing.

How? Why?

Turning, Paulie looked at Dom, looked at the small, snub-nosed pistol still in his hand on the bedsheet, and began to understand some parts of it. He looked, too, at the blood leaking through Dom's undershirt from two separate places on his chest, and he understood this as well.

Domenico managed to grin with a clown's own tragic gloom. "Hey . . ." The whisper came out in a froth of red bubbles. "You didn't remember . . . shit about . . . shooting."

The boy gazed half blindly through smoke and a sudden fall of mist. "I couldn't. I'm sorry."

Dom lay there, making pink and red bubbles. "It's . . . OK," he breathed. "Just get . . . the key and get . . . out . . . of here."

Moments later, his eyes glazed over and he gave a slow look of surprise and died.

Paulie sat with him. He thought about how he'd still be alive if he hadn't shot Tony. Why had he done it? *Why didn't he shoot me?*

Dummy, he finally told himself. *Because he'd rather Tony was dead, than you.*

After a while the boy rose, got the key from Tony's pants pocket, and freed himself from his chain. It felt strange being loose, and he walked around for a few minutes to get used to it.

Then about to call home, it occurred that having been brought here chloroformed, he had no idea where he was. So he reached the operator and learned he was in the area of Lercara Friddi, in northeastern Sicily. Of course, he thought. Home of the Mafia.

Paulie looked at a clock, saw it was 2:54 A.M. and dialed

his house in Positano. Feeling the heat of his excitement, he counted off twenty rings before finally hanging up. Then thinking he may have gotten a wrong number, he tried again for another fifteen rings with the same results.

He was attacked by a whole new range of worries. If his parents weren't home at this hour of the night, they weren't likely to be home at all. So where were they? Out looking for him, of course. Where else could they be?

Dead. They could be lying dead somewhere, like Dom and Tony. The thought hit him with such force, was so real to him at this moment, surrounded as he was by death, that he dissolved into tears.

But he cut it off right there. *Don't be a damn crybaby,* he told himself. *Get your dumb baby self together. Get going from here fast, like Dom told you. Go home. When Mom and Dad can't find you, that's where they'll go, too. That's where they'll be.*

Paulie found some maps in a desk. He saw exactly where Lercara Friddi was and tried to figure out his best way home. Sicily was an island and he would have to take a ferry from either Palermo to Naples, or from Messina to Reggio Calabria. The map said Palermo to Naples was the better choice. The land part was shorter, and the sea part longer. Which would be safer than having to spend more time on the roads, where the big *capo* would have his whole gang out checking and looking for him.

Then there was the matter of money. He would have to be traveling for at least a few days and nights and would need to pay for the ferry, too.

It made him sick but he forced himself back into Dom and Tony's bedroom and took all the money out of their wallets. There was a great deal of it, more than he had ever seen at one time. Which was no surprise to him. Since everyone knew that gangsters were rich. Why else would they be gangsters?

It was only as he was stuffing all the money into his pockets that the true awareness broke through that he had actually witnessed the killing of two men and almost been killed himself. He felt it should have been enough to shake the earth and fire up the sky. Yet it did no such things. Everything appeared as before, and somehow this didn't seem right.

Leaving the house and the two dead men, Paulie suddenly dropped to his knees on a bare patch of earth, as if to steady it or himself. Or maybe it was just something to make the ground itself take notice of those who had been here for a little while and then had gone away.

The boy didn't know or understand any of this. It just felt right to do it.

49

VITTORIO BATTAGLIA DROVE, with Don Ravenelli sitting beside him, his hands tied behind his back. Gianni and the girl, Lucia, sat together in the rear of the car. Lucia's hands, too, were tied, but rested more comfortably in her lap. Gianni held the only visible weapon, an automatic with the safety released.

There was no real conversation as such. Whatever needed to be said had been said before they left the villa. The only words spoken now had to do with Ravenelli's route instructions to Vittorio.

They were driving east on the coast road. A heavy mist came in from the sea and a fragment of moon was visible between drifting clouds. At this hour, only an occasional car appeared and passed like a ghost, and they might have been riding one of the darker rims of the earth.

Gianni glanced at the girl sitting quietly beside him. Lucia's eyes gazed straight ahead, her expression serene and unchanging. Dressed, her body showed no hint of the carnality her nakedness had projected earlier. Which made her seem another woman entirely. Were Gianni to paint her, there would be no overimages of lust in the portrait. If anything, he could far more easily see her as someone whose life's goals leaned more toward those of the spirit, rather than the flesh. Even her earlier evidence of fear seemed to be gone. In its place appeared to be a quiet composure.

Don Pietro Ravenelli's woman.

Feeling Gianni's gaze, she turned and managed a hesitant smile.

"I know how crazy this sounds right now," she said, "but I'd like to thank you while I have the chance."

Gianni looked at her. "For what?"

"Your paintings. They've given me so much pleasure. I look at them and feel and understand things I've never known about before. They move me."

Gianni felt curiously touched, almost embarrassed. *While I sit holding a gun on her.* "That's very kind."

"Do I sound childish and stupid?"

"You sound like every artist's dream of what he'd love to have happen to him. To be able to reach someone. It's *I* who thank *you.*"

It was like a random moment of grace in the midst of chaos. Then Lucia looked straight ahead once more, and Gianni heard Ravenelli give Vittorio instructions to watch for a narrow road that would be coming up soon on the left, and the moment was gone.

They reached the turn and Vittorio shifted into lower gear as the car's engine strained up a long, steep grade. The new road was winding, with a lot of sharp turns and the branches of trees swooping low in places and forming a series of arches where the opposing sides met.

The mist grew heavier, cutting visibility further, and not even the fog lights could break through for more than about twenty or thirty meters.

"How much more of this soup?" Vittorio asked.

"Not much," said Ravenelli. "Maybe two kilometers. It starts clearing as you get higher."

Gianni could feel himself growing tense. It was a perfect area for an ambush. Slow movement, a fallen branch to suddenly stop the car as it comes around a curve, and finally a few submachine guns pressing against the windows.

So what would you do? Shoot Ravenelli and the girl and

die right there? Or drop your gun, put up your hands, and probably die later? Great choices.

But Gianni was certain Vittorio knew all this better than he, and Vittorio was the one in charge. Besides, there didn't appear to be anything in Ravenelli's style or manner that gave a hint of a death wish. The man was no fanatic. Quite the reverse. If the don had impressed Garetsky with anything, it was with his air of philosophical reason. Don Pietro was a deal maker, a confirmed survivor. And he obviously cared about his girl. He wasn't likely to risk both their lives just to carry out a contract.

Then they rounded a turn, the ground fog cleared, and a house came into view about a hundred meters off to the left.

"This is it," said Ravenelli.

Vittorio parked just off the road.

They were at the beginning of a long, dirt driveway that crossed about an acre of open field with the house at the far end and dark stands of trees on both sides. The house itself was two stories high, and had shuttered windows and a porticoed center entrance. A light burned in the downstairs foyer, but the rest of the house was dark.

"You mentioned two men being with my boy?" said Battaglia.

Ravenelli nodded.

"Where are they sleeping?"

"On the second floor. Your son's room is behind those windows above and a bit to the left of the entrance. The men share the next bedroom off to the right."

Vittorio sat staring at the house and grounds. "How many keys do you have?"

"Two," said the don. "One for the front door and one for the rear. I suggest we use the front."

"Why?"

"The back door gets warped in summer. It takes some forcing. It could be noisy."

"What else?"

"Nothing. I don't really expect any problems. I know these men. They're like me. They'd much rather live than die."

"I hope so. For all our sakes."

Vittorio half swung around and addressed Gianni and Lucia along with Ravenelli.

"Here's how it's going to be," he told them. "I'm taking Don Ravenelli in under the gun. If I'm attacked along the way, or if I get inside the house and don't come out within fifteen minutes, Gianni shoots Lucia and drives off alone."

Vittorio paused. "Any questions?"

No one spoke, and in the following silence Gianni watched Lucia's face for some reaction to the possibility of her own death at his hands. He saw none. Either Don Ravenelli was being straight with them, or Lucia was far and away the world's best and bravest actress. In Gianni's own judgment, Ravenelli was telling the truth. The alternative was simply unthinkable.

"All right," said Vittorio Battaglia.

Leaving Ravenelli sitting alone in front, he went around to the car trunk and began unloading his weapons case. He took two fragmentation grenades and a pair of automatic pistols for himself and handed what remained, including a rifle and a submachine gun, to Gianni inside the car.

Pietro Ravenelli watched with clear amusement. "You guys expecting World War III?"

Neither man answered.

Vittorio opened the front passenger door and helped Ravenelli out of the car. The don moved awkwardly with his hands tied behind him, and he stumbled and almost fell.

"You've got two guns on me," he said. "How about giving me back my hands?"

Vittorio ignored him and spoke to Gianni. "I don't like this long stretch of open field, so keep us covered with the rifle. Watch the house windows and the woods on the right for movement. If you see anything, fire once in the air."

He glanced briefly at the girl. "And before you go all soft on Miss Angel Face here, just remember who she is and where you found her."

The two men stood looking at each other.

"I think it'll be OK," Gianni said.

"I know that's what you think. Stay sharp anyway."

Vittorio took Ravenelli's arm and started toward the house with him. He felt the flesh of the don's beefy arm, and breathed his cologne, and fought the anger that came with his closeness. He didn't need anger right now. He needed calm and he needed his senses. This was past thinking.

He kept the pace slow but steady. It took discipline not to rush. His eyes were on the house in front, and on the woods off to his right. The fragment of moon had vanished behind some clouds and the darkness hung heavy. Vittorio seemed to sense a new silence in the dark, a dead silence, like some stretch of the void with nothing beneath.

The grass was high, past knee length, and Ravenelli kept tripping without the use of his arms for balance.

"Goddamn grass hasn't been cut in six weeks," he complained softly. "And it's fucking paid for, too."

"Shut up," Vittorio whispered and took a firmer grip on his arm.

He felt his own tension and tried to ease it by thinking about his son. He pictured him asleep in that upstairs bedroom, his thumb inevitably in his mouth, his thin, solemn face pale against the pillow. *So close and getting closer,* he thought, and had to resist a growing need to break into a wild dash toward the house.

There was a sudden burst of light.

Someone with a bullhorn yelled "Freeze!"

Vittorio stared unseeingly at a white blaze. He slammed Ravenelli down into the grass and dived down against him. The muzzle of his automatic was hard against his throat.

"You sonofabitch!"

Rage took over. It blinded his brain as totally as the floods blinded his eyes. Then it passed and a cold calm turned him sane again.

Flat out in the high grass, the muzzle of his gun to Ravenelli's throat, he saw three floodlights coming out of the tree line.

Then the voice on the bullhorn called, "Don Ravenelli! Are you all right?"

"My son isn't here?" Like a lover, Vittorio whispered the words into Ravenelli's ear.

"No."

"Was he ever here?"

"No."

"Where is he?"

The man on the bullhorn repeated his question.

"In another house," said the don. "Around thirty kilometers from here."

Vittorio stared at him in disgust. "Answer the damn bullhorn. Tell them you're all right."

Ravenelli was silent.

Vittorio hit him in the mouth with his automatic.

Ravenelli spit blood. Then he called out the message.

"You set this up with that call before?" said Vittorio Battaglia.

"Yes."

"What was the code line?"

"When I said 'No problems with the boy.' "

"Cute." Vittorio stared through the high grass at the lights. "You want to die?"

Ravenelli spit more blood. He swallowed some and gagged. "No."

"Then tell them I'm walking you out of here with a gun at your head. Tell them if they shoot once, I'll scatter your brains like bird shit."

Ravenelli hesitated.

Vittorio rammed the gun into his ear. "Fucking tell them."

"Michael?" the don called.

"Yes, Don Ravenelli," said the voice on the horn.

"He's taking me out. Don't do a thing. One shot and I'm done. He's not fooling."

There was no answer.

"You hear me, Michael?"

The pause was extended.

Then: "I hear you, Don Ravenelli. You don't have to worry."

Vittorio gripped Ravenelli's arm. "You ready?"

"As ready as I'll ever be."

"OK. Slow and easy."

Vittorio strained under the don's bulk as he struggled him up out of the grass that hid them. It was a careful, hesitant rising, with the two men tightly joined all the way as they came into the blaze of white light.

We are risen, thought Vittorio coldly, and tried to shield his eyes from the blinding glare. It did no good. He could see nothing. And at that moment he could almost have allowed himself to slip into the beginnings of a dream in which this weighted body he was clinging to so lovingly belonged to someone other than an enemy.

Then the first shots exploded.

A ragged volley came out of the lights like something meaner than thunder, and kept crackling and groaning until the noise alone seemed to be pounding them straight back down into the grass. Except that it was a lot more than just the noise.

For even when most of the sound had stopped, they were both still flat out in the grass, with Vittorio huddled as tightly as ever against Ravenelli, who lay unmoving and would never move again, and Vittorio himself only now beginning to feel the rush of pain, after the initial shock, of the two hits he had taken. One was above the other. Left side and thigh. He felt, too, the few scattered hits that continued to impact the don's body. Which was Vittorio's only real protection at this moment, but wouldn't be protecting him much longer if something didn't happen fast.

An instant later there was the crack of a rifle from another direction, and something did happen. One of the floodlights exploded in a shower of sparks and went dark.

Gianni.

Then there were two more shots from the same direction and the two remaining floods blew out as well.

Vittorio peered through the new dark and for the first time was able to make out movement and hear voices in the area of the trees.

Do something.

Ignoring the pain, Battaglia rolled on his bad side and groped free the two grenades he had taken with him but never really expected to have to use. He pulled the pins, made his count, and lobbed both grenades within seconds of each other. Blood sloshed as he moved. His own.

The explosions shook the ground and Ravenelli's body. They drowned out the first cries from among the trees. When the sound of the explosions faded, the human cries grew louder.

Come on, Gianni, thought Vittorio, and started crawling toward his parked car. Then he raised his head and saw that his car was suddenly speeding toward *him.*

It was beside him a moment later, with the doors open and Gianni half lifting, half dragging him into the front passenger seat. Vittorio glimpsed the girl, both hands lashed to a door handle, staring out to where Ravenelli lay in the grass.

"Your Pietro's dead," he told her. "I didn't kill him. His friends did. Nice friends."

Lucia just stared out at the dark remains in the grass.

Then Gianni was back behind the wheel and they were tearing through the dark field, away from Don Pietro Ravenelli's body and the unseen bodies of those lying dead and wounded among the trees.

"Crazy bastards," said Vittorio hoarsely. "Paulie was never even here. All this shit and we're no place."

"How bad are you?" asked Gianni.

"Bad enough. I took two in that first burst. Upper leg and side." Holding himself, Vittorio's hands were sticky with blood and blood was oozing between his fingers. He felt pain crawling all over him like something that had been crouching there a long time, waiting for the right moment. "I've goddamn learned nothing. What an asshole."

They rode in silence.

Vittorio Battaglia's eyes were closed.

"I think he's passed out," said Lucia.

They reached the coast highway moments later. Gianni drove west for a few miles, then pulled off the road and parked behind some brush.

Vittorio opened his eyes. "Why are we stopping?"

"To find out if you're dead," said Garetsky.

"I've got too much to do to be dead."

Gianni switched on the dome light and for the first time saw the full extent of the bleeding.

"Jesus. We've got to get you to a hospital."

"You crazy or what? A hospital's the first place they'll be looking."

"Then at least a doctor."

"Just as bad. Doctors have to report bullet wounds to the police, and the mob's got the police in their pocket."

The girl spoke softly from the back. "My cousin is a doctor. You can trust her. She hates all police and gangsters."

Gianni looked at her. "Where is she?"

"In Monreale."

"Why would you help us?"

Lucia shrugged. "You didn't shoot me. And those pigs murdered Pietro. They've just been waiting for the chance. Especially that Michael. And if he gets me, I'll be next because I saw it happen."

"No doctors," said Vittorio. "I don't trust any of them. Just bandage me up for now. Tight. That'll cut the bleeding."

"Please listen to me," said Lucia. Her hands were still tied to the door handle and the two men seemed to have forgotten about her. "I know where the boy is."

Vittorio was unable to turn to see her, but his body stiffened where he sat. "Where is he?"

"In a house near Lercara Friddi. We can be there in fifteen minutes."

"You knew this all the time?" said Gianni.

"Yes."

"And you let that useless bloody mess back there happen?"

The girl's curiously virginal face showed nothing. "How could I stop it? I couldn't betray Pietro. Now it's different. Now I've got only myself to think about. And you gave me back my life when even Pietro was willing to put it at risk."

"What about the two men with my son?" said Vittorio. "Was your Pietro telling the truth about that?"

"Yes. Tony and Domenico are the only ones with him."

Vittorio closed his eyes and seemed to diminish where he sat. "All right," he said. "Let's try *this* house."

Gianni cut Lucia's hands free and together they laid Vittorio across the backseat. The girl sat in front with Gianni. Five minutes later, when Lucia turned to check on Vittorio, his eyes were still closed and he appeared to be asleep.

Vittorio Battaglia opened his eyes only after the forward motion of the car had stopped.

They were parked in a field at the edge of a wood. The lights of a house showed through the trees at a distance of about two hundred yards. The moon remained clouded over and the rest of the night was dark.

Vittorio half raised himself on the backseat. His groan was involuntary. "Is that the house ahead there?" he asked Lucia.

"Yes."

"Why would the lights be on at four in the morning? Are they always kept that way?"

"I don't know."

"This Tony and Domenico," said Vittorio. "How well do you know them?"

"Very well."

"Well enough for you to knock on the door and have them let you in without being suspicious?"

"Yes," said the girl. "Unless they've gotten a call from someone since Pietro was killed."

Vittorio lay back once more and thought about it. He was in pain, sweating, and breathing heavily just from the effort of raising himself. He felt his bandages and knew he was bleeding again. Still, he said, "Let's go," fought his way to a sitting position, and promptly passed out.

When he opened his eyes moments later, Gianni and Lucia didn't appear to have moved an inch.

"I guess I'd better wait for you here," he said thickly. "Just goddamn bring me back my boy."

They circled through the trees and crouched behind some brush about thirty yards to the left of the house. It was a small, one-story stone villa, and the lights were on in two rooms. High bushes made it difficult to see inside.

"Have you ever been in the house?" Gianni Garetsky asked the girl.

"Yes."

"What are the lighted rooms?"

"The one in the front is the living room. The other is a bedroom."

"And the rest?"

"Another bedroom and a bath in back, and a kitchen and an eating place in front. On the far side of the entrance."

They crouched there, listening. The windows were open but they heard nothing.

Gianni flicked off the safety on his automatic. "Wait here while I take a look."

Keeping low, he moved quickly up against the house and peered into the living room. It was empty.

Then he went to the lighted bedroom window and saw a dark-haired young man lying on one of two twin beds. His eyes were open and staring, his once white undershirt was almost entirely red with blood, and he most certainly was dead.

Gianni felt something dark and leaden take hold of him and refuse to let go.

Looking further, he saw a second man stretched out on the floor beside the other bed. A crimson pool had spread about his head and carried to the wall.

Gianni stood there, listening to the hard rush of his own breathing. He pressed his face against the cool glass of the window and felt sick beyond all reason. *Please. Not the boy, too. Whatever else, not him.*

He turned and motioned for Lucia to join him.

"Look," he told her. An instant later he heard her sharply drawn breath.

"Is that Tony and Domenico?" he asked.

"Yes."

They huddled together at the window.

"I'm going in," Gianni said.

He lifted the window higher, climbed through, and moved quietly from one room to another.

He found just two signs of Vittorio's son. A pencil sketch the boy had evidently drawn of one of his captors, and a long chain with handcuffs at one end, and the other end locked onto a pipe in the second bedroom.

Nothing.

Yet how infinitely better than the horror of the other possibility: finding the boy's body.

Vittorio clung to the borders of consciousness. Every breath he took felt drawn on the cutting edge of a knife. He lay propped on the backseat of the car, waiting for his first glimpse of his son walking toward him through the woods.

Which was how he finally saw Gianni and the girl, and how he did not see Paulie.

He half wondered if he were delirious and not seeing things as they were. And in his despair he felt a rush of sorrow like that of a child about to cry.

He closed his eyes and thought of his son, thinking of all the things he didn't know about him and now would probably never know.

When Gianni and Lucia finally reached him, he was no longer conscious.

50

HENRY DURNING WAS in his office, going through the motions of work, when he saw his secretary hurrying toward him. She was white faced, her eyes glistened with tears, and her first words were barely intelligible.

The FBI director and his wife had been found dead of gunshot wounds at their shore home. There were no more details than that. Everyone was stunned, disbelieving.

The secretary's tears were for Durning.

"I'm so sorry," she wept. "I know how close you were. How terrible for you."

Worse for them, thought Durning.

He ordered his official limousine brought around at once. Apart from his personal relationship, he was the attorney general of the United States and, nominally, Brian Wayne's superior. It was only proper that he should put in a prompt appearance at the scene. The better parts of him needed to be there anyway.

The first of the police barricades, set up a full quarter of a mile from the house, were quickly moved aside to allow the attorney general's limousine through.

Farther ahead, Durning saw every sign of a large-scale law and media feeding frenzy in progress. The FBI, state police, and locals were all there in a full blaze of whirling colored lights, with reporters and television crews yapping and going after them in packs, like starving jackals.

The limousine pulled up close and Durning got out.

Recognizing him at once, police and FBI agents backed away from his path as Durning entered the house and continued his march through the living room, the kitchen, and finally into the small back bedroom where the two bodies lay.

Police, official photographers, and an *in situ* forensics team were at work as he entered. But they made room for him at the bedside, and Henry Durning silently stood there, looking yet not looking at what lay in front of and below him.

And standing there, he felt pain. As he should feel it. If only because he had required, and was still requiring, so many people to die for his own needs. How long could he stand up to such inner beatings?

As long as I have to.

It was at that moment that he felt the tears come, felt them even as a photographer's flash went off, with one part of him imagining and approving the beautiful effect of so human a shot on the seven o'clock news, but the rest of him knowing his tears were real. Just as his pain and sense of loss were real.

He opened his mouth to relieve the pressure. But it did no good, and he felt fresh tears on his cheeks.

While more cameras joined with the first to record them.

He came home late, near midnight, to find Mary Yung waiting up for him in the living room. She took one quick look at his face, moved close, and held him.

"What do you want me to do for you?" she said quietly. "Just tell me. What will help most?"

"A bullet in what passes for my heart."

She stroked his hair, his neck, the small of his back. "It's been that bad?"

"Wouldn't you say it ought to be?"

Mary gently eased away, poured some Remy Martin into two snifters, and handed him one. Then she led him to the couch and sat close.

"I can't believe you mean that," she said.

"Only because you don't know what I've done."

"Of course I know."

Durning looked at her for a long moment.

"Tell me," he said at last.

"You shot your friend and his wife, then set it up to look like murder-suicide."

She said it matter-of-factly.

"How do you know?"

"Because otherwise they would have destroyed you." Mary Yung sighed. "And because in your position, I would have probably done the same thing."

Durning looked at her eyes with their needlepoints of light, and some of the feeling he hadn't yet been able to share with her or anyone else in more than half a lifetime of living came rising up in him like a small bomb.

It made him hug her again, but this time with all the gentleness gone. Until in the end, they were clutching each other in the kind of wild, tearful passion that can make a man and woman feel closer than anything else known. *Closer than sex,* he thought.

"Do you know what I think?" he said when the moment had passed.

"What?"

"That we're going to be finding it very hard to fool each other from now on."

"Which means what?"

Henry Durning bent and kissed her.

"That we're going to have to be either very good, or very careful."

51

DON CARLO DONATTI'S armored gray stretch moved smoothly upstate along Route 17. The don sat alone in back, enjoying a bottle of his favorite red, and watching a repeat videocassette performance by Henry Durning on yesterday evening's network news.

This was the fourth time he had run the segment, but he had picked up something new from it with every showing. Know your enemy was perhaps the single best piece of advice his father had ever given him, and the attorney general was certainly that. His enemy.

Watching him now, the don saw Durning arriving at the site of the double tragedy, striding blank-faced and imperious through the small army of reporters, photographers, and police, and entering the house of the late FBI director and his wife.

From here, one camera or another was on him all the way as he walked straight through the entrance hall, living room, and kitchen, and into the bedroom where the Waynes' bodies lay. Of course the bodies themselves were never on camera. But Henry Durning's face was long, with his tears and obvious grief. At which point Donatti hit the pause button and froze the frame.

Even after four viewings, the don remained fascinated. The tears and grief were genuine, not a performance. It was heartfelt.

It hit Carlo Donatti as a double shock. First, that a tight-assed WASP prick like Durning could actually be capable of such emotion. And second, that feeling as he did about his longtime friend and his wife, he was still able to murder them. For there was absolutely no doubt in Donatti's mind that the attorney general had done it. By his own hand.

Imagine the threat that such a man posed.

The limousine passed through the old Catskill town of Liberty at about 9:00 P.M. and pulled up in front of Donatti's cabin less than ten minutes later. Although to describe his father's great pile of half round logs as a cabin, thought the don, would be like describing St. Peter's Basilica as a church.

Simply getting out of the stretch and standing before the house, Donatti felt diminished. As if he were still the little boy, being brought up here by his father for a weekend of fishing or hunting. His favorite times, with just the two of them and maybe a couple of quiet *goombahs* for security, and his father laughing all the time. Which he hardly ever did away from here. And no women. Not even his mother.

His chauffeur followed him up onto a porch, lighted by an old electrified lantern, and into a huge, timbered, two-story main room. There was a great, fieldstone fireplace at one end, and four men playing cards at the other.

The men put down their cards and rose in respectful greeting. Don Donatti waved them down and three sat. The fourth man, a young, thick-necked bodybuilder named Sal, came forward and shook the don's hand.

"Welcome, Don Donatti. Everything's all set."

"Where do you have them?"

"The big bedroom." Sal pointed up to one of four doors leading off a second-floor balcony that covered one entire side of the main room.

"What do they know?"

"Nothing. Just that the boss is coming to talk to them. And that they'll have to be blindfolded and handcuffed while they're with you."

"Any problems?"

Sal shook his head. "Just bullshit stuff. The guy's a real wise-ass. Big talker. But we straightened him out fast. The lady's OK. Mostly scared."

"And they've never seen anyone's face?"

"Hell, no. We've been doing like you said, Don Donatti. We always wear our masks around them. They wouldn't know us from shit."

"Good. Let's go."

Carlo Donatti followed the young man upstairs to the balcony. Then he waited there while Sal put on his mask, unlocked the door, and went inside to take care of his charges' handcuffs and blindfolds.

Sal was out in three minutes. "They're all yours, Godfather."

"Lock the door behind me and go downstairs with the others," said Donatti. "I don't want any big ears at the keyhole. Understand?"

"Yes, sir."

The don went inside the room, closed the door, and heard it locked from the outside. Then he turned and looked at John Hinkey and Bonnie Beekman. The Washington lawyer and his client sat side by side on straight wooden chairs. They were blindfolded and their hands were cuffed behind their backs. It was Donatti's first sight of them, a middle-aged, undistinguished-looking man and woman going to fat, who still had no idea what they were into.

Donatti sat down facing them, took a small, rectangular unit out of his pocket, and spoke into it.

"The reason I sound strange," he said, "is that I'm using an electronic voice disguiser to keep you from identifying me later. So please bear with me."

"You're the one who had us brought here?" said Hinkey.

"Yes."

"I don't know what you're trying to do," said the lawyer. "But if you think you can get away with this kind of—"

The don cut him off. "You're not a fool, Mr. Hinkey. So stop blustering like one and just listen to me."

Hinkey's nostrils flared as he drew in air, but he remained still.

"To begin with," said Donatti, "I'm the only reason you two are still alive. If I had followed the orders given me, you both would have been dead the night you were picked up."

"My God," whispered Mrs. Beekman and began quietly sobbing.

"Whose orders?" asked Hinkey. "The FBI director's?"

"No. Wayne was a victim himself in all this. In fact he and his wife were found dead yesterday in what was set up to look like a murder/suicide but was actually a double murder."

"Fucking Christ!" For once, Hinkey was awed. "Who killed them?"

"Someone even higher than Wayne. Someone afraid of Wayne breaking under pressure. The same person who pushed me into getting rid of you both, and even now thinks you're buried somewhere."

Fresh graves, real and imagined, seemed to open in the room. Hinkey sniffed opportunity in them. "Then why are we still alive? Because you're such a great humanitarian?"

Donatti smiled. "That, and the sense that you might just possibly be able to do more for me alive than dead."

Other than for the soft sound of Mrs. Beekman's steady sobbing, the room was silent.

"OK," said Hinkey. "So exactly what is it you want me to do for you?"

"That's something we're both going to have to spend a little time thinking and talking about."

"I don't know what that means."

"It means I think you're a smart man with brass balls who knows how things work in Washington. And what you don't know, you're not afraid to find out."

"Like where certain bodies might be buried?"

Donatti was silent.

Bonnie Beekman had stopped crying. "What about my husband? Please. Can you at least tell me whether he's alive or dead?"

The don considered his answer from two perspectives . . . the woman's and his own. In neither instance was he able to see anything remotely positive resulting from the truth.

"Your husband is alive," he told her. "That's all I can say for now. So please don't ask me anything more."

"Thank you." She began crying again.

"Another thing, Mr. Hinkey," said the don. "You might like to know your son appeared on national television two days ago. Assuming you and Mrs. Beekman were murdered, he followed your instructions and went public with everything you'd dug up on the dead and missing FBI agents. He was very moving and effective. It's generally believed his revelations were what drove Wayne to kill his wife and himself."

John Hinkey nodded, slowly, his body swaying with his head. Beneath the blindfold, his cheeks suddenly appeared flushed and damp.

"But now you?" he said. "You don't believe Wayne killed his wife and himself? You think they were murdered by someone higher up who was afraid of being implicated?"

"I don't just think. I know."

"I agree. And I know who it is."

"Yes?"

"Henry Durning," Hinkey's voice was calm. "It has to be him."

"Why?"

"Because no one else in the world was anywhere near as close to Brian Wayne and his wife."

"That's no reason."

"Maybe not," said Hinkey. "But it's sure as hell an answer. And give me a little time and I'll bet you a million bucks I can dig up a reason to go with it."

Carlo Donatti looked at him. It was a beginning.

52

PAULIE WALKED QUICKLY through the dark. He was going mostly downhill toward where the last road marker had said he would reach the next town in four kilometers. It was hard to read the name on the marker because the stone was old and worn and there was only a small piece of moon. But the name didn't matter as long as he was headed in the right direction. Then his map told him the town had to be Lercara Friddi, so he was doing that part all right.

So far, only two cars had passed while he was walking. He had seen their lights and heard their engines from a long way off, so he'd had plenty of warning to get off the road until they were gone. He knew it was kind of soon for anyone to be out looking for him, but why take chances?

After a while a wind came up, and he felt cold in only a shirt and jeans. He guessed he should have taken something of Dom's or Tony's for added warmth, something to throw over his shoulders, but he'd had other things on his mind.

He walked faster. Then he jogged a little to warm himself, and it worked. When he jogged, the gun in his pocket kept bumping against his leg, so he stuck it inside his belt. He had taken Dom's small snub-noser instead of his big automatic because it was easier to hide in one of his pockets. The idea that he better take a gun along had come to him late and hard, just as he was leaving the house. The hard part was his remembering what he had just seen guns do. It was very different from seeing it in movies. Suddenly, blood was blood, and dead was dead, and nobody ever got up again for another picture.

The next thing he thought about was food. All of a sudden he was hungry and he had nothing to eat. Stupid. All that great bread and salami and cheese and fruit and stuff lying back there at the house, and he hadn't so much as thought about filling a bag. But he had money. He would buy things when he reached the next town. If he didn't starve to death by morning.

To get his mind off eating, he did an imaginary night painting as he walked, with the piece of moon turning the road ahead into a blue-green river that ran between banks of bushes and grass. He felt the mood as soft, with hardly any contrast between the halftones and darks. Except where the moon glazed the road in tiny pinpoints of light, and these caught the eye right away.

The boy loved night painting, although he had not done it all that much. It was hard to work from life in the dark, and harder still if you tried to do it from memory in the studio. But it was easy enough to do it all in your mind, without brushes and paints. And there wasn't even the mess to clean up afterward.

Then Paulie saw the faint lights of a car moving in the distance. It was hard to tell direction at first because the lights kept disappearing around curves and behind trees. Then they came along a straight, open stretch, and it was clear the lights were headed his way.

He left the road, ducked behind some brush, and stayed there until the car arrived in a rush of sound and light. The boy caught a quick glimpse of a man and woman sitting close together in front. The woman's head was on the man's shoulder, and she looked as though she might be sleeping. Then the car was gone and the road was a blue-green river again.

Those two, at least, were not chasing him.

Paulie continued his trek.

Moments later, cresting a rise, he saw the glow of what had to be Lercara Friddi.

He stood looking off at the town, envying those asleep in their beds, surrounded by families, doors closed against outside threats. The stores would not be opening for another three or four hours, so he thought it best to wait up here in the woods until then. A strange kid wandering around the streets in the middle of the night was just asking for trouble.

The boy found a broad-trunked, comfortable-looking tree and sat down with his back to it. He took Dom's snub-nosed revolver out of his belt, broke it open, and counted four unused cartridges in the cylinder. The two spent cartridges had sent their bullets into Tony. Paulie thought again about how Dom had saved his life with those two shots, and how God had rewarded him for his good deed by letting him get killed on account of the very person he had saved. It didn't seem right or make sense, but that sure was how it turned out.

He slid the snub-noser into his right-hand pants pocket, became aware of the thick bulge of lira notes stuffed into his other pocket, and felt a bit easier about things.

Paulie guessed that money and guns had to be just about two of the most important things in the world.

After a while he grew sleepy and curled up in the grass. He shivered with cold. He couldn't remember ever having been this cold. And hungry. He collected some leaves and branches and covered himself with them.

Later, after he had put his thumb in his mouth and stopped shivering, he finally slept.

53

THEY ARRIVED IN Monreale just as it was growing light, and drove through gray, deserted streets.

Gianni sat behind the wheel, with Lucia beside him to tell him where to make his turns. Vittorio was still stretched out, unconscious, on the backseat. His strips of bandage were soaked through with fresh blood. His breathing heavy, rasping.

The girl pointed through the windshield. "It's the next turn on your left. My cousin's home is the last one on the block. There's a doctor's shingle in front."

Gianni saw the shingle. The doctor's name was Helene Curci.

He pulled into the driveway and parked close to a side entrance that had a sign, OFFICE, above it. No one was in sight. The road continued past the house, but it ran only across empty fields, finally curving off and disappearing in the distance.

"Is your cousin married?" asked Gianni.

"She was. Twice. Not anymore."

Lucia got out and rang the bell beside the office entrance. A moment later she rang it again and the door opened. Watching, Gianni saw a slender woman. She was still getting into her robe.

"My God, Lucia!"

Vittorio's blood was on the girl's clothes.

"It's not me, Helene. It's a friend. He's unconscious in the backseat."

"Pietro?"

"No. Pietro is dead. His own men murdered him. This is a good one. He saved my life."

The doctor sighed. Gianni thought she had an intelligent good-looking face with disappointed eyes.

"Knife or gunshot?" she asked.

"Gunshot. Two. Side and upper thigh."

"Wonderful. Pull the car all the way up and bring him in

the back door." The doctor bent to look at Gianni behind the wheel. "Who's he?"

"His friend. He saved my life, too."

Dr. Curci slowly shook her head. "I'll put on some clothes," she said and disappeared into the house.

Gianni followed her instructions. He lifted and wrestled Vittorio out of the car, through the back door, and onto a metal examining table in her office. He was sweating and stained with blood when he finished.

Vittorio came awake as Gianni put him down. "Where the hell am I?"

"My cousin's office," said Lucia. "The doctor."

Vittorio closed his eyes. Dr. Curci took his pulse, looked at the bloody bandages, and didn't even bother to cut them open.

"He barely has a pulse. You'll have to get him to a hospital."

"No hospital," said Vittorio.

"You need blood or you're dead," said the doctor. "You want to die? Do it in your car, not in my office."

"You're all heart," breathed Vittorio.

With the roads empty, they made it to Monreale Hospital in under eight minutes. A wheeled stretcher took Vittorio through the emergency entrance. Close beside him, Gianni looked for possible watchers.

Vittorio moved in and out of consciousness. At the end, being rolled toward surgery, he reached for Gianni's hand. "Don't forget my boy," he said. "You hear, Gianni?"

"I hear."

Vittorio Battaglia squeezed Garetsky's hand one last time and disappeared through a pair of green swinging doors. Gianni stood staring after him. Feeling Lucia at his back, he turned and didn't like what he saw in her eyes. She had dark deep eyes to look into, and they told him things he didn't want to be told.

A short while later the girl's cousin came through the green doors and told him these same things in words.

"Your friend just went into cardiac arrest," she said. "We

got him going again, but he's lost so much blood he can go into shock at any second."

Gianni stood looking at the messages on the doctor's face. "Are you telling me he's going to die?"

"Only God can tell you that."

"I'm not asking God. If He was here at all, He must have left early. I'm asking *you.*"

The disappointment Gianni had seen earlier on Helene Curci's face turned sad. "I can only promise you this," she said. "Whatever can possibly be done for your friend, everyone here is going to do."

Gianni Garetsky believed her.

He watched her walk back down the corridor and through the green doors. *The next time she comes through those doors it will be to tell me whether Vittorio is alive or dead.*

Meanwhile, there were things to do.

Gianni took Lucia's arm and led her to a small waiting area off the corridor. It was empty and he sat the girl down where she would have a clear view of the emergency reception desk.

"Listen," he said. "Sooner or later someone's going to be coming in over there to check for gunshot admissions. It'll probably be one of Ravenelli's people. Do you know them all?"

"Yes."

"Do you know how to use a gun?"

The girl nodded.

Gianni took out an automatic and put it in her purse. "For emergency use only. I don't want you a sitting duck. Just remember it's on safety. Also, if you know them, they'll know you. So try to stay out of sight. At least until I get back."

"Where are you going?"

"I want to drive our car away from the entrance area before someone spots it. And while I'm out, I can pick up some Sicilian widow's weeds and turn you into a less easily recognizable old lady."

Before leaving the hospital, Gianni slipped an orderly a bunch of lire to lend him a set of whites and toss his own bloodstained clothes into a washing machine.

Outside, the sun was up and burning away the early mists.

The hospital was close to the center of the city, and the streets were coming alive with the day's business. Gianni could feel each separate sound enter him. A normal world. But no longer his.

The car was just where he had left it. Including the keys in the ignition. Stupidly careless. And in Sicily, of all places. Car theft capital of the planet. Walking around the automobile, Gianni counted nine separate bullet and shrapnel holes. Anyone looking would have had little trouble picking it out.

He drove the car a few blocks away and swung into the center of a rapidly filling, municipal parking lot. Before leaving the car, he remembered to take out not only the ignition key, but another automatic to replace the one he had left with Lucia.

I'm improving. I may even get good at this.

Walking back to the hospital, he stopped at a clothing store and bought the traditional black dress and head scarf of the island's elderly to help camouflage Lucia.

Gianni had been gone from the hospital for no more than half an hour. But simply reentering the place, breathing its air flavored with body things, drugs, sickness, he felt it an alien land that belonged to another life. He glimpsed Lucia, sitting exactly where he had placed her in the small waiting area. The girl nodded slightly to let him know there had been no disasters during his absence, and Gianni nodded in return.

Then he approached the dark-haired woman at the reception desk and wished her a good morning.

She smiled. "Good morning to you, too. How is your friend doing?"

"Not well. They told me his heart stopped beating for a while. But I'm hopeful. It's my nature."

"That's a good nature to have. You're lucky." The woman looked at him. "You speak Italian well, but not like a Sicilian. Where are you from?"

"The United States. New York. But my mother was Sicilian. She was born in Marsala."

"I have cousins living in Marsala."

"You're joking," said Gianni.

"No. Seriously. To be exact. Five cousins. And two aunts."

"Maybe we're cousins."

The woman laughed. "Stranger things have happened."

His eyes solemn, Gianni studied the woman. "Besides maybe dying," he said, "my friend has this other little problem. Certain people may be coming around asking questions."

"I know. Dr. Curci explained about that. You don't have to worry. No gunshot wounds were admitted here tonight. Not officially, and not any other way."

Gianni Garetsky found himself so moved he kissed her hand.

"Please," she said. "What are cousins for?"

Gianni went back to where Lucia was sitting and gave her the black dress and the head scarf.

"I bought the dress three sizes too large," he said. "If you stuff a pillow inside, they won't know you for sure."

The girl went into a room to change. When she returned— her hair covered by the black scarf, her plumped-out body stooped over as she walked—she might have been an aging Sicilian peasant woman long widowed and gone to seed.

They sat together through the waiting. They spoke little. They watched the green doors, a big clock on an opposite wall, and those entering the reception area and speaking to the dark-haired woman at the desk.

Gianni, having not really slept for almost forty-eight hours, occasionally dozed off. It was while he was briefly in this mode, dreaming of Mary Yung, that Lucia squeezed his arm and woke him with a start.

"I know those two," she whispered.

Gianni followed her glance toward the reception area and saw two men talking to the woman at the desk.

"They look like police," he said.

"They are. But what does that mean around here? Pietro had half the *carabinieri* on his payroll. I've seen those two at the villa at least five or six times."

The girl drew back her chair as she huddled under her old woman's shawl. Gianni fingered the automatic beneath his shirt. He watched the two cops talking to the woman and gazing about the emergency entrance area. The whole concept of the police being involved was disturbing. It brought that much more scope and depth to the search. It meant there would not be a doctor, clinic, or hospital on the island that wouldn't be checked out several times over the coming days.

Gianni saw one of the men pull over the emergency room register and examine the admissions for last night and this morning. Then apparently satisfied by what they saw and whatever the woman had told them, they turned and left the hospital.

Breathing deeply, Gianni blessed his new cousin.

He saw Dr. Curci come through the green doors. It was more than four hours since she had disappeared behind them, and her movements were slow, tired, almost trancelike in their deliberation. Watching her approach, Gianni sensed Vittorio Battaglia's death preceding her along the corridor like a dark angel. He felt Lucia stiffen in the chair beside him, confirming his judgment. When the girl put her hand on his, her touch was one of condolence.

Good-bye, Vittorio.

They both stood to receive the news. It was instinctive, a show of respect for the newly departed.

"I don't know how," said Dr. Curci, "but your friend did get through surgery."

Gianni looked at the drawn-faced woman in her rumpled and spotted hospital garments and suddenly thought her beautiful.

"Thank you for everything."

"Don't thank me yet. He can still be dead in an hour."

Gianni Garetsky nodded. "Where is he now?"

"In recovery."

"And then?"

"Surgical intensive care."

"I have to be with him."

"It's not allowed."

"I can't leave him alone," said Gianni. "They've already been here looking for him. They went away, but others will be back. They'll finish him for sure. You know these things better than I."

Helene Curci thought about it. "Come with me."

She prepared Gianni with a sterile mask, cap, and gown

and set him up behind a screen in a corner of the room. He sat there, gun in hand, listening to the small, frightening sounds of the monitors.

What I've done to this man and his family.

54

IT WAS MORNING and Peggy had decided. Today she would do it.

She lay on her stomach in bed, in the safe house, her chin resting against the backs of her hands. She thought of her husband and child and what they'd had together. Until it began tearing her apart. *I can't do that. If I do, I'll be useless.* The thought was by way of apology.

A few strands of hair fell across her eyes and she stared out the window through them.

She saw some bushes and a tree nearby and a mountain in the distance. A breeze came off the mountain and filled the thin white curtains and pressed them against her face. A stream ran downhill a short distance behind the house, and although she could not see it, she could hear the sound of the water and the sound of the wind blowing above it. The water sounded close enough to be flowing over her feet and washing them.

After a while she got out of bed and bathed in the stream. Although she was not hungry, she took something to eat because she had never started a day without eating, and she was not about to change now.

Then she set about doing all the other things she felt needed to be done. It was all part of the compulsive order by which she had always tried to live her life—as if by imposing order on the small parts, the details, she could soothe the disorder that threatened to tear apart the whole.

She had no idea whether Vittorio was alive or dead, but

she wrote him a note anyway. In case he ever did come back here, she didn't want him wondering what had happened to her. Then she left the few scrawled sheets of paper where they had long ago agreed to leave such things if it should ever be required.

At the end, Peggy moved more quickly. As if speed itself would be enough to keep her from thinking too much.

She walked out of the house, locked the front door, and left the key over the lintel.

Once, before getting into her car, she stopped and looked back at the house that was supposed to be so safe for them. Then she slid behind the wheel and drove away in the late-afternoon sun, circling slowly down out of the mountains in the direction of Ravello.

She drove stiffly, tensely, watching the front and rear with the kind of caution she knew had more to do with fear than logic. If they were out searching for her at all, she thought, it wouldn't be up here on a narrow, winding mountain road. Still, her knuckles were white on the wheel, and her eyes kept glancing back and forth between the road ahead and rearview mirror.

When Peggy reached Ravello, she made three passes through town, watching for pedestrians or cruising cars that looked the slightest bit suspicious. She had done a dry run the day before and had chosen the pay phone she thought it would be best to use. Ready now with a bag full of the necessary coins, she finally parked her car and walked over to the public phone in the gas station. There she placed a person-to-person call to Attorney General Henry Durning, the Department of Justice, Washington, D.C.

When she heard Henry Durning's personal secretary say that the attorney general was out of the office at this time, Peggy asked the operator to pass on the message that Irene Hopper would call again at exactly 1:30 P.M. Washington time, and that it was absolutely vital for the attorney general to be there to speak with her.

To ensure against possible mistakes, Peggy insisted that the secretary repeat the entire message.

She hung up and walked back to her car. Then she sat

watching the people strolling along the streets, going into and out of shops, and driving by in their automobiles.

I used to do all these things.

Henry Durning returned to his office from a White House meeting half an hour later and received Peggy's message along with a bunch of others. It had been clocked in as an overseas call at exactly 11:32 A.M. Durning told his secretary to hold all calls until further notice and got the head of the Justice Department's Communications Section on the line.

"A person-to-person call came into my office from Italy at 11:32 A.M.," he said. "I want to know precisely where it originated. City, town, switching station, phone number, location. Everything. And fast."

The attorney general had it all seven minutes later. Not only that the call had come from Ravello, but that it had been made from a pay phone, in an Esso service station, on the Via Contari where it crossed the Via Teno.

He walked out to where his secretary was sitting and put the memorandum on her desk.

"Did you take this call yourself?"

She glanced at the flimsy. "Yes, sir."

"Did you hear the woman speaking at the other end?"

"Yes."

"Was she speaking English or Italian?"

"English."

"With or without an accent?"

"Without. As a matter of fact, she sounded like an American."

Durning returned to his office and closed the door. Using his secure phone, he called Carlo Donatti's personal number in his New York office tower.

The don answered on the third ring.

"It's me," said Durning. "Are you alone?"

"No. Hold just a moment, please."

The line was silent. Durning's mouth felt like sand when he swallowed. He drank some water and turned it to mud.

"All right," said Donatti. "What's happening?"

"I've been out of my office all morning. When I returned a

few minutes ago, there was a message that the woman we're looking for had called me person-to-person at 11:32 and would call back at exactly 1:30 P.M."

"You're sure it was her?"

"Who else could it be? A woman calling person-to-person from Italy and, according to my secretary, speaking English like an American. Anyway, I had the call checked by Communications. It came from a pay phone at an Esso station in Ravello. Can you get word to some of your people in the area?"

"Of course," said Donatti. "If they can't get there themselves, they'll reach others who can. How do you want it handled?"

"The way it should have been handled ten years ago."

Donatti was silent.

"You have only about an hour and twenty minutes to set it up," said Durning. "And the chances are she's not going to be calling back from the same telephone or even from the same town. But I'll try to hold her on long enough to let your people get a trace going."

"What do you suppose she wants?"

"Her son. What else? She wants to make some sort of deal for him."

"Would you be interested?"

"Why not? At least on the phone. I'll agree to anything to keep her talking long enough for your people to reach her. After that, there's only one kind of deal that can give me some peace. And you know what that is."

"I'll call when I have something," said Donatti.

"If you have something, I'll probably know before you do. Remember. I'll be on the phone with her when it happens."

The don accepted his unexpected good fortune with the same quiet equanimity with which he had learned to accept the bad. Had he planned this latest twist of fate himself, he could not have arranged things any better for his own needs. He felt the warmth of it pulse through him in the same way he had once felt the warmth of an especially desired woman. Except that if this went right, its results would be more significant and longer lasting than anything ever offered to him sexually.

With no time to spare, he quickly made a call to Don Pietro Ravenelli's private number at his villa outside of Palermo.

The man he heard answer was definitely not the Sicilian *capo*. And as far as Donatti knew, no one else had the authority to unlock and pick up Ravenelli's secure phone.

"Who is this?" he asked.

"Michael Sorbino, counselor to Don Ravenelli." Sorbino sounded tentative, quietly deferential. "With much respect, Don Donatti, I'm at your service."

"You know my voice?"

"We've met several times, Godfather. But of course you wouldn't remember."

"What are you doing on this phone? Where is Don Pietro?"

Sorbino allowed himself a long moment before he answered. "He's dead, Don Donatti. In the middle of the night. A terrible tragedy. Along with five of our family. It was that crazyman and his friend. The two you've been after. First, they hit two guards here at the villa. Then they took out three more after we thought we had them trapped. You wouldn't believe such a disaster. And all because of the boy."

Carlo Donatti let it filter through him. They had planted a wisp of a breeze and reaped a whirlwind.

"And they got away?"

"Yes. But we believe the boy's father took at least a couple of hits. All doctors and hospitals are being checked."

"And the boy himself?"

"The boy is gone, Don Donatti. Disappeared during the night like a ghost. And the two men guarding him were found shot in their bedroom."

Donatti worked to control himself. "The men are dead?"

"Yes. Two of our best."

"You think it was the boy's father and Garetsky?"

"I can't think who else. They had Don Ravenelli's woman with them. She could have known where the boy was being held and taken them there."

Donatti didn't agree. If Vittorio had his son back, why would his wife be calling Durning? Unless they had not been in touch since last night, and she didn't know the boy was with his father. But Carlo Donatti had something more important on his mind right now and time was getting tight.

"I take it you're in charge there now, Michael?"

"I'm trying my best, Don Donatti. As you can understand, it's a sad time for us all. But if I can be of service, you have only to ask."

"As a matter of fact you *can* be of service. And it's vital. If you can help me in this, I'll be most grateful."

"Please. Just tell me what you need."

"Good. Then listen carefully because there's a clock ticking. At 7:30 this evening, your time, a woman calling herself Irene Hopper will be making a person-to-person call to United States Attorney General Henry Durning in Washington, D.C. She'll be calling from a pay phone either in Ravello or someplace not too far away. And you're going to have to get a trace going on this call from the moment it's put through. Are you with me so far?"

"Yes, Don Donatti."

"So the overseas operators in that area will have to be alerted in advance. Which means you'll need plenty of police cooperation. Can you get that?"

"No problem."

"The attorney general will be doing all he can to stretch the conversation and hold the woman on the line as long as possible. But everyone will still have to move fast to pick her up. I don't care who gets to her first, your people or the police. As long as she's not hurt. That's important. You understand that, Michael?"

"Yes."

"If the police get her, you can pick her up from them and take her to that small white villa near the Palermo airport where I once had a meeting with Don Ravenelli. You know the place?"

"I know it, Don Donatti."

"If your own people get to her first, the police don't even have to be involved. Just take her directly to the villa, call me at my private number, and I'll give you further instructions."

"I don't have your private number."

Carlo Donatti gave it to him.

"You're the only one who's to know the number. Memorize it, then put it to a match. Do you have any questions?"

"Am I to know who this woman is?"

"She's the missing boy's mother."

The line was silent for several beats.

"She doesn't know her husband and his friend took the boy?" asked Sorbino.

"Evidently not. We don't know that for sure, either."

High in his New York office, Carlo Donatti glanced at his watch. "You have only about fifty minutes to make your calls and set things in motion. I would suggest you arrange for as many cars as possible . . . police and your own . . . to be spaced every few kilometers within a thirty-kilometer radius of Ravello. Then when the trace picks up the phone's location, at least one of the cars should be no more than a few minutes' drive away."

"I'll arrange it."

"Thank you, Don Sorbino."

Forty-five hundred miles away, Michael Sorbino swelled with pride and pleasure at the first official recognition of his new status as a boss. And from no less a personage than the all-powerful American *capo di tutti capi* himself, Don Carlo Donatti.

In New York, Donatti put down the phone and carefully went over the call in his mind. If all went well and his luck held, it might well turn out to be one of the more significant conversations of his life. But his major wild card was still the boy.

Where was he?

Was he even alive?

55

Peggy drove into Amalfi at a bit after 7:00 P.M. Italian time. She made two slow turns around Flavio Gioia Square and parked with a long line of tourist shops on one side of her car, and the open sea on the other.

She had earlier chosen the phone she would use. It was in a glass booth at the far end of the square that would allow her a clear view of the area and anyone approaching. Once she was talking, she wanted no surprises.

Peggy sat stiffly in the car and watched people walking by. The sun was low and turning orange, with everyone's skin going to copper. They looked like Indians, and Peggy suddenly wished she were an Indian. She wished she were just about anything but what she was. Then not liking the way her mind was working, she stopped thinking entirely.

It had showered earlier, and puddles had collected in some of the low places in the pavement. They reflected the sky and the buildings facing the square and sometimes people walking by. They were as smooth and perfect as mirrors until someone passed through them and shattered both image and glass.

At 7:25 Peggy left her car and went into the phone booth to set herself up. It was an old-fashioned booth with a seat and a small shelf, and she sat down and tried to make herself as comfortable and well organized as possible. She took a bunch of coins from her bag and arranged them in neat piles. She prepared a pad and pencil for any notes she might have to take relating to future calls or plans. She tried to breathe slowly and deeply to calm a growing sense of panic.

Then she lifted the receiver and once more began the process of putting through a long-distance, person-to-person call to Attorney General Durning in Washington.

This time Durning's secretary passed the call right through to him, but then the line was quiet.

"Henry?" she said.

"Hello, Irene."

Nine years flew away. His voice was the same.

"Will anyone be listening in?" she asked.

"No. The moment I got on, the line became secure at this end. You can speak freely."

"I don't know how good I'm going to be at this," she said. "So I'm getting right to it. Is my son alive or dead?"

Durning didn't answer for so long that Peggy felt her son's death enter the silence. Then he said, "He's alive."

"And well?"

"Yes. He's well, too."

"All right. Then set him loose and you can have me. I'll go wherever you say. I'll do whatever you ask me to do."

Once more, Durning let the silence stretch. "Just like that?" he said softly.

"Just like that."

"I'm afraid it's not that simple."

"Why not? It's *me* you want. Not Paulie. So I'm giving you me and you're releasing Paulie. What makes that so complicated?"

"We do," said Henry Durning. "You and I. Who and what we are. The fact that lives are at stake. The kind of guarantees that would be needed to deal with our all-too-understandable mutual distrust. All these things that would have to be worked out."

What he did *not* tell her was that he was simply stalling for time to get a trace going.

"Then for God's sake, let's work them out. I just want Paulie safe in the hands of the International Red Cross in Naples. When that's been confirmed, I'll fulfill my end of the deal."

Durning's sigh drifted from Washington to Amalfi. "You used to be a damn good lawyer, but you're certainly not talking like one now. Once your son is safely with the Red Cross, what guarantees would I have that you wouldn't just disappear again?"

The operator broke in at this point to ask for additional money, and Peggy spent the next several moments clanging more of her coins into the box. By then, something from a long way back had entered her like a private, all-but-forgotten woe, and it was enough to set her off into another time and direction.

"How could you have done it, Henry?" Even her voice had changed, had gone soft with a ten-year-old hurt.

Her sudden transformation had lost him. "How could I have done what?"

"Sent someone out to kill me. I mean originally. Ten years ago."

No longer lost, he still had no answer for her.

"Didn't you know me at all?" Peggy said. "I adored you. I'd have died sooner than betray you. I'd have done anything for you. I *did* anything for you."

It took Henry Durning a long time to answer. When he did, his voice seemed as much changed as Peggy's.

"It was my own craziness that betrayed me, not you. What can I tell you, Irene? That if I had it all to do over I wouldn't have done it? All right. I wouldn't have done it. Do you think I'm proud of what I've become? I've done the worst. But taking your boy was never my idea. I hope you believe that."

"Why should it matter what I believe?"

"Because you loved me once. And as insane as it now sounds, I loved you."

Peggy sat staring with blind eyes. The lying bastard could get his mouth to say just about anything. Yet with it all she was almost ready to believe it. "That's just history," she said tiredly. "The only thing I care about now is getting my son freed. You mentioned guarantees before. You said you didn't want me disappearing once Paulie was safely with the Red Cross. All right. Tell me what kind of guarantees you want."

"I'm afraid it's more than just that."

"What do you mean?"

"It's a question of belief," Durning said. "I guess I can't really get myself to accept the idea of your being willing to—"

Peggy heard no more.

A man she had not even seen approaching had opened the booth, pulled the telephone receiver from her hand, and hung it up.

"Police," he said, and showed her a badge and ID.

She stared dumbly at them. Then she saw that there were two other men with him. All three wore plainclothes, not uniforms, and their car was parked no more than ten feet away. The car carried official plates, but was otherwise unmarked.

Were they really police?

Not that it mattered much in this country. The long arm of the mob reached into just about everything. And in this particular case, Henry Durning was clearly at the far end of the arm.

God, have I messed things up.

Then Peggy entered a small circle of calm and let it close around her. She knew that once she left it, there would be nothing.

"Would you please come with us?" said the detective who had showed her his badge and police identification.

"I don't know what this is all about, Officer," said Peggy, "but there's obviously some mistake."

"No, signora. There's no mistake."

"Who do you think I am?"

The detective just stared at her. As did the two men with him. They evidently had no identification for her other than the fact that she was talking on this particular phone at this particular time.

"I'm not a criminal," Peggy said softly, out of her new calm. "I'm Mrs. Peter Walters, I'm an American citizen. I live with my husband and son in our own home in Positano, and I'm the owner of the Leonardo da Vinci Gallery of Art in Sorrento."

She handed the alleged detective her purse. "If you'll look in my bag, you'll find my driver's license, credit cards, and any other identification you might want."

He gave her back the purse without opening it.

"I don't doubt you, Mrs. Walters. But I'm afraid you'll still have to come with us."

"Come with you where?"

"To the Amalfi police station."

"On what charges? Talking on a public pay telephone in Flavio Gioia Square?"

Then apparently out of patience, the officer in charge took her arm and started trying to pull her out of the booth.

Peggy grabbed the anchored telephone, braced herself, and held back.

"If you don't let go of me, I'm going to scream, and kick, and yell, and make enough of a scene to bring two hundred angry, frightened people running to find out who's being raped. Now is that what you'd really like to see happening here?"

The detective let go of her arm.

"Be reasonable, Mrs. Walters. We don't know any more about this than you. We're just trying to follow orders and do our job."

"What are your orders?"

"To bring in whoever's talking on this phone."

In the following moment of stillness, she decided they were police after all. If they were mob, she'd be lying quietly dead at the bottom of the booth, and they'd be gone. Which could mean little in the long run but might allow her a bit of slack for now.

"If you'll let me make just one phone call to the American consul in Sorrento," she said, "I'll go with you without further fuss."

"Sorry, Mrs. Walters. No phone calls."

"Is that part of your orders?"

The detective nodded.

"What's your name?" Peggy asked.

"Trovato. Sergeant Trovato."

"Well, Sergeant Trovato, it looks as if you're going to have to take me in kicking and screaming."

The sergeant appeared genuinely puzzled.

"I don't understand this whole thing, Mrs. Walters. All we're asking you to do is take a five-minute ride to the Amalfi police station. If there's some mistake, you'll be out of there in no time. Why are you making this so hard for us all?"

"Would you like the truth, Sergeant?"

Trovato showed a set of white, near-perfect teeth . . . a handsome, no doubt decent police officer, thought Peggy, who hadn't the faintest idea what he was in the process of doing to her.

"In my line of work," he said, "the truth is such a novelty that I've forgotten what it sounds like."

"Then I'll try to refresh your memory," Peggy told him. "You won't believe it, but the reason I'm making this so hard for us all is that once I'm in your police station, I know that no one will ever see me alive again."

He stared at her. "You can't be serious, Mrs. Walters."

"See? I said you wouldn't believe me."

"I'm sorry," he said.

And the crazy part was, she thought, that he probably *was* sorry. A polite, unusually attractive man just trying to do his day's tour of duty and go home to his family without causing unnecessary pain or harm.

So that even as he gently reached out to touch her, it seemed no more than a warm, human gesture, one member of the species reaching out to another at a moment of deep stress and emotion.

Yet an instant later she was feeling humble as a saint, as the fading evening light dimmed even more and she was entering a sweet new realm of peace and darkness.

She never sensed she was falling, because Sergeant Trovato was holding her before she was able to feel her legs starting to go.

Peggy knew she was in a prison cell the moment she opened her eyes.

She lay with her head facing a window, and the bars were dark against a translucent orange sky.

There was no pain, just a faint soreness at the pressure point on her neck where the gentle sergeant must have briefly cut off the flow of blood to her brain.

If she felt anything at all, it was rather like the exhausted state of grace that sometimes came after a long, intense session of making love, with the heavy action behind you, and nothing to do for a while but drift.

The thing was, they hadn't killed her.

It was a mark of her current view of things that this fact alone was enough to make her euphoric.

56

THE ATTORNEY GENERAL went over some papers and had lunch in his office as he waited for Carlo Donatti's call. But he was only going through the motions of working and eating. His thoughts were solely on the woman he had once known as Irene.

To have had the courage to offer herself like that.

There was a purity to the gesture that defied and broke through his cynicism. Except that it was a lot more than a gesture. It was her life. It made him reassess everything he had felt and thought about her.

You should have trusted me, Henry. Didn't you know anything at all about me?

Obviously not.

But even if he had known, that kind of trust still would not have been in his nature. Too bad. It would have saved a lot of trouble and an appalling number of lives.

Donatti's call came through on his secure line at 2:47 P.M.

"All went well," said the don. "Can we meet tonight? There are some things to talk about."

"The usual time and place?"

"If that's convenient."

"Fine," said the attorney general, and hung up.

Henry Durning felt no elation. Not even relief. In a curious way he felt diminished, as if one more vital piece of him had broken off and floated away.

This time it was Durning who arrived at the room first and took care of the dual amenities of the music and the drinks.

My ritual assignation.

It did have many of the characteristics of a lovers' tryst. With none of the accompanying joys. Still, the excitement was there, the covert tactics, the constant threat of discovery or betrayal. And although they didn't trust each other for a second, their individual power alone created a certain mutual regard.

Or so it seemed to Henry Durning.

It was hard to know about Donatti. These so-called *men of respect* were of a different breed entirely. You might sometimes think you knew them, but you never did. With their long history of tradition, their almost medieval oath of silence . . . *omertà* . . . there was no real possibility of ever understanding or getting close to them. At best, all you could hope for was an acceptable working relationship. And even this depended on a carefully weighed balanced of power.

Like keeping a gun carefully aimed at each other's head.

And when possible, Durning thought coldly, getting hold of a little something extra as backup insurance.

The don arrived moments later and they embraced and sat down facing each other. Neither of them spoke for several beats. They seemed to be making an accommodation to the event that had brought them together tonight.

Donatti crossed his legs carefully and sipped the scotch Durning had prepared for him.

"Well, it's done," he said. "You did your part well, and so did everyone else. The woman is no longer a problem for you."

"Thank you Carlo. I appreciate it."

Donatti looked at him. "You don't exactly seem wild with joy."

"I'm not. I needed her death. I can't take pleasure from it." Durning stared into his drink without touching it. It might have been blood. "How was it done?"

"Do you really want to know?"

"No. But it's better than having to keep wondering and imagining."

"It was very workmanlike," said Carl Donatti. "Nothing special. How much did you hear from your end?"

"We'd been speaking for almost eight minutes. Then the receiver was suddenly slammed down and that was it. Who was it that picked her up?"

"Three detectives from the Amalfi police department."

"And?"

"They put her in solitary. A few hours later two of our Sicilian people picked her up, drove her to some woods, and did it. She won't be found."

A surging burst of Mozart filled the silence.

"Did she know what was going to happen?"

The don shrugged. "Who can say? Anyway, who cares what she knew?"

"I care."

They sat with their usual loud music for a few moments, not talking. His eyes blank, Carlo Donatti slowly shook his head. "You're a strange one, Henry. For such a concerned and sensitive man, you seem to be getting an awful lot of people killed."

Durning was silent.

"Just to bring you up to date on the body count," said Donatti. "Our friends Battaglia and Garetsky have just added eleven more, among them, the Sicilian *capo* I've been working with."

The attorney general felt the numbers settling inside him. A slow-acting poison.

"This boss," he said. "He was the one holding Battaglia's son?"

Donatti nodded.

"Then where's the boy? Did his father get him back safely?"

"Nobody seems to know."

"What about the two men you said were guarding him?"

"Dead. And according to the new *capo*, Vittorio himself took a couple of hits in all the fireworks. They've got people checking hospitals."

"Wonderful," said Durning.

Closing his eyes, he saw dark waters washing over vague faceless bodies in a midnight pond.

Mary Yung had an aversion to the cool, arid feel of air-conditioning on her bare flesh, so Durning kept the unit turned off when they made love.

"I adore our being wet together," she had told him, "all that lovely slipping and sliding," and he appreciated what she meant.

That sweet mingling of one more set of juices.

Even in darkness, it brought him visions of her seductively shapely body shining with perspiration, climbing all over him as she invented new and ever more exciting ways to bring him off.

What were her limits?

She had to have them, of course. She was still only a woman, with the standard number of available parts . . . two hands and three body openings. But sweet Lord, what she could think of to do with them. And the way she did it.

So what are her limits?

They lay on their backs in the close heat of the night. Heavy air pressed against their faces. A car went by, its tires whispering on the asphalt. Miles away, a police siren wailed of another murder.

"You're like a seventeen-year-old," she said.

"How? In my unseemly adolescent compulsions?"

"You have this incredible sense of wonder. There's not a centimeter of a woman's body that you don't know, understand, and love. It's a wonderland for you."

"Is that good or bad?"

"It depends on how you use it."

"In that case I'm in deep trouble."

She rolled onto her side and kissed him. "As if you didn't know that."

"What I know is that when I die it's very likely to be a woman who's going to do me in." Durning reached for his cigarettes, lit one, and studied the glow in the dark. "And I must admit that right now you're probably the leading candidate for that honor."

Mary Yung tried to see his face, but it was too dark to make out its expression.

"Are you serious?" she said.

"About my own death?" He smiled. "How could I not be?"

"Then why are you keeping me living in your house and romping in your bed?"

"Because that's where I want you."

"Even knowing you might well die of it?"

Like a cat, he idly licked her breast. His pacifier.

Then he lay back once more. "Yes."

"That's insane, Henry."

"Insanity is nothing but a judgment call. And in my judgment it makes great sense for me to have and enjoy what I want most at this particular stage of my life."

Mary Yung lay still, wordless.

"Don't misunderstand," said Henry Durning. "I'm far from suicidal. I want very much to live. I love living. It's just that I'm trying to be realistic about my short-term prospects."

"Meaning?"

"That I seem to walk in the shadow of death these days. I just breathe and it's right beside me. Just tonight I learned your friends Gianni and Vittorio have added eleven more to the growing list."

Durning felt Mary stiffen beside him. But she remained silent.

"Not that I blame them. They're simply trying to get back Vittorio's son. Just as you and the boy's mother have been trying to do. And I've been told *she* died sometime this afternoon."

It took Mary a moment to respond. When she did, she spoke out of a cold dryness in her throat that had not been there before.

"Peggy?"

"Yes, though it was as Irene that I once knew her."

"So you finally got what you've been after all this time," Mary Yung said slowly.

Durning said nothing.

"And her boy?"

Durning considered his answer to this one very carefully. Though in a practical sense, there really was nothing to consider. If he didn't lie, he would lose her. And he had no intention of allowing that.

"I had it all arranged," he said. "They were supposed to let the boy go the moment they had his mother. But before that could happen, Battaglia and Garetsky blew away eleven of their people. Now it's a personal vendetta, a matter of honor. Now they refuse to let the boy go until they get Battaglia and Garetsky."

"They're using him as bait?"

"They have no other reason to hold him."

"Who are *they?*"

"My American don's Sicilian connections."

Mary Yung thought about it.

"So what happens now?" she asked.

"I'll just have to keep pressuring them."

"You can do that?"

He pressed his lips to her breast for luck.

"I'm the United States attorney general. I'm head of the entire Justice Department. I can goddamn do anything."

"Yes. But now that you've gotten rid of the boy's mother, why would you bother?"

"To keep you from leaving me," said Henry Durning. "And maybe even to keep you from putting one in my head with your little gun."

Which was probably as close to the truth as he was able to get these days, he thought.

57

THE ATTORNEY GENERAL wept again during the funeral services for Brian and Marcia Wayne.

I'm becoming insufferable.

Sitting there with the president of the United States, the first lady, cabinet members, and other dignitaries, Henry Durning listened to the late FBI director and his wife being eulogized and felt a burning sensation in his chest. It was as though something deep inside him had spoiled, turned bad, and created its own poison.

With all his mind and heart he tried to squeeze out something for his murdered friend and his wife. But what? How?

He could get nothing for them.

All he was aware of was himself. His own burning sensation, his own weeping eyes that stung.

Even prayer was of no use. What was there to pray for? Justice? Mercy?

He breathed slowly, deeply, trying to relieve the pressure he felt. He was torn and torn again.

All right. So he killed, then he wept.

But his tears were wasted.

They meant nothing.

They helped no one.

Least of all, him.

58

PAULIE FELT RENEWED.

Leaving the town of Lercara Friddi, he wore his newly purchased windbreaker against the morning chill and carried a backpack filled with food and other needs for his journey back to Positano.

For the first time in his short life, he was consciously aware of the magic of money.

He wondered what he'd have done if he hadn't thought to take it from the two dead men's pockets. Dumb thing to wonder. He'd have just been hungry and cold. Also, when he got to the ferry in Palermo, he'd have had to sneak on board and become a stowaway because he couldn't have bought a ticket.

But you had to be careful about how you showed the money. It could be dangerous. Like when he had taken it out to pay for his windbreaker, the storekeeper had looked at him kind of funny and asked what bank he'd robbed. The man had only been joking, of course. Yet he could have been suspicious about such a young boy having all that money in his pocket, and maybe called the police.

So Paulie had played it safe after that and used the smallest bills for his other purchases. Then he'd left Lercara Friddi as fast as he could, in case the man who sold him his windbreaker had thought about it some more and decided to call the police after all.

In fact he had left so quickly that he had not even stopped to eat, and his stomach was growling. He couldn't remember ever having been this hungry and wondered how long it would take a person to starve. Then he began thinking about all the great bread and cheese and salami and stuff in his backpack.

About a half-mile out of town, Paulie left the road, found a patch of grass beside a stream, and sat down to eat.

His first mouthful of bread and salami tasted better than anything he had ever eaten. It was so good that he wished his mother could be there to see how he was enjoying it. She was always complaining about how he never seemed to enjoy what he ate. Which was why he had always been so thin. Everyone knew that if you didn't really enjoy your food, it didn't do your body any good.

But just the thought of his mother took some of the joy out of eating. He had tried calling her again before leaving the town, and again there was no answer. Now he really was getting worried. Where could she be all this time?

59

SOMETHING WOKE GIANNI Garetsky in the night.

Wearing a pale-green sterile mask, he came out of sleep slowly. He was still sitting up in his special chair in the Monreale Hospital's Intensive Care Unit for eighteen hours and he had been waiting for Vittorio Battaglia's bullet-punctured body to decide whether it was going to live or die.

Gianni had left his self-assigned vigil beside his friend's bed only to eat or go to the bathroom. He not only didn't want to miss what might well be Vittorio's few final words but was still uncomfortable with the idea of leaving him helpless and unprotected against those who had put him here in the first place.

Glancing at him now, Gianni saw Vittorio as little more than a conduit. Fluids flowed into him through one set of tubes, and out of him through another set, while on the wall behind his head, the lights of monitors beeped and danced.

Gianni figured it was one of the beeps that had wakened him.

"Hey . . . "

He turned and found Vittorio looking at him with remarkably clear eyes.

"So which are you?" said Battaglia. "God, or the fucking devil in a sterile mask?"

Gianni rose, took Vittorio Battaglia's hand, and stood looking at him. He felt himself moved. He guessed he hadn't really expected him to come out of it.

"I'll get a nurse," he said.

"The hell you will. Talk to me first." Vittorio closed his eyes for a long moment. Then he opened them. "How long have I been out?"

"About eighteen hours."

"Jesus. What about the mob and the police?"

"They came looking. But you've got a few friends here."

"Who?"

"Lucia, her doctor cousin, and a nice lady in emergency who checked you in and later said all the right things when it was important to say them."

Battaglia stared at him from his pillow. "And I've got *you.*"

Gianni was silent.

"Is there any news about Paulie?"

The artist shook his head.

"What I hate most," said Battaglia weakly, "is that I'm going to have to dump the whole load on you. While I goddamn lie here pissing through tubes."

"That's what I'm here for, Vittorio."

"You don't really have to do this, you know."

"Like hell I don't. There's probably nothing I've ever had to do more."

Then a nurse heard them talking, berated Gianni for not calling her, and excitedly brought in a couple of doctors.

It was more than an hour before they were alone and able to talk again.

"Tell me what to do," said Gianni.

Vittorio's breathing was labored. The doctors had exhausted him.

"Get to Peggy at the safe house," he said. "Fast. She probably thinks we've been killed by now, and I'm worried about what she might do."

"What if she's not there?"

"If she had to leave for some reason, there should be a message. There's a bush just to the right of the back door. One of the wall stones behind the bush is loose. Pry it out. If there's a note, that's where it'll be."

"And if she's not there and there's no message?"

Vittorio met Gianni's eyes above his sterile mask. "I'm not sure what to tell you."

Gianni was silent. It occurred to him that he couldn't remember Vittorio ever having admitted to not being sure of something.

"I was about to tell you to come back and we'd talk about it," said Battaglia. "But we'd better do our talking now."

Vittorio sipped water through a straw. His face had good color. But Gianni knew it was part fever and part the new blood from his transfusions.

"See Lucia and her cousin before you go," said Battaglia. "Tell them you might be calling with messages for me. You think they can be trusted?"

"You'd be dead this minute if it weren't for them. And probably so would I."

Vittorio nodded. "I know. But an electric prod to their tits can still get whatever they've got. So you have to be careful what you say."

He stared at the ceiling as though everything he had in his mind was written there.

"If Peggy's at home, don't tell her where I am or what's happened. Tell her I'm fine and following up on some hot leads on Paulie. Tell her you've just come to give her a report and keep her from worrying. Then you'll be joining me again. Sound optimistic as hell."

"Don't I always?"

Vittorio grimaced and closed his eyes as a spasm of pain gripped him totally for several moments, then eased off.

"If Peggy's not at the house and there's a message," he said in a strained voice, "call and tell Lucia or her cousin what it is. Unless it's something so sensitive that you'd rather come back here and tell me about it in person."

Vittorio swallowed water with effort.

"If she's not at the house, and there's no message, and she doesn't appear for a few hours, come back here and we'll try to figure out our next move."

Vittorio lay back on his pillow and turned his face to Gianni. The muscles in his jaw went slack and he seemed to diminish. Even the false color in his cheeks appeared to have been lost.

"Listen," he said dully. "This is all bullshit. Let's get down to the bottom lines. If you end up with nothing. If you can't get to me. If I'm dead or whatever. Just remember what you've got."

Vittorio Battaglia gasped for air.

"You've got Durning himself behind the whole shitpot," he said. "You've got our own Don Donatti kissing Durning's ass and doing whatever else he wants him to do. And you've got this new *siciliano* prick, Michael, probably taking over Ravenelli's end of things for Don Donatti. And all of them with just one thing in mind."

Vittorio's eyes were two black holes. "To murder my wife."

As Gianni was about to leave moments later, Vittorio gripped his hand with surprising strength.

"Give me your gun," he said.

Gianni looked at him. His fever must have started rising again because his face suddenly appeared sunburned.

"If some *siciliano* walks in here in a doctor's coat to do me," said Battaglia, "I don't want to be caught with just my cock in my hand."

"Where will you keep it?"

"Between my legs. Where else?"

Garétsky took out his automatic and made sure the safety was on.

"The silencer, too," said Vittorio.

Gianni slipped the silencer from another pocket, attached it to the gun muzzle, and shoved the lengthened piece under Vittorio's bedsheet.

They looked at each other. Gianni stood there, hating to leave him alone like this.

"What a great chance to knock off a few doctors," he said.

Gianni picked up his car from the municipal parking area and arrived at Dr. Curci's house just as she and Lucia were having their morning espresso.

"He came out of it about an hour and a half ago," he told them.

Lucia pressed her hands to her cheeks. "I lit a candle for him last night."

"Was he lucid?" the doctor asked.

"Completely."

"Good. But there's still the threat of infection. I'll look in on him later."

"You've both been great. If it weren't for you two, he'd be dead."

"He still could be," said Dr. Curci.

"I know. But right now he's not."

Lucia poured Gianni some coffee and he drank it gratefully. *These two strangers.*

"I have to ask one more favor," he said. "I'm flying to the mainland this morning and I may need to get a message to Vittorio later in the day. May I call one of you?"

"I'll be right here in the house," said Lucia, and wrote down the phone number for him.

It required effort for Gianni not to hug her.

Gianni parked at the Palermo airport, caught the 8:00 A.M. flight to Naples, and arrived there less than an hour later.

The one disturbing thing was not being able to carry a piece past security. But since his face wasn't known to anyone still alive in the Ravenelli *famiglia,* he hoped there would be no need for a gun.

He rented a Ford at the Hertz counter and started the same beautiful drive south along the coast that he had taken with Mary Yung. It was only about four days ago but seemed more like a year.

And where was Mary now and whom was she fucking and selling out now?

Not that he gave a damn.

But God, what she had set in motion for her lousy million.

How did she live with it?

A woman like that.

And he had loved her.

Parts of him probably still did.

The trail to the entrance was so well camouflaged by trees, brush, and weeds that Gianni drove by twice before finally spotting it.

Easing along the trail, he mentally prayed for a happy surprise, although he'd never been big on prayer. And what he really needed here was a miracle.

But there were no visible miracles today. Only those of a brilliant sun catching the leaves, and a few bird calls, and the sight of a sky so deep and blue that you could almost swear it reached all the way to God.

Gianni did see a car parked at the side of the house. Which meant that at least Peggy was there. Until he realized there should have been two cars, since Vittorio had left his own behind.

Still, Peggy might have driven into Ravello for some reason. But it was not the most hopeful sign.

Gianni climbed the steps, knocked on the door and waited. Then he knocked and waited twice more. He felt a threatening quiet.

He tried the door and found it locked. But remembering Vittorio reaching over the lintel the night they arrived, Gianni did the same thing and touched a key.

He opened the door and went in.

"Peggy?"

There was not even an echo.

He went from one room to another of the small house. In the kitchen, there was a coffeepot on the wood stove. Gianni opened the grate and saw ashes. He touched the ashes and they were cold.

In the bedroom that Peggy and Vittorio had used, the bed had been made and Peggy's nightgown lay across it. Without knowing why, Gianni picked up the gown and breathed the faint scent of perfume. It was Peggy's scent but it made him think of Mary Yung. As did the feel of the fabric. He was ready to spend an hour contemplating both.

Idiot!

Gianni put the gown back on the bed, left the room, and went out the back door.

He saw the bush growing to the right of the door and in front of the stone house wall just as Vittorio had described it. Bending, he pushed and pulled at the individual stones until he located a loose one and removed it. In the hole was a pale-blue envelope wrapped in a clear, plastic bag. Gianni took out the bag, replaced the stone, and went back into the house.

He sat with it in the kitchen. There was a tingling in his fingers where they touched the plastic, and an oppression close to strangling in his throat.

Then suddenly disgusted with himself, he opened the plastic bag and took out the envelope. It was neither addressed nor sealed, and the stationery inside was of the same pale-blue color.

The letter was headed with yesterday's date, as well as the time, which was 6:00 P.M.

My love,

It's been more than three days since you and Gianni left, and I'm writing this letter with the terrible feeling that you may never return to read it. But just in case I'm wrong and you do make it back, I want you to know what I've done, and why.

All that matters to me now is Paulie. I want him out of the hands of these animals. I want this horror to be over for him. And as I finally see it, I'm the only one who can make that happen. So this is what I'm doing.

I'm leaving here in a few minutes to call Henry

Durning in Washington. I'm offering him a deal. Since the only thing Henry's ever really been after in all this is me, I'm letting him have me in return for his getting Paulie safely to a division of the International Red Cross.

In a way, I'm almost glad you're not here. Because I know you would have stopped me. And I don't want to be stopped.

What hurts most is how much I love you. I'm just so sorry I had to put you and Paulie through all this. Loving you has been the most wonderful thing that's ever happened to me. It makes me less ashamed of everything I was before. If someone like you could have loved me, how bad could I have been?

It's just that I feel so cheated. I'd have loved at least another forty years with you. Or maybe I'm piggish. Maybe when you get ten years as lovely as we've had, you can't expect any more. You can't measure something like that in years anyway.

Hey, love. I'd take those ten years with you over fifty years with any other man I've ever met. So don't feel sorry for me. I can't bear the idea of your feeling sorry for me. If you do, I swear I'll come back and haunt you. Unless you're dead ahead of me. Then you've got seniority and you can do the haunting first.

But dear God, I hope you're not dead. It would be terrible if our Paulie lost us both. You're the one he's always been most crazy about anyway. How he adores you. His papa. So please, please, don't be dead, love.

Oh, shit. Now I'm starting to cry. I was doing great, but now I'm starting to piss-ass cry. I can't even leave you a decent posthumous farewell note without messing it up with tears.

But I guess I've said it all, anyway. And what I haven't said, you already know.

If you're alive, you can pick up Paulie at the International Red Cross in Naples. If you're dead, he'll know to get in touch with my sister in Vermont. I've talked to him about her enough just in case something like this ever happened. But, God. Who had ever really expected it?

Please, please . . . remember me with joy.

                                          Love,
                                          Me

Gianni sat there for a while with the letter.

He guessed that some hearts just put out more love than others.

Vittorio could do better with it than he.

60

THE GALATEA CORPORATION's long-range executive jet took off from JFK International Airport at exactly 7:18 P.M. New York time. On board, besides a flight crew of four, were only Don Carlo Donatti and two personal bodyguards.

The plane's passenger cabin had been custom designed to provide the utmost in luxury and comfort, and Donatti was able to sleep for much of the smooth eight-hour flight on a full-size bed in the privacy of his own enclosed bedroom. So that when he stepped off the plane at the Palermo Municipal Airport, he appeared rested, refreshed and perfectly groomed, all of which Donatti considered important to his image.

It was 9:35 A.M. Palermo time.

Don Michael Sorbino was waiting for him on the tarmac with three black, low-profile, armor-plated sedans and a retinue of half-a-dozen men. The two *capi* embraced and went through the usual amenities. Moments later, the three-car convoy left the airport and headed south in the general direction of Partinico.

                    *   *   *

Only Sorbino and Carlo Donatti entered the classic white villa half an hour later. The others remained outside, either waiting near the cars or strolling about the grounds.

One of Sorbino's interior guards handed Donatti a large brass key, and the don went upstairs alone and unlocked a tall set of double doors. Then he closed the doors behind him and approached Vittorio Battaglia's wife, a slender, dark-haired woman sitting beside a window with an open book in her lap.

So this is the one, he thought, and felt the faint stir of an excitement he had long ago given up for dead. It was nothing sexual. Although she was certainly attractive enough as a woman. The feeling was more in the realm of who and what she was, and of all she had caused to happen. But most importantly, of course, it was born out of what she had it within her to do for him.

"I'm Carlo Donatti," he told her.

He spoke in English and waited for her response.

But there was none. All Peggy did was sit and stare at him.

"You don't know who I am?" he said.

"Should I?"

Her voice was flat, her face devoid of all expression.

"Vittorio never mentioned my name?"

Peggy shook her head.

Donatti pulled up a chair and sat down facing her. He was stunned that Vittorio Battaglia had never broken his oath of silence. And after all that had taken place. It pleased Don Carlo Donatti.

"You had good reason to know my name," he said. "Ten years ago, I was the one who gave Vittorio the contract to kill you."

Peggy sat there as it entered her. "You were his *capo?*"

"I was. And I was also the one who saved your life yesterday."

"How did you do that?"

"By not having you shot. As I'd been ordered to do."

"Who ordered you?"

"You should know by now who wants you dead."

She was silent.

"Henry Durning," he told her.

Peggy frowned. "I don't understand."

"I was to arrange for your second call to Henry to be traced, and then have you shot. But I had you brought here instead."

"What did you tell Henry?"

"That you were finally dead. This time, for real."

She sat looking at Carlo Donatti. "All right. Now tell me the important parts."

"Which are they?"

"The ones you've left out."

Donatti smiled. "What did I leave out?"

"Two things," she said. "Why someone like you would be taking orders from Henry Durning. And why you're suddenly so interested in saving my life."

The don nodded. "You must have been a very good lawyer, Mrs. Battaglia." It was the first time anyone had ever addressed her as Mrs. Battaglia, and it was not without effect. There was a whole life out there that she had not even begun to live.

"I tried my best, Don Donatti."

Carlo Donatti put on a pair of glasses and looked at Peggy more closely. Was there something about her he might be missing?

"The answers to your two questions are almost pathetically simple. I take orders from Henry Durning because he holds hard evidence that can put me away forever. And I'm interested in saving your life, because I've finally stopped being brain dead long enough to realize just how valuable you can probably be to me."

Peggy sat wordless.

"I've been a fool," said Donatti. "Durning himself told me he wanted you dead because you could effectively ruin him anytime you chose. And that was weeks ago. Yet until now, it never even crossed my mind to use you."

He paused to consider her.

"And, of course, let *you* use *me* in return."

Peggy didn't move. She was almost afraid to breathe. It might change something. And at this moment she wanted nothing changed.

"I'm not your enemy, Mrs. Battaglia. I never was. It's never been part of my code to make war on women and children. I sent Vittorio to kill you nine years ago only because Henry Durning, as district attorney, offered me a deal I couldn't refuse. Your life in return for quashing a murder indictment against me. Now that you have suddenly turned up alive nine years later, it's come back to haunt us all."

They sat without speaking. Outside, there was the murmur of voices from the men waiting beside the cars.

"You're a powerful man, Don Donatti," said Peggy. "If Henry's been such a long and continuing threat, one has to wonder why he's still alive."

"Because he's no moron. He's let me know that the moment he dies, the evidence against me goes straight from his vault to the district attorney."

Peggy nodded. "Now let's hear what you want from *me*."

"That's obvious. I want enough of a hook into Henry's gut to finally lift him off my back."

"And in return?"

"You and your boy go free."

Peggy stared down at the book in her lap. She didn't want Carlo Donatti to see her eyes at that moment.

"I know where you have *me*," she said. "But where do you have Paulie?"

"One step at a time, Mrs. Battaglia."

"Then what's the next step?"

"The reason Henry wants you dead."

Peggy cleared her throat. The dry sound of a winter leaf.

"I saw him kill two people. A man and his wife."

Carlo Donatti stood unmoving.

"You were on the scene? An actual eyewitness?"

"Yes."

"When and where was this?"

"Ten years ago. In Connecticut. In the house of a couple we'd met that same night. I was the only other person present."

"Then it was unpremeditated?"

"Yes." Peggy stared off somewhere. "At least the first killing was. I'd have to call that one manslaughter. Maybe even self-defense. It was done with a fire iron. But the second was done with a rifle and it was clearly a murder to cover the first killing."

"What happened afterward?"

"Henry staged it to look like a break-in burglary, rape, and murder. And the local police bought it."

Donatti began pacing the room, his eyes turning with him.

"You were lovers?"

"Yes."

"Did you ever threaten to go to the police? To expose him?"

"Never. I was too scared and too taken with him. He just couldn't live with the whole idea of my knowing."

"Technically, at this point, it would be your word against his. What proof would you have that it ever happened?"

Peggy thought about it. She watched Donatti's silhouette pace back and forth across the window. Finally, she put it together.

"Henry buried the murder rifle and some jewelry nearby, and I'm sure I could help you find them. Then ballistics could match the rifle to the bullet taken from the woman's body."

Carlo Donatti slowly sat down. "That should be enough. At least, as a threat."

Then he went silent.

Peggy watched him, searching for signs. A pot of water waiting to come to a boil.

"My son," she said. "When do we talk about my son?"

Donatti looked at her as though he had forgotten who she was and what she was doing there.

"Soon."

"I don't know what that means."

"Please be patient with me, Mrs. Battaglia. You're a lawyer. I'm sure you understand the subtleties to be worked out in something as complicated as this."

Complicated, she thought.

The last time she had heard the word it was spoken by Henry Durning over a telephone. And moments later she was in the hands of the Amalfi police. Between this bigshot *capo di tutti capi* and the attorney general of the United States, she felt herself being played like a violin.

"Do I have your word as a man of honor," she said, "that my son hasn't been harmed?"

"You have my word."

Peggy was almost afraid to ask the next question.

"And my husband? What's happened to my husband?"

"God only knows about Vittorio. I don't."

Donatti paused and Peggy listened to herself breathe.

"The last I heard," said the don, "he and Gianni Garetsky had blown away eleven of our best Sicilian soldiers while trying to get back your boy."

Donatti rose. He smiled but it was somewhat rueful.

"So you see, Mrs. Battaglia. I'm as anxious to give you back your son as you are to get him. He's not doing any of us much good where he is. So please bear with me. We've made good progress this morning. I'm encouraged about our prospects in regard to Henry Durning, I promise. You won't have to wait much longer."

61

ALONE IN AN anonymous rented car, Henry Durning drove north along the Potomac until he crossed into Virginia. Then he turned west for the long, final stretch on Kirby Road.

It was 9:15 P.M. and Durning had put in a full day at his office, enjoyed a satisfying dinner with Mary Yung, and reluctantly left her about twenty minutes ago for an unexpected meeting called for earlier by Mac Horgan.

Mac was the New York private investigator who had been effectively carrying out his more sensitive covert work since his first years as a district attorney. Durning had always liked and trusted the PI because he wasted no time on scruples, made no moral judgments, and did everything offered him on a cash-and-carry basis with no questions asked. It was Mac who had set up the alleged propane explosion a couple of weeks ago that resulted in the deaths of Vittorio Battaglia's pilot friend and his wife and started the chain of events that had brought the attorney general to where he was tonight.

All right. So where was he?

Not too badly off, considering.

Considering what?

That he might have been disgraced and in jail. Or dead and buried. Or any combination of the aforementioned.

He could be still.

Yes. But with Irene finally eliminated, there was no longer an eyewitness to stand up in a court of law and accuse him of murder. So he certainly was better off tonight than he'd been only two nights ago.

Better off? How? With a world-class assassin out there someplace, hoping to avenge the murder of his wife and the disappearance of his son? He wasn't better off. He was just pathetic, a walking target.

Still, he wasn't exactly helpless. He was head of the United States Department of Justice. He had thousands of armed federal agents available for his protection. If he felt himself in danger, he had only to pick up a phone to have a hundred sharpshooters closing around him.

Wonderful. And this was the lifestyle he would be looking forward to enjoying from now on?

Then disliking how he was thinking, Durning just drove and thought of nothing. Yet he was vastly excited, in a steaming emotional state. And he decided that for the time being he was either free of his brain or crazy.

The attorney general arrived at the ruined barn at precisely 9:35 P.M. He drove around to the back and found Mac waiting in his car. In all their years of covert meetings, Durning couldn't recall a single instance of the PI either failing to show up or being as much as five minutes late.

Horgan was out of his car and coming toward him by the time Durning parked and cut his lights. Woods and overgrown fields were dark all around. Other than a fragment of moon and great clusters of stars, nothing else was in sight.

They shook hands and Mac Horgan settled himself beside the attorney general. Horgan was a tall, lean man with quick eyes and hands, who always smelled of English Leather and something else; to Durning, it was like a whiff of the iodine in a piece of marine life left to bleach on the sand.

"How is the gang?" Durning asked.

"The usual," said Horgan. "With that many, there's always some new disaster of the day."

But it was said lightly, even with a certain amount of pride. The gang referred to was Horgan's nine children. In numbers alone, they were an unending source of wonder to Durning. *To make up for nonproducers like me.*

The PI took a small notebook from his pocket, flipped through a few pages, and put it away.

"Something I thought you should know about that happened a few days ago," he said. "Like you told me, I was following Carlo Donatti. One night he went all the way the hell up into the Catskills. To this big log cabin with three *goombahs* in residence. I can't get too close, but there are lights on upstairs, and I see Donatti talking to a man and woman who've got blindfolds on."

"Could you make out their faces?"

"I tried. But with the distance and blindfolds and all, it was no go. But I stayed overnight at a motel and went back next morning. I hung out in the brush, hoping they'd come out.

Horgan paused to light a cigarette.

"And?" said Durning impatiently. He knew the investigator well. If he was dragging it out this much, he had to have something.

"After a few hours they came out with a couple of the *goombahs*. It must have been a kind of exercise period for them. Though their hands were cuffed and they just sort of stood around in the sun."

"Did you see them any better?"

"Yeah. They had no blindfolds on now, and it was daylight, and I was using my best binoc. But I couldn't believe what I was seeing. And neither will you when you hear."

Durning waited, letting Mac milk his big moment. It was part of what made him so good. Pride of achievement. Each new revelation was like finding a cure for cancer.

"How about Hinkey and that Beekman woman who've been missing all this time?"

Henry Durning stared at him. Mac, of course, knew nothing about their having been terminated more than a week ago. "What made you think of *them?*"

"Hey! I didn't just *think* of them. I *saw* them."

"Maybe you made a mistake at that distance."

"No mistake, Mr. Attorney General, sir." Mac grinned as he handed Durning a clutch of snapshots and flicked on the dome light. "I took these shots with a telephoto lens just in case you had doubts."

Durning put on his reading glasses and looked at the pictures. There must have been about a dozen, but he looked at only the first three. Then there was some sort of injunction in his brain not to go on. It was as though he had lived his entire life in a blacked-out cave, and now lights were being brought in. He couldn't deal with them all at once.

Never underestimate the enemy.

A lifesaving aphorism in Vietnam, but obviously just as valuable here at home. It was just that he had somehow failed to keep in mind that Carlo Donatti was his enemy. *With my safety-deposit box rammed against his jugular like a hunting knife, how could the sonofabitch love me?*

But suddenly there were other, less abstract things to be dealt with.

"What made you think that John Hinkey and his client were so important to me?" he said.

Mac Horgan was still giving it his best, most disarming grin. "Come on, Hank. I'm not stupid."

"I never said you were stupid. And your intelligence or lack of it has absolutely nothing to do with what I asked you."

Durning switched off the interior light, and the two men sat looking at each other in the sudden blue dark.

"All I meant was, I know what's going on."

"Do you?"

The PI's smile was gone now. "Well, I don't really *know,* of course. But it's not that hard to figure out."

Durning just stared evenly at his eyes.

"Look," said Horgan. "These were the two who sank

Brian Wayne and his wife with what they were threatening to expose. And everyone knows the Waynes were your closest friends, right?"

Durning was silent.

"So like the real good friend you are, you made a deal with this head *goombah* to do a job on Hinkey and Beekman to save Wayne's career. Except two things went wrong. One, you never knew about Hinkey's letter telling his son to air his dirt on national TV if he died or disappeared. And two, Donatti decided to go in business for himself and keep Hinkey and the woman on ice. I don't know for what. But it sure as hell can't be good for *you*."

Durning nodded slowly, weighing everything.

"It's true," he said. "You're not stupid."

The PI's grin came back. "I hit it right?"

"On the nose," said the attorney general. "Now tell me this. Did Donatti go anyplace else this week that was a break from his usual routine?"

"Yeah. As a matter of fact he did." Horgan took out his notebook and checked a few pages. "He took off from Kennedy at 7:18 P.M. yesterday in one of the Galatea Corporation's long-range jets."

"Who was on board? Any corporate executives?"

"No. Just a flight crew of four and two personal bodyguards."

"Did you find out where they were headed?"

"Yeah. Sicily. Palermo airport."

Naturally, thought Durning.

He awoke in the night. The curtains at the windows were silver. The moon was a cool stone over the city. Mary Yung lay naked and asleep beside him. She had been asleep when he came to bed at about one o'clock, she hadn't wakened, and she was sleeping still. The luminous hands of the clock by his bedside put the time at after three.

Durning wished she was awake. He needed her. But for perhaps the first time, his need was more than physical. Still, he wouldn't wake her. He felt his waking her would somehow spoil it, take away the good, rob it of its magic. For it to work she had to feel his need and come to him out of herself.

A child's game.

Yet he was no child. Nor was she. Although lying there, face up in the moonlight, she was pure virgin. Clean.

Come on, love, he thought. *Come on . . . come on . . . come on. . . .*

His incantation.

I'm Merlin.

Her eyelids fluttered as if at his touch. Her eyeballs appeared blind in the silver light, without pupils. Then she saw him. He was up on one elbow, looking at her.

"I tried to wait up," she said. "But I guess I didn't."

He lay close and held her. His breath tore from his throat so quickly it burned.

She suddenly was wide awake and alert.

"What is it?" she said. "What's wrong?"

Her voice was soft, anxious. *My little mother,* Durning thought, *comforting me.* It made him smile.

"Something is funny?" she asked.

"You're so sweet."

"No one has ever called me that before."

"Only because no one has ever known you before," he said.

"Who taught you to say things like that?"

He laughed softly. "You can't be taught. It's either there or it isn't."

They lay holding each other. All the space in the room, from the walls and windows in, seemed to be composed of delicate glass. A wrong move from either of them would shatter it.

"Are you ready to tell me now?" she said.

"It seems I've been played for a fool," he said. "Which is never enjoyable. But in this case it can also be dangerous."

"Whom are you talking about?"

"My big American don. My *capo di tutti capi,* who's been the Master of the Hunt for me in all this."

"What has he done?"

"It's more like what he hasn't done," said Henry Durning.

"I've learned just tonight that a couple of supposedly buried threats haven't been buried at all but are being primed to use against me. And it suddenly looks as though Vittorio's wife falls into that same category."

"You mean Peggy hasn't been eliminated after all? She's still alive?"

"It does seem that way."

Mary Yung looked at Durning in the silver light. "Forgive me if I can't get too upset about that."

"I never really expected you to, love." Durning found himself smiling once more. "As a matter of fact, in an insane sort of way, I don't really feel all that terrible about it myself. Unless that's because I'm suddenly faced with so many more immediate threats."

"Like what? How do you think all this affects Peggy's boy?" asked Mary.

"I don't know. Other than I obviously can't believe anything the lying sonofabitch has told me about him."

62

Paulie felt the tightness all through him as soon as he entered the streets of Palermo.

He didn't like the noise, and the traffic, and the crowds of people, and the policemen wherever you turned, and the feeling that every one of them had strict orders to watch for *him*.

The feeling became worse when he reached the harbor area and walked onto the dock where the ferry to Naples was waiting to be boarded. The ship looked as big as an ocean liner, and there were all these cars, trucks, and buses lined up in rows, and lots of people with baggage pushing and yelling as if they were angry and looking for a fight.

The boy saw signs pointing to where you had to go to buy your ticket, and he headed in that direction. When he finally got to the place, he stopped a short distance away and watched to see how it worked.

There was just one ticket office, with men selling tickets at three different windows and a line of passengers slowly moving in front of each. Two *carabinieri* kept a careful eye on those buying tickets. As did three young guys with good haircuts and nice suits who could have been brothers to Dom and Tony.

Thinking it through earlier, Paulie had decided this would be the most dangerous part of all for him. They knew he would have to leave the island to get home to Positano, and there were just two places where he could catch a ferry to the Italian mainland . . . Palermo and Messina. So all they needed were a few people to watch the ticket lines in each port.

And what made it even easier for them was that there probably wouldn't be any other eight-year-old kid alone and buying his own ticket.

How could he have been so dumb?

But he had to do something pretty quick because the ferry was due to sail in less than an hour, and another one wasn't scheduled to leave for Naples until tomorrow.

Or was he doing all this worrying for nothing?

Paulie decided to find out.

He saw a boy of about his own age kicking around a soccer ball and joined in the play for a few minutes. Then he stopped and said, "Hey! you want to do me a big favor and I'll give you three thousand lire?"

"You kidding?"

"No."

The boy grinned, all curly dark hair and white teeth. "Whose throat do I cut?"

"Nobody's. All you do is buy me a ferry ticket with some money I give you, and I'll give you three thousand lire."

The kid did a fancy riff in place with the soccer ball.

"That's all I have to do?"

Paulie nodded. "Nothing to it."

"If there's nothing to it, why don't you buy the ticket yourself and save the three thousand?"

"Because I ran away from my fucking old man yesterday, and I figure he's got *carabinieri* watching for me." Paulie aimed his chin at the ticket windows. "Like those two dick-heads over there."

"No shit?" The boy's grin grew broader. "Where you going when you get off the ferry in Naples?"

"My grandma lives in Rome. I guess I'll go there."

The boy's eyes were all jealousy and admiration. "Jesus!"

"Will you do it for me?" said Paulie.

"Sure. Why not?"

Paulie counted out the money for the ticket. Then he watched his new friend deftly work his soccer ball through the crowd to the nearest ticket line, about fifty yards away.

Now I'll know.

There were about a dozen people ahead of the boy, but the line was moving well and he was soon number five.

It was when he had advanced to three that Paulie saw one of the two *carabinieri* approach, bend down to the boy's height, and start talking to him.

Damn, thought Paulie, and began slowly easing away, moving a short distance back into the crowd.

There was no one in front of the boy now, but the *carabiniere* was still talking to him. While a few of those at his back began moving around him to the ticket window.

Paulie saw the kid standing with his head low, sometimes talking, but mostly listening. At one point he had his hand open and was showing his money to the policeman, who looked at it very seriously.

A moment later the boy turned and stared at where he had left Paulie, but he didn't see him. Then he did see him a bit farther back in the crowd, and he pointed and kept pointing until the *carabiniere* saw him, too.

The policeman cried out something Paulie couldn't hear, and then he was up and running toward him with the other *carabiniere* close behind, and the three haircuts right in back of them, and all five of them running like the devil.

Paulie had a last glimpse of the kid's face. It was scared white. And Paulie was scared, too.

Then Paulie was just running, weaving in and out of the crowds, and between the great trucks with their diesels growling and gears grinding, and the slowly moving lines of cars and buses. He ran without glancing back, cutting back and forth between the vehicles and people, understanding now that everything he had been worried about was true, and the *carabinieri* had been watching the ticket lines for an eight-year-old kid, and the same with the mob haircuts and suits, and if they ever caught up with him now, Jesus only knew what they'd do to him.

Then he slammed into the side of an eighteen-wheeler that wasn't even moving, and suddenly and for several seconds nothing at all was clear.

Still, gasping for breath against the heavy tarp that lay stretched over the big, open flatbed, he felt remarkably calm. At that moment he saw no one and was sure that no one saw him. What he did see in close detail were the twisted fibers of the hemp rope that fastened a corner of the tarp to the truckbed. And he saw, too, the fine hand of God offering him salvation.

He quickly untied the rope, slid under the tarp and onto the open truckbed, and securely refastened the tarpaulin above him.

Paulie lay in the sudden darkness. He kept hearing voices passing, but no one approached him.

A short while later, he felt the truck start to move. It moved slowly, in fits and starts, part of the long snake of traffic rolling into the great belly of the ship. There was a different sound and feel when the truck hit the steel decking. It was all kind of hollow and smooth. If he had to give it a color, in his mind it would be a dark blue-green. It seemed so long since he had painted, he began to wonder if he'd remember how.

Which was kind of crazy. Might as well wonder if he'd remember how to breathe.

After a while he felt the vibration of the ship's engines, then the long rolling motion of the swells as they put to sea.

He thought it might be all right for him to leave the truck now and wander around the ship. But he decided to stay where he was for the time being.

So he lay there in the darkness under the tarp, trying to concentrate on as much good stuff as he could remember from before all this started to happen.

Which was all right for a while. It was like staring off into the pale, pink mists of memory, where things always seem just a little brighter and nicer than they really were.

What he liked best about the remembering was that his mother and father always were there. The worst was that no matter how bright and clear they seemed in his thoughts, they still couldn't touch him.

Paulie guessed that was what he missed most right now.

Being touched.

63

VITTORIO BATTAGLIA LAY alone in the night with his tubes and the blinking lights of his monitors and wished that Gianni Garetsky would come back.

The thoughts that came when he was alone were worse than the pain, and the pain was very bad. But he knew it was a sign of healing, because they were taking him off the morphine.

Pain is good for the soul.

And what idiot had said that?

An idiot who obviously had never experienced real pain or known a damn thing about the soul.

But it wasn't his pain or his soul that bothered him most in the night. It was his fear. Although even this was for his wife and son, not himself. It was the only thing that seemed real among the hallucinations of his semidrugged state. Which made it the only thing of true importance.

Gianni, bring me some good news. Please.

It was the closest Vittorio had ever come to pleading.

Despite himself, he must have dozed. Because his next awareness was of Gianni Garetsky sitting in his usual bed-side chair, staring at him.

"Did I conjure you up?" he murmured. "Or are you real?"

Gianni's smile was faint. And even that almost required more effort than he could scrape together.

"I'm real."

Vittorio's eyes searched Gianni's face for messages. They found none that meant anything.

"How long are you here?"

"About twenty minutes."

"Why didn't you wake me up?"

"I figured you needed the sleep."

"I need good news more."

Gianni said nothing, and Vittorio Battagli listened to the silence and heard everything there was to hear.

Vittorio closed his eyes and breathed slowly, deeply.

"Did you find her dead?" he finally asked. "Or was she just not there?"

"She wasn't there. But she left a message. It was where you said it would be."

"Read it to me."

Gianni hesitated. "Maybe you'd better read it yourself."

"No, I don't think I can. Read it to me." Vittorio's voice was flat, but otherwise controlled. "Please."

Garetsky took out the blue envelope. He removed the letter, spread it open on his lap, and tried to press out the creases with the flat of his hand.

Then he tried to clear the thickness from his throat. It was hopeless.

He read the date and the time of day at the top of the page.

"My love," he began.

Gianni read it slowly, quietly, the words rising and losing themselves quickly in the heavy-aired silence of the hospital room.

Vittorio lay there, listening, growing angry.

Gianni Garetsky's soft, slow voice read on. Immutably. It was impossible to stop.

Then the anger went away. It left a deep sickness in its place, an oppressiveness, a ghostly pain in his stomach. No. In his heart, his lungs, everywhere, that had nothing to do with the real bullets that had entered him earlier. And he knew that no amount of morphine would be able to make it disappear.

But then the sickness, too, subsided.

And there was nothing.

It took Vittorio a few moments to realize that Gianni had stopped reading. He accepted the silence.

Then even that became too much.

"She's gone, Gianni," he said.

Garetsky looked at him. Vittorio appeared dry eyed and blank faced. Then a tear suddenly appeared in a corner of his eye. It ran down his cheek, moving fast, like sweat on a cold glass.

"We don't really know that," said Gianni.

"You just read me her letter."

"Yes. But that's all it was. A letter."

"You think she or Durning didn't go through with it?"

"I don't know what I think," said Gianni. "But no one's dead until they're dead."

Gianni looked into Vittorio Battaglia's eyes. Until he saw the hope there. Then he had to look away.

Gianni waited until shortly after 9:00 A.M. Then, using a hospital pay phone, he put through a person-to-person call to the director of the Naples office of the International Red Cross. When he got the official on the line, a Signor Ferrare, he said, "This is Ralph Billings calling from the United States consulate in Palermo."

"Yes, Signor Billings."

"I'm hoping you can help me," said Garetsky. "We've just received word that an eight-year-old American boy, a Paul Walters, was to be left with you people for safekeeping until he can be picked up by his father. Offhand, could you give us any information about that?"

"Exactly what would you like to know?"

"Whether the boy is with you now. And if he's not, whether your office has heard anything further about him or the situation."

"I'll certainly check on it. When was the boy supposed to have been left with us?"

"We don't know precisely. But it should have been sometime during the past day or two."

"Please hold on, Signor Billings. I should be able to find that out for you right now."

Gianni stood waiting. He didn't know what he wanted to hear. If the boy was there and safe, in all probability his mother was dead and gone. If the boy wasn't there, it could mean anything. With the odds strongly in favor of nothing good.

"Signor Billings?"

"Yes," said Garetsky.

"I've just spoken with the two people who would know about such things. So far, neither of them has any information about a boy being sent here. Would you like us to call you if the boy does come here?"

"Thank you, but I expect to be traveling for the next few days. So I'll check back with you if I may."

Gianni thanked Ferrare again and hung up. Then he slowly walked back to where Vittorio lay waiting to hear.

"Nothing," he told his friend. "They haven't heard a damn thing."

Each held a separate silence.

"I'll tell you," Vittorio said. "I'm not surprised. I didn't really expect Paulie to be there."

"Why not?"

"Because it wouldn't be in that bastard's nature to make a deal and stick with it. He'd always be looking for an extra edge of some sort. And Peg wouldn't have a prayer with a man like that."

Garetsky started to say something. Then he changed his mind and remained silent. What was there to say without lying and sounding like a fool, or speaking the truth and making it worse?

"What the man's done," said Vittorio tonelessly, "is murder my wife and son. That part's finished. Now I just have to accept it. Then maybe I can get on with the rest."

Gianni turned to him. Vittorio Battaglia's eyes were two black holes and his skin appeared drained of blood. He was a ghost. His face, surrounded by hospital pillows, was the size and shape of little more than the bones beneath it. While Vittorio himself was the same color as the bones.

When did he become a ghost?

64

IT REALLY WAS a small jewel of a villa, thought Peggy, with dazzling views of the mountains and sea, and the grounds spacious and well tended. And since Carlo Donatti's visit, she had been treated with all the courtesy and deference of an honored guest. She had actually begun now to allow herself the almost forgotten luxury of hope.

Or was this just her latest self-delusion to keep herself from flying into a million pieces?

With the thought, panic came off her like a scent, dull and powerful, bringing her close to nausea. Paulie lay buried somewhere while she sat here being milked with false promises. The image itself was an extinction. She could feel all that was good in her going away.

Then she breathed slowly and deeply and put all such thinking aside before she flaked out entirely and did no one any good.

65

THE ATTORNEY GENERAL flew into La Guardia by Justice Department helicopter at about 11:00 P.M. and dismissed the crew for the night. They were to be ready to fly back to Washington at 7:00 the next morning.

An unlocked Ford Fairlane was waiting for him at a prearranged parking location. The keys were under a floor mat.

A little less than two hours later, Durning drove the Ford behind a small, abandoned factory outside of Liberty, New York, and found Mac Horgan already parked and waiting. *As usual,* he thought. This time Durning left his own car and joined the private investigator in his.

"Everything all right?" asked Durning.

"Couldn't be better."

"How far is it from here?"

Horgan lit a fresh cigarette from the butt of one he had going. "Less than half an hour. It should be a piece of cake. I don't know why you had to bother coming."

Durning opened a window to get rid of the smoke.

"Yes, you do," he said. "I bothered coming because this whole thing with Donatti has suddenly turned me paranoid."

Horgan grinned. "Hey. I'm not the fucking godfather."

"I know. It's got nothing to do with you. It's all me. You'll just have to bear with me on this one."

Mac Horgan started the car, swung past the old brick factory building, and turned onto the deserted road.

"No problem," he said.

"When did you get up here?"

"Late this afternoon. I wanted a last look around while it was still daylight. I also wanted to be sure they were still there. Loose ends we don't need."

"And?"

"Full house. Three *goombahs* and the two of *them.*"

They drove north on Route 17 for about ten minutes. Then they turned east for a short while on 52. It was a clear night with half a moon and lots of stars. There were few cars moving, and the Catskills showed high and dark above the trees.

They spoke little.

Durning had been tense but fine until now. Then as they swung onto a narrow, two-lane blacktop that made up the final stretch, he felt the first faint stirrings of dread in his stomach.

"What are you using?" he asked.

"Plastique."

"Is that smart? There aren't too many sources. Which makes it eminently traceable."

Mac Horgan shrugged. "They won't trace this. I've had it stashed for too many years. Besides, it's the only stuff practical to use on an operation like this. I wasn't about to start scraping together and lugging around five hundred pounds of TNT."

Durning was silent.

"What about Carlo Donatti?" said Horgan.

"What about him?"

"He's going to know it was you."

"I expect him to."

"You don't think he should be done?"

"He will be," said Durning.

"I mean before *this* job."

"No. There are things he has to tell me first. And I can't have Hinkey and the woman floating around for however long that's going to take. They're too dangerous."

"Whatever you say, Hank. It's all the same to me."

The attorney general fixed on Horgan as he drove. Not true. It *wasn't* all the same to Mac. He enjoyed doing the *goombahs* best. And it wasn't just the historical antipathy between the Irish and Italians. Mac's dislike for the mob reached all the way back to his detective days, when he refused to accept bribe money, personally brought down a couple of top family *capi*, and found himself framed and broken as his reward. Durning had been able to keep him out of prison, but not out of forced retirement.

Mac Horgan suddenly pulled off the stretch of narrow blacktop and parked behind some brush.

"It's about a five-minute walk from here." said the PI. "Just over that rise. You can either wait here, or move in closer with me and see the action. It's up to you."

"What kind of security do they have?"

"Only the three guards and some photoelectric stuff across the driveway. There are no fences, no wiring on any windows, and no TV monitors. It's an old hunting and fishing place of Donatti's father, hardly used."

"I'll walk in a ways with you," said Durning.

Horgan had everything in two canvas bags in the trunk, and he carried them both himself.

They walked slowly through high grass, the night quiet and silver-gray about them. There was just enough moonlight to cast shadows. With each step, Durning felt the dread grow stronger in his stomach.

Then they crested the knoll, and Durning had his first glimpse of the cabin, about two hundred yards away.

It was much bigger than he had expected, a rustic two-story building with three fieldstone chimneys and huge, half-round logs chinked together in the Adirondack style of many turn-of-the-century camps favored by the old robber barons.

They had approached the cabin from the side and rear. Other than for two night-lights, one upstairs and one down, the place was entirely dark. The moon silvered a wood-shingled, steeply pitched roof.

Durning glanced at his watch. It was close to 2:00 A.M.

"Stay down and wait here," said Mac Horgan, and quickly and quietly took off.

The attorney general watched him go with his two bags, crouching low and hugging the shadows of bushes and trees. Then Horgan was against the cabin and lost in the darkness.

Durning knelt there, listening to the great silence of the wood. Which really was no silence at all, but a thing alive with a thousand sounds and each one taking up its own separate pitch. He had never heard such a subtle din, and all of it trying to tell him something.

But what?

Then he heard the hoot of an owl off in a tree somewhere, and the rush of sound seemed to disappear.

Durning never saw Mac Horgan returning until he was less than twenty feet away and approaching from another direction.

"Exactly seven minutes to showtime," he said, and casually flopped beside Henry Durning. He was not even out of breath.

"How many charges?" Durning asked.

"Four. One on each side. Something like this, you don't want to fool around."

"What's the dynamite equivalent?"

"About a hundred and fifty pounds each charge."

"Jesus Christ," Durning whispered.

The PI grinned. "More's better, right?"

Durning hoped so.

This quiet wood.

Horgan said, "I just wish that fucking Donatti was in there too. Then I'd feel good."

Henry Durning was silent. There *were* those who took pleasure from such things. He himself just happened not to be one of them.

"Better get below the crest of the hill," said the investigator, and they moved back about another thirty yards.

Moments later there was a crackling roar that Durning felt as a shudder in the earth beneath his body and saw as a blaze of red in the night sky.

Then great chunks of things went whistling and tearing through the leaves overhead, and Durning felt the blast from the explosion roll back over him as he lay with his hands tight over his head. His face was down against the grass, and the yellow smell of the blast rolled over him in bitter smoke. Then it started raining bits and pieces of nameless stuff.

When everything seemed to have stopped falling, Durning and Mac Horgan rose and walked back to the crest of the rise.

To Henry Durning it was like staring down into the crater of a live volcano. A great hole in the earth, filled with smoldering chunks of fire, topped by rising spirals of black smoke. Nothing recognizable remained. Not a chimney, not a wall, not a piece of furniture, not a toilet, not a body.

Later, of course, Durning knew that the experts would be able to place bits and pieces of things under high-power microscopes and make some sort of human identification. But it would only be of technical and academic interest. For all practical purposes, it might just as well have been the crater of a live volcano.

The attorney general stood staring blankly into the smoldering hole. He felt numb all through himself.

Horgan touched his shoulder. "Come on," he said. "We don't want to be anyplace near here when the locals start showing up."

They heard sirens in the distance but passed only a few cars on the way back to the old factory building.

The attorney general turned and looked behind them several times as Horgan drove. He was looking for the red glow in the sky that would have been the mark of a spreading fire. But there didn't seem to be even that much left.

They reached Durning's car behind the old factory at about 3:30 A.M. It really hadn't taken all that long.

"Right on schedule," he said dryly.

"Didn't I tell you it would be a piece of cake?" said Horgan, not understanding one bit.

Durning slowly nodded. "Yes, you did."

They sat in silence.

"But I'd never call it a piece of cake," said Durning.

"What then?"

"A bloody tragic massacre in which five people were blown to bits."

The private investigator laughed. "Same thing."

"No. Not at all the same thing."

Horgan shrugged. "Shit, man. They're just as dead. What's the difference what you call it."

"A big difference."

"Yeah? Like what?"

"Like between an ape and a human being."

Horgan looked at the attorney general. "And of course I'm the ape and you're the human being."

"I guess it bothers me a little that you could do it so easily and take it so lightly."

The PI sat there with it for a long moment. He seemed to be giving these last words some deep and careful thought.

"And it *doesn't* bother you a little," he finally said, "that those five people would never have been blown to bits at all if you hadn't told me to do them?"

"That bothers me, too, Mac. I can't tell you how much. But I'm afraid that worse still lies ahead for me."

"Yeah? What's that?"

Durning nodded toward the car window behind Horgan's back. "Take a look over there," he said.

And when the PI turned in his seat to look, Henry Durning shot him twice in the back of his head.

Although, as it worked out, once would have been enough.

* * *

Working with his usual calm and control under pressure, the attorney general carefully did everything that needed to be done.

He started his own car a short distance away and left the engine idling.

He took a five-gallon can of gasoline out of the trunk, emptied it over Mac Horgan and the interior of his car, and lit a match to a long, gasoline-soaked fuse.

Then he drove off just as the flames went up. Later, he dropped the unregistered gun he had used into a nearby reservoir.

The single moment of acute depression he allowed himself was for Mac's children. But that, of course, couldn't be helped. And the idea of setting up a generous trust fund for them made him feel better at once.

Durning was home in Georgetown in time to shower, shave, and have breakfast with Mary Yung in the garden room.

He kissed her as she poured his coffee. "Miss me?" he asked.

"The truth?"

Durning's nod was tentative.

"Bad night?" she asked.

"The worst."

"Want to tell me about it?"

"I couldn't."

"Why not?"

"Because I don't want you to despise me any more than you already do," he told her.

"I don't despise you."

He was careful to leave that one alone.

Mary Yung held her coffee mug in both hands, as though needing to warm them. "It's getting easier to do and harder to shake off, isn't it?"

"What is?" Durning asked, although he knew.

"The killing."

He shrugged. "I can handle it."

"Of course you can. I know that. You're Henry Durning." A slow look of hers lighted on his face, held there for a moment, and went straight through him. "The question is, do you want to?"

"It stopped being a question of wanting a long time ago."

"I don't believe that."

"Why not?" he said.

"Because, someone like you, once you want something, you can make it happen."

Durning stroked her hair, gently, thoughtfully. "Then it's just a matter of my deciding?"

"Exactly."

His smile was as wistful as it was loving.

"What a truly lovely thought."

66

DON CARLO DONATTI was awakened by a knock on his bedroom door in Sands Point. A digital clock told him it was 6:27 A.M.; he had returned from Italy less than twelve hours ago.

"Yes?"

"Telephone, Don Donatti," said his houseman.

"Who is it?"

"The chief of police up in Liberty. He says it's important."

Warnings going off in his brain, Donatti picked up the phone. "What's wrong, Pete?"

"Sorry to wake you, Mr. Donatti. But there's been a terrible tragedy up here at your cabin."

Donatti felt the warnings spread down through his chest and stomach. "What happened?"

"Christ only knows. There's not a damn thing left but a big hole in the ground, rubble and charred bodies. It looks like fucking Hiroshima."

Donatti's hand was frozen on the phone.

"I hope no one close to you was up here," said the chief.

"No." Donatti stared at nothing. "There were no survivors?"

"Survivors? We'll be lucky if we can find half the parts."

Donatti heard voices and yelling in the background. The chief was obviously calling from the site.

"Do you know who was up here?" asked the police chief.

"Not off hand. I'll have to check around. Some of my people use the place for hunting and fishing. They don't always tell me. What about the cause? Could it have been accidental?"

"Hell, no. Not with that size hole. Some demolition people said the explosion carried a blast force of close to seven hundred pounds of dynamite. We'll know more when the Bureau people get here."

Donatti's mouth was dry. "You called the FBI?"

"It's automatic with this kind of explosive power," said the chief. "They're afraid of terrorists. You got any known enemies. Mr. Donatti?"

"I've got nothing else, Pete. You'll have to form your suspects in alphabetical lines."

The policeman's laugh was flat.

Donatti said, "I guess you'll want me up there for questioning."

"At your convenience, Mr. Donatti. I know the feds'll want to talk to you. But if you could get us some names of those in the cabin, it would sure help."

"I'll take care of it. And thanks for calling me personally, Pete. I appreciate it."

"Sorry it had to be such tragic news." The chief paused. "All things considered, Mr. Donatti, you'd best watch your ass."

"You can count on it."

"One last thing, Mr. Donatti. An unidentified male body was just found roasted in a car not far from here. He had two bullets in his head and the remains of a detonating device in his trunk."

Donatti called the attorney general on his office secure line at about noon. It had taken him that long to settle down enough to decide how best to approach the situation. Not that he felt there were any true choices available to him.

"It's me," he said when Durning got on the line.

"What took you so long? I expected to hear from you hours ago."

Carlo Donatti ignored the flippancy. "I think we'd better talk as quickly as possible. If you can make it this evening. I'll fly down to your area."

"Fine. The usual place at eight?"

"I'll see you then."

The don hung up and felt the cold stir of oppression. It was not new to him. He had been born to it, had literally spent key portions of his life chatting at one cliffside of disaster or another. In fact, he had long ago learned to judge the measure of a man by how well he could sit with danger. But sitting with this man, this Henry Durning, was the closest he had ever come to sitting with the devil. There were no fixed, no recognizable, no previously landmarked parameters of behavior. The only certainty about Henry was that he had the sharp teeth and appetite for flesh of the true carnivore.

They sat in the hotel room near Washington's National Airport.

This time there was not even the pretense of the ritual embrace and other amenities. The pistols, so to speak, were now loaded and on the table. Donatti could all but smell the gunpowder with each breath. If he had one final wish left to him in this world, it would be to be able to shoot Henry Durning dead center between the eyes and go home with impunity. Even the thought of scotch, his usually dependable spur and appeaser, simply threatened to turn his stomach.

As for Durning himself? He appeared no more than mildly amused, a man so thoroughly in control of his fate and fortune, that nothing could mar the perfect veneer of his humor. Yet beneath the veneer, something perilously close to desperation.

What a president he would have made.

"Congratulations, Carlo," Durning said. "Until twenty-four hours ago I never suspected a thing. It was all very clever."

Donatti nodded, grimly accepting the compliment.

Durning shrugged. "Then you got a little careless, and I got a little lucky."

"You're too modest. But in the meantime, five more people are dead." Donatti paused. *"Six,"* he said, correcting himself. "I'd forgotten your burned-up bomber with two bullets in his head."

They sat looking at each other in their locked room. Until Durning abruptly got up and put on the overly loud music he had neglected to put on earlier. When he sat down again, Donatti noted that he no longer appeared amused.

"All right, let's get down to it," said the attorney general. "Tell me what you've got and what you want, and maybe we can work something out."

"You already know what I've got and what I want."

"All I've got so far is supposition, and I can't make a deal on that. So let's hear it straight out, Carlo."

Carlo Donatti smoothed his hair with the palms of both hands, although not a strand was out of place. "I have the woman. I have Vittorio Battaglia's wife."

"And she's not dead, as you told me? She's alive?"

"That's correct."

"How do I know you're not lying now, and that she's really dead after all?"

Donatti took three snapshots from his jacket pocket and handed them to the attorney general. They showed him standing beside Peggy, one hand on her shoulder, his other hand holding the front page of an Italian newspaper, datelined two days ago.

"She's looking a lot different from when I last saw her," said Durning flatly. "Where have you got her?"

"Somewhere in Italy."

"And what has she told you about me?"

"The whole story."

"Which is?"

"Essentially that she was witness to your killing of a man and a woman in Connecticut ten years ago. She put it all on videotape for me. I have the cassette in the car. Would you like to see it?"

Durning shook his head. "That wouldn't add appreciably

to my joy." He looked at the don. "You realize, of course, that the cassette would be inadmissible in a court of law. That is, without the witness herself present to testify under oath and be available for cross-examination by the defense."

"I know. I'm an attorney too, Henry. Remember?"

"Just trying to keep the record straight," said Durning.

Carlo Donatti was silent under the pounding of the music. Now he was just waiting for the devil to start dancing. He could almost feel and smell the heat of him.

"I'm ready for the bottom line, Carlo," said the attorney general. "What do you want and what are you ready to give?"

"You know that, too."

"Yes, but we don't want any misunderstandings, do we? So let's hear it in real words."

"I want the originals of everything you have on me in your safety-deposit box, and you can have Mrs. Battaglia. Simple and clear enough?"

Durning nodded slowly. But it seemed to Donatti that something else was stirring in the room, and he waited for it to make its presence known.

"What about the boy, her son?" said the attorney general.

"What about him?"

"I want *him* along with his mother."

Donatti thought he had already touched the man's low point. Evidently not. "You mean you—"

"No, no. Not to hurt him, Carlo. Just to be sure he's all right."

"I don't understand."

"You don't have to understand. It's personal. You told me last time no one seemed to know what happened to him. Anything changed in that?"

Donatti had the sensation of something cold and strange blowing in his face. "Matter of fact, I had a call from Palermo this morning. Seems the boy was spotted trying to get on the ferry to Naples. Then they lost him. It shouldn't be too long before he's picked up."

"And Battaglia and Garetsky?"

"Still nothing. But better watch your back."

"Watch yours. I'm sure they want you as much as they want me. Maybe more, since you're one of their own."

They both breathed the same air of stopped-up violence.

"Well?" said the don. "Are you interested?"

"How could I not be? It's just the details that will be tricky. I mean the 'who tries to fuck whom' of it." Durning's smile was pure ice. "One would have to be crazy to buy a used car from either of us. But since we each have everything to gain from making it work, maybe it will."

Durning stared at Donatti. "But what does our Mrs. Battaglia believe she'll be gaining from her confessed indictment of *me?*"

"Her boy. Not to mention my undying gratitude. I did, after all, save her life the other day, didn't I?"

"Yes, you did. Although you've obviously lied to her about having her son."

Don Carlo Donatti studied the tips of his fingers and nodded. When he spoke again, there was something gentle and tired in his voice.

"That's true," he said. "I did lie to her. But everything considered, I can't really see it mattering all that much. Can you?"

67

I'M GOING TO die right here on this crazy ship, thought Paulie, *among these smelly barrels, and no one will ever know what became of me.*

It was the middle of the night, with gale-force winds and pounding waves, and the constant thumping of engines, and no relief from any of them. And as if all that wasn't bad enough, he was slowly being poisoned to death by the giant pizza he had pigged out on earlier.

He had been asleep for a while under his truck tarpaulin,

but had been awakened by recurring stomach cramps. The boy tried to fight down the pain. He wouldn't give in to it. He would just lie quietly and wait, and it would go away.

Then Paulie drew his knees up against his chest, the spasm passed, and he felt something very near to hope.

With it, on the tossing, rolling truck, he was able to believe that the storm would be over by morning, that Naples would be safely reached without his dying of a poisoned pizza, and that his mother and father would be waiting for him in Positano when he got there.

Instant magic. A moment's freedom from pain.

But it didn't last long. Because soon the cramps came back and they were so bad that he cried out, and cried out again, and then again. Until he became so afraid someone would hear him that he stuffed his handkerchief into his mouth to muffle the sound.

Finally, he closed his eyes. As if shutting out all sight of the tarpaulin over his head would shut out the pain as well.

But it didn't. And when he opened his eyes again, the tarp had been pulled away and a man's face was there instead.

"Holy Christ!" said the man.

All they seemed able to do was stare at each other.

The man was big and tough looking, and Paulie guessed he was the driver of the truck. Now he was in for it. Now he'd be handed over to the *carabinieri,* who'd pass him on to the haircuts, who'd give him to their *capo,* who'd shoot him full of holes for what he'd done to Dom and Tony.

"What the hell's going on?" said the man.

The boy made a muffled, choking sound against the handkerchief in his mouth. He seemed to have forgotten it was there.

The man plucked it free. "What are you trying to do, kid? Choke yourself to death?"

As if suddenly rendered mute, Paulie shook his head.

"What then?"

"I'm sick." The boy's face contorted as another spasm hit, gripped him, and passed. "I didn't want to make any noise."

The man studied him. "Where does it hurt?"

Paulie pressed a hand to his stomach.

"You running away, or what?"

Paulie was afraid to answer.

"You been hiding here since Palermo?"

"Yes."

"Where are you trying to go?"

"Home."

"Where's that?"

Paulie stared at him.

"Don't worry, kid. I won't turn you in. You got enough trouble. Just tell me where you live."

"Positano."

The trucker nodded. "If you don't die first, maybe I can drop you not far from there."

The boy felt a rush of something that made his eyes start to water. He fought it back. He hated that about himself. It was like he had a fountain in his head. The least thing set it off.

"Listen," said the man. "You don't have to lie back here with all this shit. I got a better place for you up front. Right back of the cab."

Paulie shook his head.

"It's all right. No one'll see you there. It's where I sleep on long hauls. I got some stuff for your cramps, too. What kind of garbage you been eating?"

"Anchovy and sausage pizza."

The trucker made a sour face. "Next time you want to kill yourself, try jumping off a high building. It's faster and don't hurt anywhere near as much."

Paulie could barely straighten up, and the ferry was still pitching and rolling badly. So the man carried him to his secret place behind the driver's seat and stretched him out on some nice soft padding with a regular pillow for his head. Then he gave him a swig of some pink stuff from a bottle that he promised would make his cramps go away in less than half an hour.

"What's your name, kid?"

"Paulie."

"I'm Nino. You want to sleep, go ahead. No one'll bother you here."

Paulie was tired enough to sleep, but he didn't want Nino to see him sucking his thumb. Also, the trucker's being so nice to him was beginning to make him worry a little. He'd heard all about the kind of men who liked to play around with young boys' weenies. He'd never actually run into anyone like that, but a couple of the kids from school had told stories about what had happened to them with such men.

The boy closed his eyes.

He wondered what he would do if Nino suddenly tried to fool around with him. Would he jump out of his truck and run away, or pull out his gun, or just let him do it?

Then he opened his eyes and saw Nino sitting there, looking at him, with that real tough face of his kind of smiling.

"Cramps going away a little?" he asked.

Paulie nodded.

"Good. Your mom and dad know you're coming home?"

"No."

"I guess you're going to surprise them, huh?"

"I tried to call them but no one was home."

"Well, they'll sure be happy to see you. My kid ran off once. Was gone for two days and nights. Nearly drove me nuts. I swear I wanted to kill him. Then he walked in the damn door, and all I did was hug and kiss him and start crying like an asshole."

The boy silently rolled with the truck and the ship. Somehow, he didn't think Nino was one of those men with young boys' weenies on his mind.

"Thanks for helping me," he said.

The trucker shrugged. "Shit. Who wouldn't help a kid trying to get home? Besides, I like your guts. Imagine sticking a handkerchief in your mouth to keep from crying out."

Paulie lay there, his cheek resting against his hand. He didn't think there was anything so special about his not wanting to cry out and maybe get caught. But he liked the idea of Nino thinking he had guts.

68

THE SEATBELT SIGN had just come on for the descent to Washington's Dulles International, and Gianni Garetsky thought, *I'm coming full circle.*

Leaving Palermo that morning on the earliest scheduled flight, he had spent the last twelve hours flying first to Naples, then to Rome, and finally on to Washington, where he would be landing at approximately 3:00 P.M. local time.

He hadn't taken off his clothes or slept in a bed for more than thirty-six hours, although he had dozed occasionally in the air. With his thoughts and emotions running at flood tide, he had neither the need nor the patience for serious, all-out sleep.

Finally, he was going to the source.

Gianni had made the decision about fifteen hours ago at Vittorio Battaglia's bedside, with Vittorio himself forced into reluctant agreement. Not that they had any real choices. What the two men did have in their few final nighttime hours together in the hospital was a tiny spark of hope, still fighting to hold on against an avalanche of negative logic and reason.

"I've accepted it," had been Vittorio's coldly stated position. "My wife and son are gone. I can't bring them back. But as soon as I am able to walk out of here, I'm at least going to save what's left of my sanity by making payment."

"How?" Gianni had asked. "By blowing away Durning?"

"Along with Don Donatti. I hold them both responsible."

Gianni had remained silent.

"You don't agree?" Vittorio had asked.

"We don't really know for sure that your son and wife are gone."

"*You* might not know. *I* know."

"And if you're wrong by some miracle . . ."

"I don't believe in miracles."

"If by some miracle," Gianni repeated quietly, "one or both of them are still alive at this moment, and you find out later that you gave up on them just a little too soon . . . how do you imagine your sanity would react to *that?*"

Vittorio had stared at Gianni until there was no air left in the silence.

"I can't deal with this shit," Vittorio had finally said. "I'm not worth a damn here in this bed. What do you want me to do?"

"Nothing. Just get well."

"Then what do *you* want to do?"

"I want to go to them both. First, Durning, then Donatti. But fast. Right now even miracles have time limits."

"And do what?"

"Put a gun to each of their heads and ask for answers."

"And if there are no miracles?"

"I'll squeeze the trigger. Twice. Once for each."

"You'll be able to do that?"

"Take a good look at me, Vittorio."

Battaglia had taken a good look. Then he nodded, tiredly. "Yeah, you can do it. Though that's really my job."

"I've got my own stake in it."

They had considered each other in the silent room with its hospital smells.

"Just one thing," Vittorio had said. "I'm giving you a name and a phone number. If you need help, or anything at all. Call this man and tell him it's for Charlie. You can trust him with your life. I've already trusted him with mine."

"Who is he?"

"His name's Tommy Cortlandt and he's been my company contact and chief of station for the past eight years."

Garestsky had stared blankly. "You mean like in CIA?"

"Exactly." Vittorio had written the name and number on a slip of paper for him. "Memorize this along with the code word Charlie. Then tear it up."

It had taken Gianni a while to absorb. "That's some surprise."

"No big deal. Just a need I had."

It occurred to Gianni that Vittorio Battaglia had always done pretty much as he wanted with his life. He had never just accepted what was handed him.

It was less than a week since Gianni Garetsky had left the country with Mary Yung, but coming back, he felt as if he had been away for years.

I'm back, he told his wife. And I'm alone. You never warned me. You never taught me that all women are not like you.

Well, now you know, said Teresa.

Picking up his bag and going through customs, he saw that people suddenly seemed beautiful. The girls were slender and bouncy and walked with their breasts high, half smiling as if re-membering some secret pleasure the night before. The young men looked strong and immortal. The children were laughing and energetic. The elderly were neatly dressed and appeared philosophically relaxed about whatever might lie ahead,

Among them, he felt like the proverbial specter at the feast. Come to threaten. Come to shoot and kill.

He found himself deeply weighed by his mission. So much so, that for the first time in years a few words of He-brew, learned as a boy from his father, came back to him. *Hazak, v'ematz.* Which was the order God gave to Joshua and meant strengthen thyself.

He rented a black Cougar from Hertz. Then he drove into Alexandria to rearm himself, having had to abandon his weapons before boarding the first of his trip's many planes. Vittorio had given him the address of a gun dealer who would satisfy his needs without questions. And an hour later, Gianni was on his way to Washington with a sharpshooter's rifle and scope sights in his car trunk, a 9mm automatic in a belt hol-ster, and silencers that he could attach if needed. Trying to an-ticipate his needs, he also picked up some high-powered binoculars and a pair of infrared night-vision goggles.

At shortly before 5:00 p.m., he was parked near enough to the Justice Department Building to be able to spot the attor-ney general when he came out.

Seeing a steady stream of town cars and limousines com-ing and going, Gianni suddenly felt joyless, dispirited. All this great officialdom of the world's last remaining democra-tic superpower, and everyone with their own line of dirty se-crets. The higher you went, the dirtier they got. While at the very top, a past, present, and future killer.

Gianni felt it as something beyond him, some eternal seepage from the nation's waste pipes. And the more you held your breath the more it stank.

For over a week now he had been crawling through some pretty mean streets. They tore away the pink wrappings and exposed the maggots. Blood flowed like honey, and a lot of people got their livers chopped. Memorial candles burned day and night in too many windows. Everyone had their own landscapes. His had become studded with a grotesque blend of lies, violence, and ice cream sundaes.

Gianni had been waiting for almost an hour when he saw Henry Durning leave the Justice Department Building and get into the back of an official, dark-gray, chauffeur-driven limousine. Moments later, the car drove off and he followed.

Keeping a safe interval in the heavy, early-evening traffic, Gianni tailed the attorney general out of the immediate area of working Washington and through some of Georgetown's more picturesque streets. When the limousine finally deposited Durning in front of a narrow Federalist town house, Gianni circled the block and parked within sight of the entrance.

The limousine had disappeared.

At about eight o'clock, a black woman left the house and drove off in a gray Toyota.

Gianni sat there until it was fully dark. Then he left his car and worked his way around to the rear of the house.

Lights showed in two rooms . . . one, on the first floor . . . the other, directly above it on the second floor.

Gianni eased himself between some shrubs and looked into the lower room. It was a library, with a desk, floor-to-ceiling bookshelves, an oversize couch, and some comfortable-looking chairs. And sitting and reading in one of the chairs was Mary Chan Yung.

She was alone in the room, with the same stillness of a photograph that Gianni remembered from his first sight of her through another window, in Connecticut.

I'm sleepwalking, he thought.

Yet she was there, right enough. No mistake in that. Where else should she be? The devil's own whore was simply where she belonged. With the devil. And as if the sight of her alone wasn't enough, he began breathing her perfume through the open window.

Then the attorney general came into the room. Obviously on his way somewhere, he was in dinner clothes. *An imposing man,* thought Gianni coldly. He exuded confidence and control.

He bent and kissed Mary Yung where she sat reading, an easy comfortable kiss that pretty much showed where they were.

"Sorry, love," he said, "but it shouldn't be more than a couple of hours at most. At least I got out of the dinner part."

Mary Yung rose and walked him to the door. "I'll watch you on television."

"Christ, you don't have to."

"I want to. You do it so well."

Then they were out of Gianni's sight and hearing.

Moments later he realized that the limousine had returned and then sped away with Durning in the backseat.

Gianni quickly cut a slit in the screening, reached in and opened two latches, and was waiting in the room when Mary returned.

Her eyes went wide.

"Gianni!"

Only the single word escaped.

"That's still my name," he said quietly. "What about you? What's *your* name these days?"

Mary was silent. All she seemed able to do was stare at him. *As though at a ghost,* Gianni thought. *As though I look as dead to her as Vittorio looked to me.*

"I'm surprised to find you here," he said. "I guess the one million wasn't enough, was it? Who are you selling him now? Or is it just your usual whore self?"

Gianni's hands were shaking so badly it made him ashamed. What kind of man was he? She'd betrayed him and everyone else. She'd caused God only knew how many deaths, and how many more to come? And *he* was the one standing here with trembling hands.

"Gianni."

She said his name again, this time so softly he could barely hear it. Was it finally the only word she was able to say? Was this her penance? Doomed to repeat the name of her fool through all the circles of hell?

To quiet his hands and make him feel less ashamed, he took out his piece, screwed on the silencer, and aimed it between her eyes.

"Where do you want it *love?*" he said softly and mockingly, using the endearment because this was how he had heard Henry Durning address her, thereby soiling the word for all time. "Between your lying eyes or your whore's thighs?"

He watched as her eyes flooded.

Then he watched her grip his gun hand in both of hers to steady it, and lean her forehead against the silencer.

"Go ahead," she whispered. "Do it. If it will make you feel any better, just do it."

They stood that way. The only sound was their breathing. Until something broke inside him and he brought the gun down.

I'm ludicrous, he thought. *I can't even do this right.*

"Why?" he said. "Of all the men in the world, why did you have to come *here,* to *him?*"

Her eyes still flooding, she stared blindly at Gianni. "For the same reason you came," she said. "To get him to save the boy, or to kill him."

Gianni considered her. Was it possible? Not likely. Yes, but was it *possible?*

"Durning would do that for you?"

Mary Yung shrugged. "He wants me. He seems to see something in me."

"And what do *you* see in *him?*"

"Maybe some small hope of redemption."

"In that animal?"

"He's not an animal, Gianni."

"What then?"

"A man in trouble. Who'll do anything, even kill, to get out of it."

"Is that what you tell yourself while you're fucking him?"

Mary took the question seriously. "I'll say this. I've felt dirty with any number of men, but I've never felt dirty with Henry. He says he loves me and I'm not sure exactly what that means to him. But I know he finds things of value in me that no one has ever found before."

"Congratulations."

"I didn't expect you to understand. But you asked me a question and I tried to answer."

Feeling a bit wobbly, Gianni sat down on the couch. "What about Peggy and the boy? Are they alive or dead?"

"No one seems to know about the boy. The two men guarding him were found shot to death a few days ago, and no one has seen Paul since. But Peggy is definitely alive."

"Where?"

"Someplace in Italy. Henry just found that out. After Carlo Donatti had told him she was dead. It seems he and Donatti have been playing their own little power games with her. With the don now apparently using her as a bargaining chip."

"For what?"

"I have no idea. Henry never goes into details. But I do know he and Donatti have worked something out."

"Durning told you that?"

"He implied it. Which is the best I can hope for with him. But he also asked how I'd like to meet him in Capri for an idyllic week of sun, sea, and love.

"When?"

"He'll be flying to Naples late tomorrow evening for some sort of conference. But he doesn't expect to be hanging around there long and said he hasn't had a real vacation in years."

"Then you won't be going together?"

"No. I'll be flying Alitalia, and he'll be on a government plane with the delegation."

Gianni sat staring at the gun in his hand. It was no longer shaking. "And you think this is all tied in with Peggy?"

"It has to be."

"How can you be so sure?"

"Because Henry never mentioned a word about Capri or going to that Naples conference until after his last meeting with Carlo Donatti. Which was right after he found out Peggy was actually alive. Then he suddenly turned all sweetness, light, and hope and love. Remember, Peggy is the heart of this whole nightmare for him. Only when she is dead is he finally in the clear."

"Do you really believe Durning has plans to kill her himself?" Gianni asked, stunned.

"Of course. That's why he's going to Italy tomorrow. Who else but himself can he finally trust to do it? He's learned the hard way. Ten years ago he trusted the job to Donatti, who trusted it to Vittorio, who went and married Peggy instead of killing her. Then a few days ago he again trusted Donatti to get the job done. But all the don did was tell Henry she was dead, and hold her for whatever kind of deal he was trying to work out."

Mary slowly sat down, as if the weight of all this deception was simply too much to handle on her feet.

"Which leaves only Henry himself to do it," she said. "Not someone else to squeeze the trigger and possibly talk about it later. And certainly no witnesses to be there and see *him* do it. Just Henry and Peggy. As alone together as when they started out ten years ago."

Mary Yung sat mutely, eyes stricken as though witnessing the actual scene as described. "And afterward," she said tonelessly, "if Henry's really learned from past experience, he'll make sure her body is never found."

Gianni watched her sitting motionless, fingers clasped like spikes in her lap. "You've done a lot of thinking about it."

"What else do I have to think about," she said dully. "How I made it all happen? How I destroyed a whole family for my million? You said it all when you walked in here. Except you were too kind. At least a whore gives an honest trade. Herself for the money. I didn't even sell myself. I sold others."

He felt, as he listened to her, the weight of her heart.

"How you must hate me," she said.

Gianni was silent. He had lost even that. If he despised anyone, it was himself. For being such a damn fool.

"Since Vittorio's not with you," she said, "I guess they killed him."

"Not quite. He's in a hospital with two holes and a bunch of tubes in him. But he thinks his wife and son are dead. So the best of him is dead, too."

Mary Yung's eyes, brimming all this time, suddenly spilled over and ran down her cheeks. It made Gianni feel no better, and he looked at his gun and silencer and the back of his hands.

"What are your plans?" he asked.

"I'll meet Henry in Capri and see what I can do."

"You mean besides fuck him?"

Mary nodded, her expression unchanged. "He wants very much for me to love him. Maybe that can at least help save the boy. If not Peggy."

"Do you really believe that?"

"I have to."

She wiped her eyes with the back of her hands. A little girl's gesture.

"And you?" she asked. "What are you going to do?"

Gianni just looked at her.

"I don't blame you," she said. "I wouldn't trust me, either."

Gianni holstered his piece and rose to go. "Will your Henry notice the slit in the window screen tonight?"

"He won't even be in here."

"You'd better have it fixed while he's gone tomorrow. No point in making him wonder."

Mary Yung nodded.

She walked to the back door with Gianni.

"Please," she said. "Just try to believe this. Every word I said to you tonight was true."

Gianni quickly turned away. He didn't want to have to see what was taking place on her face as he left.

He checked into a Holiday Inn not far from the airport. Then he got out of his clothes and showered for the first time in two days.

Gianni stayed under the hot water for about half an hour. When he finally came out, he toweled himself dry with almost brutal roughness. In the mirror over the sink, his face stared back at him through a film of steam. He smiled as though testing the muscles, then shrugged and turned away.

The soap he had used was scented and there seemed to be a clinging, distinctly feminine fragrance in the air that had nothing to do with Mary Yung, yet filled the room with her presence. Insanely, he felt himself begin to melt down under the bright lights, finished up quickly, and left the bathroom.

Gianni put on fresh underwear and lay down stiffly on the bed. He didn't own pajamas or slippers or a robe. These were for sickness or lounging, and he was never sick and never lounged. The moment he was up he put on his pants and shoes, put on his man's responsibilities and dignity. His wife had teased him about not knowing how to relax, but had understood his needs better than he.

Teresa. He suddenly seemed to have lived two lifetimes since she was gone. How simple things had been with her. There was love, you knew what you had, and that was that. And now? Pain and deception.

Watching the time, he waited until midnight. Then he put through a call to Dr. Helene Curci's home number in Monreale, Sicily, where it was just 6:00 A.M. But it was Lucia's voice that he heard answer.

"This is Gianni," he said in Italian. "I'm sorry if I woke you. How's Vittorio?"

"Weak, but getting better. He keeps asking if you've called. Do you have news for him?"

"Yes. And it's good. His wife and son are alive."

"Oh, Gianni!" Lucia's voice went thick with emotion. "He's been so sad, so sure they were gone. Where are they?"

"Somewhere in Italy. I don't know any more than that. But tell him I've got some leads."

"Wonderful. You take care."

"You, too. We owe you and your cousin everything."

It was later that Gianni felt the depression setting in. How much false hope had he conveyed, and how much damage would it do if and when it came to nothing?

Still, even false hope was better than none, he thought, and he was almost able to believe it for a while.

Then he turned out the light, lay back once more on the bed, and pictured Henry Durning coming home to his Georgetown house, walking into his bedroom, taking off his custom-tailored dinner clothes, and placing his naked body between the smooth, welcoming thighs of Mary Yung.

Gianni's motel bed felt damp and haunted with lumps, and his body lay rigid. He forced a yawn to fool himself into believing he was ready for sleep. But it failed to work.

Slowly, Gianni began to swear. He swore carefully, almost

fastidiously, in a low, even voice. When he had exhausted every vile word he knew in English and Italian, he dug back for a few Yiddish words and added these, reciting his bitter, trilingual litany with as much sincerity as he could muster in the solitary dark of the quiet room.

69

ABOUT TWO HOURS before Gianni Garetsky's call to Lucia, Vittorio Battaglia had felt himself trapped in a nightmare.

On his first night out of the intensive care unit and in his own room, he was suddenly dry mouthed, sweating, and unable to breathe, with some animal claw making marks on his chest, and the devil himself choking him on his own air of foul intent.

But it was no nightmare, no animal, no devil. It was just an iron hand gripping at his throat, and a pillow jammed over his face.

There was a sound of heavy breathing, nothing more, a quiet pressing and straining, pulse packed against pulse in suffocating blackness.

They've found me, he thought, and for an instant he actually was grateful. *Let it be over,* he told himself. Then a view of what was on the other side of darkness came to him: a lovely vision of his wife and son laughing in the glow of a summer evening, waiting, unhurt, whatever damage they might have suffered in their passage having been magically healed. He was weary with a most honorable fatigue. He'd had enough. What was there without them anyway? Only being alone, and more degraded clowning, and all the best of it was behind you and gone.

Vittorio was as far into himself as he had ever been. Until spasms began opening and something cried out.

Don't let the bastards get away with it.

Then the anger and hatred came, passing into him in waves. His hand drove between his legs, and he groped for what remained of his manhood. Which at this possibly final moment of his life was to be found not in his poor limp thing, but rather in the sweet hard butt of his automatic.

The wonder was that he had enough control and presence of mind at that point to remember to release the safety.

But he did.

And he aimed straight up against the weighted sheet directly above him.

Then he squeezed once, twice, hearing only the soft sound of the silencer. No more than that. Until there was a single grunt and he felt the full weight of his intended killer collapse against his chest.

Vittorio pushed the pillow off his face and sucked air. He saw flashing lights that whirled in a dream. When he felt ready to trust his eyes, he opened them.

A heavyset, dark-haired man he had never seen lay half on and half off the bed. Vittorio felt for a pulse. But both shots had entered the man's chest and he was dead.

The door was closed and Vittorio lay aiming his piece at it in case the dead man hadn't come alone. But no one entered the room, and the corridor outside was quiet.

So they'd found him. Which was no surprise. The wonder was that it had taken them this long. The mob had eyes and ears everywhere, and there were simply too many shifts and too many people working in a hospital to keep something like this quiet.

Vittorio Battaglia closed his eyes. Much of his fury had passed, and he felt no great urgency to take action. Not that there was much he could do, or even felt like doing. Although he was out of intensive care, no longer connected to tubes, and able to take short walks along the corridor, he was weak as an infirm old man and subject to recurrent bouts of dizziness. Still, unless he didn't mind being dead within the next few hours, he would have to get his pale, fevered ass out of here as fast as possible.

So Vittorio set about doing just that.

He slid the body out of sight under his bed. He got out of

his hospital gown and into his street clothes. And he quietly eased past the nursing station while the two on-duty nurses were busy in patients' rooms.

By the time he reached the parking lot behind the hospital, he was soaked through with perspiration and had almost passed out twice. Finally, he was dizzy enough to have to lean against a car to keep from falling.

Great.

Vittorio wondered if he was hemorrhaging from all the moving about. But he didn't feel a thing. Which wasn't to say nothing was happening to him. Like spirits of the dead, emotions tore at him and refused to leave. He wished he had been smarter, braver, more gifted and aware, as if it somehow were hidden failures of his own that had wasted his family.

You get what you deserve in this life.

And what kind of idiot had come up with that one?

The dizziness passed and Vittorio pushed himself away from the car and began carefully making his way out of the parking lot.

Heading where?

He had no idea.

Of course he could always call Lucia and her doctor cousin, impose himself on them, and probably end up making them pay with their lives for all their kindnesses.

But he would sooner wander off into the woods and cover himself with leaves. They deserved better. Inasmuch as the mob had found out he was in the hospital, they undoubtedly also learned who had brought him there in the first place. Which meant they would head straight for Dr. Curci's house as soon as they discovered him gone and their assassin dead.

So much for that.

He was barely out of the parking lot when he saw the lights of a motel off to his right and a few blocks down the road. With half-a-dozen stops along the way, in just under fifteen minutes, he was able to make it to the entrance of what was called the Palermo Motor Lodge.

It was a big commercial establishment and the parking area was almost full. Which was good. Because it was the kind of place where it wasn't unusual for guests to be checking in at all hours of the night.

Vittorio rested against the hood of a parked car until his breathing was easy and quiet. Then he wiped the sweat from his face with a handkerchief, finger-combed his hair, and walked into the lobby without falling on his head in front of the desk.

He registered, using one of his several CIA names and credit cards, and said he expected to stay for two or three nights. Then the clerk gave him his room key, wished him a pleasant stay, and returned to the paperback he had been reading when Battaglia appeared.

Something took hold of Vittorio and drew him toward the sanctuary. He felt as though he were in a powerful magnetic field where some force without sensation was leading him to perform one small act of survival after the other without a single contribution from anything resembling a will of his own.

Until it took him to his room, opened the door with his key, closed and locked the door behind him, and stretched him flat out on the bed without his turning on a light or taking off his clothes.

Suddenly it was all quite clear. The decision had been made for him in his hospital bed with that pillow over his face and those steel fingers clutching his throat. He wasn't going to die tonight, or tomorrow, or the next day, or the day after that. He was going to live and get his strength back, and finally do what had to be done.

He wasn't going to let the bastards get away with it. It was the thought that had kept him alive when he was nearly gone earlier, and it would go on keeping him alive for however long it took to get them.

But get them he would.

As poor Gianni would try to do. But wouldn't be able to. And would finally die of it himself.

He told his old friend good-bye.

As he already had told his wife.

And as he told his son.

Good-bye . . . good-bye . . . good-bye.

* * *

It was just 6:30 A.M. as Vittorio silently offered his final good-byes. Which was about the time Lucia was driving to the Monreale Hospital to bring him the good news from Gianni.

70

PEGGY WAS SITTING on the back terrace of the Sicilian villa when one of her guards came out with a telephone.

He plugged the jack into a nearby connection and handed her the receiver. "It's for you, signora," he said, and went back into the house to allow her privacy.

Not that she was without surveillance. Another guard sat about a hundred yards away, in the shade of a tree. They were omnipresent. It was the only visible indication that she was anything other than the pampered lady of the manor she appeared to be.

Except perhaps for the whiteness of her knuckles as she gripped the telephone, and the nest of snakes that never left her stomach.

"Yes?" she said.

"It's Carlo Donatti in New York, Mrs. Battaglia. I hope you're well."

"If you consider going quietly mad and vomiting every few hours being well."

"I'm sorry," said Donatti. "But I have some good news for you. Before too long, I believe you should be together with your son."

She felt a flutter in the lower eyelid of her right eye. "What does 'before too long' mean?"

"It's hard to pinpoint something as complex as this. But I don't think thirty-six to forty-eight hours would be too far off the mark."

Peggy took a long, deep breath. She had a horror of suddenly starting to scream and not being able to stop.

"Can I really believe that?"

"Absolutely. But first we have a few details to take care of. You mentioned buried jewelry and the murder weapon as backup evidence. You said you could tell me where to find them. I assume that's true."

"Yes."

"Then please tell me now because I must have these things confirmed."

"You'll have to write it all down. There's too much to remember."

There was a metallic sound from the other end as something hit the phone.

"I'm ready," said Donatti. "Go ahead."

Peggy gave it to him then, in full detail. She had carefully memorized it almost ten years ago, hoping she would never have to use it, but knowing, too, that if she ever did need it, the need would be a critical one.

She started with road and landmark directions that would bring a searcher to within fifty yards of the burial site, and ended up with the kind of foot-by-foot, inch-by-inch measurements that could only have been produced by a professional surveyor's level on a tripod. Which, as Peggy told the don, she actually had rented and learned to use before she and Vittorio fled.

Carlo Donatti was impressed. "You're an incredible woman, Mrs. Battaglia."

Knowing you can't get good news by asking for it, Peggy asked anyway. "Do you know anything about Vittorio?"

"Nothing. And it's just as well. With Vittorio, any news would have to be bad."

The line hummed between them and Peggy groped for a way to hold on. She didn't want the connection broken. It was her one link to hope.

"Please," she said. "You've known Vittorio since he was a boy. Up until this whole terrible business with Henry, wasn't he always loyal to you?"

"Vittorio was the best I had, Mrs. Battaglia. I trusted him with my life."

"He felt the same about you. And I know that once you've freed Paulie and me, once I've told Vittorio it was you who saved our lives, he'll respect and care about you as much as he ever did."

"Vittorio and Gianni are my *famiglia*. Like part of my blood. It would give me no pleasure to see them come to harm."

"Thank you, Don Donatti," she said, and had to consciously resist a sudden, insane urge to call him Godfather. She despised herself for it.

"We'll be meeting soon, Mrs. Battaglia. Until we do, try to think positively. Things will go well."

Donatti broke the connection.

Walking about later, followed by a guard, Peggy felt no such confidence. There were just too many unknown factors. Not the least of which was Henry Durning.

The fact of it was, she simply couldn't picture anyone, not even someone as powerful and resourceful as Carlo Donatti, forcing the attorney general to do something he didn't want to do.

71

PAULIE FELT THE throb of the ship's engines going into reverse, then the soft thumping of the prow against the dock. It was morning, and they were in Naples, and he hadn't died from the pizza after all.

At the moment he was back among the metal drums under the big six-wheeler's tarp. Nino had thought it the safest place for him to be through the disembarking, and Paulie had agreed. He knew that the police and the haircuts would be all over the place as the cars, trucks, and buses rolled off the ferry. So why take chances? Unless the *carabinieri* thought they'd frightened him off back in Palermo and that he'd never gotten on the ship at all.

The boy wondered what Nino would think if he knew the truth about him . . . that he hadn't run away from home at all, that he'd been kidnapped by gangsters and had escaped after a shootout, and that even now he was carrying a loaded snub-noser in his pocket. He could just picture the trucker's face if he ever told him. Not that he ever would. But he guessed maybe part of him did want Nino to know that he wasn't just a silly, crybaby kid who'd run off for some dumb reason, then got scared and changed his mind and started running back home. He guessed he wanted Nino to know he was more than that.

I'm more than that.

Paulie told it to himself. It would have to be enough that he knew.

He heard the truck's engine start, along with the engines of all the other wheeled things lined up in the belly of the ship. They began slowly moving off the ferry and onto land. Then the boy felt the truck suddenly picking up speed and rolling across the rough cobbles of the Naples waterfront. Until the truck stopped moments later, and Nino came around and lifted the tarp and brought Paulie up front to ride beside him in the cab.

The trucker grinned. "Well, it looks like you made it. Feeling better about things now?"

Paulie nodded.

Nino glanced at him as he drove. "You don't look too happy. You getting a little nervous now that you're this close?"

The boy shrugged.

"Don't you worry." Nino draped a muscular arm across Paulie's shoulders. "The worst can happen, they'll just hug and squeeze you to death a little."

"Sure," said Paulie, and wished again that he could tell this nice man how it really was.

An hour later he shook the trucker's hand, said good-bye to him, and stood there at the cutoff as he watched the huge eighteen-wheeler disappear on its way to Salerno.

It took the boy only twenty minutes to walk the rest of the way home to Positano.

His first sight of his house made everything go weak and soft inside him, as if he suddenly were melting down.

The house is there.

But had he expected it not to be?

He approached cautiously, not using the road but circling around through the trees and growth in back. His dream, his recurrent vision was, of course, of coming home to his parents' arms. But the hard core of him recognized this as little more than a child's fairy tale. Since his mother and father had never been home to answer his calls, he didn't really expect them to be home now. If anyone was waiting for him, he thought, it was more likely to be a couple of mafiosi.

But after crawling around the place twice through the brush, it appeared to Paulie that not even the gangsters were there. No windows were open and no cars were in the parking spaces off the road. Finally, he worked his way to the front door and found it locked. As was the side door. Then he found the secret family emergency key in its special place under a rock and was able to use it to get inside.

The boy quietly closed and locked the door behind him, and stood there breathing the air of the house.

He listened to the silence.

The first thing that caught his eye were the folding easel, paint box, and half-finished canvas he'd been working on when Dom slugged him and carried him away. They lay together in a corner of the entrance foyer, where Paulie figured his father had left them after finding them down near the water.

He walked over and touched the canvas to see if the paint had dried. It had.

Opening his paint box, he saw that all the dirty brushes he'd been using that afternoon lay wrapped together in a rag. Which was what he usually did with them when he finished painting for the day, but which his father must have done for him this time before carrying his things home.

Paulie took the dirty brushes down to the basement, rinsed them in turpentine to soften the half-dried paint, then washed them with brown naphtha soap in one of the two washtubs he and his father always used for cleaning their brushes. In the basement, the smell of paint and turpentine slipped over him like an old shirt, familiar, warming. Down here, as in his father's big studio upstairs, were things he knew about, that he was prepared for, that he had spent more than half of his eight years learning to handle.

With something like courage, the boy forced himself upstairs into his father's studio. He was there for several moments before he noticed the hole in the great picture window that made up almost the entire north wall of the room.

Although to Paulie, it was far more than just a hole. It was a tear in the fabric of his life. The size of it alone was daunting. Wanting to close his eyes and cry out, he just stood there staring at the way the jagged edges of glass, tinged with patches of dried blood, caught the light.

His mother and father were dead.

Numbly, the boy walked to the window and gazed out for his first glimpse of his parents' bodies on the rocks far below.

But nothing was there except rocks.

There was not even the broken glass.

Nor were there any signs of it on the studio door.

God had taken Mom and Dad to heaven.

Along with the glass.

72

GIANNI GARETSKY CAME awake in a cold sweat on his lumpy hotel bed after less than three hours' sleep.

He had a deep headache behind his eyes and every nerve was alive with messages of alarm. Suddenly ambush was everywhere, and even the air seemed to come into his lungs with the fading warmth of the newly murdered dead.

He saw Vittorio strung out and hanging like a chicken by his intravenous tubes.

He envisioned the boy, Paulie, staring wide-eyed at the sky from a freshly dug, open grave.

He heard Peggy's poor cries blight the darkness as Henry Durning finally laid the last of his paranoidal fears to rest.

While I do what?

What can I do?

Vittorio had already told him.

If you need help, anything at all, call this man and tell him it's for Charlie.

Gianni had, as instructed, memorized the name, Tom Cortlandt, and the number, which was Cortlandt's direct line at the American embassy in Brussels.

It was 4:22 A.M. in Washington, and 10:22 A.M. in Brussels. Gianni hesitated. Then he dialed the number.

I can't believe I'm doing this.

"Cortlandt here," said a man's voice in English.

Tempted to hang up, Gianni took a deep breath instead.

"You don't know me, Mr. Cortlandt, but a man named Charlie told me to call you if I ever needed help."

Several beats passed in silence.

"What's your problem?"

"Keeping Charlie and his family from being terminated."

"Where's Charlie now?"

"In a hospital in Sicily. With two gunshot wounds."

"Who are you?"

"An old friend."

"Your name?"

"Gianni Garetsky."

"The artist?"

Gianni sighed. "Yes."

"What names do you have for Charlie's family?"

"His wife is Peggy. His son is Paul."

"How old is the boy?"

"About eight."

"Where are you calling from?"

"A hotel room near Washington's National Airport."

There was a long pause.

"All right, Gianni. Here's what I'd like you to do. As soon

as you hang up, go over to the airport and call me collect from a pay phone. It'll be this same number, but with the last four digits reversed so that they read from right to left. Do you have that?"

"Yes."

"Then let's do it," said Cortlandt, and broke the connection.

Twenty minutes later, Gianni was at a public telephone in National Airport with the Central Intelligence Agency's Brussels chief of station back on the line.

"So what's this all about, Garetsky?"

"You're going to find this hard to believe."

Cortlandt waited in silence at the other end.

"It's all about Henry Durning," said Gianni.

Cortlandt barely missed a beat. "I assume you're talking about the attorney general."

"I am. He is trying to kill Peggy Walters."

"You're right," said the agent flatly. "I do find it hard to believe. But considering who you are and who told you to call me, I can't just dismiss you as some kind of nut. But you're still going to have to tell me about it."

Gianni stared out at the predawn emptiness of the terminal and said nothing.

"Well?" said Cortlandt.

"It's such an ugly story."

"That seems to be about the only kind I ever get to hear."

"All right," said Gianni. Then suddenly wishing he had a large snifter of brandy between his palms to help oil the telling, he went into his dark, corrosive tale for an audience of one, four thousand miles away, whom he had never even met.

Tommy Cortlandt listened without question or comment. And when Gianni finally finished, the silence at the other end went on for so long that the artist began to wonder whether the agent was still there.

He was.

"That's twice you've been right," Cortlandt said. "It *is* an ugly story. Almost too ugly not to be true."

Gianni again felt himself bleeding for a brandy.

"But before we go any further," said the agent, "there are a few things you should know. We operate under a limited mandate. We have nothing to do with matters of criminal justice or internal security at any level. Those are strictly FBI and police functions. Officially, what we deal with are threats to the national security from the outside. Such as from foreign governments, individuals, and the like."

"And *unofficially?*"

"There's no such thing." Cortlandt paused. "Which doesn't mean we aren't always being accused of doing things our own way without regard for little obstacles like laws, mandates, and such. Still, if we feel the safety of our own people and their families are being threatened, we're not indifferent. And of course there's always the sanction of general authorization."

"What does that mean?"

"That if we feel it's right and necessary, we'll do whatever the fuck we want. So now that we've got the bullshit out of the way, let's get down to specifics. Exactly what sort of help are you looking for?"

Leaning against the smooth plastic of the pay phone, Gianni Garetsky felt a rush of warmth for this faceless man way off in Brussels.

"First," he said, "there's the matter of Vittorio. I mean, Charlie. I had to leave him helpless and alone in the hospital, and I've a bad feeling about it. Sooner or later they're going to find him."

"What hospital?"

"Monreale Municipal. It's about thirty kilometers southeast of Palermo."

"Under what name was he admitted?"

"Franco Denici."

"And his doctor?"

"Helene Curci."

"Does she know the truth about him?"

"Only to a point. Only that the mob wants him."

"I'll put a few people on him," said Cortlandt. "What else?"

"Henry Durning will be leaving for Naples on a government plane sometime late today, Washington time. I'd like to know exactly when he'll be taking off, his estimated time of arrival, and where he'll be staying while he's there."

"I'll have to get back to you on that in around five hours. How about Durning's itinerary in Naples?"

"Yes, that, too," said Gianni Garetsky.

"And I guess you'll be wanting the same information on Carlo Donatti's movements."

"You can get that, too?"

"Gianni, we can walk on water."

The artist was half-ready to believe it.

Five and a half hours later, Gianni was back at the same airport phone, calling the same Brussels number. Collect. In between, he had been lying in his motel room . . . thinking, dozing, and staring at the ceiling. This time, the terminal was in its more common manic state.

"Cortlandt here," said the chief of station.

"Garetsky."

"Here's what I've got," said Cortlandt. "To begin with, Charlie's no longer in the Monreal Hospital."

Gianni felt a sharp stab of light enter his eyes. "What do you mean? Where is he?"

"No one seems to know. But a local enforcer was found shot to death under his bed."

"What about Helene Curci? His doctor. Did they go after her, too?"

"She and a woman living with her were worked over pretty good. But apparently they didn't know anything, either."

Gianni leaned his forehead against the cool surface of the phone. It didn't calm him one bit. "How bad are they?"

"Not too. They got away lucky. It's mostly bruises and lacerations. I have them being watched in case Charlie or the goons show up."

Gianni was silent.

"Here's the rest of it. Durning leaves from Dulles at 9:00 P.M. tonight your time. He arrives in Naples at 10:30 A.M. local tomorrow. He and his delegation will be staying at the Amoretto Hotel in Sorrento. They have meetings scheduled there for the next four days."

"And Donatti?"

"One of his Galatea corporate jets has a flight plan filed to leave JFK for Palermo a few hours before Durning takes off for Naples."

For several moments neither of them spoke.

"What are your plans?" Cortlandt said at last.

"I don't really have any. I'll be playing it mostly by ear. But I appreciate all you've done."

"If you'll let me, I can do more."

Dimly, Garetsky was aware that people were hugging, kissing, saying good-bye, and hurrying to catch planes.

"How?" he asked.

"I'll give you a number that can reach me twenty-four hours a day. I'd never be farther away than the nearest phone. Just keep me informed. Then, if you need it, I can get you backup or information faster than you'd believe possible."

"You'd really do something like that?"

"I just said I would."

"Then I accept. What's the number?"

Cortlandt gave it to him and Gianni wrote it down and put it in his pocket until he could memorize it.

"It's best that you stay in touch anyway," said the intelligence agent. "I may have something for you soon on Charlie or his boy. In the meantime, be careful. I love your paintings. Good luck."

Gianni thanked him again, hung up, and went to check the flight schedules to Naples.

Including a change of planes in Rome, there was a 5:00 P.M. Alitalia flight from Dulles that would get him into Naples at least three to four hours ahead of Henry Durning. He booked space on that.

Then he went back to his hotel to prepare once more for Italy.

Vittorio, don't die on me. I'm getting closer. I just need a little time.

73

HENRY DURNING WENT down into the bank vault with an attendant and felt himself breathing the still, lifeless air of a tomb.

It was all in his mind, of course. The air down here was no different from the air upstairs. Yet a cold breath seemed to come up over his face as if he had blundered through an invisible barrier and into a place of death.

It became even worse when he was left alone in a private viewing room with his tin box. Because now he had the box open, and all its viscera of past deaths were set loose on him at once.

This was it.

This was the original, not a copy, of the evidence collected against Carlo Donatti. It had been Durning's insurance against sudden death for more than ten years, and Donatti had finally deceived him into surrendering it as his price for escaping a more direct and immediate threat.

The attorney general knew he would deal with it, of course. Those who wouldn't or couldn't bend to the inevitable simply broke, and he had no intention of breaking. Yet sitting here alone in a vault with the cost of Donatti's betrayal fixed him somehow in a mood he didn't dare to ignore or reject, for it hinted at an additional and far worse penalty on his flesh if he took it too lightly.

With someone like Carlo Donatti there were threads everywhere. It was impossible to know where his reach began and ended. Carlo had only to pick up a phone and someone could die in a remote city on some distant shore. He could touch anyone from a poor hophead in some back alley to a head of state in a gilded palace.

What Henry Durning knew, and accepted as fact, was that for him to surrender what was in this tin box to this man would for all practical purposes be the end of him. At best, he would be a monkey on Carlo Donatti's chain, at worst a block of cement at the bottom of the Potomac.

He sat in the small, tomblike room thinking about it. He heard his heart going like a pump in the bilge of a sinking ship. He could have been drowning, or smothering in smoke, or having his brains beaten out by a sawed-off bat.

He sat until he wanted no more of it.

He wanted to be free of murder and free of dread. He wanted to be some sort of decent, reasonable man again, taking pride in himself and his future. He wanted to love Mary Yung in ways he had never loved any woman before; he knew he had it within him to love.

He sat until he felt confident he would somehow manage to get what he wanted. He had not gotten where he was out of nothing. His discipline was still of iron. He wouldn't fail.

All right, he thought, and finally got to work transferring the necessary papers from his safety-deposit box to the leather briefcase he had brought with him.

It all seemed so much easier now that he had decided.

I can do it, he told himself, and felt something near to exultation. Perhaps as someone might feel, he thought wryly, who had gotten past those first formidable barriers of fear and gently accepted the inevitability of death.

Consider.

How monumental could the act of dying really be?

Who, finally, had ever failed to accomplish it?

They would be parting in a few hours to leave for Italy on separate flights, so Henry Durning came home early and made love to Mary Yung.

Yet he found himself curiously surprised. With so many deep-rooted calls for attention drifting through his brain, he hadn't expected to react this strongly to her.

I should have known better by now.

But he knew it was more than that. There was something totally new growing inside him that was very different from his usual blend of erotic compulsions. He had enough hope to believe it might actually be the beginnings of love.

Then the thought occurred that there was a very real chance that this might be the last time for them. Or at least, for him. Which created enough of an internal disturbance to make him lose it and go soft.

Mary drew back and looked at him.

"What's wrong?"

Durning smiled. "It can happen, you know."

"Not to *you*."

He lay there holding her. "I'm afraid even with me, it's still mostly mind controlled."

Her kiss was light.

"Does that mean I'm *not* the only thing on your mind?" she said.

"You're the only *important* thing on my mind. But in this case even the distraction had to do with you."

"How?"

Durning reached for his cigarettes, lit up, and considered how much to tell her. Not everything, of course. But certainly more than he had told her so far.

"For one thing," he said, "how, if I don't end up nearly as lucky and brilliant as I'd hoped on this trip, this could well be the last time I'll ever be making love to you."

Mary Yung was silent.

"Something else you should be aware of," he said, "is that among the odds and ends I took care of earlier today was adjusting my will. You now happen to be the legal heir to more than eighty percent of my estate. So for God's sake, don't just disappear if anything happens to me over in Italy. Not unless you want to leave around fifteen to twenty million bucks to be haggled over and divided among dozens of rapacious lawyers and overstaffed charities."

"Henry—"

He gently covered her mouth with his hand.

"Please," he said. "No false cries of protest and gratitude. I loved the idea of your being honestly hungry, greedy, and clever enough to work that million out of me on our original deal. The only thing that bothers me about making you so rich is that you'll probably lose all that tough, streetwise ingenuity that intrigued me, and ruin everything by turning sweet and lovable."

She worked his hand loose.

"Fuck you, Henry! And fuck your fifteen to twenty million."

"Ah, you're still my girl."

"And you're still a mean, fucking sonofabitch."

"Absolutely," he said. "Isn't that lovely?"

"No. It's ugly and I hate it."

"That, too, " he said. "But just remember this. If you live to a hundred and end up dozing and tied to a wheelchair, parts of you will still know that no one ever even came close to loving you as I did."

74

VITTORIO BATTAGLIA HAD awakened in the motel with a bad fever, and it steadily became worse as the day wore on.

Dozing, he crawled through nightmares. He tried to get out of bed, but his head spun and he fell back. Nausea collected all through him.

At midafternoon, stumbling, falling, and finally crawling, he reached the bathroom, knelt on the tile floor, and tossed the best and worst of himself into the toilet. Each separate strain and retch tore at his less-than-healed incisions, doing their best to rip them apart.

And maybe they were.

Because back in bed, he saw a variously colored ooze beginning to drain from them. And being far from inexperienced in such things, having survived no less than nine individual puncture wounds over the years, he had a clear idea of his options.

He could stay holed-up right here in this motel room until he died of infection or internal bleeding.

He could have an ambulance take him back to the hospital and give Don Sorbino's soldiers a second chance to get the job on him done right.

Or he could try to make it to Dr. Curci's house, figuring that Sorbino's people had already checked the place out and found it clean.

Helene and Lucia were his only sensible choice.

He felt bad at having to involve them again, but he just wasn't ready to die.

Alternately sleeping, sweating, and shivering with fever, Vittorio waited until after dark to prepare.

Then he cleaned himself up, checked the local telephone directory, and found Dr. Helene Curci's address listed as 846 Via Tomaso. Next, he called a taxi and asked to be picked up in ten minutes at the ground-level entrance to room 16 of the Palermo Motor Lodge.

When the taxi arrived, he told the driver to take him to 826 rather than 846 Via Tomaso, so as not to have to stop right in front of Helene's house. Vittorio just hoped he'd be able to walk the extra hundred yards.

They were there in a little more than ten minutes and Vittorio paid the driver and watched the cab make a quick U-turn and disappear. Then holding himself as though he were put together of very fine crystal, Vittorio began walking the short distance to what he dimly remembered as the last house on the road.

There were no streetlights. There were only lights from some of the houses, and those were yellow and dim. By contrast, the glow from television sets was bright and colorful. Vittorio glanced in and saw whole families gathered around the sets . . . watching, talking, laughing. The sight was too much for him. He had to turn away.

His fever was passing through its chilled-out mode and he shivered as he walked.

Only fifty yards more.

Coming closer to the house, his eyes probed the shadows for watchers. If they were here, these would be the places for them. His automatic was in his belt and he kept his hand on the butt.

The way I'm shivering, I couldn't even hit a house if I had to shoot.

He was seeing bright, floating spots now, and he hoped he

wasn't going to fall on his face before he got there. It was as though he had just stared directly into an exploding flash-bulb.

Then Vittorio was at the house and half stumbling into the driveway. Lights were on in the downstairs rooms. But the blinds were drawn and he couldn't see in.

He walked around a parked car and approached the back door. When he was no more than twenty feet away, he felt his arms grabbed from behind and a big, hard hand go over his mouth.

Oh, shit, he thought, and found himself being dragged behind a row of hedges and onto a patch of grass. There were three hands, so there had to be at least two men.

Great thinking.

"Listen," whispered a man's voice. "We're friends. When I take my hand off your mouth don't cry out. Nod your head if you understand."

Vittorio didn't understand a thing but he nodded anyway, and the hand came away from his mouth. Then the other two hands came away from his arms and he was able to turn and stare into the faces of two men he had never seen before.

The shivering had stopped. Now he was sweating.

"We figure you're Charlie," murmured the man who had spoken before. "If you're him, you'll know who we are and who sent us."

"Holy Jesus," said Vittorio, and silently blessed Tommy Cortlandt and Gianni.

"Now you got it," said the second man.

"But how did you know I'd be coming? I didn't know it myself until a few hours ago."

"From what we heard, there's no place else you could have gone in the shape you're in. Besides, we had to be here to keep the two women from getting worked over again."

The man saw Vittorio's face.

"I guess you didn't know about that," he said.

Battaglia shook his head. "When did it happen?"

"A few hours after you did the job on that hitter in the hospital."

Vittorio stood in the grass pouring sweat. He thought of Lucia and Helene helping him. He thought of their reward.

"Do they know you two are out here?"

The first man nodded. "We thought it would make them feel easier about things." He looked at Vittorio's face. "You'd better get your ass inside. You look like shit."

Battaglia stood there a moment longer. Then he lightly touched each of the two men on the arm, half stumbled the rest of the way to the back stoop, struggled up the steps, and rang the bell.

Lucia opened the door and he saw three spinning faces. They were all equally beat up, swollen, and discolored.

"Vittorio!" she said.

He had a vague idea that something was going on with his mouth. In his mind it was trying very hard to smile. He just hoped it might somehow be doing it.

Then he walked into the kitchen, took exactly two steps, and passed out on the floor.

75

THE PACKAGES ARRIVED at Carlo Donatti's Sands Point home just a few hours before he was due to leave for Palermo.

Excitement thumping his chest like a fist, he carried them into his study and took off the wrappings.

What he had in front of him was a rifle wrapped in clear plastic, and a large, unmarked bag of what appeared to be expensive jewelry. They were the items described by Peggy Walters as having been buried ten years earlier by Henry Durning in the rich woodland soil of southeastern Connecticut.

There also was a brief typewritten report outlining the packaged contents along with the key elements determined from them, namely

* * *

That several sets of fingerprints taken from the rifle and other enclosed items matched those of Attorney General Henry Durning as currently carried by the FBI's national computer file in Washington.

That ballistics tests had shown that a bullet held by the Connecticut State Police in regard to an unsolved, break-in burglary and murder had been fired by the weapon described above.

That insurance records indicated that all of the enclosed jewelry had been the legally owned property of the victims of this same break-in burglary and murder, and that their estate had received settlement payments for whatever claims had been made for their loss.

There was more, but Carlo Donatti didn't bother reading any further. This was enough for his needs.

The initial excitement he had felt at the packages' arrival had faded to no more than mild satisfaction. There certainly was no real pleasure here. Pleasure had little to do with anything related to the deadly series of unpleasantries initiated by this man, a series that Donatti hoped would soon end with him.

Still, there did remain the business of the boy. And if that worked out as well as he hoped, there might yet turn out to be some good in it.

In this regard, Carlo Donatti glanced at his watch and put through a call to La Sirenuse Hotel in Positano, where it was after 11:00 P.M. and Frank Langiono was likely to be in his room.

When the hotel switchboard connected him to Langiono's room and he answered, Donatti told him to hang up and call right back from an outside line.

The don slipped a fresh cigarette into his holder, lit up, and tried to relax for a few minutes as he waited.

Frank Langiono was part of Donatti's long-held theory of security and survival: it was always best to keep a few people going for you that nobody else knew about.

In this case, Langiono, a former NYPD lieutenant, had

chosen to take early retirement and triple his earnings by working for Donatti in situations that could be best handled by someone outside the inevitable jealousies, loose tongues, and infighting of mob politics.

It had worked out well for more than eight years. It was still working out well. And this situation could prove to be its most important yet.

The telephone rang, and Carlo Donatti picked it up and heard Frank Langiono's voice greeting him in Italian, because Langiono always enjoyed speaking and practicing the language.

"How is everything?" said the don.

"Quiet. I just came in from watching. I swear the kid's unbelievable. He's so damn careful he won't even put on a light."

"How does he get around in the dark?"

"Mostly he seems to stay in one place. But when he does have to move around, he puts a couple of socks over a flashlight. It leaves him enough of a glow to cut the dark, yet can't be seen from outside. I only noticed it myself because I was right up against a window." Langiono grunted. "You sure hit it on the nose about his coming straight here after he was spotted at the ferry. But I guess where else would he go but home?"

Carlo Donatti was silent.

"Still figuring on the same time for tomorrow?" asked Langiono.

"Roughly. But it can easily go off by a couple of hours in something like this. Especially with all the road and air time."

"No problem. I got no other appointments."

"What about Sorbino's people?"

"Nothing. At least not since before the kid came in this morning. And like I said. All they did then was take a quick look around the house and grounds, then drive through town and talk to some of the shopkeepers. My money says we don't see them again."

"No drive-bys at all?"

"Not that I was able to spot."

The line was silent.

"Any last-minute questions?" said Carlo Donatti.

"No. I'm as set as I'll ever be."

"Then I'll see you tomorrow."

"Good luck, Don Donatti."

"You, too, Frank."

Donatti hung up and checked a number in the small, leather-bound notebook he always carried. Then he called the villa outside of Palermo where the woman known as Peggy Walters was staying.

One of the guards answered and Donatti heard a television commercial going in the background. He identified himself and asked to speak to the *signora*.

It seemed like a long time before he heard her voice.

"I hope I didn't wake you, Mrs. Battaglia."

"Is something wrong?" Her voice was tight. "Has something happened to my son?"

"Your boy is fine. I'm calling with good news. You should be seeing him within twenty-four hours."

Donatti heard nothing from the other end.

"Mrs. Battaglia?"

Still nothing. He gave her another few moments.

"Are you all right?"

"I'm sorry," she said. "I'm just having a little trouble dealing with this."

"I understand. I can imagine how this has been for you."

"How is it going to work?" Peggy asked. "Will Paul be brought here to me, or what?"

"I'll be flying over and taking you to him." Donatti paused. "But just so you're prepared, Henry will be meeting us there as well."

"Oh, God," she whispered.

"I'm afraid it's necessary."

"Why?"

"Because we'll have to be exchanging the evidence we have against each other."

Donatti could hear her breathing.

"As long as I get my boy," she said.

"That's not in question, Mrs. Battaglia."

"I'm not by nature a vindictive person," said Peggy softly. "I know we're all God's creatures and less than perfect. But for what this man has tried to do to me and those closest to me, for the fear and anguish alone . . ."

She stopped briefly.

"I'm almost ashamed of my feelings," she went on. "But I swear, Henry has so reduced me, has brought me so far down to his level, that the greatest joy I can imagine at this moment is pressing a gun to his head and . . . God help me . . . happily squeezing the trigger."

Donatti left her alone with it for several seconds.

"There's something I don't quite understand," she said.

"What's that?"

"You said you'd be exchanging evidence against each other?"

"Yes."

"I know what he's giving you, but what are you supposed to be giving *him?*"

Donatti was silent. Talk enough and you end up choking on your own shit. He sought to cover any possible damage.

"I never did tell you," he said. "Everything worked out perfectly with the buried evidence you described. Henry's fingerprints were on the weapon, and ballistics matched the murder bullet to the gun's barrel. The whole thing is solid."

"But if you give it all to him, what have you got left for an indictment? We decided. My word alone against his wouldn't be enough. He'd be in the clear."

"Not really," said Donatti.

"Why not?"

"Because I won't actually be giving him the evidence. Just a better-than-reasonable facsimile."

Peggy made a sound that might almost have been a laugh.

"I like that," she said.

So did Carlo Donatti.

76

Pᴀᴜʟɪᴇ sᴀᴛ ɪɴ the midnight dark of his father's studio and stared up at the stars through the jagged break in the big window. It was less hurtful in the dark because he couldn't see the dried blood on the edges of the glass.

After crying for a long time, the boy had begun to work his way out. The blood didn't have to be that of his mother or father. It could have belonged to some gangster. And the more he thought of it this way, the more he was able to believe it.

Paulie pushed the idea further.

With the mobster dead, this was why his parents had to leave the house. This was why they were never home when he called, and why they weren't home now. If they'd stayed home, other haircuts would have gotten them when they came around to find what had happened to the first one. Also, this had to be why his mother and father had cleaned up all the broken glass and everything and carried the dead haircut away someplace. They didn't want anyone to know what they'd done.

The boy sat on his father's painting stool in the dark studio, holding himself still and telling himself all the other things that it was necessary for him to believe.

His mother and father were alive somewhere. They weren't dead. They were busy running from the haircuts and trying to find him.

When they couldn't find him anyplace, they'd finally realize he might be home. Then they'd come here looking for him because they'd know there was no place else for him to go.

So one thing was sure. He had to stay here and wait for them. Otherwise, they would never find each other.

But he had to be careful not to put on lights or give any other sign he was in the house. Because the haircuts weren't stupid and were probably thinking all these same things.

Sitting there on the stool, Paulie began turning his head from side to side, trying to fool himself into thinking he was looking for something. As if smothering in the silence, he breathed deeply and felt his lungs fill to the point of dizziness.

Eat, he told himself. He hadn't eaten all day and it was making him weak, dumb, and dizzy. He'd better get something into his stomach right now.

Spurred by the prospect of so positive an act, Paulie groped his way into the kitchen.

He switched on his flashlight with the two socks over it, and opened a can of Beef-A-Roni. He ate it right out of the can, cold, to avoid having to light the stove. Then he had some cheese for dessert. He was surprised at how good everything tasted.

Finishing, he felt a stir of satisfaction at how well he had managed the meal, and he considered what he would do next. He had been upstairs earlier, and he didn't want to go up there again. His first visit had been very bad, with him going up into his parents' bedroom, curling up on their bed, and crying like a baby.

Even now, thinking about it, he felt ashamed.

I have to be better than that.

He knew he could.

So Paulie made himself go back upstairs.

Then he came to the hard part.

He went into his parents' room and lay down once more on their bed. But this time he didn't cry or whimper. Instead, he thought all the good stuff about them.

And he slept.

77

TOMMY CORTLANDT FOLLOWED CIA Director Lessing into the Oval Office and shook hands with President Norton and White House Chief of Staff Michaels. It was 5:25 P.M., and the fact that he and Lessing were being squeezed in between two other appointments gave Cortlandt a fair idea of just how seriously the whole thing was being taken.

Just the four of them were present.

When they were all seated, the president spoke directly to Cortlandt.

"I know just the bare bones of this mess, Tommy," he said. "And for obvious reasons I don't want to know too much more. But I do have a few questions I need answered."

"Yes, Mr. President."

"To begin with, do you believe what your telephone source told you?"

"I can't corroborate a thing at this point, Mr. President. But if I didn't give it at least reasonable credence, I'd still be in Brussels, not here."

"Then how do you see my options?"

Cortlandt looked at the chief executive. Norton was seated behind his desk in the big oval room, the American flag proudly unfurled at his right, the presidential banner at his left. It was an impressive sight. Yet all it did was make the intelligence agent wonder why anyone in their right mind would ever want to be president.

"As I see it," Cortlandt said, "you have three choices. You can do nothing and just let whatever happens, happen. You can let Durning know he's being tracked and give him a chance to do something about it. Or you can go proactive and give us orders to have his tracker neutralized. It all depends on how important you feel it is to keep Durning functioning as attorney general."

It was Arthur Michaels who answered for the president. "That happens to be very important. Durning's the best we've had at Justice in fifty years."

"Even if he's a murderer?" asked the president.

"We don't know that yet," responded the chief of staff.

"And if we did know it?" asked Lessing.

No one was ready to touch that one, and the room was silent.

Cortlandt saw Lessing and Michaels exchange quick glances, and there was something between them, something they both knew and that Cortlandt could only guess at. Still, it was an educated guess, born out of long experience, and the intelligence agent tended to trust it.

President Norton broke the silence.

"Another question, Tommy. If we were to take action at this point, when would it have to be initiated?"

"Within the next few hours," Cortlandt said. "The sooner the better."

Cortlandt saw another look pass between the White House chief of staff and the CIA director. It helped him understand that as far as these two were concerned the matter was settled.

The president didn't seem to notice. "That's really not very much time, is it?" His voice was cruel and he suddenly seemed tired.

"It's no time at all, Mr. President," said Michaels. "Certainly not time enough to investigate what could turn out to be a bunch of wild, unsubstantiated charges against no less than the attorney general of the United States."

"Meaning what, Arthur?" asked the president.

"Meaning, I don't really see us as having much of a choice as things stand. If we do nothing, there's an excellent chance Henry could be innocent and end up shot in the head by some nut with an imagined grievance. If we tell him what's going on and he's actually guilty, we've warned a murderer in advance and given him time to either get away or kill others to cover his tracks."

The chief of staff looked evenly at his boss. "So I say we have to do what Mr. Cortlandt listed as a third choice. Which is to say nothing at all to Henry and just neutralize his tracker by picking him up and holding him. Then we'd have time to properly investigate the charges and do whatever has to be done long-term."

The president brought his fingers together and let them touch. Then he studied them.

"One more point," said Arthur Michaels, sensing an advantage. "I know this isn't a moral, ethical, or even a legal consideration, but it does affect the well-being of this administration. Whether Henry turns out to be innocent or guilty, we all know the political fallout if even a hint of this ever leaks out. Come on. We're talking about the fucking head of the Justice Department. So let's not kid ourselves. If Henry's shit ever hits the fan, not even raincoats will keep us clean."

The president again put it to Cortlandt.

"What do you think, Tommy?"

"That certainly says it as it is."

"That's all?" asked the president.

The intelligence agent shrugged. "In my line of work, there's not much else. But I suppose there are a few things we might do well to bear in mind."

"Such as?"

"No matter how careful we try to be, neutralizing Durning's tracker could still end up going wrong and killing the tracker."

Cortlandt paused for so long that the president had to prompt him.

"And?"

"And the woman and boy, too."

78

GIANNI GARETSKY ARRIVED at Dulles Airport about an hour and a half before flight time, selected his seat at the Alitalia counter, and picked up a copy of *The New York Times*.

Then he sat down far enough away from his flight's boarding area to let him check out the passengers already there and those still arriving, without much chance of his being seen himself.

Twenty-five minutes later, he saw Mary Yung appear.

It was no surprise. Considering Durning's own scheduled departure plans, and the fact that Mary would have to fly to Naples in order to get to Capri, this was the most logical flight for her to be taking. So he was prepared for the possible sight of her.

What he wasn't prepared for was its impact on him.

How stupid, he thought, because it bordered on the physically insupportable. As if everything he had begun to feel for her was still draining from the wound.

He watched her sit down near the departure gate, take a magazine out of her carry-on bag, and begin leafing through it. Then he changed his seat on the off chance that she might just happen to stare off in his direction and see him.

And if she did spot him? Did he really expect her to point him out to Durning's agents waiting nearby? Wasn't it she who had told him about Durning's plans in the first place? Why would she betray him now?

Idiot. You're looking for logic again. Who knows why this one would do something?

Then for half an hour he sat reading the front page of the *Times* without absorbing a word.

He heard the boarding announcement and turned to watch Mary enter the ramp with the first-class passengers.

Naturally. How else but first-class would the attorney general's millionaire whore travel?

The aircraft was a two-aisle 747 wide-body, with most of the first-class seating laid out fore of the boarding hatch. So Gianni was able to reach his coach seat at the rear of the plane without having to walk past and be seen by Mary Yung.

In his mind it seemed a major victory. Until another part of his brain said she had seen him from the beginning.

He had finished eating dinner two hours later and just closed his eyes when she sat down beside him.

"Why are you here?" he said, without opening his eyes.

"To see if I can keep you from being dead by tomorrow night."

Gianni opened his eyes and looked at her. The cabin lights had been lowered for sleep, but Mary Yung's face was still luminous.

"You're no match for him," she said. "He's more dangerous, has more reach than you could ever imagine."

Gianni said nothing.

"I don't want you to die, Gianni."

"What's so special about *me?*"

"The way I feel about you."

"I'm sorry. I'm unmoved."

"You didn't want any part of me after what I did, and who could blame you? But I've never stopped wanting you."

He stared mutely at her.

"Come with me, Gianni."

"Where?" he said. "To Capri? To fuck with you and Henry?"

"We could just take off from Naples and go anywhere you want. I've got all the money we'd ever need and you could paint anyplace."

Before her eyes, Gianni felt himself shrink in size. "And spend our lives hiding from Durning?"

"If we leave him alone, he'll leave us alone."

"You mean leave him alone to murder Vittorio's wife and boy?"

"He doesn't have Paul. Besides, he promised he wouldn't hurt him if he ever found where he was."

"And Peggy? What did he promise about Peggy?"

She stared hopelessly at Gianni Garetsky.

"Please, Gianni. Your dying isn't going to help Peggy one damn bit."

Gianni closed his eyes. It was easier when he didn't have to look at her.

"Do me a favor," he said softly to the new dark. "Don't bury me until I'm dead."

They sat silently together at thirty thousand feet.

"All right," Mary Yung said in a voice as soft as Gianni's. He opened his eyes and looked at her.

"I've decided," she said. "If you won't come away with me, then I'll go with you."

It took him a moment to realize what she was saying.

"You're either joking or you're insane."

"I'm not joking and this may be the only really sane thought I've had in my life. I never should have let you drive me away the last time. I was just so sick with what I'd done that I couldn't stand up to you."

Mary paused for breath. She might have just been running, her cheeks were so flushed.

"This time," she said, "I'm not letting you push me away."

"You don't know what you're talking about, Mary."

"I know exactly. I know better than you. I've lived and slept with this man. I've seen parts of him that no one has ever seen. I told you. He *cares* about me."

Gianni shook his head as if to clear it. Emotion was clogging his brain. "He cares about no one. He'd kill you as fast as he'd kill me. Faster, once he knows you've betrayed him."

This time Mary smiled full-out. She was truly luminous.

"You can say what you want," she said. "It doesn't matter. I'm still going with you."

"It's impossible."

"You'll see how possible I'll make it."

"I won't let you," he said.

"You can't stop me. Whatever *you* do, *I'll* do."

"Durning will be calling you at Capri. He'll be wondering what happened to you."

"He won't have to wonder," Mary Yung said. "He'll know."

79

At about twenty minutes before boarding time, there was a warm holiday spirit, a pleasantly relaxed air of festivity in the VIP lounge at Dulles Airport.

Like a bunch of kids off to summer camp, thought Henry Durning, chatting, laughing, and casually moving among them in his role of unofficial host. Except that these "kids" happened to include a fair cross-section of the country's leading jurists and Justice Department officials. And since this was an all-expenses-paid conference at a luxury resort on the sparkling Bay of Naples, a great many spouses were present as well.

Testifying to the distinguished, high-level nature of the group was the presence of two Supreme Court justices, who would be addressing the international symposium, and White House Chief of Staff Arthur Michaels, who would not be making the trip but had come down to wish them all bon voyage on behalf of the president.

The attorney general had been surprised to see Michaels appear earlier. He was close to and knew the chief of staff from way back. Artie Michaels was a tough, hardworking political strategist who probably had the single most important and influential job in the country after the presidency. Some said, *before* the presidency. And he rarely wasted five minutes of his average fifteen-hour-a-day work schedule on this sort of ceremonial nonsense. This was strictly vice-presidential-caliber glad-handing.

Durning wondered why he was here.

He stopped wondering when Michaels suddenly draped an arm across his shoulders, walked him to a quiet corner of the lounge, and said, "We've got us a little problem, Hank."

Then the attorney general stood impassively, champagne glass steady in his hand, while Arthur Michaels gave him a quick rundown of pretty much everything that had been said in the Oval Office a few hours earlier.

Durning was silent when the White House chief of staff had finished.

"Does anyone know you're telling me this?" he finally asked.

"Are you crazy? Norton would have my head if he so much as suspected such a thing. But I feel it's important for you to know what's going on."

"I appreciate it, Artie."

"Fuck that shit," Michaels said softly. "I'm not doing it for you. And I don't give a damn whether you're innocent or guilty of whatever it is those *goombahs* want to blow your head off for. All I care about is keeping you alive, in office, and free of scandal."

A short, chunky man with narrow eyes and bad skin, Michaels squinted resentfully up at the tall attorney general's handsome face. "You have any idea of the odds against the president's getting reelected in November if his personally chosen head of Justice gets publicly accused of murder?"

Durning sipped his champagne and said nothing. Good old

Artie. Ever the quintessential pragmatist, he'd happily appoint Jack the Ripper attorney general—providing, of course, that Jack could guarantee the serial killer vote.

"So I've warned you," said the chief of staff flatly. "Which doesn't mean one of those crazy Guidos won't manage to blow your head off anyway. But at least you'll be watching out for yourself. And with Tommy Cortlandt's CIA spooks out there protecting your back, you shouldn't be too badly off."

Michaels squinted curiously at Durning with his little pig eyes. "Interesting," he said.

"What?"

"All those wild stories about you. All those accusations. You know the single, overriding effect they have on me?"

Durning slowly shook his head.

"I have no idea whether they're true or not, but they sure do humanize the hell out of you."

Michaels displayed the crooked grin that was his best feature. "Ever think about making a run for the Rose Garden when Norton's finally out of there? You suddenly seem to have all the necessary qualifications."

High above the black Atlantic, Henry Durning was indeed thinking. Although his thoughts had nothing to do with the concept of running for president.

Imagine the goddamn CIA being involved.

Who would have expected anything like that?

Not to mention the idea of Vittorio Battaglia covertly working for them all these years.

It was simply too much. He had been careful. He had done all those ugly, violent, but always necessary things one at a time, hoping each would be the last, yet finding there always seemed to be just one more that absolutely had to be done.

And now?

Now, no less than the president himself, sitting with his three wise men in the Oval Office, openly discussing the very things he had done everything humanly possible to bury.

In the government aircraft full of sleeping officials, Henry Durning pressed his face to the cool glass of a window and watched sheets of rain rip across barely visible clouds. His nose, chin, lips and forehead left prints on the glass.

According to Artie Michaels' recital, Gianni Garetsky had requested this flight's departure and estimated arrival times, so Mary Yung had to have told Garetsky.

So much for Capri and Mary Yung.

Well, what had he expected? It had been little more than a dream anyway. She had simply come to him one night out of nothing and gone off the same way. You can't tie up or nail down a dream.

Still, there were moments he felt he was touching her. In some crazy taunting way he felt close to her even now.

Or was he just twice mad?

Henry Durning stared out at the dark banks of clouds through which they were flying. He stared until a single puffy mass took on the imagined shape of her, a presence as fragile as a shadow on air. He tried to make the image come together, tried to actually see her face. He tried as hard as he knew how. But it never became anything more than a night-time sky.

Durning guessed he must have drifted off because he came out of it with a sour taste in his mouth, cold panic in his chest, and the memory of Michaels' horror story beating at his brain with a dozen hammers.

He found most of an earlier brandy still waiting for him and took it down with the desperate urgency of a man escaping from a desert. It may well have been the single best drink he'd ever had. For like a gift from the gods, it brought him a new clarity of thought and vision.

Maybe Artie Michaels' horror story wasn't all that horrible.

It didn't have to be.

With the proper handling, he might even turn it to his advantage. No less a force than the White House chief of staff himself had shown him the way.

Everyone from the president on down *wanted* to keep the thing quiet. It was absolutely essential that they did. If they kept him pure, he'd be one of the administration's prime assets during the coming elections. If he was turned into a major national scandal, he could drag down the president, who'd take a goodly share of the party's House and Senate seats right along with him.

They had no evidence. They wanted none. And he would make absolutely certain they got none.

At this point they had only a mob-related artist's unsupported allegations of his guilt. That was all. Period.

Henry Durning found himself on a sudden high. His flesh literally tingled with it. He was sure he had only to close his eyes and a fall of soft, velvet warmth would drape itself around him.

They would even make things simpler for him in his dealings with Carlo Donatti.

How could he have it any better?

He had the government itself looking out for his safety.

With the president's approval.

80

STILL WITH THE delirium, thought Vittorio Battaglia dimly, *still with the goddamn hallucinating.*

Stretched out in a small second-floor bedroom of Dr. Helene Curci's house, he had become so accustomed to the parade of wild fantasies marching through his fevered brain that he dismissed the sound of Tommy Cortlandt's voice as just another of his overheated, totally illogical imaginings.

Even when he saw the slender, fair-haired chief of station enter his room, approach his bed, and stand there grinning at him with his fucking perfect, no doubt capped teeth, he considered him nothing more than his latest visiting apparition.

"No visiting hours for ghosts," he whispered vaguely. "Tell your friends to stay away."

"Bullshit," said Cortlandt, and took Battaglia's wasted hand in both of his. "You're the ghost. Not me."

Vittorio blinked and looked at him more closely. "Tommy?"

"Damn right. Who are *you?*"

"A useless piece of shit," Vittorio mumbled, and passed out completely.

When Vittorio opened his eyes, Tommy Cortlandt was still in the room. But Cortlandt's back was to him and he was sticking colored pins into a large wall map that hadn't been there before.

"What the hell's going on?" said Vittorio.

The intelligence agent pressed in his last marking pin and turned. "If you can stay awake and lucid for at least three minutes in a row, I'll try to fill you in."

"Don't pick on me. I'm fucking dying."

"No, you're not. Your nice lady doctor says you just like hanging out in bed."

"My wife and boy," said Vittorio. "Just tell me. Are they alive or dead?"

"We believe they're alive."

"What does *believe* mean?"

"It means no one we know has actually seen them, but that to the best of our knowledge they haven't been terminated."

Vittorio lay there, concentrating on his breathing.

"OK," he said. "Now you can fill me in."

Tommy Cortlandt started with Gianni Garetsky's first call to him in Brussels, went on to his own need to bring it to the president's attention, and finished with the decision reached in the Oval Office to neutralize Gianni Garetsky and keep Carlo Donatti and Henry Durning under surveillance from the moment their respective flights landed in Palermo and Naples.

Vittorio listened without interruption until the chief of station went silent.

"Explain neutralizing Garetsky," he said.

"Putting him on ice so he doesn't mess things up by going after Durning and Donatti himself, and maybe killing them or getting himself killed in the process."

Vittorio Battaglia's gaunt, fever-flushed face stared, hot eyed, from his pillow.

"Listen," said Cortlandt gently. "Your wife and son are dangling right smack in here someplace with Durning and Donatti pulling the strings. What we absolutely don't need right now is an emotion-driven amateur with a gun blundering around in the middle."

Vittorio lay there with it, filled with an old stillness that seemed to be holding him down.

Then as if suddenly forcing himself to the surface, he pointed to the intelligence agent's oversize wall map with its clusters of little colored pins.

"You've brought me your command post?"

Cortlandt shrugged. "Why not? If I've got a phone, I can command anyplace. And this should make it a little easier on you. You won't have to lie here wondering what's going on."

Bunched muscles showed in Battaglia's jaw.

"You're a real doll," he said. "Just don't try to crawl in bed with me."

81

PAULIE WOKE LATER than usual from his first night of sleep at home. He was shocked to see how high the sun had risen.

I guess I was tired.

The thought was by way of explanation and apology, as if the mere fact of his being in bed past the hour of eight broke some holy commandment.

To compensate for the lapse, he showered and dressed in record time.

Paulie had just finished eating the scrambled eggs he had made for breakfast, when he glanced up and saw the man.

The man stood in the kitchen doorway, grinning as if they were old friends and he was very happy to see him. He seemed kind of old, with mostly gray hair and a lot of lines on his face. Especially around the eyes, from grinning.

"Hello, Paulie," he said. "Don't be scared. My name's Frank. Frank Langiono. I'm an old friend of your dad's from America, and I've got nothing but good news for you."

The boy watched Langiono walk over to the table and sit down opposite him as he talked. He spoke Italian, but with an American accent that made some words hard to understand. Up close, Paulie saw that his eyes were very blue and had tiny moving lights in them where they caught the sun. Paulie was still shocked and was watching him very carefully. But he wasn't frightened. The man wasn't a haircut, and if he'd wanted to hurt him or anything, he could have already done it.

"The doors and windows were all locked," Paulie said. "How did you get in?"

"With my special burglar's friend," said Langiono, and held up a ring full of slender, lock-picking tools. "Ever see one of these?"

The boy shook his head.

"If you know how to use this stuff," said Langiono, "no door is closed to you."

"Are you a burglar?"

Langiono laughed. "No. But I was a New York cop for twenty years so I got to know a lot of the B and E boys real good."

"What's B and E?"

"Breaking and entering."

Paulie stared gravely at Langiono. He had so many things to think about at once that he wasn't sure where to start. He understood that the man was being especially nice so as not to frighten him, but this in itself tended to make him cautious.

"How did you know my father in America?" he asked.

"We were from the same neighborhood. It was in New York. A place called the Lower East Side. A lot of Italians. I was a lot older than him and a cop besides. He was a real tough kid. But we liked each other and always got along great."

Paulie thought about it.

"How did you know I was here in the house?"

"I'd been watching the place for a while and finally saw you come home yesterday."

"How did you know I'd be coming here?"

Langiono grinned. "You sure you're not a district attorney or something? You sure got questions enough."

The boy didn't smile back. He just waited.

"You were seen trying to get on the Palermo ferry to Naples. Which meant you were trying to get home. Right?"

"What did you mean before when you said you got nothing but good news for me?"

Frank Langiono put both his hands on the table where Paulie could see them. They were big hands and some of the knuckles had been broken and had healed in crazy ways. Langiono looked at them as though seeing them for the first time. Then he looked up at Paulie with his blue eyes, which had turned quiet now and serious.

"I'm going to take you to your mother," he said.

The boy just sat there. His brown eyes went wide, then blinked rapidly for a moment, then looked gravely into Langiono's blues.

"Where is she?"

"Not too far from here."

"You're not just telling me that?"

"Why would I do that?"

The boy looked at Langiono without answering.

"I guess you've been having it kind of tough lately, huh?"

Paulie was still silent. He was suddenly finding it a little hard to breathe. What he didn't want was to do something stupid in front of this man, whom he kind of liked but didn't know one damn thing about.

Langiono dug into his pocket, took out a woman's brooch, and put it on the table in front of Paulie.

"Ever see this before?"

Paulie picked up the pin. He held it in the center of his palm. He felt it with the tips of his fingers.

"It's my mom's. Where did you get it?"

"She gave it to me."

"Why?"

"Because she knows you're a smart boy. She was afraid

you might not believe me without seeing something like this."

Paulie sat staring at the brooch. He remembered touching it on his mother's dress as a young child. He remembered that she almost always wore it.

"Is my mom all right?"

"She's fine. She just can't wait to see you."

"And you're taking me to her?"

"That's right."

"When?"

"Soon. When I get a phone call. That's when I'll know how soon we'll go."

Paulie closed his hand around the brooch. He seemed to have forgotten Langiono was there.

"You sure don't look very happy," the ex-detective said.

Paulie said nothing.

"What's the matter, kid?"

"If my mom's so fine and can't wait to see me, why can't she come *here* to see me? At home."

Langiono nodded as if he had been expecting precisely that question. "Because a deal's been cut with another man and these are the arrangements."

"What about my dad? Why haven't you said anything about my father?"

"Because I don't know anything about him."

"You mean you only know about my mother?"

"That's right. Maybe that's something she knows. When you see her, you can ask."

Then it was quiet in the kitchen. It was quiet in the whole house. Outside, too, nothing moved.

Paulie sat looking across the table at Langiono, who sat looking at his hands again. The boy began to understand. Whatever this Frank Langiono's job really was, he didn't like it very much.

82

GIANNI GARETSKY'S AND Mary Yung's Alitalia flight landed at the Naples airport at 7:05 A.M., which was about three and a half hours before Henry Durning's government charter was due to arrive.

They disembarked separately, without visible connection. Then they picked up their bags, went through customs, and rented their cars from two different agencies, with the same absence of noticeable ties. Both cars were telephone equipped, and they exchanged numbers by leaving them on slips of paper in an outside phone booth.

Gianni led the way out of the airport complex. At the first turnoff, he pulled to the side of the road and waited until he saw Mary Yung approaching behind him. Then he continued on with Mary following at a hundred-yard interval.

Suddenly, all their precautions seemed rather ludicrous to Gianni, strictly overkill. Who could possibly be watching them at this stage? Durning was the only one he had reason to be concerned about, and the attorney general was still someplace high over the Atlantic.

On impulse, he picked up the phone and hit Mary Yung's call number. "Just checking you out," he said when she answered. "Everything OK?"

"Yes. But I'd like it better if we were in the same car."

Gianni Garetsky was silent. He wondered how much of his tension had to do with Mary being along. It had all happened so fast. One minute he had been more alone than ever. Then suddenly there she was, right in his lap.

So?

So why kid himself? He loved it. She could still do this to him, he thought, and was smart enough to leave it alone for now.

"Where do we get the hardware?" she asked.

"About ten minutes from here. Vittorio told me about this guy. He's safe."

They drove for a while with the line open.

"It might be a good idea to call your hotel in Capri," Gianni said. "Tell them you'll be a few hours late checking in. Then if Durning tries to reach you when he gets to Sorrento, he won't start thinking the wrong things."

"I'll do it right now," she said, and broke the connection.

Fifteen minutes later, Gianni stopped in front of an old stucco house on the outskirts of Naples and saw Mary park a few blocks back. Traffic kept moving in both directions. No other cars stopped.

Gianni was in and out of the house in less than twenty minutes with everything in a large canvas bag. Having learned from Vittorio and recent experience, he was prepared for the worst.

He stashed the bag in his car, walked down to where Mary Yung was parked, and slid in beside her.

"All set," he said, handing her a 9mm automatic and an extra clip of ammunition. "It's fully loaded and the safety is on."

Mary Yung looked at the piece, checked the clip, and slid the weapon inside the belt of her slacks.

Gianni watched her accept the gun as part of everything that had already happened and would happen next.

"If it reaches the point where you have to use this on him," he said, "are you sure you can do it?"

"Yes."

Gianni waited for something more than the one word answer, but Mary Yung was silent.

"There's still nothing that says you have to do this," he told her.

"I know."

She blinked at him, her eyes looking slow and tired.

"Any more dumb final remarks?" she asked.

"I'll try to think of some."

"Don't bother."

They sat looking at each other, and Gianni Garetsky saw that everything was settled.

"All right," he said. "You saw where their buses were parked, waiting for them?"

Mary nodded.

"I'm sure Durning will be riding to Sorrento with the rest

of the delegation," Gianni said. "It's only about fifty kilometers from the airport to their hotel. But if for some reason he doesn't get on one of the buses with them . . . if he gets into a limousine or anything else and the buses leave without him . . . make sure you stay with him and call me at once."

Mary sat listening.

"If he's on a bus as expected," Gianni told her, "there's no problem. You'll just follow them at a distance. But remember. They'll have police cars leading and tailing the convoy. Some of the cars may be unmarked, so you'll have to stay way back to avoid getting trapped someplace in the middle."

"Exactly where will *you* be?"

"I can't answer that until I get to the hotel area and see how things are laid out. I'll call you as soon as I know."

They sat watching the traffic going by.

"You're still sure Durning's going to handle this alone?" Gianni said.

"Absolutely." Mary looked at him. "Why? Are you having a problem with that?"

"A bit. What you said in Washington yesterday makes sense. And you sure know the man a lot better than I. It's just that I can't see him going to meet Carlo Donatti without security."

"I didn't say he wouldn't have security. I said he wouldn't have witnesses."

"But if he has no backup, what's protecting him from Carlo Donatti?"

"The same thing that's been protecting him all these years. His safety-deposit box."

"How do you know that?"

"He as much as told me."

"When?"

Mary Yung stared off somewhere. "During one of his more vulnerable moments."

Gianni didn't press it.

"You remember the way back to the airport?" he said.

"No. I'll probably get lost and no one will ever know what happened to me."

He said nothing.

She turned and looked at him. "You don't have to worry about me, Gianni."

"I know."

"No, you don't. But it happens to be true."

Their eyes met and held.

"So?" she said. "Are you going to at least kiss me good-bye, or just sit there like a half-Jewish schmuck?"

Gianni leaned forward and kissed her.

It may not have been the sweetest kiss he'd ever had, but it certainly was the most knowing, with something in it of the unfilled hopes of the numberless men she must have kissed and finally left behind. And all it did as he walked back to his car was make him sad.

83

CARLO DONATTI'S LONG-range corporate jet landed at Palermo Municipal Airport at 8:20 A.M. and was met on the tarmac by a single gray sedan.

No one but the driver was in the car, and no one was standing any place near it. The closest vehicle was an airport service van parked about two hundred yards away, and the only people in sight were working mechanics and other airport personnel.

Donatti appeared to be the sole passenger. He disembarked alone, carrying a single piece of luggage, and entered the waiting sedan.

The car made a brief, ritual stop for the special passport accommodation always accorded the don, drove out of the airport, and headed south in the direction of Partinico.

Nothing followed.

Don Donatti knew this because he was watching his side-view mirror every foot of the way.

What he did notice a few minutes later was a nondescript

sedan pulling out of a cross road and falling in behind them at a distance of about a quarter mile. The car maintained this interval for perhaps fifteen minutes before finally turning off and disappearing.

But it was replaced almost immediately by a dark service van of some sort, which also maintained a steady, quarter-mile interval. The van stayed with them until they left the road and entered the long driveway that led to the white villa where Peggy Walters was being held. Watching, Donatti saw the van pass the turnoff and just keep going. But he was almost certain another vehicle would take over within minutes, park somewhere, and watch the house.

Donatti wasn't especially concerned. He was usually expecting and prepared to deal with this sort of thing. But in this case it was a bit puzzling because he knew the surveillance wasn't likely to have anything to do with Henry Durning. Which meant it was either a few of Sorbino's people operating on their own, or some other local *capo* jealous of Sorbino's inside track with the American *capo di tutti capi*. Not that it mattered. He would be losing them soon anyway.

The driver carried his bag inside the villa.

"Leave the car where it is," Donatti told him, "and get yourself something from the kitchen. I'll let you know when I need you. It won't be for a while."

The don found Peggy having breakfast on the terrace.

"A lovely morning, Mrs. Battaglia. Perfect for all good things. I hope you slept well."

Peggy's eyes searched his face for signs, ready to fly off if what she saw there appeared to be bad news.

"Is it now?" she asked. Her voice, too, was hesitant.

"Not right this minute. But we should be leaving before too long. Are you ready?"

"I've been ready since the second I got here."

Carlo Donatti's smile was the warmest he had. "Of course. One of my more stupid questions."

On impulse, Peggy reached for the don's hand and pressed it.

"Thank you," she said to the man who had once sent Vittorio Battaglia to kill her, but who now was offering life to her and her son. "Thank you."

84

THERE HAD BEEN strong tailwinds for much of the flight over the Atlantic, so the government charter out of Washington touched down at the Naples airport forty minutes early, at 9:50 A.M.

Henry Durning left the plane, picked up his bag, and walked through an all-but-automatic customs and passport check with the other passengers. He chatted pleasantly with the two Supreme Court justices in the group and made a point of being especially charming to their wives.

Then, leaving them, the attorney general put through a call to the Donatello Hotel in Capri. It was pure impulse. Like the need, he thought, to keep touching a fresh wound to make sure it was still there and hurting. It was and did.

He knew as sure as he was breathing that Mary wasn't going to be at the hotel, yet here he was, calling. It had to be something primordial, he thought coldly, first put together by a bunch of cells gone wild in his mother's womb.

When he had the hotel on the line, he asked the operator to connect him with Melissa Lee, the name on Mary's current passport. Then he waited.

"I'm sorry," said the operator. "Ms. Lee hasn't checked in as yet. However she did call with a message. She'll be arriving several hours late."

Durning slowly hung up.

Which meant what? he wondered, and left the terminal.

The four motor coaches were lined up, engines idling, exhausts turning the air blue. Around them, a large, highly visible police presence was set up to protect the visiting dignitaries from possible incidents.

The attorney general tried to see if he could pick out some of the CIA people that Artie Michaels had said would be in place to watch over him. He came up with either half a dozen or none at all.

Naturally.

When they were good, Henry Durning thought, you could be looking right at them and never know it.

Then he boarded the lead bus for the drive to the Sorrento hotel.

Tommy Cortlandt listened to the voice at the other end of the line, asked a few questions, and hung up.

"Durning just arrived at the Naples airport," he told Vittorio Battaglia. "So we've finally got them all here."

Vittorio watched from his bed as the CIA chief of station worked the little colored flags on his wall map, shifted some, added others, removed a few entirely. A kid with a new board game, thought Battaglia. Except that all those little flags he kept shoving around just happened to be real people.

Cortlandt glanced over to be sure Battaglia hadn't drifted off again. "You with me?"

"Yeah."

Cortlandt had opened and straightened out a wire hanger and was using it as a pointer. "Right now Donatti's our wild card. We're not sure what the devil he's doing way over here in this Sicilian villa. But the general feeling is that he might have your wife there."

Vittorio half opened his mouth, changed his mind, and said nothing. *Just listen,* he thought.

"Anyway, the don's not going anyplace unless we want him to. And we've got the same kind of lock on the three others. Durning and Mary Yung at the airport, and your friend Garetsky patiently parked near the Amoretto Hotel in Sorrento."

"When do you pick up Mary and Gianni?"

"As soon as the buses leave the airport area and Mary follows. We don't want Durning noticing a possible fuss and getting suspicious. And we can't pick up Garetsky ahead of time because he and Mary rented cars with phones and he might warn her before we're able to cut him off."

Vittorio Battaglia lay there with it. Fear, anger, and frustration came off him like a poisonous odor. He was sure that if he breathed deeply enough it would choke him.

"Any chance my son could be in Donatti's villa with my wife?" he said.

"Hey, come on. I don't even know whether your *wife* is really there."

"What the hell *do* you know?"

Cortlandt's eyes stayed soft. "Enough to settle for one small step at a time and not push it."

85

At a bit past 10:30 A.M., Carlo Donatti stood at a second-story window, gazing out from the front of the sparkling white villa.

He saw the wide, manicured lawn sweeping down to the road, and the circular Belgian block driveway leading up to the house, and the gray sedan that had brought him here earlier, still parked in front of the doorway.

Moments later Donatti watched as two men and a woman quickly left the house and got into the car. One of the men was his driver, the other man was wearing his clothes and was of a similar build, and the woman was the villa's slender, dark-haired housekeeper, who could easily pass for Peggy at any distance over a hundred yards.

Donatti saw the car drive off, reach the road, and turn right in the direction of Palermo. After a while, a dark service van passed the villa, going the same way. Then the van, in turn, was followed by what appeared to be the same nondescript car that Donatti remembered having seen behind them for a while on leaving the airport.

Good, thought Carlo Donatti. But he continued to perform as carefully as if he knew for certain that the house was still surrounded by watchers.

Collecting Peggy and his bag in the kitchen, Donatti led the way down into the basement, through a hidden door, and into a well-lighted passage that seemed to stretch to infinity but was actually just a little more than a quarter of a mile in length.

When they came out of it, they were in a small stone hut at the edge of a field surrounded by woods.

And in the field, a helicopter and a pilot were waiting.

My God, thought Peggy. *How lovely that this most resourceful of men, this* capo di tutti capi *to end all* capi di tutti capi, *should suddenly turn out to be on our own ever so sadly needful side.*

86

PAULIE HAD BEEN counting the minutes for more than an hour. He was waiting for the call to come, almost not believing it ever would come, afraid that even Frank Langiono's promise of a call would turn out to be just another in the long list of lies that all these people had been telling him from the beginning.

So when the desperately awaited ringing finally did come, when Paulie heard the shrill jangling suddenly explode against the quiet of the house, he turned white and cold and absolutely froze in place.

He stared helplessly at Frank Langiono.

"The phone." He was barely able to get the words out. "The phone is ringing."

Langiono looked at him deadpan. "What phone? You hear ringing? I don't hear a damn thing."

The boy could only point.

Langiono grinned and picked up the receiver.

"Yeah," he said. "No problems. Everything's on target. The boy's right here. He's great. What about your end? Two hours will be fine. Don't worry. I'll get set up early."

Langiono listened for several moments. Then he checked his watch. "I've got exactly eleven oh-six. Right on the nose.

Yes, sir. I know every second can make a difference. We'll go for one oh-six. Sure. Here he is. I'll put him on."

Langiono held the phone out to Paulie. "You interested in talking to anybody? Or maybe you're too busy right now."

"Huh—who?" the boy stammered.

"Your mom. Who else?"

Paulie stared at the phone in Langiono's hand. It might have been a snake.

"Take it," said Langiono, smiling again now that he was addressing the boy. "It won't bite."

Paulie gripped the receiver with stricken fingers. He heard a roaring sound and tried to shout above it.

"Ma! Is that you, Ma?"

"It's me, baby. It's me. How's my Paulie?"

"I'm great." The boy licked his lips and a deep red flush surged up over his collar and stained his cheeks, his ears. He looked straight ahead at nothing, hopelessly. "How . . . how are you?"

"I'm fine . . . really fine."

"What about Dad?"

"I'm sure he's fine, too."

Paulie swallowed hard. If his mother said she was sure, it meant she didn't know. "What's all that noise?" he shouted because he suddenly was afraid to ask or hear anything more about his father.

"I'm up in a helicopter. I can't wait to see you, darling."

"Me, too."

"It'll only be another couple of hours, sweetheart. I have to hang up now. I love you."

Paulie's tongue seemed to freeze between his lips. "I . . ."

Then the roaring noise became louder and the connection was broken.

The boy stood there, unmoving. The blush seemed to have settled like a permanent blight on his cheek, and he stared blankly at the dead receiver until Langiono took it from his hand and hung it up.

"Your mom OK?" he asked.

Paulie didn't seem to hear him. Tears started from his eyes and rolled down his cheeks.

"What's the matter?" said Langiono.

The boy barely managed to get it through despairing lips.

"I don't know."

A lie.

Because he did know.

They were never going to let any of this happen.

87

MARY YUNG CAUGHT her first glimpse of Henry Durning as he came out of the airport terminal and knew instantly she was not immune to the several ways he had reached her.

What a godawful waste, she thought, and was moved.

She watched him board and take a window seat on the first of the waiting buses, and found herself remembering things that would have been better left forgotten at this particular time.

She had told Gianni she could use a gun on Henry if it ever came to that, and she knew she could. Yet her deepest hope was that she wouldn't have to. God, the man had so much. And indeed there had been moments when, despite everything, she had felt a more genuine tenderness rise from him than from any other man she had ever known.

Such was love with Henry.

And now?

And now, as his one true love and chosen heir, I sit spying on him with intent to betray, entrap and, if necessary, perhaps even to kill.

Moments later, Mary Yung saw the doors close on each of the four luxury motor coaches and the lead coach slowly pull away.

Giving them time to gain some distance, she picked up the phone and called Gianni.

"They just pulled away from the terminal," she said.

"And you saw Durning get aboard?"

"He's on the lead bus, third row from the front, right side, window seat."

"Good. The thing you have to watch out for now—besides being spotted yourself—is the chance he might get off before they reach Sorrento, and switch to a waiting car."

"What about you?" Mary asked. "Are you in place at the hotel?"

"I'm parked about a hundred yards past the entrance, just off the main road. I can see anyone entering or leaving."

"I'm moving out now. I'll call again in a little while," Mary Yung said, and put down the phone.

Led by two marked police cars, the four big motor coaches were rolling slowly along the road that would take them out of the airport. Behind them, Mary saw another marked police car and two unmarked sedans. Then for a long stretch there was no traffic at all. When the entire convoy of four motor coaches and five security vehicles had traveled about half a mile down the road, Mary Yung set out after them.

Watching her back, she saw nothing behind her. She rolled her head on her shoulders to ease the tension she felt forming.

It took her almost ten minutes to maneuver into the position she wanted. When she finally had it, she was about three hundred yards behind the last security vehicle, with a civilian pickup and a van between them as buffers. There wasn't a thing at her back that she felt she had to worry about.

Suddenly feeling the need, she picked up the phone and put through another call to Gianni.

"Tell me something nice," she said.

"Why?"

Mary thought for a moment.

"Because sometime during the next few hours, one or both of us might be dead."

"Is that your cheery thought for the day?" Gianni said. "Or are you just trying to build up my confidence?"

"It would be nice if you could say you love me."

Gianni Garetsky was silent.

"What would be so terrible if you said it?" Mary Yung asked softly. "Are you afraid it might upset some kind of divine plan the Lord might have in store for us?"

"Do you really think now is the best time for this?"

"When would be better? When we're dead?"

Gianni sighed.

"Don't you dare sigh at me. We're not even married."

He laughed.

"Would you like to hear one of the nice things Henry told me the last time we were together?"

"No," said Gianni Garetsky.

"Well, I'll tell you anyway. He said if I lived to be a hundred, parts of me would still know that no one ever came close to loving me as he did."

It took a while for Gianni to respond. When he did, his voice was quiet and without the wryly mocking spin it had held just a moment before.

"That's a very lovely, very moving thought," he said. "Do you believe it's true?"

"Yes."

"Then why are you here with *me?*"

"Because that's not how *I* feel about *him*. It's how I feel about *you*."

There was only silence from the other end. Mary Yung was still waiting for Gianni's reply when she suddenly realized what was happening around her.

"Gianni!" The cry was involuntary.

"What?"

"I'm in trouble."

The wonder, to her, was her calm. It was as if she were responding in slow motion.

"What is it?" Gianni's voice was a shout.

"They've got me boxed in."

"Who? What?"

"An unmarked car with one man in it. He is waving me onto the shoulder."

"Does he have a gun?"

Mary noticed it only then, and even that seemed dreamlike and slow, with the driver using the automatic to wave her off the road, motioning with it as though the pistol was merely an extension of his hand.

"Yes. He has a gun."

"Damn them!" Gianni swore furiously.

Mary Yung heard it all in the two words. "Who is he?"

"Probably another of Donatti's Sicilian connections."

"Gianni, if someone's on me, you need to watch out. Get away from here fast."

An instant later she heard him swearing again. "Sonsof-bitches! You're right. Someone is moving in now."

Then Mary heard a sharp burst of static as the phone must have fallen out of his hand or been struck by something.

"Gianni?"

There was no answer. Only the blasting of static. Which had gotten louder.

The man waving her off the road with the automatic was shouting something at her that she couldn't hear, didn't want to hear, and wouldn't have paid any attention to even if she did hear. She was too wild with rage and anguish.

Murdering bastards, she thought, and was torn by a bloody vision of Gianni, riddled with bullets, lying slumped over the wheel of his car.

Then the calm was on her again.

Except that this time it was cold as she felt herself enter it . . . and as she felt, too, the sudden weight of the automatic in her hand.

A certain far-off feeling settled and Mary Yung saw it happen from this same distance away, saw herself roll down her window, aim the automatic at the man speeding along beside her, and carefully squeeze off one, and then two shots.

The first shot struck the driver in the head, he struggled to control the wheel. The second shot hit nothing, because by then the car had veered wildly out of lane and crashed broadside, at a hundred kilometers an hour, into Mary Yung's car.

She felt the impact.

She felt herself lifted and riding through the air.

She felt herself rolling once as they went off the shoulder and into the fall.

Just before she hit, her eyes were open and looking some-place a thousand miles away that she couldn't see.

Gianni Garetsky had heard the worst of it, had heard the gunshots and the first sounds of the crash that came explod-ing out at him as his car phone broke loose and clattered around the floor. But even more chilling was the deadness of the silence that came afterward.

Even now, tearing across a rough dirt trail with the car in hot pursuit and closing fast.

How?

It was as if they had known everything in advance . . . flight, car rentals, weapons stop, separating to cover both airport and hotel. They had to have been with them every step of the way. Then why had they waited so long before they moved?

An idiot's question.

None of it meant a damn now.

Now there were just Durning and Donatti laughing somewhere, a carload of mafiosi about to blow him away, and Mary gone.

Mary.

He let the best of her burn through him.

She could have been safely on Capri. She didn't have to do this. Yet she did.

Gianni didn't even try to figure that one.

"I love you," he told her softly. "I never stopped. I never could."

Marvelous.

Now that she can't hear.

With that done, he focused on those at his back.

All right, he thought. *Let's make it cost them.*

He still had about a quarter mile of lead, so he went about it coolly, without panic or rushing. This much he had learned from Vittorio.

Opening the canvas duffel on the seat beside him, he took out what he needed and carefully thought it through.

He was going to get only one shot at it.

The conditions were about the same. A car coming up behind him on a rough, single-track dirt trail, with thick growth pressing close from both sides. It could be great if it worked, or a full-blown catastrophe if it didn't.

Goddamn do it.

Gianni eased up on the gas and let the car slow without hitting the brake pedal and setting off any red warning lights.

Watching the mirror, he saw the car coming up on him fast through his own trail of dust.

At about thirty yards, he pulled the pin on a grenade and counted to six. Then he leaned out the window, lobbed it back in a high arc, and saw it hit an overhanging branch, angle off, and disappear into the brush.

Oh, shit, he thought, and waited for the explosion.

It didn't come. He'd bought a fucking dud.

Gianni picked up speed, activated another grenade, and tried again, making sure there were no low branches.

This time the grenade went off over the car with a crackling roar and a bright orange flame. Dust, smoke, and flying debris shadowed the sun.

He braked to a stop and got out. Then he pulled the pin on his third and last grenade, calmly counted to ten, and looped it over the heart of the carnage.

"This one's for her," he told them, and dived flat out into the brush an instant before the explosion sent shrapnel whistling through the foliage over his head.

Gianni lay there until things stopped raining down. Then he pulled the automatic from his belt, released the safety, and slowly walked back through the drifting smoke.

There were two men in what remained of the car, and they each appeared to be dead.

Gianni Garetsky stood staring at one of the men. Gianni was no longer angry. How could you be angry at the dead?

The dead man opened his eyes. He looked at Gianni without expression, lifted the pistol he was holding, and shot him.

Gianni felt the familiar stillness of falling.

It wasn't a bad feeling.

It was almost like floating.

And it was quiet.

88

THE LEAD BUS was just approaching the hotel grounds when the conference coordinator on board came over to Henry Durning and handed him a telephone.

"A call for you, sir."

The attorney general put the unit to his ear. "Durning."

"My name is Cortlandt, sir," said a controlled, New England voice Durning didn't know. "I'm a company station chief and I'm asking you to please accept everything I'm about to say at face value. Are you hearing me all right?"

"Yes."

"With the authority of the president, I've been handling security on you for the past twenty-four hours. And there have just been some negative developments."

Durning let several beats pass. "Like what?"

"We've lost Carlo Donatti and Gianni Garetsky."

"Where?"

"Donatti slipped away from us someplace in the Lalermo area. And two agents were just moving in to pick up Garetsky near your hotel when he must have been warned. Because he suddenly drove off like a wildman."

"Didn't your people follow him?"

"They followed, sir. But according to their calls, he left the road and took a dirt trail cross-country. I haven't heard from them again, and I still can't raise them from my end."

Durning felt a pull on him. "You said Garetsky must have been warned. By whom?"

"I'm afraid that's something else. About half an hour ago, another of our cars was closing in on this woman who'd been tracking you from the airport—"

"What woman?" Durning cut in.

"Mary Yung, sir."

Naturally, thought the attorney general.

"She was on her car phone, so we guessed she was warning Garetsky. Then she started shooting and the cars went off the road. When it was over, one of our best men was dead and she was close to it. And it was all unnecessary. She evidently thought we were a mob hit team out to get her."

Durning let it settle on him. Why should I feel such loss when I'd already lost her?

The bus was pulling up in front of the hotel and the passengers were stirring.

"I thought it best to alert you," said Cortlandt. "Until we get you some decent coverage, please don't leave the hotel. Donatti and Garetsky could be anywhere, and they're obviously dangerous."

Durning sat there, the other passengers starting to crowd the aisle as they moved toward the exits. "This Mary Yung," he said. "She was very badly hurt?"

"Apparently, sir. Her car went into a gully. We meant her no harm. We simply wanted her in custody. It was all a misunderstanding."

"A misunderstanding," the attorney general echoed dully.

"Yes, sir."

"What did you say your name was?"

"Cortlandt, sir. Tommy Cortlandt."

"And your position?"

"Chief of station, Brussels."

"Thank you, Cortlandt. I appreciate your efforts, if not your results." Durning broke the connection and returned the phone to the conference coordinator. Then he left the bus and walked into the hotel lobby with the two Supreme Court justices and their wives.

Trying to concentrate on one thing at a time, the attorney general picked up his key, found a bellhop to locate and get his bag, and was changing his clothes in his room ten minutes later.

When he left the room, he was wearing a jogger's warm-up suit and running shoes and carrying an Adidas athletic bag that held all the evidence against Carlo Donatti that he had taken from his Washington safety-deposit box the day before.

Durning left the lobby through a rear exit and found his car, a blue Volvo, waiting at the northeast end of the parking lot, exactly where his Naples connection had said it would be.

The keys were in a magnetized box under the front bumper, and the weapons bag was in the trunk. Durning entered the car and did what had to be done.

There were three fully loaded handguns in the weapons bag: a small .25 caliber revolver in an ankle holster, a 9mm automatic in a shoulder holster, and a naked .357 magnum. Durning strapped the shoulder holster under his warm-up jacket, set the ankle piece low and tight on his right leg, and placed the magnum loose under the top layer of evidence in the Adidas bag.

This time, one way or another, he would get it done.

And alone.

Ironically, other than for Mary's part, Cortlandt's news had been more positive than not. At least for him. He had planned to lose his company security watchers during this final phase anyway. Garetsky had just saved him the trouble by drawing them off. As for Carlo Donatti's losing them, that had been a foregone conclusion. The don knew his way around such things.

Then with his neat, carefully drawn map spread out on the seat beside him, Henry Durning drove out of the parking lot and started toward the prudently selected site where it was all scheduled to happen.

89

PAULIE AND LANGIONO were able to walk to the site from the boy's house in less than half an hour. And as Langiono had planned it, they were the first to arrive.

The place was a surprise to Paulie. He had lived in the area all his life, and he had never known anything like this existed: a bright, delicately green clearing in the foothills beneath a line of cliffs that might have been home to a new breed of gods.

The silence alone was awesome. It made the boy want to whisper. And when he glanced up at the sky, it seemed enough like heaven's gate for him to expect a flock of Tiepolo's more delicately rendered angels to come gliding out of the blue.

The clearing was closed in by brush and trees, and Langiono quietly led Paulie in a wide circle through the growth. The boy didn't understand until Langiono told him, "I just wanted to make sure nobody got here ahead of us."

Then the former lieutenant of detectives picked a spot about ten feet inside the brush from where the clearing began, and they sat down there together.

Paulie sat very still, listening for some forest sounds. But he heard none. Not even those of insects. Then he heard a bird call from one of the upper branches of a tree, and it seemed to tear through his head like a siren. They were in the shade and it wasn't hot, but the boy found himself sweating.

Why am I so scared?

He knew why.

The same reason he cried after speaking to his mother.

They were never going to let any of this good stuff happen.

The boy knew this as surely as he had ever known anything.

What he didn't know was who *they* were.

"Paulie?"

The boy looked at Frank Langiono. He saw the way the sun broke through the trees and touched Langiono's mostly gray hair and made it shine like he was some kind of holy person in an old religious painting.

"I got to explain a few things, so listen carefully," said the ex-cop. "In a little while your mom's gonna be out there in the grass with the man I talked to on the phone before. When they come, you can go right out to her. But not me. I got to stay back here in the bushes, out of sight."

"Why?"

"To wait for the other man in the deal to come. To make sure he don't bring anyone with him or try anything funny."

The boy stared long and gravely at Langiono. "You mean you're supposed to be like a bodyguard?"

Langiono gave him his grin. "Something like that. So when the man's out there with you, just be careful not to look in my direction, or say anything about my being here. You got that? Because it's important."

Paulie nodded. "What would happen if he saw you?"

"Nothing good."

Paulie suddenly felt his heart going very fast, and he began yawning, dryly, nervously. He was starting to see why Frank Langiono didn't like his job very much.

They sat there together, leaning against the trunk of a big tree and looking out toward the clearing. The bark of the tree felt rough and solid behind Paulie's back, and he watched the way shafts of sunlight struck down through the foliage and lit the tops of bushes in shiny gold. He squinted his eyes almost closed to bring everything down to masses of light and dark, and thought about his father teaching him how to capture the true feel of the gold with paint, picking up great gobs of cadmium yellow and zinc white together on the brush, not blending, but leaving the color broken to catch the vibration of the light.

The boy wondered if he was ever going to see his father again.

Then he heard the first faint sound of a helicopter and forgot everything else.

90

HENRY DURNING HEARD the distant sound of the helicopter at almost the same instant as Paulie and Langiono.

The attorney general was just getting out of his car where the dirt road ended, and he still had a good-size walk ahead of him to the designated clearing. Checking his map for a rising path through the woods, he found it about twenty yards off to his left and started the climb.

He moved lightly and carefully, carrying his evidence bag in his left hand and his 9mm automatic in the right. The sun flickered in small, bright stains among the leaves, and the air was piney and aromatic after a nighttime shower.

Then he thought of Carlo Donatti and had instant visions of snakes and demons setting off delicate warning systems in his path.

It made him smile.

Other than for the don bringing Irene, they were both supposed to be coming alone. But Durning thought he knew Donatti better than that. In all likelihood Carlo would have one or two people planted in the woods as backup. Which was exactly how he himself would have handled it if he hadn't felt compelled to do it alone and finally be witness free.

Mutual distrust. What better basis for a lasting relationship? Except that one way or another, this one was about to end.

The sound of the helicopter suddenly was loud enough to make Durning look up.

He swore softly.

It's him, he thought, and a spasm of something near to illness lifted from his stomach and touched his brain.

Through a break in the trees, he saw the copter circle down out of the sky like some creature from another age. Sunlight flashed from the rotors and reflected from the bubble. Sudden gusts whipped leaves. Bushes leaned and bent as the aircraft hovered for a landing.

Keeping low, Durning dashed the rest of the way.

When he reached the level of the clearing, he saw the two figures almost instantly. They knelt in the brush about twenty-five yards away, watching the helicopter touch down. They were a man and a young boy. And although Durning had never seen either of them before, he knew that the boy had to be the long-missing Paulie.

And the man?

Definitely not Battaglia or Garetsky. This was an older man with graying hair and a tough, lined face. Probably Donatti's backup.

Durning crouched behind some brush and waited to see what would develop. What he understood least was what the boy was doing here and where he had come from. But he guessed he would soon find that out, too. Still, there was an element of confusion for him simply in the boy's presence, and this was something he had never liked.

Just watch and stop bitching, he told himself.

He saw the helicopter lightly touch down at the center of the clearing. The wash whipped the high grass. The rotors screamed and slowed, and a hatch opened. Donatti and the woman Durning had once known but could no longer really recognize as Irene Hopper climbed out, ducked low, and ran to the far side of the clearing to escape the wash.

Almost immediately, the engines roared up to speed again and the helicopter took off, sweeping low over the trees and rising quickly into the distance. In thirty seconds it was nothing more than a speck fading against the sky.

Then Henry Durning saw the boy running out into the clearing. He ran like he was all skinny arms and legs held together by rubber bands. His hair stood straight up, pressed by the breeze he made as he ran.

How small and thin he is, thought Durning. *I never imagined he would be so small and thin.*

The boy's mother didn't move at all. She just stood frozen beside Carlo Donatti, both hands covering her mouth, watching her son struggle toward her through the high summer grass.

Insanely, Durning felt a hard dryness in his throat.

Jesus Christ, how did I ever get to this?

That same stupid question.

With its same irrefutable answer.

Trying to keep afloat.

When I should have just let myself sink a long time ago. I can still do it.

For an instant, in the imagining, he was stirred. But then, considering what it would mean, all it finally did was make breathing difficult for him.

Across the clearing, the boy and his mother held each other as Carlo Donatti stood watching.

Durning rose, quietly came up behind Frank Langiono, and shot him once in the back of the head. With a silencer in place, the sound was barely more than a whisper.

The attorney general holstered his gun and circled around through the brush before revealing himself to those in the clearing. Then carrying his bag of evidence, he walked toward the man, woman, and boy who stood silently watching him approach.

He saw the long bag in Donatti's hand and recognized the beginning of it all.

He saw Irene's surgically altered face and found enough fear and loathing there to make him believe in demons.

He saw Paulie's eyes and they froze his heart because he knew he was going to have to kill the boy, too.

So, of course, he offered them his best smile and warmest, most winning manner.

"It's been a long time, Irene, and you look just as lovely this way as you did nine years ago. Carlo, I've never seen a more dramatic entrance. Imagine dropping out of the sky that way. You make even the gods jealous."

Then Durning bent to the boy. "And you must be Paulie. Where have you been all this time? Didn't you know half the world's been looking for you?"

Paulie stared into Henry Durning's eyes as though he were trying to crawl inside them. "Where's my father?" he said. "What have you done to my father?"

Henry Durning stayed level with Paulie's eyes. For one long moment he felt himself in the same place with him. "I'm afraid I don't know where your father is. I've never even met him. But I hear he's a good man."

"He's better than *you*."

"I'll bet he is."

The attorney general rose slowly, feeling a less-than-rational urge to stroke the boy's hair. Then he turned and looked at Carlo Donatti.

"You have all the material, Carlo?"

The don nodded. "And you?"

"Right here in this bag."

"Then let's do it."

There was no visible drama in the exchange. All things considered, thought Durning, the whole business seemed rather mundane. If there was any touch of the exotic it came from the setting of a glorious sunlit clearing under an azure

Mediterranean sky. Otherwise, there were just two aging men opening their bags and handing each other assorted papers and objects, while an attractive woman and her young son stood silently watching, and an unseen dead man lay staring up through the trees.

When Durning finally tired of pretending to examine the plastic-wrapped rifle, jewelry, and forensic material he was squatting beside in the grass, he looked up and found Carlo Donatti gazing at him over the blued steel barrel of an automatic.

The attorney general blinked. It was pure reflex.

"You always did have a rather bizarre sense of humor, Carlo."

"I know. That's why I never tell jokes."

"What would you call this?"

"I'd say it was real serious stuff, Henry." Donatti's eyes were steady, cold as black ice. "You see, I'm not giving you Mrs. Battaglia and the boy. I figure we're all squared away now. And, sweet Jesus Christ, finally, enough has got to be enough."

Durning squatted there in the grass. Among other things, he felt utterly foolish. He looked at Irene and Paulie and saw them staring back at him with such gravity that even the air and grass seemed charged with it. So he laughed. He had no idea what the laugh meant. It was just that at this particular moment it was the only thing he could think of that might make him feel a bit less ludicrous and restore a measure of grace.

"Why not?" he said, and offered another smile as well. "I have no problem with that. As long as everybody is happy."

No one seemed convinced.

"Fair is fair," said Donatti. "You've got the rifle and forensic evidence, so there's no real case against you. And Mrs. Battaglia's assured me she just wants to forget the whole miserable thing."

Durning turned to her. "That's true?"

"I told you when we spoke on the phone," Peggy said. "You should have trusted me before. I would never have given you away."

"And now?"

"Now I just want to be with those I love and get on with my life."

Henry Durning slowly nodded. *How lovely,* he thought, and felt a quiet desperation in just how much he ached to believe that this sudden pathway to light, to some vague hope of redemption, could still be possible. He felt he had good things in him that were yet to be done. He was sure he had them.

He looked at Paulie, standing close against his mother, and saw it all in the incredible solemnity of the child's face. *Such a serious little boy,* he thought, and wondered whether he ever laughed, or even smiled. He looked at those dark, tragic eyes, still level and steady on his, and felt them enter his heart. He had promised Mary he would save the boy and wondered if he might yet be able to do it. Except that it suddenly seemed to be less for her than for himself.

Durning smiled at the kid.

"And what about you, Paulie?" he said with that quiet, half-grave, half-facetious manner with which he had never failed to charm children of all ages. "Do you think there's some hope for me?"

The boy gazed at him. He didn't understand facetiousness. He had a natural depth of perception that dug beneath and had no use for charm.

"I don't know what you mean," he said.

"Do you think if I tried real hard, I might get to be even a little bit as good as your father?"

Paulie considered the question. "Are you an artist?" he asked, because regardless of whatever else his father might do in the course of his life, to Paulie he would always remain first and foremost an artist.

"No. Though I sometimes wish I were."

"Then what are you?"

"A lawyer."

"I don't like lawyers."

The attorney general laughed. "Who does?"

Then Durning suddenly remembered the dead man behind the bushes and felt it all go bad inside him.

Wait till they discover this one.

So much for dream time.

The whole thing had been crazy anyway. He had come too far on blood to suddenly start counting on good will to keep him going. Too many knew about him. He might be able to handle those in Washington because they depended on such niceties as legal and political considerations. But people like Donatti, Battaglia, and Garetsky were limited by no such constraints.

Too bad, he thought, and felt something near to total despondency, as if such heartfelt remorse made him better in some way. Finally, you were nothing more or less than what you did. And he knew exactly where that placed him.

"So that's it?" he asked the don.

"*You* tell *me,* Henry."

"I'm not by nature a villain, Carlo. I didn't enjoy it and I had to work very hard at it. Since my basic survival needs seem to have been met, I'm more than happy to retire as the heavy in all this."

"Good. *Tutto buono.* For all of us."

"Can I count on your getting the word to Battaglia and Garetsky?"

"As soon as I find them."

Kneeling in the grass, Durning had started gathering together the jewelry and forensic evidence Donatti had brought him, and putting the separate pieces in his bag.

"Will they listen to you?" he said. "Will they accept an armistice? Or will I be living with armed guards for the rest of my life?"

"No problem. All Vittorio ever wanted was his wife and son. Now he has them."

Henry Durning nodded as he put the last of the forensic evidence in his bag.

And I have you, he thought, and fired the big .357 magnum through the canvas Adidas bag, its full-scale, unsilenced explosion filling the clearing and echoing from the cliffs. The don went over backward as if slammed by a bat. Durning saw his automatic fly loose and disappear into the grass. Peggy and the boy stared blankly, stunned by the explosion, trying to understand what had happened. Then Henry Durning stood up with the magnum out of the bag and in his hand, and they understood.

Paulie felt his mother grab him, but he didn't look at her. He was too busy watching the two men. The explosion had filled his head and overfilled it until there was nothing else.

He saw the man called Henry standing with the big gun in his hand, and the other man, Carlo, down in the grass with his shirt getting red all around his right shoulder.

But Carlo's eyes were still open and he was pushing himself up with his left arm so he could see Henry better, and maybe know what he was going to do next. Which was pretty dumb, the boy thought, because anybody should know that what Henry was going to do next was shoot Carlo right through his head.

Then something else suddenly seemed even dumber. Because where was Frank Langiono? If he was supposed to be Carlo's bodyguard, why wasn't he out here doing something?

Because he was dead.

Paulie understood this even as he thought it. Just as he understood that Henry was going to kill Carlo, then his mother, and then him. He didn't know why. All he knew was that it was going to happen.

Except that Henry somehow seemed in no rush to do any of it. He just stood there with the big gun in his hand, looking at Carlo while Carlo looked back at him with this funny expression on his face.

"If you're going to do it, then goddamn do it," Carlo said. "I just hate all this messing around."

"I'm sorry, Carlo."

"I know. You're always sorry. Every time. Only it never seems to stop you, does it?"

Henry stood there without answering.

Watching him and moving very carefully, Paulie took his snub-noser out of the pocket where he'd been carrying it for the past two days and nights. He lifted it with both hands and aimed it at the back of Henry's head. His mother was no longer holding him, but he felt her eyes and hoped she wasn't going to say or do anything to make Henry turn. He knew that Carlo was able to see him from where he lay sprawled in the grass, but he wasn't worried about Carlo. He was someone who would understand exactly what he should and shouldn't be doing.

"How did you know about my man back there in the brush?" Paulie heard Carlo ask, to keep Henry talking.

"Because it's how you think."

The boy took a deep breath, as Dom had taught him, held it, and began to squeeze the trigger.

I'll get only one shot, he thought, and it was exactly then that Henry turned and looked at him.

Paulie saw something funny on his face, almost like the beginnings of a smile. As if they had some secret joke that only the two of them knew about and understood.

Then the revolver fired and blew it all away.

91

GIANNI GARETSKY SLOWLY regained consciousness.

He could see the sky through only one eye. He was on his back in the dirt. But he wasn't dead. Yet his head burned like hell.

He pushed to a sitting position. With his one good eye, he saw the wasted car a few feet away, and his own car, intact, farther down the trail.

Then he remembered the man with the bloody face lifting the gun, and felt again the familiar stillness of falling.

Gianni touched his head where it burned, and touched his blinking eye. He felt dried blood in both places. If the bullet had hit a quarter inch lower, he wouldn't be sitting up. Ever.

His watch said he had been unconscious for almost two hours.

On his feet, he stumbled over to the man who had shot him. This time he was as dead as his companion. Finally.

With effort, and touches of dizziness, Gianni made it back

to his own car. He lost about ten minutes sitting there. It occurred to him that it was all lost.

It was another five minutes before he was thinking clearly enough to pick up the car phone and call Tom Cortlandt's direct line in Brussels.

A woman's voice answered.

"I'm trying to reach Tom Cortlandt," said Gianni. "It's important."

"Who is this?"

"Charlie's friend."

There was a long pause.

"Hold on, please," said the woman. "I'll check it."

She was back in a moment. "I have another number for you to call."

Gianni wrote the number down, hung up, and sat staring at it. Either the scalp wound had addled his brain, or this was Dr. Helene Curci's home number in Monreale, Sicily. It certainly was the number he had called when he last spoke to her cousin, Lucia. It made no sense. But what did, lately?

Gianni Garetsky called it.

"Cortlandt here," said the intelligence agent.

Gianni felt a new madness enter him. "Gianni Garetsky," he managed, and waited.

The phone hummed.

"Where are you?" Cortlandt's voice had changed but held its calm. "And tell me what's happened?"

Coldly, flatly, feeling like a recording and holding back his own questions, Garetsky told him.

"You're sure both men are dead?" Cortlandt said when he had finished.

"Yes."

The agent sucked in air. "This is all terribly unfortunate."

Gianni sat there feeling sick.

"It's not your fault," said Cortlandt. "You had no way of knowing. And it was all handled very badly. But those were our people you totaled."

"Your people?" Gianni echoed dumbly.

"Yes."

"What the hell were your people—"

"They were just supposed to get you and Mary Yung off Durning's back. Not start a goddamn war."

"Where's Durning now?"

"We don't know. He's not in his hotel. He must have taken off when our people were chasing you."

It all became too much for Gianni.

"You and your fucking people! What have you goddamn been doing to us? I don't understand all this shit. I thought you were trying to help Vittorio and his family?"

"I was," said Cortlandt. "I still am. Vittorio is right here in the room with me. But Henry Durning's the attorney general of the United States. I had certain obligations to the national interest."

Gianni felt his control going completely, and he let it.

"Fuck you and your goddamn obligations!" he shouted. "You had no goddamn right. I *trusted* you, damn it! You know how many lives this national interest crap of yours has cost? Those Company idiots of yours even went and killed—"

Gianni stopped himself right there. He was only assuming the worst. He absolutely didn't know for sure.

But Tommy Cortlandt was with him all the way.

"Mary Yung isn't dead," he said. "She's not all that great, but she's alive and being cared for."

Gianni let it filter through him.

"Where is she?" he said thickly.

"Sorrento General."

About to hang up and start the car, Gianni stayed with it a moment longer.

"What about Carlo Donatti and Vittorio's wife and boy?" he said. "Did your asshole *people* at least do any better with *them?*"

"I'm afraid not."

"What the hell does that mean?"

"Donatti somehow evaded them. And they never did find Mrs. Battaglia and the boy."

"Absolutely terrific," said Gianni.

His eyes cleaned, and the wound in his scalp treated, Gianni sat in Mary Yung's hospital room, waiting for her to wake up.

The late-afternoon light drifted in, and streaks of sun fell on her face, on that incredible nose and mouth, still visible among the bandages.

When she opened her eyes, she saw a nurse, a doctor who had just stopped by to read her chart, then Gianni.

"Gianni?" It came out as a confused whisper.

He reached for her hand, feeling himself grinning and nodding insanely, a mute maniac clown.

"You're not dead?" she said.

He shook his head.

"I thought you were," she told him.

"And I thought *you* were," he said, feeling dry, helpless tears somewhere deep in his throat. "That's what it took. That's when I was finally able to tell you. When you were no longer there to hear it."

"Hear what?"

"That I love you. That I never stopped. That as far as an idiot like me can tell, I never will."

Later, as she slept, Gianni explained it all to Teresa. Not that he had to. Who would know any of this better than his wife?

Things were being done to Mary Yung. So Gianni Garetsky, his head bandaged, was out pacing the corridors of the emergency area when he passed the small group heading in the opposite direction.

Abstracted, he was vaguely aware of a man being pushed on a wheeled stretcher, with a young boy holding his hand on one side, and a woman walking beside him on the other.

"Gianni?"

They must have been about twenty feet past him by then, and the woman's voice was tentative, questioning. Then he turned, and any faint remaining doubt was removed.

"Gianni!"

To Garetsky, it came almost in the nature of a private nonreligious epiphany, with Peggy clutching him, and the boy, Paulie, staring with his dark, serious eyes, and Carlo Donatti half raising himself from the wheeled stretcher like a grayfaced, suddenly resurrected corpse.

Then everyone but Paulie seemed to be talking at once, all

with their questions and stories, but only the two most vital parts finally breaking through and holding.

Vittorio Battaglia, dearly beloved father and husband, was alive.

And Henry Durning, attorney general of the United States, was not.

When Paulie did at last speak, it was to ask one question, "When can I go see my dad?"

"I'll have the copter take you and your mom right now," said Donatti. "You'll be in Monreale in an hour."

The don was still holding Paulie's hand. "You see this boy, Gianni? You know what this boy did?"

Gianni knew exactly what Paulie had done. He had just been told. But this was nowhere near enough for Carlo Donatti. He had to tell it again.

"He just goddamn saved the three of us. That's all. At eight years of age, *questo fanciullo,* this boy had the *coglioni* to draw down on that *assassino,* blow him away, and turn himself into a made man."

92

PAULIE DIDN'T FEEL much like a *made man* when he walked into his father's room in the doctor's house in Sicily. He felt more like a baby.

The thing was, finally seeing his father was nothing like he had thought it would be during all those days and nights of imagining it.

The boy had many different visions of his moment of return, but his most transcendently joyous was the one in which his father would be alone and hard at work in his studio. "Papa?" he would say. And as his father turned and looked at him with eyes worn red from worrying and not sleeping, Paulie would run across the studio and jump into his arms. In the fantasy, all movements were slow, silent, dreamy, a ballet without music, in which his father's paint-brushes were thrown into the air and floated, and he and his father hugged and kissed and sailed right along with them. Then the only sound was that of his father laughing, and when Paulie looked at him, his eyes were no longer worn and red but were bright and laughing.

Not so.

When Paulie actually walked into the room and saw his father, Vittorio Battaglia lay asleep in bed, his face so pale and thin and old looking that the boy almost didn't recognize him.

What had they done to his father?

He heard his mother make a small sound behind him, a sigh like that of escaping steam. It merely confirmed the tragedy.

"Papa?"

He barely got the word through the sudden flood of tears.

A baby.

The boy pressed his lids together to stem the shameful flow. What was wrong with him? Hands fluttering like birds, he brushed angrily at his cheeks. Quick. His father mustn't see.

But his father saw.

First, his son. Then, his wife. He saw.

Yet with all the fever, not even near to believing it.

Then finally, somehow, believing it.

When something close to rational talk was at last possible, Vittorio Battaglia said to his son, "So tell me, Paulie. Tell me where you were and what you've been doing."

The boy told him.

He told him from the beginning, from the moment Dom whacked him over the head and carried him away, to the squeezing off of that single final shot in the clearing. He left nothing out. A son telling a father a bedtime story, a fairy tale, a dream of magic landscapes peopled by dragons and a lone giant. Who really was just a little boy.

Vittorio felt weak, confused, baffled. His little boy, his se-cret thumb-sucker had done *this?* While he, his father, had been doing what? Shooting up the wrong people, getting shot up in return, and lying here dreaming of death.

He had proven unfit, unprepared. He had owed things to his wife and son that he hadn't been able to provide. Wild beasts roamed loose in the streets.

Yet, somehow incredibly, he had raised a tiger, he thought, and felt the first faint stirring among the tombstones in his chest.

It made the best of him want to lift up and fly.

93

It was Vittorio who told Tommy Cortlandt. But Peggy was the one who had to take the CIA chief of station back to the clearing where it had all happened.

Cortlandt was alone as he looked at Henry Durning in the grass. Peggy had just pointed the way and stayed in the car. The high grass moved in a breeze. The attorney general did not move. Over the years, Cortlandt had looked at a lot of bodies. Sometimes they looked as though they were sleeping. But not Henry Durning. This was not sleep.

Cortlandt returned to the car and asked Peggy to please leave him alone for a few moments. Then he used the cellular phone to call Arthur Michaels on his secure line at the White House.

"Just listen," he said, and told the White House chief of staff where he was and what had happened.

Uncharacteristically, it took Michaels several beats to respond. "I'm afraid we're going to need the president on this, Tommy. Hold on a moment."

It turned out to be a lot more than a moment. But when the president did finally get on an extension, Michaels had already briefed him.

"I hear it's ended up as just about the worst," President Norton said tiredly.

"Yes, Mr. President," said Cortlandt. "But if you'll let me act fast, the damage can still be controllable."

"How?"

"By turning the whole thing into a tragic accident."

The president's voice was hesitant. "That's possible?"

"It happens all the time on these crazy killer roads."

"I don't know, Tommy. That kind of cover-up can be awfully dangerous if it backfires."

Cortlandt was silent.

"Exactly who would know the truth?" asked Arthur Michaels.

"The boy and his parents, Gianni Garetsky, Mary Yung, Carlo Donatti, a few of our own agents."

"Good Lord," whispered Norton.

The CIA agent said nothing. He looked at Peggy Walters where she stood a short distance away, staring at some trees. She might have been on the rim of the earth. Less than two hours ago, she *had* been. It occurred to him that it had all started with her.

"How can we trust that man to keep quiet?" asked the president.

"It's not really a question of trust."

"What then?"

"The national good, Mr. President. Also, none of these people has any reason to want to cause trouble. All they want is to forget it and get on with their lives."

"And if they someday decide they don't want to forget it?"

"Then all they'd have is this wild story, without a shred of hard evidence, that no one in his right mind would ever believe."

"Maybe so," said Norton. "But I still don't think I'd feel comfortable with that many people knowing." He paused. "What's your feeling on the subject, Arthur?"

"Very different from yours, Mr. President," said the White House chief of staff.

"Why?"

"Because if we don't go this route, we are left with only the ugly truth. And dear, sweet Christ, I do mean ugly."

The connection was silent for what seemed a very long time.

"Since in this particular case," Arthur Michaels went on, "what the truth really means is either a special prosecutor or a congressional committee enjoying a yearlong field day of digging up smelly murders, and cover-ups, and abuses of government office, and who knows what else. And all carried out by a United States attorney general carefully selected and appointed by *you*.

"Not to mention exactly how much of this shit you yourself might allegedly have known before, during, or after the fact."

This time the following silence seemed even longer than it had before.

"Tell me, Mr. President," said the White House chief of staff. "Do you really want to put us through all that?"

Norton's sigh was barely audible. "You're wasting your time here, Artie. What you should really be doing is selling rugs."

94

IT WAS A strange period for Paulie.

He was happy, of course. Why shouldn't he be? His mother and father were alive and they were all together again. But there also were times when he was sad. And this bothered him. Because it was almost as if it wasn't enough for him that his parents weren't dead. That he somehow wanted more. Which wasn't true.

Still . . .

At moments he could be sitting alone, or standing, or doing something, or just lying in bed at night, and suddenly there would be all these people. They would sort of come drifting by, maybe one at a time, or a few together, or even all at once . . . and there would be Dom, and Tony, and those three kids with their knives, and Nino the trucker with his flatbed, and Frank Langiono, and Carlo Donatti, and Henry Durning.

No, thought Paulie, not just *and* Henry Durning. It was more like *mostly* Henry Durning. Because he was the one who seemed to come around so much more than any of the others.

Which was the craziest part of all. Because he had never even heard of Henry Durning before those few moments they'd spent together in the grassy clearing. And even then, he didn't know who Henry was. It wasn't until late the next day, when he and his father were watching the television news in his father's room, that Paulie began to learn certain things.

Delivered in somber tones, the announcer's lead line described it all.

The attorney general of the United States, Henry Durning, was killed in a tragic accident last night when the car he was driving went off the Amalfi Drive not far from the Sorrento and exploded in flames.

There were pictures of the fire-blackened car being lifted by crane from the bottom of a cliff, and of a smashed guardrail, and of an olive-green body bag being carried to an ambulance.

Shots of Attorney General Durning talking to reporters at the Naples airport as he arrived earlier with the American delegation to the Sorrento Justice Conference.

A close-up of the attorney general laughing at a question one of the reporters had just asked.

Afterward, Paulie had questions of his own.

So his father tried to explain how it was better if everyone believed that the United States attorney general had been killed in a car crash, instead of being shot by an eight-year-old boy he was about to murder, along with the boy's mother and an American *capo di tutti capi* named Carlo Donatti.

Paulie understood some parts of this, but not all. And what he didn't understand, he tried to imagine. Beyond the few facts offered by his father, there really wasn't much more he could do.

Then watching Henry Durning's funeral by satellite some days later, there was even more that Paulie didn't understand.

It was a very grand funeral in Washington, D.C., with a lot of important people present, and the president of the United States himself standing up and talking about Henry Durning. The boy listened carefully to every word. Since the president was talking about the man that he, Paulie Walters, had blown away with his snub-noser, Paulie felt that the president was really talking to *him*.

And what did he hear the president saying while so many people sat listening?

That Henry Durning was an outstanding American patriot and one of the great men of his time.

That Henry Durning was a war hero who had put his own life at risk to save the lives of others, and been decorated with his country's highest military award.

That as head of the United States Department of Justice, Henry Durning had brought fresh meaning to the word *justice* throughout the free world.

That Henry Durning's death was a tragic blow that couldn't help but lessen the lives of people everywhere.

So that listening to all this and more, Paulie thought, *How can this be?*

When it was over, he spoke to his father, who had been watching and listening with him.

"Does the president of the United States know what really happened to Henry Durning?"

"Yes," said Vittorio.

"How does he know?"

"Because I told a friend who's an American intelligence agent, and he passed it on to the president."

Paulie looked at his father, still so pale and weak in bed. "Why did you have to tell him?"

"Because he would have found out anyway. And I figured it would be better if he got it from me."

The boy felt the full chill of it enter him.

The president of the United States knew that he, Paulie Walters, had shot to death this famous man.

What could be worse?

The answer to that one came very quickly.

What could be worse was having this famous man shoot his mother, and him, and Carlo Donatti to death.

It made the boy both frightened and angry.

"Fuck!" he said, using the terrible *F* word in front of his father so he'd know how he felt.

"What's the matter?"

"Why does the American president have to be such a liar?" he said. "Why did he have to make up all those lies about Henry Durning just because he's dead?"

Vittorio Battaglia looked at his solemn-eyed tiger, at this overly serious miracle he had raised.

"Those weren't lies," he said. "The man really did all those things. And a lot more that the president didn't even talk about."

"He did?"

"Yes."

"But how could he?"

The boy's eyes were wide and troubled. He understood a lot, but this was way beyond him.

"He was going to murder us all," he said. "I swear, Papa. In another minute he would have *done* it."

"I know. I believe you. But people aren't just one way. There are different parts to us all. Some parts can be real great. But other parts can stink to high heaven."

For Paulie, it was a mixed-up, suddenly frightening thought. And it stayed with him.

He didn't like the idea of there being different parts to everyone. It made him feel sad. He didn't mind shooting the bad part of Henry Durning, but what about all that great stuff he had blown away along with it?

Lying in bed that night, it made the boy remember the famous man turning to look at him during those last few seconds.

It made him see again that funny look that was like the beginning of a smile.

As if they had some secret joke that was for only the two of them.

Except he now knew it wasn't a joke at all.

It was the great parts saying good-bye.

Instead of laughing, Paulie wept.

95

GIANNI GARETSKY FELT none of Paulie's need to weep. Instead, he felt the sweet spring of his brush against a tightly stretched linen canvas and remembered what it was like to be an artist.

Better than being a shooter, he thought.

People were, of course, still shooting one another. He supposed they always would. But this no longer had anything to do with him. Not directly, anyway. What he was interested in mostly was Mary Chan Yung and the substance of their days. The ones still ahead. Considering all that had happened during the past weeks, he felt himself ahead on points. From here on he had the same odds going for him as anyone, the same chances for joy and sorrow. He was pleased to accept them. As was Mary.

Gianni had taken her directly from Sorrento General to a villa on Capri, where the light was soft and steady on most days, and the limitations on artists and lovers were strictly their own.

Although Mary was still wan, weak, and convalescing, Gianni had already started her portrait. How could he stop himself? Never mind all that had gone out of her. To Gianni, what remained in the drawn, hollow cheeks and sunken eyes, in the hurt, vulnerable lips, added up to far more than anything she might have lost to pain.

Stepping back, the artist absently wiped his brushes and squinted as he studied what he had done so far.

It was a rough-hewn, boldy rendered oil portrait, with the brush strokes showing strong and sure, the paint heavy, and the colors bright and broken. Mary's eyes burned darkly from hidden places, her cheeks shone pale and gaunt above ridges of bone, and her mouth was a full-lipped, scarlet bow with the barest suggestion of a smile. Yet the painting seemed touched, all of it, with an almost inexpressible sadness.

"Is that the way I look?"

Mary had quietly slipped out of her chair and come up behind Gianni.

"I don't know," he said. "Is it? You'll have to tell me."

She stared at him. "But you're the one painting it?"

"No. I'm just holding and moving the brushes. You're the one who's making it whatever it is."

Mary stood there for a long moment. "Then I'm sorry," she said softly. "I didn't know I was making it like that."

"Like what?"

"So sad," she said, and pressed herself to him.

Holding her, Gianni felt how frail, how weightless she had become.

"And I shouldn't have," she whispered.

"Why not?"

"Because I love you too much to be looking so sad."

Yet it really was not that strange. Gianni had long been noticing that those who loved the most, often had the saddest eyes. Even when they were happy, parts of them seemed to be preparing for hurt. He supposed it was a kind of protection they used. They found it hard to trust what might lie ahead. Don't get yourself too worked up, said the eyes. Don't be too happy about your love because it's not going to last. You're going to lose it. In one way or another, it ends.

Which was true, Gianni thought. Love was terminal. Sooner or later one of you, either you or your love, changed, faded, went away, or died. And the eyes knew it.

But of course, with Mary, Gianni knew it was more than simply that.

So that sitting together high above the water later, with the setting sun turning the sea crimson and a flight of gulls crying overhead, Gianni felt compelled to touch upon their common ghost. There was no escaping him anyway. Even unseen, Henry Durning still had a certain presence.

"He won't leave you alone, will he?" Gianni said.

Mary was silent for several moments. "It's getting better."

Gianni doubted it. Actually, the late attorney general seemed closer to becoming omnipresent in death than he ever could have while alive. And the official lawyer's letter, received only that morning and telling Mary she had been named Henry Durning's prime beneficiary, was doing nothing to lessen her brooding absorption with him.

"It's not that I don't understand how you feel," said Gianni. "But let's not forget what the sonofabitch was."

"Are we all that sure we ever really knew?"

Gianni looked at Mary Yung and saw the remains of the day reflecting in her eyes.

"We're sure," he said. "Unless you feel a body count of about two dozen still isn't enough to remove all doubt."

Mary was silent and this in itself gnawed at Gianni.

"Or maybe it's his apparently unforgettable claim," he went on more softly, "that if you lived to a hundred, parts of you would still know that no one ever came close to loving you as he did."

Mary Yung sighed. "I guess I never should have told you that."

Yet what woman could have resisted the telling? he thought.

It was simply the nature of love. And of Mary Yung. And of course, of Henry Durning. Who, with all he had caused to happen, Gianni had never met. Not that they had to meet for Gianni to know about him. When it came to love, Henry Durning couldn't be that different. No one was.

Who didn't goddamn love to talk about his love?

At one time or another, over the years and a few drinks, Gianni had listened to gangsters, murderers, leg-breakers, the rich and the poor, the foolish and the brilliant. And their single common denominator, the one thing they invariably shared, was a compulsive need to let him know how truly and deeply they had loved.

Look at me! was what they were shouting. Pay attention. Never mind how I look or seem. Never mind what I've done.

Never mind what anyone says about me. I feel. I care. I love. And that in itself has to make me fucking lovable.

Then more softly, the eyes said, Listen. Please love me. Forgive what I've done. I didn't mean it.

But try as he might, Gianni Garetsky could scrape up nothing for Henry Durning. Too many were dead who should not have been.

Maybe time will soften me and I'll change.

Gianni didn't know.

What he did know was that whatever gifts of grace Henry Durning's troubled soul might be pleading for these days, they would have to come from Mary Yung. He could think of no other heart big enough to pump out the required amounts of love.

Gianni looked at Mary where she sat, quietly waiting for him to stop his foolish judging and just start loving her again.

He smiled and saw her slowly smile back.

There are harbors left.